Praise for

William P. Wood

GANGLAND

"Compelling . . . A bloody showdown between manipulative killer and dedicated prosecutor from which no one emerges unscathed . . . Wood knows the intricacies and ironies of the legal system."

—*San Diego Union*

"Suspense-filled . . . Realistic, fast-moving . . . Molina is the kind of criminal that you love to hate."

—*Daily Press* (Newport News, VA)

"A unique legal thriller . . . Wood knows the ins and outs of prisons, courts, government witness programs . . . *Gangland* demonstrates graphically the tensions, frustrations, and personal dangers often endured by the families of crime victims."

—*Deltona Enterprise* (FL)

RAMPAGE

"One of the better courtroom dramas in recent years."

—*New York Times Book Review*

"Clear and compelling."

—*Newsday*

"Superior! . . . Please do not miss this one."

—*Cleveland Plain Dealer*

Also by William P. Wood

Sudden Impact

Gangland

Broken Trust

Pressure Point

The Bribe

Stay of Execution

Rampage

Quicksand

The Bone Garden

FUGITIVE CITY

WILLIAM P. WOOD

FUGITIVE CITY

A NOVEL

Turner Publishing Company
424 Church Street • Suite 2240 • Nashville, Tennessee 37219
445 Park Avenue • 9th Floor • New York, New York 10022
www.turnerpublishing.com

FUGITIVE CITY

Cover design: Maxwell Roth
Book design: Glen Edelstein

Library of Congress Control Number: 2014948621

ISBN: 9781620454718

Printed in the United States of America
14 15 16 17 18 19 0 9 8 7 6 5 4 3 2 1

Deliver me, O Lord, from the evil man:
preserve me from the violent man.
—Psalm 140

FUGITIVE CITY

PART
ONE

ONE

AT FIVE A.M. ONE MORNING about two months short of her forty-third birthday, Carol Beaufort was startled awake by a telephone call.

The phone rang joltingly, twice. She groaned, snapped her arm out, fumbled the receiver into her hand. She had a heavy, pounding headache. "'Lo?" she mumbled.

"Carol?" a man shouted back.

Before she could answer, the man went on exuberantly, "Guess who? I'm on my way!" and hung up.

She lay back on the pillow, the receiver pressed against her ear for a moment. Another wrong number. Her heart hammering, her head stinging. A perfect start to another perfect day in her new home in this new city.

Carol got a lot of odd calls because her telephone number was similar to the Glass Pheasant restaurant and the Santa Maria Riding Stables. Out of irritation lately, she had started taking reservations for tables and answering breeding questions when people called.

She banged the phone down disgustedly. The man's

voice just now sounded familiar, but was hard to make out against the background clamor of music, laughter, shouting. Where was this one calling from? Truck stop? A party? Bar?

Her hand went out to the other side of the cold mattress and found that side of the bed empty. The guy knew her name, and she thought for a moment it might be one of her boozy companions from the night before, during that long, hazy marathon at the marina bar.

At least I didn't bring him home this time, she thought. I'm showing some discrimination suddenly.

She lay still, unable to sleep, fighting it, then giving in. She was too jangled to get back to sleep without some help.

Carol got up and shuffled to the kitchen. She didn't turn on the lights. The throbbing behind her eyes wouldn't take the shock.

Going through the living room, she stubbed her toes in the dark. She stopped, cursing, bending down to rub the pain. All the furniture was new, including the hassock that had caught her. Although she had moved to Santa Maria four months ago, she still hadn't unpacked completely, and the tables, chairs, sofa in the living room were strangers.

Limping a little, she went into the kitchen and found the Gilbey's bottle with practiced fingers. Some parts of the new house weren't strangers at all. She found a glass in the cupboard to the right of the sink. Everything looked slightly luminous, faint in the darkness. She poured a shot and drank quickly.

It was so quiet in the neighborhood at that hour, she heard a dog barking miles away and the rising and falling lament of the train passing through town.

Big day today, she thought, lots of good old work at the office. I need my rest. But the vodka hadn't quieted her enough. Something more was needed, much better than the glass of warm milk Mom would certainly have made sure she drank.

Into the darkened bathroom, Carol felt her way around, pushing bottles on the sink around until she felt the fat Xanax. Just like Valium, just as much deadening, soothing blankness. One five-milligram, she thought, taking it with water she slurped from the faucet. Two Xanax would be greedy.

She got back into bed, leaving the covers off, breathing in the night's fading air. "I'm on my way," the caller said. Who isn't, she thought? Look at me, I'm well on my way.

I look ten years older than I should, she thought. That's why no lights now, why I don't look at myself in the mirror in the morning or at night or any time when you can't hide it. My figure's good, I'm slim, I look perfectly fine, until you see that face giving it all away. Getting old, older, oldest. Mom gave me her face and her figure. Thank you.

Carol was almost six-two barefoot, with reddish hair and sturdy features. Even though she wasn't homely, she didn't like the way she looked. I look like I should be behind a goddamn mule-drawn plow, she thought.

Her head banged less now, her breaths jerked. Think of something pleasant, drift off with a dream.

This house was hers. That was a dream realized. It was her first home, not something bought or rented for her by Mom and Dad. She had moved away from them finally, putting hundreds of miles between them and her. She coughed uncomfortably. All right, they're both ill, in Mount Calvary Convalescent, but the rest of the family is there. Let someone else spend the years tending and watching them. I did my share, tied into the whole family and Dad's business pals, everybody watching, weighing and judging. *So Carol's still alone, maybe that's why she started this drinking thing. Is Carol afraid to work for a decent lawyer, some firm in town? She afraid to go out on her own?*

Carol sat up, heart thudding, her throat tight. Not sick, not again, once a night was more than enough and

I did mine after the marina frolic. She heard the unseen dog barking somewhere, smelled the thick oatish-scented breeze blowing across fields outside the city.

She forced herself to calm down, let the pill and the liquor work. She had been a lawyer for fifteen years, always working for small firms or solo practitioners who needed a diligent, discreet attorney who had a horror of going into court. Carol was intelligent and worked hard in the law office and library.

But finally, about four months before, the lifetime of being so close to a tight-lipped, unbending family and career had become enough. I ran away from home after I was forty, she thought wryly, smiling in the dark, sitting cross-legged on the bed.

Right now her employer was Brian Reilly. She imagined him later that morning, a squat, bustling bundle of unscrupulous energy, coming into her office, sinking down into a soft chair. He would hand her the files and motions to prepare, ask her what he had to worry about in court. On today's docket were interrogatories for a deposition one of his many developer clients had been trapped into giving and a divorce action a police lieutenant was bringing against his wife of six years. Reilly represented some cops. He also represented the most dynamic and risky elements in Santa Maria's building boom.

And I tell him where to go and what to do every morning. I hold his hand. I know where all the bodies are buried, she thought. And Reilly had a lot of buried secrets to watch over.

She did not particularly like this aspect to her new life, but Carol was practical. She could not uproot herself, set down, and hope to find everything as respectable as Mom or Dad would want. I've got a lot of dead years, wasted days to catch up on.

She lay back on the pillow, the soft hand of the barb and

vodka closing around her burning head. A vivid memory of Mom came to her, one of those that seem to point toward revelation and rarely do.

It was their old kitchen, on Mesmer Avenue, the same red-brick waxed floor and Mom was retying one of her shoes. Much huffing and sighing. Carol could see Mom's broad back bent over her shoe. She was always losing her shoes and she must have been in the third grade about the time this one came off. They were always expensive shoes, too, the best from Dad's stock.

That's why losing her shoes was so embarrassing. It made her seem slow, stupid, ungrateful. *Carol Beaufort can't even keep her shoes on. And her Dad owns Beaufort's Best Shoes with four stores in Riverside, Banning, and Beaumont, California.*

Mom gave her retied shoe a light tap. Red strap model. The same reddish color picked up in Mom's hair and coarse features, but they looked suitably maternal on that face. Carol, Mom said in her usual, always patient, unassailably wise voice, you are the unluckiest little girl in the whole world. Don't you want to pay attention? You've got to watch what you're doing. Listen to me. You have got to pay attention.

Maybe I was unlucky, Carol thought, the ideas growing more indistinct and her breath slowing. Blamed for every accident, taller than everyone until high school, no boyfriends, no friends really. But I've got my own house now, a good job.

And I pay attention. Brian Reilly's connected to everyone and I write his motions, his briefs, his arguments, questions, even the little speeches he sometimes gives to community groups. I know all the details. I'm not unlucky anymore on my own.

Carol finally fell asleep, thinking of Mom and those lost, lonely days. She didn't think about the errant phone call again.

The day did not begin well. She was so knocked out that she slept through the alarm at seven, and only woke up when the bright morning sun sent hot bars through the half-open blinds in the bedroom windows.

It was past eight. She was due in the office at nine and Brian had gotten testy lately about her increasingly frequent lateness. She didn't like him very much, but didn't want to irritate him.

She swallowed back a recurrent tremor of nausea and went to the bathroom. Behind the aspirin bottle were her Ritalin pills and she took two, which should be enough of a jangle to shake off the liquor and Xanax languors.

A quick shower made her clammy and unsettled. She was only a little late, no tragedy. Carol liked to think of herself as a survivor and these uncharted deviations in her routine bothered her.

Out of the shower, she critically looked at herself in the steamy mirror, another departure from routine. I am a survivor, she thought, but the taint was already there in her flesh, breasts poised to fall, the tall, firm figure bending beneath the assault of nights like last night. Okay, she vowed, cut it down, keep the playtime to a minimum. She could do it. Just cutting down on the highs and lows of tranquilizers and uppers would help.

She put on a pink fluffy bathrobe—hair still wet— and made a quick cup of coffee in the kitchen. She could just squeak into the office before Reilly made his daily appearance.

The coffee was too hot and she winced, hurrying back through the living room. Four months ago the TV, stereo, the tasteful traditional furniture was new. New newspapers and books, unread magazines and dishes lay in the dust covering them. Got to clean this place up soon, she thought. I live here now.

She was debating whether to wear a pastel-blue outfit that Reilly had admired or stick with something basic in a simple skirt and blouse when someone knocked on the front door.

She only opened the door to tell whomever it was to go away. No one with any good news came to the front door at eight-fifteen.

The door was partly open when two men pushed inside. Carol dropped her coffee cup, felt the hot liquid splash against her bare feet.

One man grabbed her, his arms flung around her. The breath rushed out of her.

"Carol honey! I'm here! I'm here! I said I'd come!" and he began kissing her roughly, his hands under her buttocks, lifting her bodily into the air.

She squirmed, tugged backward, tried to move away. The grip was too strong. "Kenny? Let me go, Kenny." She said it loudly and he dropped her back to the floor.

His lightly bearded face had scratched her cheek. The other man, a gnomelike figure in a black suit, went to the front door and gently closed it, as if from a sense of modesty.

Kenny was chattering happily. "If you could see your face. You got the funniest look I ever seen on you." He pointed, gaping with amusement. "You look like you going to drop." He turned gleefully to the little man, "Don't she look like she's going to drop, Dave?"

"You made your point," the little man answered solemnly. "Tell her who I am."

"Yeah, yeah. Carol honey, this is my old cell-buddy Dave Lisio. Dave, this's my Carol."

Lisio put out a small white hand. "How do you do?" he asked formally.

Carol had begun to regain her inner balance. She had recovered enough equilibrium to swat away Kenny's groping hand. "What the hell are you doing here, Kenny?

When did you get out? I mean, you've just come out of nowhere." She tried to make it sound as if he'd overlooked a social grace. "You didn't let me know or anything."

She was trying to discern the point. Looking at the solemn, dark little man, sunlight hitting him and almost vanishing into that black suit, and the taller, boyish Kenny babbling at her, Carol sensed something unspoken. This was not a simple visit. How could it be?

As far as she had known until a minute ago, Kenneth James Trask, age twenty-eight, having abandoned his wife and child, was still incarcerated at the California Institution for Men at Chino, three hundred miles to the south. My old neighborhood, Carol thought. The prison was close by Riverside.

Kenny should still be in a cell finishing the last twenty-four months of a seven-year sentence for a very inept robbery of a Sambo's restaurant. She had represented him on a thus-far unsuccessful appeal of that sentence. She was his lawyer, and for nearly a year now, his clandestine lover.

It was a gross weakness, a terrible vanity to have undertaken the odd love affair she and Kenny had. Gropings in the prison visitor's room when guards weren't looking, letters back and forth where she played out sex and fantasy and he tried to match her. His violence moved her, she admitted; and part of its attraction was the shameful pleasure it gave, so shocking to her family if they ever found out, so damaging to her career as a lawyer if revealed.

"But, Carol honey," he said, reaching for her, "I did call. I called you from some shithole outside of town couple hours ago. I called soon's I got a chance. I been driving pedal to the metal all damn night," Kenny wheezed theatrically.

So much for the odd call. The major advantage to being in love or in lust with Kenny was that he was not leaving that cell on C-Block anytime soon. They could be as passionate as distance, letters, and guards permitted. She could delight in manipulating his desire, knowing he would always be there for her, never leaving like the others, innocent, ironically, in many more ways than she was. It had been, until this moment, very secure, very safe for her.

But now here he was, hands out, the improved Kenny Trask.

"Well, it's wonderful to see you," she said without much conviction. "You look wonderful now, Kenny. I wish we had more time."

"We got all the time in the world. It's going to be just like we been talking about, honey. I swear to God to you. Just like we been dreaming." He tried to put his hands around her back again.

He was blond and strong. His face was clean, even handsome in an unformed way. He looked like he had been only partly stamped out, the features still to be fully filled in. She saw that prison really had been good for him. Regular food and exercise had transformed the weak, skinny amphetamine addict she first saw in his court file's booking photo into a tolerably put together young man.

She wondered, with all his impatient, jittery talk and movement, if he was using speed again.

"No, what I mean," she began with a false smile, "is I've got to get out to work now. Right now. How about we meet for lunch? I could take you out. A celebration for your release."

Kenny giggled loudly. Lisio said coldy, "Not now, Kenny. Remember, I've got to talk to her now."

Carol had the growing, uneasy feeling that the unspoken, threatening thing was nearing her. She saw the way Kenny obeyed Lisio, almost reflexively. Something was going on.

"Okay, I wait my turn," Kenny said, hands dropping from her.

"I really don't have time," Carol said firmly. "You can sit here and we'll leave together, but I have got to get ready." She started to turn.

"I must talk to you," Lisio said without raising his voice.

"Not now," she said.

"Carol honey, you better talk to him. It's important for us," Kenny sighed deeply. "You don't know what I'm feeling now, seeing you all wet, out of the shower."

Carol had taken a step. I bet I do know what you're thinking. All this emotional talk of the two of them annoyed her. Kenny seemed to think he could barge in and they would run off. It was ludicrous.

"Now, just a second." She watched the little man peering at her. "You didn't even let me know you had a release date, Kenny. You can't show up and expect everything to stop."

"There isn't much time. I must talk to you," Lisio said firmly again.

The cold tone, so different from Kenny's heedless joy, pricked her. He's the bad one, she thought. He's the one with the bad ideas. He was so short he looked like someone doing a Toulouse-Lautrec impression, except he was clean-shaven.

"We can talk on my way out," she said.

"I promise to be brief." Lisio was behind her as she walked toward the bedroom. "It is in your vital interest."

"Carol honey. Please. Just take the minute."

She decided a quick resolution was best. A quick interview to hear the pitch for a loan, then throw them out. The Ramirez kid next door was revving his motorcycle again, high-pitched and grating. But this morning she didn't mind it. For the last few minutes, everything else had become too strange.

"May we talk somewhere?" Lisio asked. His white flesh was shiny like wax.

She pointed to the kitchen. "In there. For a minute. I mean it."

"That's her lawyer voice," Kenny said merrily. "Can't she crack that whip?"

Lisio turned to Kenny. "Why don't you take care of the cars while I'm doing this?" He tapped his watch.

Kenny saluted. "Carol honey, you're going to love this. It's all going to be just like we wanted."

She went into the kitchen, Lisio following her. These two were an annoyance she intended to end immediately. I don't need this today, she thought.

Behind her, as he opened the front door, she heard Kenny say a little apprehensively, "You ain't said you're happy to see me yet."

She stood against the kitchen sink, arms folded. Lisio waddled in and she suddenly realized how misshapen he was. His right hip was thrown up and out, giving his small body a twist. He gripped a thin black stick to maintain his balance.

"Do you have a legal problem? Do you want money? Is that why Kenny brought you here?" she asked brusquely. "I'm not interested in your case and I don't lend money."

Lisio didn't answer at once. He laid his stick by the kitchen table and sat down. Actually, he hoisted one side of his body onto the chair, then used his hands, like a child, to pull the rest of him into the seat. It was a repulsive sight, she thought. Like something that's been half-squashed and still moved.

"No," he said with a faint smirk, "I can see you don't lend money."

She disliked the quick, intense perusal he made of the kitchen, the heaped unwashed plates and clothes left by the washer. He took in the yellowing linoleum and cracked white cupboards, judging and unforgiving. It was like her mother, making her feel stupid and clumsy.

"Hurry up. I've got to get out of here. Make your speech. Whatever Kenny's told you, I'm not giving you anything."

Carol had learned a few tricks doing indigent appeals for cons over the years. The paramount rule with cons, in the joint or out, was never let them think they could ride you or dictate to you.

And this one, she saw, loves being in charge.

Lisio grimaced, his little white hand on the Formica tabletop. "Don't speak again unless I ask you a question. I want you to listen very closely because there isn't much time." He quickly looked at his watch again.

Her anger boiled up and out. It was a combination of indignation, the bad night, and the false courage the charge of Ritalin gave her. She snorted at him. "That's it. Get out of here. Get Kenny and both of you get out of here right now."

He didn't react. Carol thought she probably looked a little less than formidable in a pink fluffy bathrobe, her hair tangled and wet, but her anger was clear.

Even as she moved from the sink, pointing at Lisio, she cataloged his dark hair and high forehead that suggested a reptile's fragile, thin skull. The dark eyes stayed on her.

He reached into the shapeless black coat. "I have a gun." He brought out a small gray automatic. It was compact enough to fit in his small hand, but it looked real.

"I don't have anything," she said. "If Kenny told you I've got money or something valuable, he's lying. You can see that."

"I can see that," he said.

The back of the countertop pressed into her spine as she tried to move away. The little man's eyes were on her—not hostile, not friendly—clinical almost.

He laid the small gun on the table, beside the ketchup bottle. "I want you to listen to me. I'll shoot Kenny and then I'll shoot you if you don't. Do you understand?"

Carol's head beat with her pulse. She had to be at work in twenty-five minutes. Reilly would be demanding her. She was in her own kitchen, still wet from a shower, the Ramirez kid playing with his motorcycle. She could shout and he'd hear her. But she looked at Lisio and saw he would do it.

"Answer, please," he said sharply.

"Yes, I understand. Don't do anything. I'll listen."

"Sit down," he said.

Carol heard her mother's pronouncement, the unluckiest girl in the world. And that was over lost shoes.

TWO

WHEN SHE SAT DOWN, Carol discovered her legs wouldn't stop twitching under the table. A fright response, she thought objectively, looking at the little man, his little gun, and hard, beetlelike eyes.

"First, your part in this wasn't my idea," Lisio said. "It was Kenny's. He insisted. I need Kenny and he needs you." He spoke with the distaste of a builder forced to compromise on the steel in his girders.

"I can talk to him," she said, "if that'll help."

"Don't answer. Listen. In thirty minutes, you, me, and Kenny are driving to the Pacific Security Bank in the Del Paso Shopping Center. Do you know where that is?"

She shook her head. The twitching in her legs slowed. I can beat him, she thought, I'm a survivor. Just listen, nod, the moment will come.

Lisio was slightly annoyed. "I thought you'd know. I've made a map for Kenny to follow anyway. I've idiot-proofed it for him."

She nodded. His hand was beside the gun. The Ramirez kid abruptly stopped revving his motorcycle. She heard Kenny's harsh command.

She watched Lisio. "I'll be in your car," he said. "You and Kenny will be in his car. You will drive. You'll drive to the drive-up teller. Kenny will get out and demand money from the teller and you'll drive away at a normal rate of speed. You'll meet me a few blocks away. It's marked on the map." He raised his eyes to her. "Questions?"

"You're going to rob the bank?"

"What did it sound like?"

"You don't need me."

"Kenny insisted," Lisio said again peevishly. "I've made very careful plans and Kenny's forced me to change them to accommodate you." His hands flapped on the table, he squirmed in his chair like a precocious pupil who thought everyone else was an imbecile.

"I'm not going anywhere," she said evenly. Her legs twitched badly. "I am not helping you rob a bank."

Lisio touched the gun, then stuffed it back into his coat pocket. "I should have started out by saying how much, much more I know about you than you know about me. For example, I know you are afraid of getting old. I know you've left the support of your senile parents to your brother. I know you've worked for five different attorneys, always doing the scut work, never going to court. I know you're going through a midlife crisis," he was derisive. "I know you think you're sexually very impressive."

At the last he was caustic, sneering at her. She felt a little sickened by the intimacy he forced on her. Carol got up. She wasn't going to let a con manipulate her.

"You read my letters to Kenny. That doesn't get you anything. Get out right now."

Carol thought briefly about trying to use Kenny, but she was utterly uncertain what his motives were now.

He had exposed her to this man without reservation, apparently.

"I read your letters. I helped Kenny write his. Did you notice how his grammar improved? How the quality of imagined orgies got more detailed and creative?" Lisio momentarily forgot the bank scheme. He was boasting to her again, flaunting himself.

She had detected a change about seven months ago, about the time Kenny stopped using tiny swastikas to dot *is* or make periods.

"If you leave now," she said, tensing, "I won't call the police."

Lisio grinned mirthlessly. "You should also know that Kenny escaped from Chino yesterday. He stole a car and beat up a man, pretty badly he says. He drove here. Of all the places in the world he came straight to you. You understand me?"

He was impatiently looking at his watch.

She already ran through the scene with the Santa Maria police. An escaped convict drove three hundred miles from prison to see you. Had you planned his escape with him? How long have you known Kenneth Trask? How long have you been frequently corresponding? How long have you been passing escape plans back and forth?

Carol knew it would be impossible to explain the letters in public without intense embarrassment or worse. They were private lusts and longings between her and Kenny. How could she explain them to Reilly? To the police? She was a lawyer engaged in shocking behavior with a client.

The least sanction she'd face was losing her license to practice law. And that assumed the police found it reasonable she had no prior knowledge of Kenny's escape.

She thought of the letters, in a blue metal box in the back of her bedroom closet, lonely dreams. Safe dreams while Kenny was locked up in Chino.

She heard the front door close, Kenny clumping around in the living room. Like an expectant father, anxious about the delivery.

"If Kenny's a fugitive, you're in trouble," she said. She used her lawyer's voice, cold and impersonal. "You're an accomplice."

"You're not as smart as Kenny said." Lisio held up his hand imperiously. "Anybody brighter than a turnip sounds like a rocket scientist to Kenny."

She noticed sweat beading on Lisio's high forehead, and suddenly realized he was scared, too. She recognized things in him. Never had a woman, no real relationship anyway. The lonely boy without dates, the loner who told himself he preferred solitude to the jeers or pity of others. He couldn't maintain a social contact, even this threatening one, for very long. People scared him.

So she said, "I'll give you some time. You and Kenny can get away. I won't call the police right away."

"I won't call the police. I won't tell. I won't tattle." Lisio struggled to his feet, swaying toward her balefully. "Listen. I will swear that you and Kenny planned his escape and took me prisoner. You planned a series of bank robberies here. That's why you moved here. Kenny told me about it. And he'll say so, Carol honey." He repeated Kenny's light drawl bitterly.

"No, he won't. I know him," but she wasn't sure any longer. Showing up on her doorstep demonstrated how little she knew him.

"Kenny's got a gun, too. If you threatened him, do you really think he'd walk away?"

"I don't believe he'd hurt me." She turned toward the window. Kenny's criminal history was full of revenge violence, stabbings for insults, fights over poor-quality meth, and he liked to boast of what he'd do to others. He might hurt her. That, she admitted, was part of his attraction. He was unpredictable and dangerous. I'm not the first one to find that appealing, she thought.

Lisio tugged at her bathrobe. "You're lying. You're stupid. All you have to do is drive a car."

"Let go. What happens afterward? It's a bank robbery," she snapped.

"I will leave. You and Kenny come to any arrangements you wish. I'm satisfied."

"You don't care if he turns himself in? If I convince him to do that?"

Lisio nodded. He barely came to her waist, staring up at her. "Do anything you wish. I've made secure plans to leave Santa Maria. This is all very simple, very foolproof."

"I want to think about it," she said.

"No." He was furious. "There is no time. We must be at the bank as soon as it opens."

She stepped back, bumping a chair. "I'll tell Kenny you threatened to kill him."

Lisio laughed suddenly, holding onto his black stick, his misshapen body shaking. "Tell him. I'd like to see your reaction when he answers. He thinks I'm a joke. He thinks I'm kidding." And Lisio suddenly blotted the sweat on his forehead with his coat sleeve. "I won't need anymore time than that."

She had heard enough bragging and lying from cons to pierce much of it. Looking at the bitter, bright, tautly wound little man, she realized he was not bragging. There was a turbulent center in him, darker and worse even than Kenny's thoughtless violence. He is the bad one, she said to herself again.

He had the little gun out again, held toward her. "It's a seven and a half minute drive to the bank from here in this traffic. I've timed it. You have eight minutes now to get dressed."

Carol made her decision. She had the choice of running out and hiding at the Ramirezes'. She could call the police.

But there were all the complications and terrible doubts. And she admitted instantly that she didn't have the courage to run by someone with a gun.

"All right," she said. "I'll get dressed."

He put the gun away. "Hurry."

She walked out of the kitchen, Lisio trailing closely, the black stick making a faint clicking on the floor.

Her reasoning was basic. Get out of the house and away from this little man. Alone with Kenny she could persuade him to call it off. I can't rob a bank, she thought incredulously. This is crazy.

Kenny bounced off the couch, his face lighting up. He was watching antic, loud cartoons on the TV.

"Ain't it great, Carol honey? Ain't he a genius?" Kenny asked in a rush.

Before she could reply, Lisio interrupted. "Let her dress. We can do this later. Time." He tapped his watch.

Kenny's face fell. "Okay, you right. Okay. Boy, boy." He rubbed his hands together.

Lisio came behind her into the bedroom. She didn't like him mocking the rumpled bed, prints hung on the walls, her disordered life.

"I'll be right out. I'm not going anywhere," she said coldly, turning on him.

He smiled crookedly, almost ashamed. "I don't care about how you look. Kenny says you sometimes wear a wig."

"Sometimes."

"May I see it?"

She opened the closet, exhalation of mothballs and dust, and reached onto the top shelf where a moderately expensive brunette wig sat on a Styrofoam head. "You want to wear it?" she asked.

He looked at it, nodded. "It's fine. Please bring it with you. And any sunglasses you have."

He waddled out without looking back. Kenny had the cartoons up again and he gaily babbled at Lisio. She dressed, trembling, thinking of some way out. She thought of Reilly missing her soon. I can get clear, she said, I can get out of this.

She combed her hair, then took another Ritalin on impulse. She went to the bureau, scooping change into her purse. House keys, and she panicked because her car keys were missing. She went down on her hands and knees, searching. Last night? Had she lost them somehow last night in all the bleary confusion?

She got up, took the wig and sunglasses, forcing an impassive expression on her face. She didn't know what Lisio would do when he found out she had delayed him.

Kenny was half-bent, talking to Lisio. He tugged at the too-short sleeves of the Raiders jacket he had on. Where had it come from? She wondered how big the man was who owned it and what Kenny had done to get it away.

"I can't find my car keys," she began.

Lisio jingled his pocket and smiled. "Try the wig on, Kenny."

"I picked the keys up while you two were gabbing." Kenny jammed the wig onto his short blond hair.

"Why don't we just call it off?" she said, startled by their foresight. She was part of a plan she didn't even know. "I'm telling you as a lawyer, this doesn't work. We can go our separate ways now."

"Come on, Carol honey," Kenny tugged at her roughly, like an impatient older brother, "Dave's worked this out to little-bitty pieces. We just follow his lead."

She was pulled out the door. "Lock it, please. As you always do," Lisio said.

She did so. She looked at her driveway. A dented, small yellow car was parked behind her station wagon. Up the street, salsa music, neat rows of single-story houses, and she had no one to help her.

"You have the map?" Lisio asked Kenny.

"Check."

"You follow that route exactly."

"Check, check."

"To make this work, you've got to get back to where I'm parked in under five minutes."

"Check. I know the fucking drill, Dave," Kenny said.

Lisio said to her, "Does your car have any quirks I should know about? Does it stall?"

"No, no, everything works fine." She saw that Kenny had already opened the station wagon doors. Everything was ready. All prepared.

"Then we're off," Lisio said, sweating. "Give her the keys, Kenny."

Carol numbly took the keys to the dented car from Kenny.

THREE

RUSH HOUR WAS JUST OFF its peak as Carol slipped unnoticed into it, driving south on the main north-south artery, Fairview Avenue, toward the other side of Santa Maria.

Her hands slid a little with sweat on the steering wheel. She only had about four miles to drive. Every so often, Kenny, who was quiet, would tell her to change lanes or speed up.

He sat beside her, a map of Santa Maria on his lap, the route Lisio wanted marked out in red felt pen. He had a bag of peanuts on the dashboard and a thin shoe box and neatly folded shopping bag at his feet.

She watched the overhead signs vanishing as they sped down the crowded, broad avenue. Camper and car lots, new apartment complexes, the gray block of a franchise technical school passed her. Now is the time, she thought.

"Kenny," she said, hands slippery, knuckles white, "if it's a question of money, I can give you my checking account. There isn't a lot."

"Money?" his head jerked up. He was studying the map, his watch, cracking peanuts and tossing the shells out the window.

"It's just a lot easier, a lot safer for me to get whatever you need from my bank."

"I appreciate that, Carol honey. Sure, sure we'll get your money. It all goes into that communicating property." He sounded moved.

"You mean community property." She couldn't resist correcting him even now. "That's only if there's a marriage, Kenny."

"Sure there'll be a marriage." He grinned, rubbed her leg. "You better scoot over to the left lane, we got to turn at the next light."

"You're still married. You never got a divorce."

"It ain't no big deal." He waved it aside, offered her a peanut. "We going to be together like we married."

Reluctantly, she slowed down. The car stank of old cigarette smoke and apples and she wondered what Kenny had done to get it. She glanced at him, bent over the map intently. He should look preposterous in her wig, sunglasses, the short Raiders jacket. But it all gave him an innocent vulnerability, a kid clowning around. Fat chance, she thought, Kenny's about as vulnerable or helpless as a baby viper.

"I'm suggesting we go to my bank instead," she said, her voice unnaturally calm, "because we're both in a lot of danger."

"From what?"

"That little maniac threatened to kill you and me," she said roughly. "He showed me a gun. He says he'll kill us."

Kenny, to her surprise, laughed like a kid after a good football game. "Yeah, he kills us, he kills people crowd him on the freeway, kills people make noise in a movie, kills guys in the chow line."

"Then you know he's dangerous. Let me turn off at the light and we'll figure out what to do."

"No, no you keep driving," his voice had an edge. "See, Dave's always talking like that. But he don't do nothing. He never does nothing. Who protected him in the joint? Me. He can't do it himself. He's scared, he hides. He don't do anything like that himself."

"Kenny, you're fooling yourself," she began, hoping to break through his new and disturbing self-confidence. The one thing she had counted on was Kenny's uncertainty. He seemed to have lost that since she last saw him. Her spirits fell.

"No, I know things," he said sharply. "I know Lisio. He's got these great little hands, he can make anything, but he can't get it up to do anything. Guy wants to hurt somebody, Dave makes a little thing, tiny, tiny out of staples from a goddamn comic book. Drop that in a guy's ear, he goes crazy getting those teeny hooks out, digs it in."

"He's a monster, Kenny. We cannot go through with this."

"Just listen," he glanced around. "First, you only got about a half mile to go here." His finger traced the blood-red line on the map. They were in a landscape of concrete buildings and wide parking lots, stores and fast-food monuments spreading out in cheery testimony to the city's startling growth.

"I'm going to get us out of a very dangerous, risky—" she said, but he interrupted harshly.

"Now, Carol honey, be quiet. It ain't dangerous. Dave's planned and we talked and he planned. Look, he made a bomb out of matches. You believe it? Guy wanted to blow up his buddy, Dave made a little bomb out of match heads, magazine paper. Blew the whole damn sink out of the cell. See, he *thinks*. He got this all set up and it's going to work for us." He suddenly yawned.

"You're tired. You should let me think this through," she said.

Ahead was a large sandstone sign announcing the Del Paso Shopping Center. They were being fed inexorably toward it.

"Carol honey, remember you told me, you wrote me, you

go, Kenny, you always got to do what you got in your heart is right? You tell me, Kenny, they hate you in prison, all the guards and everybody because you got courage and they don't?"

"I didn't mean to be stupid or foolish," she said. He pointed for her to turn left into the shopping center. Two glass-fronted department stores dominated the asphalt expanse and she couldn't see any bank, only an arcade of stores.

"Now I'm doing what's right. For both of us. I see it. I know it. You look out for me when I was in the joint, right? Okay. I'm out. I look out for you, both of us now. You the one being stupid now."

There was an unshakable firmness in his voice. Her heart pounded with desperation. She had turned into the shopping center, following a short line of cars crawling toward the stores. Kenny was directing her, businesslike and purposeful. She raged because those efforts to improve his self-esteem—her pep talks, letters, and hidden caresses in the prison interview room—had worked so well.

Although she'd only seen Lisio's gun, she assumed Kenny had one, too. Maybe in the shoe box between his feet.

On a Thursday morning, there were people wandering all over the shopping center and she couldn't call out. Not if he had a gun.

"See? There it is. We here," he pointed, and she spotted the blue-tiled roof of the bank at the west end of the parking lot, a fringe of palms around it.

She kept her hands tightly on the wheel. "All right, I'm going to drive out of here, Kenny."

His hands flashed out, freezing the wheel. The peanuts jumped to the floor as he jostled the bag.

He said, "You drive us over to the bank. You hear me?"

He wouldn't release the steering wheel. They were starting to make other cars back up behind them. A horn sounded. There was, she realized, no give on this for Kenny. He had made a decision, hard for him to do, and impossible to undo.

She took a slow breath, ignoring the honking. She put her hand on his. "I'm getting out of the car."

"You ain't."

"I've got to."

"I say no."

She reached for the door handle and Kenny's hand came across her waist. He was pressed to her, his face tight and implacable. She saw herself dimly in the lenses of his sunglasses. She looked frightened.

At least I know where I stand. I'm a prisoner, she thought.

Other cars joined in the honking. But Kenny stayed fixed on her. She recalled his strength when he lifted her up.

"I'm not driving anymore," she said.

He grunted angrily, sat back, upright. "Okay. Park over there," he pointed toward the store arcades.

They stopped in front of Petland, which still offered a good view of the bank. He swore, looking at his watch.

"Okay, okay it's okay. They got couple of cars in the drive-up line ahead, so this works out."

It was not, she saw, a decent spring morning after all. It was warmer, the sky near the east violet-hazed and heavy. Rain, she thought. A lot of rain today.

Kenny got out of the car, walked behind it, and came to the driver's side. He tapped on the window. Carol started. She had thought of Reilly and where she was supposed to be now and it made being so frightened easier.

She opened the door and Kenny, lithe and quick, slid in, forcing her over to the passenger side. Through the open door, the screeching of gaudy parrots in the pet store seemed to taunt her.

Kenny twisted, bobbed his head, the wig flouncing a little. She had nothing more to say to him. He was going to rob the bank and she would have to try to find some way free of him later.

She had, though, worked out a very good defense of duress for herself. I was being held prisoner and in fear of my life. That's the only reason I was in that car, she would say to the police. Sooner or later, Carol realized she would have to account for this morning and she needed her wits to save herself.

"I hear what you're saying," he said, starting the car again, "but I got to tell you, Carol honey, you made this a lot harder than it's got to be. You just got to trust me and it's going to be okay, but you causing me a hell of a lot more trouble than you need to and the only reason I ain't getting more mad is because I know you ain't thinking this in the right way, so I got to think it for both of us."

Fat chance, she said to herself. He drove toward the bank. There were two cars going through the drive-teller. They passed an Albertson's supermarket, strollers idling in and out and over to the arcade of jewelers, liquor stores, pizza parlors, real estate agencies, all indifferent to them. A tiny Campfire girl vainly tried to sell cookies to people ambling from the supermarket. Nobody sees what's happening, Carol thought.

"You pouting?" he demanded.

She laughed.

"What's funny?" he demanded again.

"That isn't the question I expected from a bank robber."

"Well, it wouldn't be asked if someone wasn't adding to the burdens of someone else who's only trying to do the best for her."

"Something bad's going to happen," she said. They were in the drive-up teller lane, and Kenny had slowed. It was humid and cool under the roof, like a covered bridge.

"Nothing bad if you don't do nothing," he said. He reached into the Raiders jacket and she tensed. It was his gun. No, his hand came out with a folded piece of paper. He reached down for the shoe box and shopping bag. "You stay put or I swear, I come running for you, you get out of this car. I swear."

"I believe you, Kenny."

"Okay." He turned his attention to the teller. A green light flashed above the glass-enclosed booth.

"Can I help you?" came the teller's metallic voice from behind the mossy-green glass window.

Kenny smiled, his most boyish and charming, and passed the folded paper into the metal tray pushed out by the teller. Carol sank back toward the door. The young woman in the teller's window paused in an abstract, routine counting of cash. She hadn't looked up. She unfolded the paper.

Kenny was out of the car, the shoe box held out. He flapped the shopping bag once, with a snap, opening it. The teller could look into the shoe box as he raised its lid.

Carol didn't know why the teller dropped the paper and a look of amazement, then terror came over her. Something Lisio did is in the shoe box, she realized with instant clarity. The little hands put something in there.

Kenny closed the shoe box. His lithe, hard body jittered, and he made quick, agitated surveys around him. With one hand, he gestured at the teller as if beckoning.

Carol's hands were balled into fists on her lap. The car's engine rumbled and vibrated through her.

It was over in a moment. The young teller dropped rubber-banded bundles of cash into the metal tray and pushed it out to Kenny. He held the shoe box under one arm, scooping the bundles into the shopping bag with hard, effective motions.

A car came behind them and Carol realized that Kenny had done everything without saying a word, without showing a weapon to anyone except the teller. He turned, the wig fallen a little to one side.

"Open it, open it," he snapped. His door had closed. She reached over, opening it, and he thrust himself back into the car, stuffing the heavy shopping bag onto her. The city map crackled beneath her feet along with peanut shells.

He drove out slowly, nervously shifting in his seat, swinging out into traffic on Brighton Boulevard. "See how easy? See how that goes? No fuss, no nothing." He had his mouth open, even when he wasn't speaking.

A hideous clamoring bell began, rising into the air, so loud Carol imagined everyone in the city could hear it.

She bent to look in the shoe box. "Leave it," Kenny shouted. "You mind reading off the streets? You do that anyway? That too much?"

"All right," she said, trying to calm him. That bell must draw someone, she thought. She craned her head, looking for the police. She called off the street names.

"Bannister, Castor, Marvin," she said. No police and the bank's alarm had already faded into insignificance against the city's other commotions.

"They ain't coming," he seemed to know her mind. He yanked off the wig, rubbing his hair fiercely, making it spike up. "Two more blocks, then I turn right," as if repeating a memorized lesson.

"You and Lisio worked this out in a lot of detail," she said. She called out two more streets.

"You bet we did. Ain't I said so? Right? Look in that bag." He nudged her hard. "Look. Look."

She opened the shopping bag between them. The bundled cash sent up a musty, old smell. Whatever Lisio had planned worked, she thought. There's the proof. She swallowed dryly, feeling the fear.

"I kiss the first cop's ass I see if there ain't six, seven thousand in there. And that's what Dave says we get from that bank so he knows." Kenny banged the steering wheel with his fist.

"You got what you wanted," she said.

"You kidding?" he snorted. He swung the car right, off Brighton and headed up a residential street of new mock-Tudor homes, identical on small gleaming green lawns with infant trees.

Carol carefully folded the shopping bag closed. Ahead on the otherwise deserted street was her own car. All right, the bank's been robbed and I've seen it all, she thought. Now we'll go back to my house, they'll divide up this money. Lisio will leave. I'll have to figure some way to make Kenny leave.

She couldn't accept the idea that Kenny had entered her life so absolutely and irrevocably.

Kenny parked the small yellow car. He checked his watch several times. Lisio, fifteen feet away, opened the driver's door on her car.

"Hurry, hurry," Lisio breathed.

Kenny roughly took her hand, yanking her. She was taller and could have hung back, slowing him, but he was stronger. Kenny had stuffed the wig into the shopping bag and he carried the shoe box in his other hand.

They quickly changed cars. Lisio drove hers, his face barely clearing the dashboard for him to see. Kenny sat with her in the backseat.

"What time did you drive out?" Lisio asked, his large head tilted back to hear.

"Nine-ten," Kenny answered.

"Then four minutes here. Traffic?"

"Okay. Perfect, Dave. You look in the bag, you see."

Lisio wasn't very interested in the shopping bag, Carol noticed. She tried to sit farther away from Kenny, but he pressed his thigh against her, his face pointed at her and he kissed her again and again.

There was a brightly colored child's lunch box beside Kenny on the car floor. Maybe we're going to have a snack, Carol thought sourly. She didn't try to stop his slow kisses.

"No problem?" Lisio asked, glancing in the rearview mirror.

"No problem. Perfect deal. Just what you said." Kenny kissed her again. "Don't say anything, Carol honey. Don't get him upset," he whispered coarsely.

"Carol?" Lisio asked. "Any comment?"

"You wouldn't be interested."

"I am. Absolutely."

"Maybe I'll mention it when you leave." She leaned a little from Kenny, who settled on her like a tired kid, and saw they were driving back along Brighton Boulevard, toward the shopping center.

"Where are we going?" she asked fearfully.

"To the bank. To watch," Lisio said. Kenny grinned up at her.

"We can't go back," she said loudly. "There'll be police, they'll see us."

"They are looking for a late model yellow car and two women," Lisio lectured her. "We have to go back so I can check the police response time to the robbery. It's essential I check it for tomorrow."

"Tomorrow? Why?" Kenny snuggled into her shoulder.

"Tomorrow is the main event. Four banks tomorrow morning, all within fifty minutes." Lisio was smug. "Didn't Kenny mention it?"

"You're going to rob four banks tomorrow?"

Kenny grinned at her. "Ain't that something?"

"It's impossible," Carol said in panic. "You can't."

"You see how that gal handed over the money?" Kenny asked.

"Yes," Carol answered.

"You wonder why she gave it to me, I show her this little shoe box and it ain't even got no shoes in it?"

"You had a gun. She saw a gun," Carol felt the panic rising.

"I got me a gun," Kenny kicked the lunch box, "but I ain't showed it." He put the shoe box on her lap and opened it.

No gun. Carol stared into a maze of red and blue wires in a coiled mass, running into a formless chunk of tan clay, and a rapidly changing digital timer. A black switch lay near one end.

Shoes, she thought, even as she saw the mechanical thing. It always comes back to shoes and I haven't run so far away.

Kenny said, "She gave it up because she's afraid she'll get her head blown off. Her ass, too," he whooped gleefully and Lisio chuckled.

"It's a bomb," Carol heard herself shout. Oh, Jesus, I'm sorry and I'm going to lose it. He's put a goddamn bomb in my lap and who gives a damn about a duress defense in court or what I say to the police when I've got a bomb in my lap?

She swatted at it, a dumb reflex, and Kenny giggled. Lisio sharply told them to be quiet so he could accurately time the police and how long it actually took them to get deeply involved in checking the Pacific Security Bank.

When Carol found herself frantically trying to push open the door to get out of the car, traveling at forty miles an hour in rush-hour traffic, Kenny grabbed her, pinning her flailing arms, and pressed her head to his chest, stroking her.

FOUR

MILES AWAY, four blue-and-white Santa Maria Police Department squad cars surged through downtown traffic, red-and-blue lights flashing to force trucks, cars, and anybody else off to one side. The squad cars pulled up in a ragged line in front of a long, fingerlike, emerald green building. The building was thirty stories high, pointing upward into the humid sky like a manmade taunt. It was visible for miles beyond downtown.

Out of the first squad car came Robby Medavoy, a tall, graceless man with black hair who acted undefeated. He carried a sledgehammer. The other cops quickly came to him. Three were in uniform. A heavy-gutted older man in blue police overalls lugged video equipment, a smaller man held a toolbox as if it contained surgical instruments. The other men, like Medavoy, wore black nylon jackets with POLICE stamped in bright yellow on the back.

"Hustle, guys." Medavoy was impatient, looking at his watch. He pointed at two uniformed cops. "You guys are on the back entrance, okay? I'll radio down if Reilly leaves his office or he sends someone down."

The uniformed cops nodded. They gazed dreamily, warily up at the tall office building.

"I always wanted to see how they fixed it up inside." Jimmy Zaragoza, another detective on Medavoy's Robbery Detail also looked up at the tower.

"Shut up, Jimmy."

"Sorry, Robby." He was a squat, dark-haired man in his late thirties and his thin, graying moustache only concealed a few of the acne pits on his cheeks.

Standing beside him was Arnold Geffen, lean and loose with a runner's easy slouch. He was a year younger than Zaragoza and Medavoy's closest friend in the police department. He kept tensing his shoulders and seemed preoccupied, which surprised Medavoy. Geffen was usually very much into the electricity of a raid.

"Same thing for you two," Medavoy said to the other cops, "you watch the front entrance here. If I want you to hold Reilly, something happens upstairs, you be ready for me."

"He going to run?" asked a young cop.

"You don't know what he's going to do," Medavoy said to all of them. "So watch out. Don't talk to people if they're stopping to ask why cops are in front of the building, okay?"

The younger cops nodded. Medavoy knew they listened to him because he had a reputation in the department, some guys hating him, others saying he was a hero. They like the way I'm juiced up about being here, too, he thought.

He liked the early dampness at his arms and back, first rush from the excitement. He enjoyed slowing the chaotic morning traffic on the street. Even the exhaust stink from so many cars and trucks seemed pleasant as it hung in the thickening air. Medavoy wondered where all the harried, bumper-to-bumper cars had come from. There never used to be so many.

He had to talk loudly over the booming, jolting jackhammers up the block where three more towers, rust-red girders teeming with men, rose from fresh rubble.

"You all read the search warrant?" he called out. "We're going into a lawyer's office. It's a tough place to search so don't grab anything that's not listed, okay?"

The men laughed a little and a civilian, standing at the edge of the group, held a finger in his ear and winced at each jarring jackhammer rattle.

"We got Mr. Santarelli here." Medavoy pointed at the wincing civilian. "He's coming in, he's the Special Master. He'll check out how you search. You got a question, come to me." The lawyer smiled nervously in his designer glasses, jiggling his leather attaché case. He looked out of place, more at home with the men and women who stared, murmured as they passed into the tower's entrance.

"And we got Ely Willy, ace locksmith, along for insurance." And the smaller man with his precious toolbox politely nodded.

Medavoy looked them over a final time. "Okay. We're on the eighteenth floor, suite three-ten. Let's go."

He lifted the sledgehammer and started for the tower, Geffen at his side. A voice behind him said, "Are we going after evidence on guys in the department? We doing shit work for Internal Affairs?" It was one of the uniformed cops.

Medavoy lowered the sledgehammer. Geffen, his stubble already dark, glowered at the other cops. Medavoy said evenly, "You read the search warrant affidavit."

"I read it," the cop answered sharply.

"Okay. Brian Reilly's a defense attorney. He's tough and he's an asshole. He's representing the fence who's tried to deal some property from three two-elevens a week ago. He's dealing on his own. We're looking for that stolen property."

"I heard they're trying to lay the two-elevens off on cops," the uniformed cop, a young man, said savagely.

"Robby just told you," Geffen broke in. "Let's go."

Gef always backs me up, Medavoy thought. There was no other man, except Zaragoza or Masuda in Robbery, he'd trust so completely.

"Any of you have problems getting evidence on dirty cops?" Medavoy asked, waving Geffen back.

"I'm not nailing other cops," the young uniformed cop said truculently to Medavoy.

"Any other deserters?"

A hand went up.

"You two head back. Get another assignment. I don't want you here." Medavoy had no hesitation about his harsh command.

When the two turned and strolled to one of the squad cars, Geffen barked, "Get your asses out of here."

The young cop swore, then said, "They got you made good, Medavoy," and the car's lights went up, its siren blared, and it tore into traffic, other cars honking and rocking to sudden stops.

He quickly got hold of his temper, a skill he had painfully learned over the years. He was acting supervisor of the Robbery Detail today and this was his operation. He apologized to the civilian, then abruptly hefted the sledgehammer. "That's it for office bullshit. We go in fast now."

He led them, more or less in a single line, into the tower's black marble lobby. Zaragoza was calming the nervous Santarelli, telling him a kid could handle this kind of search.

To Geffen, who walked briskly beside him, Medavoy said, "You, me, and Jimmy'll do the inner office, okay?"

"Sure. What's the hammer for?"

"Little visual excitement." He looked at the preoccupied expression on Geffen's face. "You tired or something?"

"I don't sleep too well lately."

"You'll sleep tonight." Medavoy wanted to perk him up. "We're going to bag Reilly. I know it."

Geffen looked disdainfully at the startled lawyers and investment bankers in the lobby as they passed by. "You want Reilly or the bad guys in the department?"

Medavoy grinned fiercely. "I want both."

"Hey," Zaragoza said worriedly, "we got anything going here if this guy's clean today?"

Medavoy shook his head, said low, "Jimmy, if we come up dry we're in a deep hole and we don't get out."

Zaragoza sighed dejectedly and smiled wanly for the civilian.

Medavoy said to Geffen, "You going to be okay when we get up there, Gef?"

"I'm okay, Robby. I ever let anybody down?" Geffen was offended.

"I just wanted to hear you're up to speed." Medavoy, with all the problems in the department now, didn't want to worry about someone he liked as much as Geffen.

Medavoy led them to a row of shining gold-doored elevators. When one opened, he held up his hand to stop the people waiting for it. "Next one, sorry. We need it." And he squeezed his crew inside. It was a tight fit with all of them, the tools, and equipment.

"Hit eighteen, Gef," Medavoy said.

He and Geffen had not always been friends. They had begun as antagonists.

Medavoy came to Robbery after a dreary, dead eighteen months on Auto Burg. He spent most of the time running down altered license plates, chopped cars, and fidgety kids—black, white, and brown—who liked to hot-wire anything they found in a theater parking lot or municipal garage.

It was boring, tedious work and seemed to mean very little. He hated it.

Medavoy had come through the department, gradually losing the spring-gun temper that had been one of the ugly legacies from his old man. By the time his assignment to

Robbery came through, he had been a cop for nine years, and like a rehabilitated alcoholic, he could restrain the impulse to instantly use his temper or fists. But he still had the impulse. His old man was a bare-knuckle cop for the Southern Pacific, quick-fisted, a bully often cited by the railroad for roughness, but kept on for the same reason. The old man's advice, which it took all these years to unlearn, was simple: "One of you, one of them, use your gun. Two of you, one of them, use your baton. Three of you, one of them, beat the shit out of him. They the only numbers that matter."

So when Medavoy walked into Robbery on the first day, he came laden with some baggage, a rap as a fighter and grandstander. Things didn't get off to a great start.

Geffen, feet up on his desk, lanky body stretched out, was going through a typical breezy war story about a puke he'd caught who only stole women's underwear from stores.

Medavoy introduced himself to Zaragoza, Stan Masuda, the supervisor Ornelas, and a couple of other guys. Everybody shook hands. Except Geffen. He waited, silent and annoyed, stared Medavoy down, and went on, without missing a beat, with the story.

Medavoy was a little miffed when Geffen didn't talk to him at all for two weeks. Just dropped reports on his desk, or time sheets, or rap sheets. Jimmy Zaragoza told Medavoy, "Gef's the steadiest guy here. He doesn't know you, he hears you're an asshole, so he's keeping some distance."

"Thanks for the rundown," Medavoy said.

"We got a lot of assholes around here," Zaragoza said.

In fact, the assessment dispirited Medavoy. He was intimidated by the Robbery crew. Geffen, Masuda, and Zaragoza were all several years older and Vietnam vets. Medavoy had gone to community college rather than enlist or be drafted because by that time, it was painfully clear what was happening over there and the war was over. He now regretted his decision because he had missed something important they were all part of and could share, even if it was hateful or sad. Geffen's aloofness increased Medavoy's sense of separateness.

He couldn't blame Geffen for caution, though. The rumors and bad feeling about departmental corruption were just starting. You didn't know who was doing what or to who.

About a month after he started in Robbery, things broke.

Geffen was called out on a follow-up investigation. It was a dippy attempted robbery and all he was supposed to do was check in a few boxes on the reports.

Zaragoza and Masuda had been working on him, so he said Medavoy could tag along.

It was a blind case; a neighbor calling the cops said somebody fired a shotgun the night before. A patrol unit checked and located a man named Hardy who admitted firing a warning blast into the air to scare away someone climbing through his bedroom window.

Medavoy and Geffen went out and interviewed Hardy in his furniture warehouse. He was a cinnamon stick of a man, belt cinched tight, with a sour look. He lived on the second floor of the warehouse. They asked him what happened. He said he was awakened about three when some kid tried to crawl through the window. The kid had a gun. Hardy grabbed his own shotgun, sitting near the bed, and fired a shot over the kid's head to scare him away. The kid took off running.

They left him, and at that point Geffen wanted to head back. There was nothing more. The patrol guys had checked the area and found nothing. They had filled in Hardy's incident report.

Medavoy, though, didn't like Hardy or the story. He had seen that same smug, half-arrogant, half-frightened look on his old man when the railroad caught him lifting a couple of lamps off a freight.

So he and Geffen took a look. The warehouse sat almost alone in a thinly settled neighborhood.

"Satisfied? You see anything worthwhile?" Geffen asked.

"It bothers me he had a shotgun so handy."

Geffen swore and went back to the car. "I'm out of here in five minutes, I don't care if you're with me."

Medavoy didn't get mad. Or he didn't show it. He concentrated on going over the same ground the patrol guys claimed to have checked the night before.

About a hundred yards from the warehouse was a heavily leafed planter bordering the alley, and Medavoy found a pair of feet in sneakers. Hidden by large leafy ferns was a kid, lying on his face, as if asleep. Medavoy shouted for Geffen.

"What're you shitting around for?" Geffen snapped.

"I'm not shitting. Look in the ferns."

Geffen bent down. The kid had on jeans, high-topped black sneakers, and a green parka. Carefully, so he didn't disturb things, Geffen lifted the inert shoulders.

"Jesus. I know this kid. It's Archie Linares."

"Who's he?"

Geffen stared at the dead, sleeping face. "Archie Linares. He's like about seventeen now. He steals buses." He let the face drop softly into the dirt again. "He stole school buses. I busted him half a dozen times. Last time, I put him in my squad car, I'm going to take him out to Juvenile Hall. I turn away for like five seconds, Archie's got my ignition wires out, he's stealing my squad car. He must've been only fourteen." Geffen shook his head.

"The citizen's lying," Medavoy said.

"Show me." But Medavoy could tell Geffen had already spotted it.

He pointed and walked around the planter. "He shot the kid. It's hard to see through the ferns but there's a real heavy blood flow here." They followed it into the alley. As though abandoned, a pink ant- and fly-covered mass lay on the concrete. "I make you a bet the shotgun hit the kid, took the top of his head off, and that's his brain."

Lying under the ferns, Archie Linares simply looked damp.

There was no blood, apparently, near him. It had all run down into the alley.

Geffen was angry. "The old fucker shot Archie while he's running away."

"I don't see any gun, either."

"Fuck no. Archie didn't use a gun. He steals buses. Dumb little fuck. He couldn't do that and he's sure a washout as a burglar."

Medavoy looked away from the mess in the alley. He wasn't especially squeamish, although he had never seen anything as surgically lethal before. But the whole scene was pitiful, a kid lying dead in the ferns, brains in the alley, his sneakers sticking out, all because he tried to climb into the wrong warehouse window.

"He probably figured nobody lived in a furniture warehouse," Medavoy said.

"Okay," Geffen said, still shaking his head. "We bust the old fucker. You want to take it?"

Medavoy shrugged as if it didn't matter. "No. You bust him. You know the kid."

Which made everything work out very well. Medavoy knew Geffen appreciated the arrest. If they'd left, as Geffen insisted, someone else would have discovered the body sooner or later and Geffen would look as though he had done a very sloppy job. Geffen came out this way as being uncommonly thorough.

Hardy ended up copping to shooting the kid and plead guilty to involuntary manslaughter, which came out a six-month jail sentence and a few thousand hours of community service.

Geffen called the Santa Maria Unified School District and told someone their school buses were no longer at risk.

Life was much easier in the Robbery room after Geffen loosened up. He and Medavoy became friends. Medavoy was still married to Annie, Geffen still married to Robin at that point and the two couples began seeing each other, having dinner at each other's homes. It was a matter of grim satisfaction to both men later that their former wives disliked each other.

Annie was in her "growth phase," as Medavoy put it. She was eating constantly and grew wider before his eyes. Sex with her stopped dead. "It was getting like riding a stack of pillows and I never did anything right she said," he complained to Geffen.

"I don't know about your rack time," Geffen said. "Remember when Annie'd bring out that casserole thing she always made?"

"Chicken. She said chicken was less fattening."

"Maybe if you only looked at it. That casserole was heavy duty. We get home, Robin says to me, sweetest voice too, 'You eat what you want, Arnold. But, I'm on a strict no-shit diet.'"

"No shit?"

"Strict," Geffen grinned. He was running marathons then, at Robin's urging, and they ordered their lives around high-carb foods and training days and miles per week. Gef lost a lot of his running intensity when they broke up.

Medavoy was best man at Geffen's third marriage and organized the bachelor party. They held it at Lil Ed's, a strip joint made of cinder blocks in the middle of wheat farms near the north edge of the city. There were plenty of strip joints closer to downtown, but Medavoy rightly figured that a roomful of drunken, rowdy, and increasingly libidinous law-enforcement types should have as much open space around it as possible. Lil Ed's also featured the best minestrone in Santa Maria, which was an undeniably odd combination of sensual attractions.

When his own marriage to Annie collapsed, Medavoy slept on the Geffens' couch for almost a month. He remembered never sleeping past six in the morning because one or more of the kids—a mixed brood of three girls and two boys—would sneak out and manage to scare him awake by tickling him, dropping ice cubes on him, or jumping on his belly.

About eight months after the Archie Linares thing, Geffen found a chance to return the favor.

He and Medavoy were attending the regular Friday-night-to-Saturday-morning discussion group that met at Rainey's Bar on Merrimac Avenue, way down in the older heart of Santa Maria. Rainey's was one of Medavoy's sentimental favorites since the city had begun an inexplicable and unstoppable growth spurt, wrecking neighborhoods and homes and bars. There were very few like Rainey's left.

The discussion group consisted of off-duty cops and sheriff's deputies and a few beer-bellied marshals from the county courthouse. Medavoy felt at home on those incoherent, loud, and friendly nights and he matched Geffen's war stories with his own or tales from the Southern Pacific his old man had told.

This particular session drifted apart at two A.M. The cops, including Zaragoza and Masuda from Robbery, stumbled out into the dewy night under ancient oaks and elms. A black kid on a ten-speed rode up to the bunched, swaying cops, pointed a gun at them, and shouted for their wallets.

Medavoy had enough wit left to doubt that anybody in his right mind would point a gun at a bunch of drunk, belligerent cops. So he instantly produced his wallet; the kid snatched up three more, and started pedaling away down the street like distant lightning.

Medavoy and two other cops had their own guns out and started shooting at him. Luckily, it was late enough that no one was on the street or sidewalk and the yelling, furious cops got off a dozen shots before Geffen shouted, "Stop firing, assholes! You can't even see him!"

Geffen, in perfect training then, took off after the kid. It was much later that Medavoy sobered up enough to realize the kid didn't know they were cops—everybody was out of uniform—and was probably much surprised himself when these drunks began shooting.

He watched Geffen, striding rapidly, head down Merrimac. "Gef needs backup," Medavoy shouted. The others agreed and they all lumbered and wheezed after him.

They lost two marshals within a block. When they did catch up to Geffen, he had knocked the kid off the ten-speed and was bending one arm behind his back. It took some doing for Medavoy to keep himself and the other members of the discussion group off the kid, but Geffen quick-marched him back to the bar and a phone. Medavoy was startled to discover that the kid's gun was a water pistol and he wasn't black, just tan, and he wasn't a kid, but probably about thirty.

Which proved it was fortunate Geffen had been in such good shape since none of those trained police observers would have been able to give a usable description of the guy and he would have gotten away with their wallets and shields inside. And that indeed would have been highly embarrassing.

And later, Geffen was content to fall into Medavoy's shadow when events made Medavoy well known. So why was Gef getting sloppy in his reports, blowing interviews, and losing investigation requests from the DA all of a sudden? He rarely talked about Vietnam or the Marines, but lately bits and pieces of his experience started creeping into his cop stories.

Medavoy admitted Gef was probably wrapped too tight for his own good. Three marriages proved that if nothing else. The last few weeks showed something was bothering Gef and this concerned Medavoy. He was, though, rebuffed every time he tried to help.

The other guy in Robbery he got along with well was Jimmy Zaragoza. This was no trick. Everyone got along with Zaragoza, who had one of the easiest, most unassuming natures Medavoy had ever encountered.

Zaragoza was married to Candace, who was called Sugar. They had two daughters and lived in the same two-bedroom home in Laurel Acres as they had when Zaragoza joined the department fifteen years before. In the summer, there were barbecues every other Sunday and all Zaragoza and Sugar insisted on was that everyone bring something to cook. Zaragoza coached his oldest daughter's softball team, he attended Holy Martyrs regularly, and Medavoy often complimented him on the smoothness of his life.

"Smooth? You don't know the problems," Zaragoza would moan. "I got more stress than anybody here."

So one afternoon, when Zaragoza was taking time off, he and Medavoy went over to Rainey's, Medavoy's treat. Zaragoza never had any real vacation time built up or any sick leave. As the hours accrued, he took them off, and nobody had stopped him so far.

He was smoking with Medavoy and he only smoked when he drank, so he coughed a lot.

"Jimmy, you have the best deal going of anybody I know," Medavoy said to needle him.

"Jesus, you know what I got to live with. You know my rep," Zaragoza hacked, grimaced at his cigarette, and took another shaky drag on it.

"What rep? Nobody remembers that old four-fifty-nine deal." Another needle. Medavoy ashamedly admitted he took advantage of Zaragoza's good nature as much as anybody. Ordering him, needling him. He was so good-tempered he seemed to invite it.

"Nobody? Hey, I go to serve a subpoena last week for the DA on some dumb Seven-Eleven stop and rob. Me. Serving a subpoena because the dumb lady DA thinks her reluctant witness will pay attention if he knows it's me. And hell, Robby," Zaragoza drank, sucked on the cigarette, and sighed, "he did. I hand him the paper. He says, you're the cop who nailed that guy in the nuts. You're a mean son of a bitch, my man. He showed up in court. Word gets around a town like this, Robby. They all hear it."

When Zaragoza was a patrolman, years before, he had

chased a burglary suspect from an auto parts store. The man turned on him, raising what later proved to be a crescent wrench. At night, Zaragoza didn't know what it was and fired his gun. As Zaragoza explained it, the man instantly dropped the wrench, missing how terrified the cop was, his gun wiggling with fright. The man glanced down at his bloody pants and said, in a mournful, reproachful voice, "How come you had to shoot me in the balls, man?"

Zaragoza claimed to feel very guilty about his bad aim.

"It's like the wild West, Robby." He waved for another round, ground out his cigarette. His olive-colored face was sad. "You get a rep and they come after you. I had four guys, four, try to shoot me after that deal. They wanted to see if they're tougher than the cop who turns four-fifty-nines into sopranos."

"I bet you scared off a lot more pukes than came after you," Medavoy said. "A bad rep can be a good thing."

Zaragoza shook his head, lighting another cigarette and coughing. They were nearly the only normal people in Rainey's at three in the afternoon. "Well, you watch yourself. You getting a pretty bad rep, too. Then you start worrying. Then you get upset stomach all the time, heart hurts, you can't shit."

Zaragoza's catalog of nervous symptoms was well known. He always complained of some kink or ache, never crediting the source.

"Okay, Jimmy, everybody says you fucked up the Alseki search. Right?"

"I never live that down. Never." Their drinks came and he swallowed half of it.

"So what happened?" Medavoy wanted to hear from the prime actor how the famous *People v. Alseki* went wrong. It was Zaragoza's chief claim to fame, and one he would not live down.

"You want to hear? Okay. First, I didn't fuck up the case. I had this snitch who comes to me. He says Alseki's dealing crank from his house on North Casement. And he's got a bunch of stolen guns in there, including a stolen Uzi. This's a couple of years ago, Bobby, and an Uzi showing up in town was hot. Now, this snitch's one of my very best; he's dead now, he got hit by a garbage truck, which is sad and kind of funny. But, he's good. So I take my partner who was Frank Katouzik over to North Casement."

"No warrant?"

"For what? I got to check things out a little myself. Hey. Give me a break. Everybody does this, like I should know what the damn Supreme Court's going to do before. Like I'm supposed to know they'll change the rules in the middle of the game."

"Take it easy, Jimmy. I just asked."

Zaragoza ground out the cigarette. Medavoy was sorry he'd upset him. "Okay, so here's what happened. Me and Katouzik sit on the house for an hour, it's like five in the afternoon. There's Alseki, strutting around, he goes out on the lawn, bullshits with some pukes, passes some cash, struts back inside. We see him strut out to his car, he's taking out these things in canvas. I say to Katouzik, fuck this. The snitch's right, Alseki's dealing and he's got those guns inside, so let's knock on his door."

Medavoy grinned. He had read the Supreme Court's factual summary of the case. Every cop had to now, and every prosecutor, because what Jimmy did became enshrined as police misconduct.

Zaragoza and his partner went to the door, knocked, and were admitted by Laurice Alseki. They told him they were worried about rodents crawling all over his open garbage cans. And as they talked, they moved from room to filthy room, taking it all in. Zaragoza spotted the white methamphetamine in one bedroom, sitting on a bureau guarded by a young woman with stringy hair. In an open hall closet he saw a sawed-off shotgun propped up.

At that point, he assumed his plain-view observations justified a more extensive search and seizure, so he and his partner put Alseki and the woman under arrest and began searching. They eventually seized two shotguns, the sawed-off, a .32 and .22 automatic, and 143 grams of crank, which was not much, but more than you could use in a single sitting.

"But, we didn't find the goddamn Uzi and I wanted to find that," Zaragoza told Medavoy earnestly.

The long and the short of it was that Alseki appealed the search contending that the police violated his Fourth Amendment rights. The California Supreme Court, to Zaragoza's shock, agreed and even named him directly in its opinion. *"This officer,"* wrote the stern Court, *"had no authority to continue his search past the point of his observations of alleged contraband"* ("Alleged!" Zaragoza squawked to Medavoy in the bar) and *"Detective Zaragoza should have ceased his search and attempted to obtain a warrant in order to validly seize any property."*

What really hurt, though, was the rest of the opinion in which the Supremes dumped all over Zaragoza's snitch. No good to enter this man Alseki's property on a ruse prompted by an unreliable, untested informant, and so on and on. For a long time Zaragoza was known as "Bad Search Zaragoza" in many police agencies. "Which could've been worse," he told Medavoy. "I could've been called BS."

"You ever get the Uzi? I didn't see it mentioned anyplace."

Zaragoza grinned slyly. "I got it. That shithead didn't mention it because he'd have burned no matter what the Supremes said if he yelled about it."

"How'd you find it? You see it?"

"He gave it up," Zaragoza said. "Katouzik and me get Alseki downtown. I'm not like you, Robby, I never hit guys."

This nettled Medavoy, but he agreed it was fair turnaround for getting to Zaragoza. "I never hit anybody in custody, Jimmy. I never hit anybody who didn't go after me first."

"I hear things, too."

"This is what I'm telling you."

Zaragoza slicked down the edges of his moustache, moist with spit and liquor. "Okay, forget it. You know how I got that Uzi? I put Alseki in a chair by the Xerox machine. I got this colander Sugar gave me because I brought some grapes to wash for lunch. I stick the colander on Alseki's head, stick his hand on the Xerox. I tell him, Laurice, this here's the latest in police science. It's like the world's greatest lie detector. You know why? 'Why?' he asks. Because the goddamn Japs made it."

"He bought that?"

"Alseki's not the greatest brain I ever met. Maybe amongst his peers, he's like a genius, but you put him up against any moron, he's going to come out second."

Inside the copy machine, Zaragoza had already put a page saying NO. So he told Alseki that whenever he told a lie, the machine would immediately know it. And then he and Katouzik questioned him about the Uzi. Each time Alseki answered, Zaragoza pushed the copy button, out slid a copy with NO on it and he'd sorrowfully tell Alseki things were getting blacker and blacker. The Japs were too good.

"Finally, he's sweating bullets and he goes, 'Yeah, I got this Uzi, I got it as part of deal with some bikers in Placerville, I can't lie to you.' So he gives it up and I went back to his house and found it in the attic, stuck under the insulation."

"That was a bad search," Medavoy said merrily. "You know that."

"Robby, that's the secret of this work. You know it's bad, I know, even the puke knows it. But what's he going to do, make a big deal of it because he got outsmarted by a kitchen utensil? I mean, I took a fucking Polaroid of the guy sitting at the Xerox machine with my wife's colander on his head."

This was Zaragoza's general approach to life, far less intense or physical than Medavoy. He asked, "So how's your sex life, Robby?"

"Okay."

"That's bullshit. You say it's great or you got a lousy one. It's never okay."

"It's lousy." He and Annie were becoming terminal. They were sleeping in separate beds. He only saw her in the morning and that was when he went into the bedroom to get his clothes.

"Robby, look, I'll give you my proven secret for a happy marriage. You want to hear it?"

Medavoy leaned forward. "Sure, Jimmy."

Zaragoza fiddled with a final cigarette, holding it without lighting it, like a conductor's baton. "The secret of great sex is first, you never fool around on your wife. Or you don't do it much. Some guys think they got to have variety to keep in shape."

"No?"

"It's crap. Stick to the one you know. Most of the time. And the second part, you got to set up a schedule. You screw your wife every Monday night, nine sharp. Get it?"

"Sounds like it'd get boring. Suppose you're not home. Suppose you got work."

"That's the beauty. See, you both start thinking about it, Sunday night, then Monday morning, then after dinner, and by nine, she's going to start going for you like it's your first time with her."

"I don't believe it, Jimmy. It's too predictable."

Zaragoza waved the unlit cigarette. "Who's got two kids, a happy, satisfied wife. Who's looking forward to Monday night?"

Medavoy had to agree that of all the cops he knew, Zaragoza had the most stable, apparently solid marriage. There was no chance to try the theory with Annie, but Medavoy had thought about the virtues of stability and predictability lately since he started seeing Jane.

"Jimmy, what happens if once a week is, you know, not enough? I mean, it's got to be tough about Wednesday, right?"

Zaragoza rolled his eyes. "Then you add another day. No

problem. It's the schedule that counts," he paused worriedly. "I got to tell you, sometimes you get a lot of stress doing it this way."

And that, Medavoy thought, was probably the first time Zaragoza had used the magic word that had so dominated his vocabulary in the last few months.

The litany of bodily ailments and sleeplessness had gone on and then the department brought in Dr. Bernard Junkin, who was to address the troops on "Stress Management or How to Stop the Hidden Killer."

It was, for Zaragoza, an event akin to visiting Lourdes. He heard the esteemed psychologist describe his very symptoms, heard their cause linked to the rigors of his job; his worries and fears over Alseki or the soprano burglar translated into heartburn and muscle spasms.

"Robby, I tell you, I never knew I had so much stress until I listened to this guy," Zaragoza said later with fervor.

The department's attempt at stress management through education resulted only in Zaragoza refusing to work overtime and taking more sick time and a general upswing in the number of workers comp claims filed against the department by cops who said their sore elbows, aching backs, and piles were caused by crime fighting.

So now, crowded into an elevator with Geffen and Zaragoza, Medavoy knew he could trust them. They were going on a raid that could go sour and he needed that trust. In a department where corruption and uncertainty about loyalties had taken root, he had faith in the guys on Robbery. He had to hang onto that today.

FIVE

THE ELEVATOR DOORS OPENED at the eighteenth floor, onto a corridor of pale walls, fluted lights, and quiet, heavy carpets. Medavoy shouldered the sledgehammer.

"Okay. Everybody inside quickly, guys. Don't slow down. I want to secure that office as soon as we're inside."

"Now, Robby?" asked the heavy-gutted police cameraman.

"When I knock and go through the door. Get the knock-notice."

They walked past double doors, law firms and bankers, investment firms, suites of offices. Medavoy was very pleased because he had wanted to confront Reilly for a long time. And he loathed the idea of corrupt cops. He did not, in fact, know which he wanted to destroy more, a crooked lawyer or crooked cops.

He grinned at Geffen, stiff and even nervous, alongside him. Whatever was bothering Gef would have to wait.

At the high-doored, gold-lettered law firm of Brian Reilly, Medavoy paused, got out the search warrant, self-consciously

56

straightened his shoulders, and knocked loudly, then pushed the door open.

"Police. Santa Maria Police Department and I'm coming in."

"Hey, hold it, Robby. I missed it. I didn't get the thing on."

"Jesus, Ron," he swore, closing the door quickly. The handy-talkie he and Geffen wore hissed and rasped with faint radio traffic.

"Do it again. I'll get it this time."

Zaragoza said to the Special Master, "I wish he'd bust the door in. Wouldn't you like to see that?"

"You don't have to break anything."

"You'd be surprised."

Medavoy slowly repeated the notice of his intention to enter. A brief glance at the camera. "Okay?"

"Beauty," Ron said with a high sign.

He went inside. Three people sat on the surprisingly cheap couches in the waiting room. Reilly's secretary was already on her feet, hurrying forward.

"Are you from *60 Minutes* or something?"

"I'm Detective Robert Medavoy, Santa Maria Police. These men are police officers. We have a man here, he's a lawyer, he's going to observe while we execute the search warrant."

"Oh, my God. Oh, my God," she said with growing vehemence. She was young, thin-faced and thick-waisted.

"Jimmy, Gef, help those folks out, then secure the door." Medavoy noticed the young couple, in jeans and fatigue jackets, avoiding his glance. Shake them a little and I bet everything falls out, he thought merrily. Reilly's bread-and-butter dopers.

From behind a large fern, a woman said, "Excuse me, I've got an appointment."

"Sorry, everybody's leaving," he answered firmly. The young couple and the woman were gently forced from the office. This dramatic urgency wasn't really necessary, he knew, but it helped to keep people being searched off-balance. I am my dad's son, he thought. He put on an act and enjoyed it, too.

"We'll give you new dates. I'll call," the secretary sang. "My God!"

"Where's Mr. Reilly?"

She breathed in short, startled gasps. She stared at the videocamera, the toolbox, the sledgehammer in Medavoy's hand.

Before she could answer, he marched forward, through the receptionist's office, into the inner office. Reilly sat behind a desk far too large for him, and he looked up from the tuna sandwich he held in one hand.

"What do you people want?"

"We're searching your office. Get up, please. I want you outside with your secretary." Geffen, Zaragoza, and the cameraman had pushed in behind Medavoy. They were tensely alert.

The plump attorney daintily lowered his sandwich. His scarlet-veined cheeks were damp suddenly, his manner still calm. He wore his suit, as though he had just come from court.

"Let me see the warrant. Robby? That's what they call you?" He held out a white hand.

Medavoy gave him the warrant with enjoyment.

It was very specific, based on what a reliable informant had told Medavoy. Three drug dealers, two handling cocaine, one manufacturing and selling methamphetamine, had been raided by the Special Weapons Unit of the Police Department. But, no one had been arrested. Only cash, some drugs, and a few odd and striking items, like a gold nugget, had been taken. Reilly had offered to sell the nugget back to the dealers.

There had been rumors for several months about things going wrong with the Special Weapons Unit. But this warrant was the first opportunity to link them directly with a crime. What Medavoy couldn't determine was whether the informant was one of Reilly's drug clients who felt let down or was it simply a lucky tip.

"Come on, somebody's going to help you out." Medavoy nodded to Geffen, who moved toward the lawyer.

"Wait a minute. Hold it," the famous Reilly stammer, imitated in courtrooms in five northern California counties was vivid. "Nielda! Where are you?"

His secretary timidly peered at the bunched men from the doorway.

"Nielda, have Carol step in," Reilly gestured, stammered, holding the warrant. "I want her to make notes."

"Nobody's interfering while we search," Medavoy said. Geffen had taken Reilly's thick arm.

"Carol Beaufort's my assistant. I want an unbiased observer involved."

"Carol didn't come in," the secretary said.

"Call her at home."

"No answer. I tried an hour ago."

"Call her again. Tell her to come down here immediately."

Medavoy held up his hand. "Don't waste your time. I'm not letting anyone else into this office until we leave."

Geffen began tugging at Reilly. The slender, wiry tough runner tacked a little, like he was drawing down a kite in the wind.

"I want to talk to you alone," Reilly said to Medavoy.

"Take him outside."

"Give me a minute. We'll take care of everything."

Geffen looked at Medavoy.

"Okay. Close the door and keep the camera going, okay?"

"Don't screw around with him, Robby. Let's do what we got to do." Geffen's lips were dry, his face tight.

"I'm just showing we're going the extra yard to cooperate," he spoke directly and solely to the camera.

The four men retreated, the solid door shut softly. Medavoy was struck by how impersonal Reilly's inner office was, pictures bought thoughtlessly to cover the light walls, brass fixtures, thick-pillowed chairs, all random and mass-produced. A Little League Coach of the Year award on his desk stood out as uniquely personal. The office safe, listed in the search warrant to be opened and gone through, lay blue-black and dense under a stereo receiver. The informant said everything was in the safe. Medavoy wouldn't search there first or even single it out. He didn't want Reilly to pinpoint the identity of the informant by his knowledge of something so specific.

The office belonged to a man, Medavoy thought, who didn't care too much where he worked.

"You've got a fast minute," he said and he leaned on the sledgehammer handle.

Reilly laid down the search warrant. He was a fat man who managed to look dour, his brown-framed glasses giving him the dusty indifference of a druggist.

"So what do we have to do here?" Reilly calmly asked.

"You tell me."

"I'm asking you seriously."

"You think I'm wired?"

Reilly smiled faintly. He stammered more. "You've got a videocamera outside. It'd be a kind of waste."

"So how about you? You getting this down?"

Reilly nodded appreciatively. "Only for clients. My kind anyway." It was said without apology. He ostentatiously opened a lower desk drawer, revealing a tape recorder, its spools slowly revolving. With equal ostentation, he shut it off. "Now tell me what we have to do."

"I'm going to search your files. Then I'm looking in your desk, your safe, whatever you got here. Anything you have is mine."

The lawyer pointed. "Are you going to use that?"

Medavoy gripped the sledgehammer. "If you don't open something when I want, yeah."

"I'm going to be the victim of the famous Medavoy roughhouse?"

"Your choice. Hey, so what do you want?" Medavoy realized in years past he would have stood at the door to a speakeasy, ax raised, wood splintering. Today it was all disappointing show and barter.

"Robby. You want me to say the magic words?"

"I want to hear something."

"All right. I can give you ten thousand now and another ten maybe tomorrow if your search here comes up dry."

Medavoy's grin was warm and deep. "That's what I wanted to hear."

"You'll take care of it?"

"Fuck no. I'm going through your whole damn office and I'm going to love it now."

Reilly suddenly sat down in one of the pillowed chairs, almost sinking away. His damp, blotchy face was drawn and cold. "I represent other cops. I do divorces, tenant cases. I plead for them when they default on bank loans. It's the only civil work I do. I've got friends all over the department."

"I bet you know a couple of guys in Special Weapons."

"I know a lot of cops. They come to my Christmas party. Maybe you will this year. You can meet some of the people who are making this city grow. They get into trouble, drunk driving, minor assaults, their kids do things they shouldn't. These are important people and I take care of them." He tried coaxing as he stammered. "You'll like my parties. My wife makes peach ice cream. There are rewards here, Robby. Things you can do for yourself. For the men in your unit."

"Give me the names of some cops."

Reilly smiled, relaxing. "Tell me who the snitch was for your warrant."

"Ask me in court."

Reilly's face tightened again, the scarlet veins drawn into a complex webbing. "Don't play games. What do you want? You can get it. It can be done. Great things are happening in this city." His small foot, in a handsome brown leather shoe, tapped up and down suddenly.

Medavoy knew, from his father, that there were all kinds of corruption. Reilly's was love of money and power. The crooked cops in Special Weapons were corrupt that way, too.

There was the corruption of loyalty, holding his men above everything else. And finally there was the corruption of hate. It was that one he didn't think he could resist.

The jagged, striking new skyline of Santa Maria, like a black paper edge stuck to the horizon, loomed outside the great window in Reilly's office. Medavoy no longer had a doubt about the warrant. Reilly wouldn't have tried to bribe him if there weren't things to hide.

"Get up," he said brusquely to Reilly.

Reilly stood. There was not a great contrast in their height, but the cold fury in Reilly's face passed Medavoy's hotter anger.

"You've got a past like everybody," Reilly said. "You've got things you're ashamed of."

"Not me. I'll tell you, you do anything outside now, I'll arrest you for interfering."

"There's one case, right Robby? There's one secret."

Medavoy let go of the sledgehammer and caught Reilly by the shirt front. He twisted the cloth firmly and patted Reilly's coat with one hand.

"You're a violent son of a bitch. Everybody knows it. That medal doesn't matter. You're an idiot," Reilly spat angrily. "You're no hero."

Medavoy held the fat lawyer as easily as a dog with a captured bird. He pushed forward until they were at the door, opened it, and released Reilly.

"I just thoroughly searched him for weapons. He's clean," he announced into the camera. Geffen paused in stacking files inside a cardboard box. He sighed and Zaragoza smiled broadly.

Reilly took three steps into the middle of the room, raised his hands above his head, folded them behind his head, and lay down on the carpet.

"Is he ill?" Santarelli asked suddenly, watching wide-eyed, standing beside Geffen.

"Maybe a heart attack," Zaragoza said.

Medavoy bent over Reilly's prone body. He looked down speculatively. Reilly's visible eye was open, balefully staring up.

"He's resting. He doesn't want to participate." Medavoy straightened up. Willy, the locksmith, was sitting in the waiting room, reading a magazine.

Reilly's office looked like he was moving, the cops sorting and sifting through each book on the shelves, opening every drawer. Everyone made exaggerated efforts to avoid stepping on the man on the floor.

Geffen asked Medavoy, "What's the deal?"

"We're golden. It's here. I'm going to gradually get to the safe, like it's just part of the search. He's dirty, Gef."

"You sure?"

"Fat fucker tried to bribe me, then blackmail me."

"Blackmail?" Geffen held two files tightly.

"I think he knows about Baladarez."

"You know who told him."

"Sure," Medavoy tried to make it sound inconsequential, "same guys we're going to bag right now."

Geffen lowered his voice. He was a boon companion after work, making the rounds of bars, drinking little and talking a lot. He was master of the deadpan. But Medavoy didn't like the frightened, strange face he saw.

"This is getting a little out of plain old robbery. You think we should back off?" Geffen wasn't kidding.

"You want to?"

"It's your call, Robby. We're here with you. It's your case."

"Then I want to make it."

"Okay." He returned to the open file cabinet, going over it with too much concentration. Medavoy thought again that Geffen was spooked about something unsaid.

Zaragoza, practiced hands sorting through the cushions in Reilly's chairs, blithely told an inattentive Santarelli about all the stress in his job. Medavoy grinned. Jimmy had a new audience.

He went into Reilly's inner office again, finding a small bathroom. It gave him a little time alone to think. He opened the medicine chest, aspirin, hair oil, combs, blood pressure medication, tubes. Closed the mirrored door, checking the sink, the drain, finger swiveled around, then a thin wire down the drain, probing.

Medavoy was ashamed of one case. There were probably others he would regret, but Baladarez was bad and a year old. He had hoped it was a fading memory, known to a few in the department. But if a man like Reilly had it, thought it could be used as a weapon, then it was common knowledge among his enemies. Who else knew and cared? Baladarez was a sin of omission but one man was in prison and there was no way to mitigate or undo it.

He looked in the toilet, flushing it, checking the tank for anything that could be taped inside. The nice part of this search was that its scope was broad. Drugs and the nugget could be hidden almost anywhere. While some cops disliked searches, Medavoy did not. He found nothing embarrassing or prying about the hidden caches in homes—pictures stuck behind bureaus, small bindles in flour bags or cookie jars, intimate letters folded inside books or under stereos. Reilly was right on that score. Everybody was ashamed of something or wanted to wall off some part of their lives from anyone else. A cop needed a constant link to victims and predators and perhaps a secret shame was as good as any.

He called Geffen and Zaragoza in, bringing the cameraman to stand in the office door. Always in view was the safe, but Medavoy worked around it. While Geffen jiggled the locked file cabinets, he opened Reilly's desk. Onto the very ink-stained blotter went pens, pencils, clips, more pill bottles, torn wallet calendars. From drawers he took file folders, put his hand up and around the corners in the drawers, finding nothing.

"This sucker won't open," Geffen said, giving one of the

file cabinets a final rattle. A steel bar ran from the top drawer to the bottom.

"Get the key."

"Reilly's still just lying there. He won't give up anything."

"You want me to get the locksmith?" Zaragoza asked.

"Naw. I'll bust it."

Medavoy picked up the sledgehammer. The other men waited, grinning. He flexed his arms, holding the sledgehammer like a baseball bat, aware of the easy way he had with physical things, how they customarily yielded to his strength and stubbornness.

"Stand clear," he ordered.

He swung, the heavy, solid impact reverberating through his body, the sound wild in the office. The cabinet rocked. The bar bent.

"One more, Robby. You got it," Zaragoza said.

Santarelli and the locksmith ran in. "What's wrong?" the lawyer asked frantically.

"I'm demonstrating how to get into a locked file cabinet." He swung a third and last time, the steel bar breaking, slipping out with a dull thump to the carpet. "And that's how you do it."

"Jeez, Robby, you coulda let me. I coulda popped it." Willy looked with dismay at the crude work.

"We're doing the safe now, Ely. Get your drill and let's get inside."

He had circled the safe long enough to allay any hint it was the real object of the search. The informant was protected.

Reilly's secretary stood behind the cameraman and she nibbled fiercely on her fingernails. With a determined bustle, Willy hurried back with his toolbox, gently unpacking fine-tipped drills, plugging them in. Geffen and Zaragoza took the stero off the safe.

"I'm all set," Willy announced.

"Last chance, Mr. Reilly. You can open the safe now if you

want," Medavoy called out. He could just see Reilly's shoe heels and the cops guarding him in the next room.

"Open it, Ely," he ordered.

The drill whined, Willy pushing his slight frame into it, the smell sharp and instant, a ferrous musk. Medavoy watched. There had to be something inside after all this. The rule was always good. Look long enough, look hard enough, and you'll find something on anyone. He had never, in twelve years as a cop, been disappointed.

Willy was working on one side of the safe's combination lock, trying to avoid the tumbler pins. Suddenly, Medavoy went to his knees, picking up another drill. He began working on the opposite side, the two men bent to the safe.

"Jesus, this's a hard mother," he grunted, pressing as he drilled.

"We do three on my side, three holes on yours. I oughta be able to pop this lock off and work the pins from inside."

Zaragoza nudged Santarelli. "You feel the tension?"

"It's been an instructive afternoon."

"Sure. And we do this all the time."

"Hey, shut up, Jimmy," Medavoy snapped.

"Sorry." He was as unchastised as a clever child.

They drilled for another ten minutes, the other men silent; only the noise and smell of the drills filled the office. Geffen held the log on which all the seized items were listed. He was ready to note anything from the safe.

Medavoy sat back on his heels. A bright drop of sweat rolled down his temple. The office was full of strange smells, as though a metal foundry had dropped into a church. Ink, paper, and flowers competed futilely with sweat, hot oil, and metal.

"Come on. Why you screwing with it?" Medavoy said to Willy. Willy's tongue was part out of his mouth as he threaded wires into the safe's raw holes.

"Get off my back. I'm working, okay? I got it."

Medavoy looked at his watch again and again.

"Takes a few minutes, Robby," Geffen said.

"He's taking all fucking year with it."

"You know, it just occurred to me that if someone came walking in right now, he might mistake us for burglars," Santarelli chuckled slightly.

Medavoy, Geffen, and Zaragoza looked at him. He blushed.

"Let it go, honeybaby, a little click," Willy blew out a loud breath. "It's open, Robby. It's all yours." He slid back, unplugging the drills, tenderly wrapping the electric cords, only half-interested in whatever was in the safe.

"Ron, bring the camera closer. I'll show you anything I find." Medavoy felt a quickening fear. There had to be something inside. He was an impatient man who did not like to have his certainties postponed.

Geffen and Zaragoza were down on their knees with him. He squinted and reached in, his hand falling on a dully yellow, heavy stone.

"That look like a nugget?" he held it out.

"Looks like damn big one to me," Geffen said. He began writing.

"I'm holding a large stone, smooth surfaced, possibly gold, about seven inches long. Heavy. Read me the last report, Gef."

Geffen flipped to find the theft report on his clipboard with the log and search warrant. "You have an item listed in number 89-74233. Victim held up by three armed men, among the items taken was a gold nugget, value about three thousand dollars." He grinned at Medavoy. "It's a family heirloom."

Medavoy grinned back. The victim was a coke dealer with arrests and convictions going back eleven years, the earliest a juvenile offense when he stole a carton of telephones.

Medavoy held in his hand the first physical evidence in a community of corruption. Dealer to rogue cops to Reilly. He was pleased he had not been disappointed. He was never cynical.

"Jimmy, you're the bagman. You take charge of this stuff." He passed over the nugget and began removing more from the safe—paper bindles of white powder, baggies of crystalline powder, a loaded .22 automatic pistol listed by serial number as taken from another dealer. His fingers closed on something else.

He retrieved the last, unmistakable thing from the safe.

"Most lawyers don't keep things like this, Mr. Santarelli?"

"No. No. Is it real?"

"Gef?"

Geffen stared at the thing in Medavoy's hand. "It's pretty real. It's a gas grenade. I got rid of a couple myself."

"What'd you use them for in Vietnam?"

"Same thing we do here. Crowd control, clearing an area, moving people away from someplace you don't want them to be." And on Geffen's grim face, Medavoy saw a memory of cool highlands, thickly green, over which spread smoke, stinging and nauseating. He saw a glimpse of Geffen's new fear.

"Will it go off?" Santarelli had backed away slightly.

"Ask Reilly." He gingerly handed the grenade, black-green and weighty, to Zaragoza. Geffen took it, held it for a moment, then gave it to Jimmy. "Our Special Weapons Unit has tear gas grenades in its arsenal. Like Gef says, you use them to clear a building or force the bad guys into the open. You don't give it to lawyers."

"How did Reilly get it?"

"Yeah, how did he?" Medavoy was coldly sarcastic.

"Oh," Santarelli looked unhappily from cop to cop.

"Right," Medavoy said. He started walking toward the shoe heels in the next room so that he could give Reilly the good news.

Zaragoza said behind him, "Robby, you got your talkie on?"

Medavoy fumbled with the handy-talkie clipped tightly to his belt. "I turned the volume down so I could think."

"Dispatch wants you out on a two-eleven in the south area, some bank deal."

"Shit. I'm not done here."

"You're the supervisor. They want you."

"Let me call in. Maybe I can tell them I'm only acting super."

He called downtown but couldn't persuade anybody over the radio that his presence at the scene of an armed robbery at the Pacific Security Bank wasn't vital. He swore again. "Gef, you come with me. Jimmy, you finish up here. Okay? It's not too much stress?"

"I know how to manage it." Zaragoza took the clipboard from Geffen, and said to Santarelli, "I been taking this class. It's great."

With Geffen following, Medavoy went to the outer office. Reilly's secretary had half-risen from a chair where she'd retreated at the sight of the grenade, a fingernail caught in midbite. Medavoy looked again at the cheap furnishings. He hoped Reilly spent the money someplace, that the rewards of wickedness at his level were not so meager.

He wanted Reilly to say something. Geffen warned him quietly. He got down on one knee, almost like he was proposing. Reilly had stretched his clasped hands in front of himself on the carpet, his eye open on Medavoy, savagely pensive.

Medavoy bent lower. "You're busted," he said viciously.

SIX

THE CHIEF WAS LATE by three minutes. He rubbed a hand over his thin, gray hair, trying to subdue it, failed and walked more quickly. He was the only man hurrying in the languidly elegant Santa Maria Hilton. Everyone around him seemed lulled by food, drink, the palms and ferns and soft music.

He had out his daily schedule and made a quick tick beside his late lunch. Now almost four minutes behind. The Chief didn't want to go to this late lunch and he always disliked unpunctuality.

A pinstripe-suited man tried to halt him.

"Steve, keeping busy? Got a minute?" the man asked.

"Sorry, Pat. I'm running late. Give me a call later." He didn't pause. Someone else waved and mouthed his name.

He strode by the still-full meeting rooms, loud laughter and applause emerging from their closed mahogany doors. The Chief was tempted to peek inside. Santa Maria Rapid Transit Task Force, Downtown Community Business League, Rotary and Kiwanis both, Friends of the New Library, Friends of the

Old Library, Convention Center Bureau Managers, retirement luncheons for two senior City Hall clerks, Santa Maria Cable Television Commission, the South Delta Unified School District's monthly board meeting, all people and things he knew and who knew him. He had only been Chief of Police for a year, but Stephen McNeill had appeared on civic letterheads for twenty years.

He stopped at a private dining room, took a breath, and went in.

"Sorry I'm late, Vin," he said to the younger man sitting alone at the white-linen-covered table. The fourth councilmanic district, running from the port back downtown, embracing the new, vibrant heart of Santa Maria, lay spread across the picture window.

City Councilman Vincent Prefach looked up from the papers he had been writing on. His tautly athletic features were merry.

"Are you? Jesus, only a couple of minutes, Steve."

"I got held up on a long-distance call."

"You have to relax. A few minutes doesn't matter in the long run."

The Chief sat down, fidgeted, threw his linen napkin across his lap. He took the newspaper from his suit pocket. It was opened to a headline: CHIEF WANTS MORE COPS.

"How does it look tomorrow? Have you done a head count?"

Prefach had stood up, gone to a buffet table, uncovered several silver chafing dishes, and started carefully putting food on two plates. "The first thing on the agenda is Mason's stupid airport noise ordinance. The man is an intense moron. So we'll have to play with that for an hour and get that out of our system."

It continually amazed the Chief that Prefach could say the most indiscrete things and never be called to account for them.

"I've got to have a new substation, Vin. My men can't patrol the Pocket area now."

"Everybody agrees things are getting tight. City's too big." He served the Chief. "We're having poached salmon. You like salmon?"

"Looks very good."

"You want another vegetable? I can get green beans if you don't like the peas."

"No, thanks. Peas are fine."

"How about some hot bread?"

"Please." The Chief quelled his impatience as Prefach went through the ritual of serving him. As though the councilman hadn't made him Chief and remained his bulwark on the City Council, as if he worked for me, the Chief thought sourly.

When he was satisfied the Chief had a full, attractive plate, Prefach himself sat down. He inhaled the steaming food. The councilman was young enough to be McNeill's son.

"I have Hanson, Lindow, Stubbs, LeMesiuer, Cline down as definites." Prefach ate without tasting. "Meredith, Her Honor, Mason as nos."

"So I do get the substation."

"There's going to be a little trade."

"For what?"

"I can't get them to swallow a nine-million-dollar increase. I know that means you can keep two officers per one thousand population. They just don't want to spend the money."

The Chief's food went down hard. He had come through the department as an expert in resource management, budgets, force deployments, criminal statistics. He appeared often before the City Council and yet he always had to beg.

"I'm spreading that increase over five years, Vin. We need it. The city's growing too fast for us."

"The problem's most of the council still thinks we're a small town. They don't see what's happening all around them."

The Chief didn't think Prefach understood the urgency.

"We're stretched to the very limit from one end of the city to the other."

"I know," Prefach said.

"It means the response time for a patrol unit is going way up, Vin. That's got to matter to the council. We can't respond to emergency calls like we should. We get overloaded."

"You're preaching to the choir, Steve."

"I'll tell you what's going to start happening. People will call for a cop because someone's breaking in and it's going to take us ten minutes, maybe even a half hour to show up. We don't have the men or cars."

"When voters start complaining because the cops are slow, the council will listen," Prefach said bluntly.

"Would it help if I made another pitch to them, hit this particular issue hard?"

Prefach shook his head. "If I can't make them go for it, you can't." He reached over absentmindedly and speared peas off the Chief's plate. Another reason to dislike eating with Prefach. Food was fuel and he never cared whose he ate. The Chief again pretended not to notice.

The Chief recalled a common Prefach story. There were dozens around town. During his first campaign, the unknown youngster, only twenty-two, went to a rally. One hundred people showed up. He greeted them all. After his speech, Prefach waded among the people and shook hands with each one. He spoke to each by name, all one hundred. It was a feat everyone talked about. The Chief thought there were prodigies in politics just as in music or science. Prefach was one.

He had run for every office available in high school and college. Now, in his third term on the Council, there were people in Santa Maria who boasted they had voted for Vincent Prefach a dozen times already.

The Chief pushed his plate away, toward Prefach, who was now working on the potatoes. "This is going to make life very difficult. The department's got to look to the future."

"Work up another analysis." Prefach laid down his fork and rapidly doodled on the immaculate whiteness of the tablecloth. "I'll give them a full-court press next month."

"I need the additional officers now."

"Can't have them." Prefach caught the Chief's annoyance at the dirtying of the tablecloth. "Coffee?"

"Thanks, Vin. Black, please."

Prefach rose, and with a menial flourish, filled the Chief's china cup from a silver urn. "I have some good news. Actually, it's more good news. TGB Properties is going for my proposal to upgrade the port. It's going to be a sixty-five-million-dollar improvement."

"I should buy more shares?"

"After the announcement, definitely. I wanted to cheer you up, Steve."

The Chief saw the insect-frail derricks and cranes at the port looming miles away. He sipped his coffee. "The Fourth District's going to sink. I don't even recognize half the places I grew up with in it anymore."

"I feel pretty good about that. It's a lot of hard work. I've got six big-scale office buildings, the Mayhew Industrial Park, Norton Tech Center, three other corporate parks going up. This port deal will just draw the business."

Vin Prefach wouldn't see the sadness in upheaval or the pangs as old neighborhoods shuddered, sundered, and were reborn. The Chief couldn't avoid bringing up another matter. "What about my internal problem, Vin? What's your advice?"

"The bad cops?"

"Yes."

"Who is it again?"

"I don't believe it's more than a dozen men. Most of them are in the Special Weapons Unit."

"And they're really rotten? There's no way out?"

"I'm going to be getting more evidence."

"It's not changing the basic picture, right?"

"No."

Prefach swabbed his mouth with the linen napkin, tossing the cloth down like a gauntlet. "Cut them out, Steve. Do it right away."

"I suppose I'd like to wait."

Prefach shook his head. "It doesn't get easier or go away. That's the one thing I've learned. If you've got a bad chore, do it fast, get it out of the way."

"There's going to be a scandal if I start firing men or even investigating."

"Steve, that's nothing compared to what'll happen if you wait. No. Get the names, get them out of the department. Do it today if you can."

"I'm worried the Council might hold back on the budget."

"As long as you're decisive, you act like you're in charge, they'll love you."

"Then I'll clean house."

"Bad cops. Makes me feel sick to my stomach. You trust them. They're supposed to be on your side."

In truth, the Chief didn't know how he would react to actually dismissing or confronting police officers committing crimes. Personnel had never been his interest except in a statistical sense. He finished his coffee.

Prefach was instantly half out of his chair. "More?"

"No, that's fine for me."

"You going for dessert or watching the calories?"

"I'll pass today, if it's all right." He had another appointment and the stale victory in the Council didn't please him. He would not have asked for what he did not need. And they will only give half.

Prefach stood, glancing at the humid, white sky, its vague threat. "You like opera?"

"Not much."

"What do you do for recreation, Steve? Got a hobby?"

The Chief had to humor these meanderings when they

came up. "Model boats. Sailing ships. I buy the kits and they're fun."

Prefach nodded without interest. "Gina's got me tied up on this City Opera thing. I'd like to give away my ticket."

"Not to me. I don't listen to much music."

"I don't listen to any. Okay. So, you'll come to the meeting tomorrow about eight-thirty. We'll be done with Mason's bullshit."

"I'll be there." The Chief wiped his lips. Ambition, he wanted to tell Prefach, was a fickle guide. It nearly always led away from where you thought you wanted to go. I wanted to be chief, he thought, and now I don't really know why.

"Make an announcement about cleaning the bad apples out of the department," Prefach grinned. "Might change some minds and get you the new cops you want. Who knows."

"I appreciate the advice, Vin. I'll make a list today."

SEVEN

KENNY WAS NOT SURE why Lisio drove them out along the river and parked instead of going back to Carol's place. He would have preferred her place, to tell the truth, because he needed to curl up on her bed for couple of hours and catch up on the missing night's sleep he'd lost when he escaped from Chino.

It wasn't much of an escape, Kenny admitted. He was in the work furlough program, spending six hours a day at Art's Plumbing and then back to the prison at night. He intended to steal Art's dune buggy to drive to Santa Maria, but Art took it to pick up a load of cheap PVC pipe his cousin was selling him. "You watch things, Kenny," he said, that smirk on his face, "I'll be right back." As a work furlough inmate, Kenny was paid far less than anybody else Art could have gotten at the store.

It was, of course, strictly forbidden to leave Kenny alone like that. But Art couldn't resist a deal. So he saved getting tied up, maybe hit a few times, and having his dune buggy stolen.

Kenny went up the street instead, to the Circle K store

where a fat kid named Arthur sat and read *Football World* behind the cash register. It wasn't difficult to get Arthur's dented yellow two-door and the .45 he kept beneath the counter for protection. Kenny really didn't want to hurt him at all, but Arthur tried to run, which he couldn't do very well. He ended up with Kenny hitting him on the head twice with the .45 since Kenny didn't want to shoot him.

Kenny had some experience with being hit on the head. As a kid he had been walloped enough, but when he tried to rob the Sambo's restaurant in Riverside five years before, the manager had snuck up behind him and bopped him with a metal rolling pin. It was quite painful and knocked him out. He was sure Arthur would stay quiet after being hit on the head. He tied Arthur up and left him in the small storeroom beside the dairy freezers.

The only good thing that had come out of the Sambo's mess was meeting Carol. If he hadn't been caught blindside by the manager, he wouldn't have gone to Chino and Carol wouldn't have come to help him.

Or, it was also possible to believe that if he hadn't been so wired on fairly bad quality crank, he wouldn't have been jumping and jittering around in the Sambo's and missed the manager. It was possible, in a way, to say that his overuse of methamphetamine was making a new life for him now.

And now was when Lisio insisted he had to be in Santa Maria. He had to escape from Chino on Wednesday to be in Santa Maria Thursday so they could make their bank scores Friday. Lisio had it all planned.

It had taken some time to quiet Carol down after she tried to take a dive through the car door the first time. If he had any inkling she was so worked up, he never would have dropped Lisio's phony bomb in her lap. He had to shake it, poke it, show it to her again and again to prove it was only one of Lisio's clever frauds, something those nimble little hands had put together.

Carol still tried to get out of the car again, this time while they were parked across Brighton Boulevard in front of a Chinese dry cleaners and Bob's Donuts. They were watching the four cop cars driving around the Del Paso Shopping Center, around the Pacific Security Bank, cops getting out, getting back in. And all the while, Lisio was checking his watch, nodding, saying this was exactly how he thought they'd behave. After about fifteen minutes of seeing how the cops got so excited by the bank robbery, Lisio said they could go. They had a lot to go over.

So, here they were, out in the middle of no place beside a very wide, very slow-moving river. "It's the Tuolumne River," Lisio said as they drove along the road. "Fifty miles long, deepest point, sixty-five feet. Crests at just over fifty feet," and so on. Lisio was a blabbermouth when it came to showing off how much he knew and he knew a lot.

Kenny had been occupied with trying to comfort Carol. He was worried about the way she cringed away from him on the backseat, as if his touch were offensive. He told her the .45 in the lunch box was just for insurance, the real trick to these bank scores was Lisio's phony bomb. He held her and stroked her and wished he wasn't so inarticulate, unable to use words or tell her what he felt. All he could do was hold her and hope she loved him still.

He really did wish Lisio had driven back to her place. Kenny wanted to take Carol to bed right now, not wait for tonight. He wanted to pull her into bed with him, with all her clothes on and undress her with his teeth.

"You okay now, Carol honey?" he asked softly when they parked.

"How could I be anything other than just perfect, Kenny?" she said, a little spirit back. She sounded like her old self again.

They stood in the empty roadway carefully loading everything into the trunk of her car—the wig, sunglasses, shopping bag, shoe box, and lunch box. Then Lisio locked it because Kenny insisted there were greedy people even along this deserted piece of road.

"I'm not much of a nature lover." Lisio was propped on his black stick, eyes going up and down the primitive undergrowth and the soft hiss of the river nearby. "But when I saw this place the other day, I thought this would be the spot to finalize our plans for tomorrow."

"What plans?" Carol asked.

"The banks. You know. Getting the money," Kenny said helpfully.

"Oh. Your plans," she said sarcastically. "They're not mine."

Kenny grumbled good-humoredly and stripped off the sweaty Raiders jacket, which he'd taken from Arthur and which fit him poorly, and when he was down to his T-shirt, he squeezed his right bicep until the vein popped out on the round muscle. Carol had her eyes on him and he liked the way she looked at him.

"I bench two-fifty," he said proudly, making the muscle bunch up. "I can curl forty-five."

"You're a lot bigger since I last saw you," she said.

"I worked a little," he said modestly, although he was delighted at her interest. She was responsible for this new look. He started working out in the exercise yard seriously only a year ago when she commented that he still looked like a strung-out cranker. It was bad for his self-image, she had said. It ate away at his self-esteem. Kenny hadn't touched anything in the joint, not even the prison home brew, largely because he'd discovered how much any dependency on candy, smokes, or sex put you at someone's mercy.

So when Carol said that, he made some resolutions. He would eat better, exercise. It was time for a change in his life. Lisio made fun of him when he'd come back into the cell, sweating and pumped up. Lisio would be lying on his bunk, on his side to take the weight off his rotten hip. He'd be reading, too, always some book or technical magazine and he'd look up and say, "Kenny, you just lifted a couple hundred pounds. You're still in the same cell. I just went to the moon." And he'd show off the cover of some magazine with a big moon on it.

Those cracks stopped when Lisio's release date was about eight months off. Suddenly, Lisio saw a use in Kenny's new strength and he began to sketch out the plan for a quick, devastating strike at some banks. Kenny's new confidence and muscle would be essential.

Kenny at that point also straightened out his own act. He stopped fraternizing with the white brothers, trying to curry favor with them. They wanted him to beat up or cut blacks or Mexicans. He didn't mind as long as he believed he was going to stay in prison.

But Lisio showed him a way to get clear of everything in his life that had been wasted, pointless. Kenny became a model inmate. He got so many brownie points he was able to get into the work furlough program. He was picked up by the prison bus, taken to his job in Riverside, and brought back at night. It was much easier to escape from prison while you were outside the walls than inside them.

Kenny looked at Carol and Lisio with an almost heart-breaking fondness. Lisio was giving him a chance to start over again. Carol was the new start, the first woman who had cared about him and really loved him. His wife, who he didn't like at all, was living someplace in northern California. He had married her when he was barely eighteen, abandoned her at nineteen. Only Carol mattered to him.

It ain't a new life I'm starting now, he thought. I was dying before. I'm starting to live today.

"Follow me," Lisio said, clumping ahead on his stick toward a dark-green archway of branches in the heavy stand of pines, oaks, and elms along the road. "We'll have absolute privacy back here."

"Take my hand, Kenny," Carol said.

He took it and they followed Lisio's slow waddle into the trees. Lisio had been in Santa Maria for the past week, investigating things, figuring details, ever since he was released from Chino.

They walked on a well-worn path, Lisio panting with the effort. Through the dense trees, Kenny saw the speckled white, humid sky breaking through.

Just as they broke from the trees, the path was blocked by a fallen cypress. Kenny agilely hopped over it. He reached for Carol. She tucked her skirt between her legs in a thoughtless motion. He inhaled deeply. First time he'd seen her legs bare, more tanned than he imagined, slim. He thought of the time he first put his hands between them in the prison visitor's room. He and Carol sat close together, like they were conferring on his case, and he slid his hand up and into the heated place at the top of her thighs. He was astonished he got away with it. She was his lawyer, she was older, but she told him to go on. He loved the flush that spread over her face, the abrupt shine of moisture on her lip.

Another time, she opened his pants and tried to give him a hand job, but it didn't work very well. He was nervous. It didn't seem right for her to be doing it to him.

"What's wrong?" she asked, stepping over the wide cypress. "You're looking at me funny."

"Sorry," he said, embarrassed. "I didn't mean to."

Lisio waited behind Carol like a kid in line at a ride. He watched them blandly. He then vainly tried to swing one short leg over the fallen tree. "Some assistance, please," he said.

Kenny had trouble turning his attention from Carol. He was so close to being with her all the time he could touch it. He felt his heart thumping, jumping, almost like a high of crank spooned into your coffee.

"Jesus," he grunted to cover his excitement and confusion, "you can't do anything yourself." There was no anger as he bent, Lisio's arms going around his neck like a trained chimp.

The two of them huffed over the tree. Carol wandered onto the short stretch of yellowish sand that ended suddenly in green water. The other side of the river was easily a hundred feet away.

"Now isn't this relaxing, all this beach to ourselves?" Lisio took off his shoes, one much thicker and heavier than the other. He patted the sand. "Sit here with me, Carol. Kenny, map please."

Kenny fumbled in his jeans and took out the map on which Lisio had drawn the route to the Pacific Security Bank. Lisio scooped out a small hole in the sand and grinned like crazy.

"You not mad?" Kenny asked Carol because she was watching him so closely, with that lawyer vision, like she could see into the back of his head. She's thinking, he realized, figuring it all out, seeing how this is going so simple.

She answered as if reading his mind, "No, I'm not mad. I'm getting my bearings back. Everything's been so confusing for a while."

"Bearings, honey?"

"I'm getting an idea of where things stand. Where we stand."

Kenny nodded with pleasure. Good, good. She was coming into focus, running with him on this deal. She went on giving him the lawyer X-ray eye.

Lisio said, "Kenny, match please." Then to Carol, "I'm not supposed to have matches."

"He's a real firebug," Kenny agreed, fishing out a matchbook and handing it to Lisio.

Lisio grinned at Carol. "Nobody will see. We're completely alone." He struck the match and dropped it onto the map which lay in the scooped-out sand. It caught and burned with a dull flame. Lisio sighed and struck five more matches quickly, adding them. Then he threw in the whole matchbook and breathed deeply when it flared up.

This business with matches and fires was another strange

thing about his former cellmate that Kenny never understood. He recalled Lisio that first day, stumbling, shuffling into the cell, holding his bedding and two heavy books on chemistry. Sitting on the lower bunk, fearful, shivering. Kenny ignored him at first. He was such a pathetic mess. Then that night, first thing, Lisio started in with all the people he'd take care of, guards, cons, people he'd worked with, people on the street. He ran down lists of people he'd burn or kill in some way. After a while, Kenny gave up and assumed it was more con babble.

They got to know each other better, as you had to. Kenny respected Lisio's intelligence. But Lisio made him carry matches if he needed them and he never went near anything lit himself. "I'm like an alcoholic," he'd say. "Better to stay away from temptation." Which was peculiar, because as far as Kenny was able to tell, this was Lisio's first time in the joint and it was off a bad-check beef in San Bernardino. He kited a few grocery checks, then one for a car, then a dozen or so for apartments he rented around town. But Lisio had nothing in his rap about arson or fires.

And Lisio never talked to him about his past. Never. Nothing about his family, where he worked, how he made ends meet when he wasn't passing bad checks. So Kenny, who was acting as the little guy's protector by then, simply chalked this matches thing up as one of the eccentricities of the very smart.

"Now," Lisio wiped his hand of some sand, took off his black coat and spread it on the sand gently, sitting down, "we can congratulate ourselves on a very successful first stage. Based on what I just saw, the cops and the tellers will act exactly as I predict tomorrow."

"How many banks?" Carol asked coldly.

"Four."

Kenny nodded. "All the money we need."

Carol shook her head. Kenny didn't like that tone. Maybe Lisio had put the whole deal to her too harshly. Maybe I should have done it, Kenny thought. Lisio said, though, that she would listen to a more objective presentation and Kenny was just too close to her to make it.

"I'm sure I can knock holes in whatever you've planned," she said, sitting up straight, combing her hair back a little.

"I doubt it," Lisio said sharply. His lips were white. Bad sign. He hated being challenged.

"She just means she's real interested." Kenny tried to be conciliatory.

"I know what she meant. All right. Listen to me and learn." He fussed with his coat and took out another city map. "These are the four banks and their times. Watch, Kenny." He had a red felt pen and began making circles on the map. The circles were spread out, about three miles between them. Lisio numbered each circle.

"Okay. I see," Kenny said. He patted Carol. She stared at the map hard.

"At nine," Lisio said, licking his white lips, "the Merchant's Commercial Savings. At nine fifteen, Central Valley Savings. Nine thirty, Santa Maria Federal. Finally, Citizens Savings at nine forty-eight." He sat back on his haunches.

Kenny had known the mechanics of the plan for a long time. This was the first time, though, Lisio named the particular banks. He had selected these banks this week after checking them.

"Then what? You've just robbed four banks, the cops are looking for your car. What then?" She couldn't catch Lisio's eye.

Lisio took out a green felt pen. "Watch, Kenny. We will have three cars placed within two blocks of the first banks. We will change cars after each bank. Most robberies fail because transportation isn't thought out." He circled the map in green. "This is where we'll place the exchange cars tonight."

"Where do you get them?" she asked coolly.

"We steal them. I have several overnight parking facilities picked out. Most stolen cars aren't reported until the morning anyway. It takes approximately thirty hours for a stolen car report to become available to patrol cars."

Carol raised her eyebrows for the first time. "I didn't know that."

Kenny thought this was a good moment to inject his enthusiasm. "I can get into a car, two seconds, Carol. No sweat to get the cars."

"I know your talents," she said to him.

"And your next question," Lisio said arrogantly, "is what happens after the last bank, after Citizens Savings?"

"That was a question."

"There are two reservations at the airport for flights leaving Santa Maria at ten-ten and ten-fifteen. One goes to Dallas, the other to Los Angeles. You can take your pick."

"We just fly away?"

"We just fly away," Lisio said.

Carol shifted her legs, stretching them out on the sand, smooth skin against the grainy beach. Like she's posing, Kenny thought. He liked the pose, the insouciance of her attitude. This was the Carol he knew, always on top of things, always ready with a rule or law.

"How much do you expect to get?"

Lisio winked at Kenny. "You're interested?"

"Curious."

Lisio said, "Well, we know that tomorrow's Friday. Payday. The four banks I've chosen, in addition to their other qualifications, all provide checking services for several major new businesses and construction projects around them. These banks have much more on hand every other Friday than anybody else."

"So they'll be more careful."

"No. They're all in shopping malls, like the one just now. The malls have security guards, but the guards patrol the stores. Not the banks. The banks rely on electronic surveillance, cameras, alarms, timers for the vaults. Frankly, they just don't expect this kind of assault."

"It's like all new, like something really different," Kenny said. "And Dave got the idea from a guy on our tier, guy who used to swipe suits from Sears."

Carol smiled thinly. "I can see the origin of the idea, Kenny. So how much money? What are you hoping to get?"

Lisio bobbed his head as if calculating. Kenny knew he'd done all this way before, they'd talked about it for so long. This was to tease Carol. "Each bank ought to have between thirty and fifty thousand at the drive-up windows. Or that the teller can get hold of quickly. Maybe more. I couldn't get precise figures," he grinned at her.

"So your total might be like a quarter of a million?"

"With some luck. For a little more than two hours' work tonight and tomorrow morning."

"We got a great head-start with half that, Carol honey," Kenny said, reaching for her, but she stood up, dark against the humid white sky. She seemed to be looking off toward a green tower, misty and faint, somewhere downtown.

He didn't mind her taking Lisio on. The more she poked and jabbed at the plan, the more she'd see how solid it was.

What was she looking at, though? What was so fascinating about some damn green skyscraper downtown? She sighed longingly.

She said to Lisio, her back to him, "The money's going to be dye-marked or booby trapped."

"I can disarm any booby traps or dye markers," Lisio said. "I'm very good with my hands."

"Jesus, you should see him, Carol," Kenny said, upbeat and pleased.

"You'll have to fence the money. You can't use it."

Lisio sniffed, winced as he sat over to one side, favoring his good hip. The Santa Maria map, green- and red-circled, was held down on the sand with his black stick. "I've checked it out. These banks are soft. They don't expect this kind of drive-up robbery. They have a rapid cash disbursement through the drive-up windows so the money's clean. We don't fence it."

"Well, I know the Santa Maria cops. They won't lie down for you. You saw them just now."

"The city police are part of the plan. The most important insight I had is about the cops."

Kenny blurted out, "Tell her about Lansing, Dave. Tell her how you got the idea." This should impress her. It was such a simple thing, something he'd heard probably a dozen times at the California Youth Authority or jails he'd been in and it took Lisio to see how valuable it was.

Carol turned from the green tower she'd been gazing at. "The cops will be on you after the first bank."

"You'd be right if we stayed in the same car or only tried for one bank," Lisio said, grunting as he sat back. "It's the multiple robberies that make it work."

"How?"

"Well, the idea for the blitz tomorrow came from John Maynard Lansing."

"Big John," Kenny said. Lansing was a tall, gangly guy who dealt cigarettes and grass.

Carol listened, arms folded, head down a little. He wanted to touch her, but she was concentrating on Lisio.

"John Lansing was a retail store burglar. No finesse, no plan really. He parked his car at the side entrance to a Sears or Montgomery Ward, Penney's, nearest the Men's Department generally. He then ran inside and grabbed a dozen suits off the closest rack, ran out, and drove away."

"How impressive," Carol said. She moved her toes in the sand. Kenny playfully pushed some sand toward her and she irritably shook it off.

He said, "Big John get maybe twelve, fourteen hundred dollars of suits, one good grab. Get maybe two hundred bucks easy when he dealt them."

Lisio snapped back at Carol, "It is impressive. The whole

insight here is that stores or cops can't handle very fast, very mobile thieves. They're set up to deal with one problem, one emergency at a time."

"City cops aren't store security guards."

"Sure they are. They just protect the goods."

"I've heard a lot of cons talk like that."

Kenny halfway wished Carol would find some flaw in what Lisio was saying, at least take him down a little. Drop that superior bullshit, the condescending way Lisio would talk to him when he tried to pronounce some word in *National Review* or *Scientific American* or *Journal of American Chemists* or any of the books stacked neatly on Lisio's side of the cell. "This isn't for you, Kenny," Lisio would say. "It's not for any jerk in this place."

So he only half-listened to Lisio explain it again. This part he'd heard over and over. He lay back on the sand.

Lisio was saying in a rough voice, "I'm sure you've heard a lot of things. But you don't know anything. You don't think. You don't observe. I looked around for a long time to find California cities of no more than five hundred thousand people, no less than one hundred thousand. Cities that also had heavy growth recently, easy access to parts of the city by surface streets or freeway. Airports. I found five cities that fit my requirements."

"Why were we so lucky?"

"I told you," Lisio said brittlely, "coming here wasn't my idea."

"I made him promise," Kenny looked up at her from where he lay, "I go, Dave, you check out this place, you want me in on it. It's got what you need. It's got what I need and we go there, you want me with you."

"Why is the size of the city so damn important? Why not LA? They've got a lot more banks."

"And more cops. Listen. At these population levels, there are sufficient numbers of banks, handling businesses, payrolls, banks with more drive-in customers than walk-ins. And fewer cops than a big city."

"You don't need many cops."

Lisio swished his black stick over the map on the sand. Kenny put his hands behind his head, feeling strangely relaxed, as if the bickering were a pleasant background noise. He felt the same mixture of fear and joy, hate and longing he got when he was in his mother's bedroom and she wasn't sick or drunk. She was rocking him, hands around him, protecting him from Trask who was shouting and pounding on the door. He was safe with her. He was safe with Carol and Lisio, too.

"I know about the cops in this city," Lisio said to Carol. "They drive standard modified Ford cruisers. In traffic, with lights and siren, they can reach a maximum fifty miles an hour. If they're lucky. If everybody gets out of the way. They patrol by sectors. Look at the banks." He jabbed at the map, excited. "Each of our banks is in a distinct sector. The cops will draw down that sector and everything nearby to get us. We'll have gone on to a separate sector."

"So what?"

"The cops will run to banks we've left, drawing their patrols away. We'll be moving very quickly tomorrow. In a city this size they don't have the manpower to flood every sector."

Kenny added, "It's like we outrun them, honey. We go too fast."

Lisio broke in, "I've run it over and over. We saw it just now. The cops cannot respond faster than seven minutes. To anything. We'll always be on to the next bank within five minutes."

Kenny saw Carol's mind working behind her impassive features. Her eyes gave her away. She was playing lawyer, the way she did when he was in prison and she'd tell him what to do. That ice layer she had. She stared back into Lisio's challenging, beetle eyes.

"You get delayed for any reason, you're dead."

"We won't be delayed."

"All you need is one teller to say fuck off."

Lisio smirked at Kenny. They'd talked about this part a great deal. It's what made Lisio's little hands so important. "This is why the threat of being blown up is potent. After the first bank, the cops will not only be confused, they'll treat each successive report with extreme caution, slowing them down more. No teller will balk either. Anybody can be courageous against a single man with a gun. But nobody outruns an explosion."

She shuddered, obviously recalling the shock of that shoe box landing in her lap. Lisio had made his point. Kenny reached for her, said he was sorry again. Stupid, stupid to scare her like that.

A humid breeze rustled through the trees around them and across the river. ⁓oming for sure. A pheasant or mourning dove soft

"This stuff abo   onse times, where did you get it?" s   bbing her wrists.

"They talk a   I did a little research and I kept my   sio said crisply.

"All right.   h of you listen to me. Nobody's been ки.

"Not that I know o.

"But if one person dies, for ⸱ ⁄ reason during this romp tomorrow, you go to Q. You go to Death Row."

"We will be done within an hour and on planes out of the city. No guns. Just good planning," Lisio said.

"I've got a little money in the bank. There's the cash in the bag in the car. Why don't you take that?" she said to Lisio.

"You must be joking."

"No risk. You'd have more than you came here with."

"Why don't we ask Kenny?"

Carol looked down at him. He could hear the slow river hitting roots and trees, making a hissing sound.

"I'm ready for it, Carol honey. It ain't no big deal."

"You're risking everything, Kenny. Any life we might have."

"No risk, honey," he said lazily, then added firmly, "but I do it if it's what we got to have."

Carol shook her head angrily. "I know the cops here. I've dealt with some of them. They're not jerkoffs."

"They won't be a problem," Lisio said confidently.

"They don't play games."

"We don't either."

"Where will I be?"

"With us. Even if you choose not to take an active part."

"You must be crazy."

Lisio wiggled his toes and straightened part of his black coat on the sand. "Until this is over tomorrow and we go our separate ways, we're staying together."

Kenny didn't want to let Lisio know Carol had refused to drive at the bank. He was prepared to force her now so they could be happy later. Later she would have time to understand things more clearly. He would act and plan for them both until after tomorrow morning.

"Lovely," she said, almost to herself.

"What, honey?"

"I said, lovely, Kenny. This whole half-assed thing is lovely."

Before he said anything else, she flung off her skirt and splashed into the river, standing there like it was hers, looking up at the sky, the wilderness around them. Jesus, she looks so tough, he thought, like she wants to take everybody on.

He propped himself up on his elbows, admiring her.

Lisio watched her too. "She bothers me," he said.

Kenny glanced at him sharply. That same superior tone because he'd won. Outside of Chino, he thought, Lisio acted much more arrogant, like he didn't need me for protection or help. Like he could make it on his own.

"It's okay. She's okay with me," he replied to put Lisio back in his place.

"All right. As I told you, she's your responsibility until after ten A.M. tomorrow."

"I keep an eye on things."

"I won't let her cause any trouble."

"Don't mess with it."

"Fine, Kenny. Calm down. You should study the map here now. I'll be with you as navigator, but you need to know the streets yourself."

"I don't want to now," he was looking at Carol, who had an impenetrable, contemplative expression on her face. She had waded into the river until it was up to her breasts.

Lisio saw where he was looking. "All right. I said we needed a little relaxation. Big night tonight getting the cars. We have a big day."

"Yeah, yeah," Kenny stood and started stripping his jeans and T-shirt off. Carol slowly unbuttoned her blouse, uncaring if Lisio saw her. Her skin was pale, freckled against the darker water. A vague, sublime image shifted, floated in Kenny's mind. Carol waited for him.

She was unexpectedly graceful in the water. He sensed she was claiming her independence, even from him possibly. Kenny stamped into the river, raising wavelets, felt himself tugged at by the current. He half-paddled to her, growling in her ear.

"We can't do this tomorrow," she said, putting her arms around him.

Just then, the image that had floated in his mind solidified. He looked around, past Carol, to the trees and sky. It was that picture hanging in his mother's bedroom. She had it over her dresser. She was a plump, small woman, who smelled coppery, like a new penny. The picture was a chromo of John and Robert Kennedy ascending into heaven. His mother had picked it up at some church rummage sale. She was still pretty religious in those days, alternating between salvation and a perpetual liquor-fueled stupor. His slight drawl came from her. She was a South Carolina girl.

Kenny liked looking at the picture, the serenity and promise of joy on the two brothers as the earth, heavy and doom-laden, fell away beneath their feet in black wing-tips. Sometimes when his mother was sick or dulled, bottle beside her, she wanted him nearby and he stared at the picture, imagining life like that, wishing it could be so. Sometimes it comforted him, when his mother shouted obscenities back at Trask, locked out, bellowing and pounding on the bedroom door. Kenny had just gotten another beating, his eyes unfocused from being hit. To float away into the sky like those two famous brothers who endured suffering and gained paradise.

Trask was only Kenny's stepfather. He believed his real father was a man who lived with them for about a year when he was young. He wished he remembered that man better. His mother was married four times. He rarely thought of her anymore. All he really thought of from those days was hitting Trask, after one painful beating, with a short wooden chair and knocking him out.

"Did you hear me?" Carol asked, and they turned slowly in the green water. "We can't go through with this."

"Yeah, we can. We can do anything," he said fiercely. They floated and he buoyed in her embrace, breathing with her and against her. He cursed himself for being unable to tell her how he felt at that moment with her—like the Kennedys drifting into the clouds, lighter than air, on breaths of pure spirit.

Kenny kissed her deeply. She pushed back at him, responding. On the shore, like a sick kid abandoned by his friends, Lisio sat on his black coat, the map held down by one stockinged foot as he watched the two of them twirl blithely in the river.

Kenny pitied Lisio, who had nothing. I got it all, he thought.

All he had to do was steal a few cars tonight, stash

them, and go home with the woman

anybody in his life.

Carol whispered to him as they t
struggled in him, he couldn't say
groaned with shame and frustration

She didn't seem to notice his stru
the deal, like she could talk him out
thing for the two of us, Kenny. Jus

"No," he managed to say.

"We'll go back into the city. W
and he even momentarily though
sway him by getting so close.

"No," he said tensely again.

"Then we'll both be destroyed

He shook his head, straining to
anything else she was thinking al
right now, not her. He put it as cle

"I. Love. You," he said fervent
after that.

MEDAV

dow, o

himself

the first

with his

the free

develop

"Re

Medavo

"Lik

"I g

to be a

then I w

for the n

"Thi

"I'll

Maybe h

on the V

EI

FU

HT

Y DROVE EASILY, one hand hanging out the win-
the way to the Pacific Security Bank. He found
arrying more than his share of the conversation for
few minutes. Geffen fiddled with the radio, fiddled
tie, fiddled with his fingernails. Then they were on
vay heading south, passing the Delta Pointe Estates
nent.

ind me to get something for Jane before we leave,"
said.

what?"

t to get her something, a little present, this is going
ad day. Whatever we got here with this bank deal,
ant to check on Reilly, make sure he's all settled
ght."

k he'll bail tonight?"

o a support affidavit to the judge to jack his bail high.
'll spend the night. Then I got to do that photo ID
ss deal." It was a violent gas station robbery.

"I can go. I don't have a girlfriend with a kid to treat gently." For the first time that day, Geffen smiled.

"Don't give me shit about being married, Gef. You're not the expert."

"Two times. You marry Jane, you'll be up with me. I got more kids than you do."

"I'm working on it."

Geffen settled in his seat. His legs were long enough that he had to bend them slightly under the dashboard. "I'd like to make Reilly roll over on some of the guys he's got in the department."

Medavoy grinned. "Brutality is my rap. You don't have enough complaints for excessive force to scare anybody."

"I'd still like to make Reilly give up some names."

"We leave this bank, I'll check with the DA and see what kind of deal he's thinking of. Reilly's got enough heavy stuff now they can squeeze him pretty good."

Geffen was back to fiddling with his nails. "They been asking about you again."

"Who?"

"Easter. The other guys in Special Weapons."

"Who they asking?"

"Me. Sometimes Jimmy. Masuda, too. Anybody who works with you."

"The same bullshit?"

"Yeah. You know, anything solid about your excessive force complaints. They ask about Baladarez—did you really fuck that up? Who's got the paperwork? They really want to dirty you up, Robby."

"Well, I think any cop who's been on for twelve years and doesn't have a couple of excessive force complaints hasn't been doing his job." Medavoy drew his arm in, still driving one-handed. "I wish I hadn't screwed up Baladarez. I wish the Menefee kid hadn't been shot. Nothing I can do to change it."

"We all told them to go to hell."

"We're a real tough unit," Medavoy chuckled. "Jesus."

"It frosts my ass," Geffen said bitterly, "guy like Easter making fun of you, your medal."

"I love my medal."

"He's pissed because the Chief loves you."

"We play golf a lot." Medavoy swung off the freeway at the Antelope Road exit. On his right was an empty field of high grass and nettles, green and luxuriant. A sign in the middle of the field announced the imminent construction of the Summit Shopping Center and Department Stores. "My dad should have bought some land around here when he had the chance."

Geffen looked out his window, again lost in thought. He said, "You want to go out and get really loaded tonight?"

"How loaded? Like fucking anything that moves or you can't stand up?"

"Stone-cold loaded, Robby. Like the old days."

"I got my responsibilities. I don't think Jane'd go for it."

"Forget it."

"Some special occasion?" He wanted it to sound flippant and insignificant. With Geffen and other cops, the most important things were purposely made to appear unimportant. Life was controllable in that way—its jagged, tearing edges sheathed.

"Nothing special," Geffen answered. He had the bank's address jotted down on a slip of paper. "You want to make a left here at the next light. It's one of these new shopping centers."

Medavoy slowed for the light. Their radio had been venting a hissing stream of comments for cars around the city. Possible domestic disturbance, possible knife fight, possible burglary in progress, man with a gun, woman with a knife, regular checks with other squad cars to see where they were and what they were doing. To Medavoy this never-ending chant was the caption of daily life in Santa Maria. Underlining everything was the disruptive and violent, the unexpected event that transformed and deformed.

"I'd like to get out," Medavoy said, answering Geffen's request. "We'll do it some other time. What's-her-name'll let you out?"

"You know her name."

"It's a joke, Gef. Lighten up. Life's too short."

"Yeah. We'll go another time." Geffen studied the address again, as if it held some deeper interest. "I mean, you know, I'm kind of scared lately. For no reason."

"Scared of what?"

"I don't know. That's the deal, Robby. Everything scares me all of a sudden." He tried grinning and failed badly. "It just happened."

The tone and pleading warned Medavoy and he instinctively moved from the danger. "That's bullshit. There's nothing wrong." He acted as if Geffen had been joking.

"Yeah. It is bullshit," Geffen said and slumped slightly. "It's got to be over there, Del Paso Shopping Center." He pointed out his window.

"I see a couple of cars there." Medavoy slowed, turning right into the parking lot. A small cluster of people, fluid at the edge as watchers and gawkers came and went, had formed around the squat bank building. Yellow-tape barricades had been wound at either end of the drive-up teller's lane.

"Don't forget, remind me to get Jane something before we go," Medavoy said. He flashed his red-and-blue lights to startle other cars out of the way as he drove toward the bank at the other end of the parking lot.

"I won't forget. Annie know about Jane?" Geffen had resumed their normal bantering conversation. His thin runner's face, ambiguously the image of health or sickness, was masked.

"I haven't asked her."

"She still taking karate lessons?" Geffen grinned.

"I'm still paying for them."

"You do like to live dangerously. Annie's going to beat

your ass when she finds out about Jane and you buying gifts."

"I ain't telling her." Medavoy had his attention drawn to the police squad cars and a black van blocking the Pacific Security entrance. Men in black uniforms, with assault rifles and gear hanging from their belts, milled beside the van.

"Special Weapons showed up. Doesn't look like anything's happening," Geffen said warily.

"Whoopee doo. Whoopee goddamn doo. Don't tell them Reilly's been busted, okay? Play it real serious, okay? Let's make it a surprise." He parked alongside two squad cars, banging his door against one as he got out.

"I'll play it real straight. You make a buy, you ever tell a dealer, howdy, I'm from the police? I would like to buy narcotics." Geffen got out, fussily adjusting his coat and pants.

"You're kidding." Medavoy squinted in the bright haze.

"Some lawyer asked me that in court. I told him no, you dumb shit. You don't tell everyone the truth."

"Let's be nice. I don't want to make anybody mad," he chuckled.

"These guys are all my pals. Hi. Hi." Geffen saluted the Special Weapons cops in black, their ungainly black weapons pointed into the sky, as he and Medavoy went by.

Medavoy was disquieted by Geffen's admission in the car. Fear was an accepted fact, unavoidable and bare. To be unafraid was impossible or dangerous. But Geffen admitted more, something that couldn't be dismissed or overwhelmed. He couldn't be a coward. It was inconceivable. All he needed were some of Zaragoza's stress management lessons. It had to be that simple.

A hesitant breeze rattled, rustled through the stiff palms around the bank. An advertising clock on the supermarket flashed 3:12, then 74 degrees like signals.

Medavoy smelled rain coming.

Medavoy took a quick, thorough impression of the two worlds inside the Pacific Security Bank.

People in one lined up to have their accounts updated, to withdraw money. Men and women holding bankbooks stared at what was happening a few feet away. Some nibbled on the bank's complimentary cookies and sipped from paper cups of coffee. It was a light, cheerful world, with optimistic slogans taped to the walls.

Medavoy entered the other world alongside.

Four cops in dark-blue uniforms talked, gestured to several people. A stocky, gray-suited man nodded, wiped his glasses. A cop wrote on a clipboard while he talked. Another cop stood by a woman in a lemon-yellow and-white striped chair. She shook her head, crossing and uncrossing her legs. A photographer took pictures from the drive-up teller's window and a technician slid almost sinuously, looking for possible fingerprints.

"There's Easter," Geffen whispered.

"Be nice, be nice." Medavoy strode up to a solid, square-shouldered man, dressed in a black uniform with POLICE in silver on his back. He was older than Geffen or Medavoy, his whitening hair in a crew cut. The leader of the Special Weapons Unit brightened falsely when he saw Medavoy.

"Hey now, here comes a hero, Mr. Seymour. How you doing, bud?"

"I'm good today, Ralph. I'm Rob Medavoy, Santa Maria Police Robbery." He put out his hand to the gray-suited man.

"How do you do. I'm the president of this bank. Wilson Seymour."

"This is Detective Geffen. He's also with Robbery."

"How do you do." The bank president shook hands mechanically. Geffen nodded and watched Easter.

"You have any suspects in the area?" Medavoy asked Easter.

Easter shook his head. He held a black helmet under one arm as though he had come from playing polo. "Long gone, bud. I had a check of the area run, nothing. I got out a description of the car."

"So why's Special Weapons here?"

"That was my request." Seymour kept glancing at the young woman, who was obviously upset, sitting in the striped chair. "Given the nature of the theft, I thought some expert help was needed."

"What's unusual, Mr. Seymour?"

"A bomb was used."

"Is it still here?"

Easter winked at Geffen. "They took it with them. Flashed it at the teller and then ran."

"Guess there's no need for you to hang around," Medavoy said to Easter. "Thanks for bringing me down here."

"Hey, my pleasure, bud. This is your kind of case, lots of excitement, media's going to love it. You're lucky, sir," he said to Seymour. "You have got a certified hero investigating your case. He's going to solve it right away."

"I didn't realize," Seymour began.

"I'd like to talk to the teller."

"My boys'll start cleaning up. I'll be in the van for a while, Robby, if you need a hand," Easter said and grinned. He was an exuberant, oppressive man who held the local speed record in water skiing. He had been a cop in Santa Maria for close to twenty years and had shot five men while on duty, two off-duty. He slapped Medavoy on the back, just hard enough to convey menace.

As he walked away, Geffen pulled him up. Medavoy couldn't hear what they said.

"She's not very calm right now. I'd like her to be clear for you, but I don't know." The bank president wiped his glasses again quickly, uselessly. Then they walked over to the young woman in the chair.

"Alice, this is a detective. Please tell him everything you can. He understands you're upset. You do understand?" he asked Medavoy.

"Can I get you something?" Medavoy asked her.

The woman looked up, frowned. She was small-faced and pink, with an unlined, unworried expression. "I'm fine. I'm absolutely fine."

The bank president nodded to her, raised his eyebrows for Medavoy. Just then, Easter let out a loud, pointed laugh and slapped Geffen on the back. Geffen's voice rose angrily. Heads turned toward the disturbance, uneasy eyes watching.

"Excuse me." Medavoy hastily left the teller. He heard Easter saying with calm, deadly certainty, "He's supervisor today because Gordo's shitfaced on the floor someplace."

"Tell me when and where. Name it."

Geffen was white, spring-tense.

"Get out of here," Medavoy said, low to Easter.

"I'm just telling the guy why you got such a sick little unit, bud. He's getting all clenched sticking up for you."

"You're done here, Easter. You know how bad this looks? Get out." Medavoy felt Geffen's barely checked anger.

"Well, bud, the day comes I can't take both of you heroes, I quit, okay?" Easter, in all those years of service and street commotion, had never earned more than a departmental commendation. He was head of an elite unit, but it was not the same. There had been no ceremony or city tribute at a long banquet table, with warm, praising speeches and cameras like Medavoy had gotten. It was unjust.

"Maybe today's your lucky day," Geffen snapped.

"No more, Gef."

Easter exhaled contemptuously. "You put in that transfer application to my unit when you get sick of Robbery, Gef. I'll hold a place for you. We do things in my unit." He walked out, a black solid figure, stern, jealous, and intemperate.

"I didn't tell him." Geffen stayed tensed until Easter was

gone. The people waiting for tellers stirred nervously at the outburst.

"Do me a great big favor. I don't want to watch you, Gef."

"Cross my heart, Robby." He grinned sadly. "I'll put a lid on."

"Great. Find out what they've worked up outside so far. I want to know what kind of physical evidence we got here."

Medavoy was acting supervisor only because his nominal superior was lost in a bar somewhere in what had become an almost daily event. It galled Medavoy to be chided by Easter about it.

"Two women?" Medavoy asked Alice, the teller.

"I only saw two in the car. A passenger, then there's the driver who got out with the bomb."

They sat at a small oak conference table in the bank president's glass-lined office. Medavoy watched the stately movement of bank customers and the counterpointed activity of cops searching for evidence. Seymour sat beside Alice. He nodded, made frequent sympathetic noises, mimicked her gestures. He distracted Medavoy.

"What about the driver's clothing?"

"I wasn't really looking. They came up to my window; I was counting some bills." She glanced at Seymour who nodded paternally. "Then I got that note."

"What did you see?"

"Jacket. Sports jacket, maybe football. I can't tell. Sunglasses. Like the passenger."

"That's the description she gave me immediately," Seymour said.

"I'd like to hear what Alice saw, sir."

"Absolutely." He watched her like she might calve.

"Give me an estimate on the age for the two women."

"The one with the bomb was about twenty. You could tell. The other one, I kind of feel was older. Thirty? I don't know."

"The security camera was working during the robbery?"

"We maintain it very strictly. I'm proud of the protection this banks offers," Seymour said.

Medavoy made notes on a small pad. He nodded. "Have you retrieved the tape yet?"

"I can have it ready for you any time."

"Do you have someplace to watch it here?"

Seymour shook his head dismally. "I'm very sorry. We haven't had any reason to look at the security tapes before."

"That's okay. I'll take it with me." Medavoy half-smiled at Alice. "You have any idea about height on either woman?"

"I'm bad at that."

"Please try, Alice," Seymour coaxed.

"Well. Maybe about six feet for the one with the bomb. I didn't really look very much at the passenger and she never stood up," she shrugged apologetically.

"Okay, now describe this bomb for me. I mean, what made you think it was a bomb?"

"It was a bomb. That's what the note said."

"This note?" Medavoy held up a plastic-covered single-typed page. On it was written: PUT THE MONEY IN THE CHUTE OR I'LL BLOW US UP. "And it looked exactly like a bomb, you know, timer and things moving inside. It scared me." She stared at the note.

"You knew what the chute was? That wasn't confusing?"

"I thought she meant the slot we pass things back and forth with."

"I know Alice would like to be clearer," Seymour said.

"She's doing very well, sir."

"I mean," Alice went on, "I assumed anybody who'd blow herself up would be crazy. I believed her right away. It all fit. I gave her all the cash in my drawer, no questions."

"How much was that?"

"My last total showed four thousand five hundred twelve dollars."

"Did either of the women say anything? To you? Each other maybe?"

"I didn't hear it. I think I heard something, but I got down behind my counter as soon as I passed the money through the slot."

"I'm sorry," Seymour said.

"Please let her speak, sir."

Seymour wiped his glasses again. And again.

"Give me a description of the car, please." Medavoy wanted to lose Seymour if at all possible. Alice tightened every time he spoke and his presence was slowing things up.

She took a breath. "A two-door car. It looked like a compact. It was yellow, dirty yellow kind of. It hadn't been washed."

"California license or out-of-state?"

"I couldn't see. I don't know."

Seymour sighed. "That is too bad."

"Would you mind getting me a glass of water, sir? I'm a little dry," Medavoy asked.

"Certainly. That's no problem. Alice?"

"No. I'd like to go home."

"You have the rest of the day off. You were very brave and the bank appreciates it." Seymour bestowed the comment grandly and left the room.

"Okay, Alice, is there anything you can recall about these women? Anything they did? Something that sticks in your mind now?"

She frowned in thought. "Well. It's kind of odd. I don't know. It's about the one with the bomb, how she walked kind of."

"What about the walk?"

"I couldn't think about it while Mr. Seymour's been breathing down my neck. I feel funny, too."

Medavoy detected the start of panic. "It's okay. You forget a lot of things sometimes when you get a shock."

"I thought I was okay until just now."

"What about the woman with the bomb?"

"I think it was a man. With a wig on."

"How about the passenger? Could the passenger be a man, too?"

"Sure. It could've been two guys wearing wigs. Jeez," she breathed heavily, "I'm really feeling it now."

Medavoy smiled at her. He knew the right words. "You did a wonderful job. And I tell you, I don't mind guns or knives or shotguns, but I really hate the idea of getting blown up. You did a lot better than I would have."

She eased a little, the terror fading slightly. "Really?"

"A twelve-year veteran cop does not lie, Alice."

When he came out of the bank, Medavoy couldn't see Geffen at first. He gave the bank's security videotape and the extortion note to a cop and told him to take it to Robbery immediately and get someone to look it over for a better description of the car and the two people inside. Then he checked with the technicians and two cops working the drive-up teller's lane.

"Can you bring up that tire tread?" he asked, pointing at a track laid in oil and grease on the concrete.

The technician was on his knees, as if to sniff the striated pattern. "Tricky, tricky."

"I'd like to have the tire tread."

"I'm going to work my heart out on it." The technician got up and began carefully protecting the fragile treadmarks with tape.

Medavoy looked along the busy stores and supermarket in the shopping center. He could not see the Special Weapons van either so Easter must have left. That was a shame. Medavoy had developed a distinct wish to look at the armaments inside the van, particularly the tear gas grenades and to find out from

Easter how those weapons were handled.

Geffen stood on the sidewalk arcade waving at him. He had two more cops nearby.

"What's up?" Medavoy asked when he trotted over.

"I got a witness," Geffen said. "In there." He pointed at Petland. A small white dog yipped up and down in the window. Brazen parrots obligingly screeched.

"Is this a Dr. Doolittle, Gef? Talk to the animals?"

"Don't be funny. It's the owner. He's a crack-up. You'll love him."

They went inside. It was strangely dim, rank with urine and seeds and the faint briny smell from a large fish tank. A very tanned man with a thick white mustache stood beside a cage full of rodents running madly around a wheel.

"Mr. Dickranian, this is Detective Medavoy. Would you tell him about the car parked outside your store this morning?"

"Howdy doody. Yes, I'll tell you. I was in first thing, to feed the stinking beasts. I hate animals. I am running this business only because my restaurant bellies up two years ago. It's a terrible thing to lose your business, you know?" He peered at Medavoy.

"I really don't. I've been a cop all my life."

Dickranian grunted and Geffen grinned. "So, I'm putting out their stinking food. Then I'm shoveling out their stinking cages and this car parks in front of the store."

"What time?"

"Probably nine-fifteen. Not too much more. I don't shovel their damn cages too long, you know? I don't care how they live. You have any pets?" He looked to Medavoy, then Geffen.

Geffen shook his head.

"I've sort of inherited a dachshund." It was Jane's pet.

"A small stinking beast."

"I'm getting fond of him," Medavoy said. "How many people in this car?"

Dickranian wrinkled his large nose. "Oh, this odor. Well,

they are sitting in front of my business; I think they are interested in pets. Everybody stops to look in the window, they make faces at the stinking little dogs. Oh. Shut up!" he cried at the parrots.

"How many people?" Medavoy asked again.

"There are two. Two in the car and they stay in the car while I put out the damn meal, the damn seeds, the damn crickets. I tell you, I only have enjoyment giving the mice to the python." He smiled evilly.

"Men or women?"

"At first, I pay no attention. I have my own problems. Then I think it's two lousy women taking up my parking space. I am ready to go out and tell them. Then I think no. One of the women scratches under his hair, like this? So, it's phony."

"A woman wearing a wig?"

Dickranian spat on the floor. "A man. A man driver, a woman passenger. They sat there for three, four minutes, they spit peanut shells on my parking space. Like these stinking animals who are leaking from every hole."

Medavoy said to Geffen, "Go bag the shells. I'd like to find out where they came from. Maybe we got enough for saliva, too."

"The guys outside are picking up each little piece."

"What about the car?" Medavoy was writing in his small notepad now.

Dickranian shut his eyes. "A Nissan Sentra, a two-year-old model. Two-door. Yellow, very untidy. A California license plate. Oh. Oh. Like, 25DDM400." He opened his eyes.

"That's very impressive, sir. You have a good eye."

"They sit there taking up my space. Of course I saw them."

He gave Medavoy a direct description of both people in the car. One of the parrots shrieked and rose unsteadily from its perch to Medavoy's left. It wobbled, then landed on his shoulder and a large beak stuck into his head. He froze.

"Would you take this bird off me, sir?"

"Of all these stinking beasts, I like that one even a little. They are very instinctive. A parrot loves you or hates you. They all made holy hell when that car was parked outside. But this one, has a good sense for you. You are a good man."

Geffen tried talking to the bird. It snapped at his finger and dug tiny claws deeply into Medavoy's coat shoulder.

"You made a friend, Robby."

"Maybe I should buy one for Jane."

"If they like you, they are wonderful pets. People tell me this anyway."

"The dog would probably eat it." Geffen studied the red-green bird.

"Can you get it off my shoulder? Please?"

Dickranian made soft noises with his lips, putting out his hairy forearm. The parrot screeched into Medavoy's ear, deafening him. "This is a very affectionate creature. It lives sixty years."

"I don't want it on my shoulder that long."

Dickranian sighed helplessly. "You can't afford to buy it. I never sell any of these things."

"How much?" Geffen asked out of curiosity.

"Brutus here is a cheap bird. Twelve hundred dollars."

"Jesus." Medavoy felt the bird brushing his hair. "I'll find Jane something in my price range."

"I should *give* these stinking animals away."

"Tell Detective Medavoy about the map," Geffen urged. He continued to poke his finger at Brutus the parrot. The bird nipped and shrieked at him.

"The one with the wig, I see a city map he carries when he gets out of the car. He leaves peanut shells, he changes places with the driver. I think they are lost, they have no food because they have a map and eat peanuts."

"Did you see where they went?"

"They drive away, they haven't come in, I've got these stinking beasts to worry about."

Medavoy twitched his shoulder when the parrot tickled

him. "Have you talked to any other police officers today?"

Dickranian shook his head. "No. No."

"You know the bank at the other end of the parking lot was robbed?" Geffen and the parrot were raising and lowering their heads together.

"To hell with them. They all treat me like a leper here. I don't talk to anybody."

"Well, thank you, Mr. Dickranian. You've been very helpful." Medavoy carefully put his notepad away. "Now, can you get the bird off me?"

Dickranian sighed. He went behind the counter, dug around, and returned with a small rubber mouse. He began slapping it on the counter.

"This will work. See the mouse? See the mouse, stinking parrot? See? See?"

Medavoy and Geffen checked with the technicians in the bank, those outside working on the tire tread, and the cops picking up each tiny peanut shell in front of Petland. It was nearly five, but the white sky only dimmed slightly, the breeze swift and damp from the west. A few lights went on around the Albertsons and a Japanese restaurant.

"We got time for me to get Jane something here." Medavoy looked up and down the stores in the large arcade. He started walking. He paused in front of a sports fashion store. He paused again in front of a jewelry store, but only for an instant.

He went into a cluttered store selling auto supplies.

"You getting her some spark plugs?" Geffen asked. He poked at the bins of small metal parts. There was no one else in the store.

"Don't be funny. They got videotapes here. She likes movies. We watch them all the time." Medavoy spun a rack of movies.

Geffen came over and studied the rack and handed a box

to Medavoy. "Here. This's the one. It's family entertainment."

Medavoy didn't like the photo on the box. It showed a woman being held by some sort of walking vegetable. The vegetable was peeling her clothes off and she didn't enjoy it. "Well, it says Filipino with English subtitles."

"All the movies are from the Philippines, Robby."

"Jane likes foreign movies." He frowned. "This looks like porno, though, right? She's real careful about that because of the kid."

"Ask the guy." Geffen gestured at a man, elbows supporting his head, who stood behind the counter reading a newspaper.

"Say, hello. Is this movie okay? Is it porno?"

The man, who might have been very old because of his wrinkles, looked at the police badge in Medavoy's coat pocket and smiled. "No. Is a very exciting dramatic movie. You been to the Philippines?"

"No."

"You know some Filipino people?"

"No."

"You want to learn a new language?"

Medavoy shook his head. "It's a gift. I want to rent it."

The man took the box, looked at Medavoy's badge with puzzlement and smiled again. "Take."

"How much?"

"No. Take. Take." He smiled again.

"You're sure? I don't mind renting it."

"I like cops. I have a cousin in Cebu City. He's a cop. Like you."

"I need a new headlight. I got a busted left front one on a Chevy Cavalier," Geffen said.

"Shut up, Gef. Well, thanks. You're sure this isn't dirty?"

The man smiled again. "It could be. You want it dirty?"

"No, I just want a fun picture to watch. You know, family watch it, too?"

"You tell other cops I got movies," the man said. "I got

everything for cars. I give them good deals. I give them good fuck movies."

Medavoy thanked the man again and he and Geffen went out. The commuter traffic was heavy along the widened boulevard, the hiss and swish of car after car rushing home. Medavoy looked at the movie box again. "I'll let you know tomorrow," he said to Geffen.

They walked back to the bank. "You going to call the FBI in?"

Medavoy laughed. "Jesus, if the ID is as bad as the teller's, they'll kick it back to us. If the ID gets good, they'll squeeze us out. I want to keep it."

"So it's a couple of women from out of town; they eat peanuts, they rob banks with a bomb. Sounds swell, Robby."

"Or it's a guy. Or two guys who wear wigs, eat peanuts, rob banks with a bomb. Maybe they're leaving Santa Maria, that's why they got the map out. Or maybe they're looking for another bank." Medavoy watched the cops finish collecting peanut shells. "I'll know what we got after I see the bank's security tape."

"Tonight?"

"Tomorrow. No overtime today." Medavoy was firm. He wanted to get home to Jane.

"Yeah. Call it a day."

"What're you doing tonight?"

"Maybe we'll go drinking, maybe dinner. Maybe I'll stay home and swallow my gun."

"Don't be funny, Gef." He refused to acknowledge Geffen had any real problem. It was only more dry, black humor—the profession's universal antidote to the day's pain. Medavoy felt only a twinge of genuine worry.

"Just kidding around," Geffen said. "You know what used to be here? Right where we're standing?"

Medavoy glanced around at the shopping mall. "No. I don't remember."

"Nothing. This used to be fields. You could play ball, hit

one like past third and never see where it went. That's how open it was. Little farmhouses. I came down here with my brothers after school and we played ball every day in the summer. They had pheasant, wild rabbits, all kinds of shit in the brush out here." Geffen looked around wonderingly at the cars flashing by on Brighton Boulevard and the crowded stores.

"No kidding? I never got down to this part of town much."

Geffen grinned. "Well, what we got here, Robby, is proof of real progress in the world. Right here used to be open fields couple years ago. Now we got a bank robbery and you got a dirty movie. Who says this town isn't going someplace?"

Medavoy nodded. He looked at the white sky, going gray, hinting at black.

"We got a lot of rain coming," he said.

NINE

IT WAS PAST SIX before Medavoy actually turned up his street. He could drive the route thoughtlessly now. A few people were still out, misty dark shapes tending to lawns and cars. Several waved at him and he waved back. He had only started to learn who his new neighbors were a few months ago. They liked having a policeman living on the block.

One very good thing living with Jane had taught him; she drew the line on work at five. It was the rare evening she got home late and he tried to follow her example. He had taken care of the evidence from Pacific Security, called the DA on Reilly's case and satisfied himself that the bail would stay at three hundred thousand at least until the hearing tomorrow morning. Then, with a feeling of guilt, he canceled the photo lineup with Mrs. Voss. He could not face seeing her son tonight and there were so few leads, the possibility of an identification from pictures could wait until the next day. And finally, he got out the car description Dickranian had given, sending the license to the Department of Motor

Vehicles in Sacramento by teletype with a rush request. He might get an answer tomorrow.

Jane's car wasn't in the narrow driveway but all the house lights were on. Medavoy parked, got out, and felt his gun cut into his side. Jane worried the kid might find the gun, so Medavoy kept it close by all the time.

She lived on the east side of Santa Maria, out where the development boom hadn't arrived yet. Medavoy liked the new city, all the bustle and clatter and confusion, the dynamism. He liked to watch the landscape change almost overnight. Jane wasn't impressed. They'd drive along and she would play name-what-used-to-be-there with him as a tease.

From her small lawn, when he paused now, he could just see the field at Madison High School. Four years of baseball there, mostly shortstop. He pitched only once, a disastrous game against Bella Vista that old classmates sometimes liked to taunt him about. He liked being able to see the high school field again and see those games again with Jane and the kid in early spring. They walked over—he carried the kid on his shoulder, Jane held his hand—following the sound of cheers from the high school field. He spoiled the kid every game with soft drinks and candy from the machine, but that felt like the right thing to do. He enjoyed doing it.

If he were not living with Jane, he didn't have any idea where he'd be tonight. His first house, still mortgaged, still drawing four hundred fifty-two dollars a month from his paycheck, was in Annie's hands—his former wife—lost in the early evening dark, miles away. He rarely spoke to her or saw his son. They were a separated term in his life, remote now and unreachable.

He stepped on the wet grass. The streetlights snapped on miraculously. It was a quiet neighborhood, all single story around Jane.

It was good to have a house again, a family routine, a front door that was yours, even by sufferance. He used his key and went in. It smelled right, too—frying meat, something boiling; there was a dark blue carpet that was worse off because of Natty, the dachshund. Jane had on a rock station.

He took off his coat, thinking he'd annoy her, dropping it on the sofa. Then he remembered Natty's fondness for his clothes and picked it up again. Almost everything he wore now had a thin covering of short, stiff dog hairs.

Jane was singing softly in the kitchen. She was a court reporter. She sat hour upon boring hour tapping out the truth and lies from witnesses and lawyers in whatever trial department she was assigned. She had her own business, too. Civil attorneys hired her, at a terrific hourly salary, to tap out the truth and lies from people with lawsuits.

Medavoy met her when he testified as the arresting officer in the Frito Bandito trial. Three illegal aliens robbed women walking down the street. They would drive their stolen pickup alongside some woman, one of them leaned out, and grabbed the purse. If the woman had no visible purse, they reached out and grabbed her coat, dragging her until she fell out of it.

Jane was the court reporter, sitting just below him on the witness stand. He noticed her when he came in, took the oath, and started talking. He noticed her for the next four hours. Delicate features, rich dark hair that caught the sunlight like coal. She fooled him. Dressed in pastel, small hands tapping on the steno machine, she looked utterly retiring and fragile.

The "Dresden Doll" a judge called her. Medavoy thought that was one of the greatest jokes he'd ever heard. She was tough and bright and rarely cowed by people or events. There was nothing doll-like about her beyond the way she looked in the morning, still asleep, first light on her pale, slightly freckled skin.

That day in court, she asked him out for a drink. They went out again. His divorce was still pending and Jane had not begun to show her pregnancy. She didn't make a secret of it. Nor did she marry the father. Medavoy didn't move in with her until the kid was a few months old.

He went into the kitchen. It was not possible to sneak up on Jane. The moment Medavoy came in, the dachshund skittered over the linoleum to him.

"The dog's got my shoe again," he said.

Jane turned from chopping up lettuce. "Natty. Down. Sit. Do something." The dachshund growled and went on chewing fiercely at the toe of Medavoy's shoe.

"I had a parrot on my shoulder. I come home, I got a dog on my foot."

"Dumb animals love you," she grinned. He still held his coat, and he kissed her, one hand on her neck. It was complete and full to love her and be loved in return, as though he had achieved something his first marriage made seem ugly, pointless. They ended the kiss reluctantly, putting it aside for later.

He fished in his coat. "It was just a thumper of a day. Got you a movie. Maybe we watch it later?"

She took it. "Thanks. It looks . . . odd." She set it on the counter.

"My car went out again." Jane finished with the lettuce, stirred something fragrantly boiling on the range. "It's the transmission so Oscar'll keep it for ten years. I need a ride in the morning."

"You going downtown first thing?"

"Right to the courthouse. I'm still doing the homicide with Moskowitz."

Medavoy opened the refrigerator. "Righteous Ron. You want a beer?"

"God. Give me two."

"Seriously?"

"I've been listening to the dumbest judge in the whole courthouse tell dumb jokes all day, Robby. And my car's dead."

He grabbed three bottles. Even though they shared life, love, and work, Jane had carefully segregated the refrigerator. His food was on the left, hers on the right. He didn't like yogurt or tofu or natural cheese anyway.

They clinked bottles and took the first drink simultaneously. Natty had slunk away, satisfied with her kill.

"How's the kid? Asleep?"

"If you go look in, give him some of your beer. Maybe
it'll keep him quiet for a while." She took another drink and
licked a finger after dipping it in a pot.

"Do I have to eat that?" he asked.

"Eat out if you want."

He leaned forward and kissed her again. "I'll be right
back. Keep the wonder dog here, okay?"

"Natty. Stay," Jane said without much hope.

He walked down the hall, humming the tune from the radio.
Natty began clicking along the linoleum toward him and he
heard Jane's command to stay again. He felt tired but pleased.

He sat down on the large bed, rumpling the patchwork
quilt Jane had made, took off his shoes, stripped, and changed
into jeans and an old Police Baseball League sweatshirt. The
closet was arranged so that he had a third or so at one end
for his few clothes. Jane's neatly stored shoes, blouses, coats
took up the rest of the space. She was an accumulator, unlike
him. Already their bedroom was too crowded with framed
pictures, Jane and Robby at Disneyland with the kid, Jane and
Robby holding hands against a garish sunset, Jane and Robby
and another couple at the beach, laughing at something off
camera. She had no hesitation about asking people to take
their pictures.

He went into the kid's bedroom without turning on the
light. Johnathan, a year and a month old, was asleep. He had
Jane's delicacy of feature, someone else's blond hair. Medavoy
hoped that the part of himself he gave to the kid wasn't as
obvious. He did not like the internal legacy from his own
father. With this unmarked, unmade child Medavoy thought
he had a chance to add something decent and good.

He felt Jane brush gently up to him.

"Didn't hear you," he whispered.

"I like to watch you look at him."

"He's pretty quiet now."

"They gave him a cookie or something at day care. He bounced around here for an hour."

Medavoy turned to her. "You've got that look again. I'm in for it later, right? Long night ahead?"

"You bet. Johnathan's not going to be an only child if I can help it." She kissed him again.

"Oh, God."

"Come on. Dinner's on." She took his hand and led him back to the kitchen.

While they ate, he told her about the Reilly search and the parrot. He did not mention Easter or Geffen's melancholy. She was doing dailies on the homicide trial, which meant no lunch breaks and early mornings so that the attorneys could have transcripts every night.

"Somebody called," she said. "About five."

"Who was it?"

"I don't know. A guy asked for you, asked if you lived here. I said you did. Then he hung up." She looked at him.

"You recognize the voice?"

"It wasn't Geffen or Masuda or any of the usual suspects."

Medavoy chewed slowly. "I don't know if it's such a great idea telling somebody I live here."

"You do. I'm not going to say you don't. You want me to say you just stop by for your dinner?"

Medavoy could tell she was peeved. "You know what I mean. We don't exactly have the right setup. According to the department."

"Well, maybe it was a burglar. He wants to know if I'm alone." She grinned at him. At the end of the kitchen, face buried in her water dish, Natty glanced up, huffed, and splashed her snout in again.

"You got the wonder dog to take care of burglars."

"Only if they wear your shoes. Natty loves everybody else."

"She's jealous."

"Sure she is. I don't blame her."

Medavoy finished his beer and got another. Jane was good for about four, maximum, and she stretched her second out at dinner. He said, "Okay, so let's not broadcast I'm living here. Get a number and I'll call back. If it's legitimate, that'll work."

"What's wrong, Robby? Something happen today? You started acting antsy." Jane reached for him.

"Nothing. It's okay."

"You better tell me, Medavoy." She scratched the back of his hand lightly.

"It's the case I got working on Reilly. There're bad cops in it. They're digging around on me."

"Who is?" She was slightly alarmed.

"The bad guys."

"Bad cops, bad lawyers, bad politicians. You do any digging in this town, you find bad guys. I hear about it just like you do."

"Well," he said reluctantly, "there's something they can find."

"Not on you."

"I didn't tell you everything about Baladarez."

"Tell me if you're worried." She let go of his hand.

In truth, Medavoy was no longer scared of Baladarez for himself. Its sad revelations, if made widely public, would hurt or embarrass Jane. Or so he thought, and it was that concern which bothered him more than his own guilt.

About a year before, just as his first marriage was imploding, on a night when he worked late as acting supervisor in Robbery, Leroy Menefee ran up to Mrs. Concepcion Baladarez as she walked home from the American Market on the corner. It was fairly dark, the sidewalk cracked, unlit. Menefee grabbed her large black handbag, which was hooked in her arm, and tugged mightily.

Mrs. Baladarez screamed and dropped her groceries. She

held onto her purse, which contained, she later told Medavoy, a silver crucifix from her aunt, her library card, and the only photo of her late husband, Humberto. She held onto that purse with all her strength.

Menefee was a tall, strong black kid. He yanked, tore, whipped her around, breaking the strap on the purse, and fracturing her elbow. He fell back a little when the purse came loose, and then ran. He was in high-top sneakers and he ran fast.

Mrs. Baladarez screamed so loudly that people from the market came out. They called a patrolling squad car. Forty-five minutes later, the Santa Maria police arrested Leroy Menefee at his home four blocks away. On the front step, open and empty, lay Mrs. Baladarez's purse.

Although there was an ambulance ready to take her to the hospital, Mrs. Baladarez waited long enough, in some pain even with medication, for the police to bring Menefee back to her. He was in handcuffs. She looked up from the stretcher and shouted that he was the one who stole her purse. She identified him as her former newspaper delivery boy.

When she saw the empty purse, she demanded he tell her where the crucifix was, the photo. She hinted she might even forget everything. Menefee only said she was crazy. She cried and was taken to the hospital.

Medavoy was working overtime that night. He had worked overtime every day that month and joined the 80 Club. It was open only to officers with at least eighty hours of overtime in a month and was celebrated with a Friday-to-Saturday drunk.

He was, in a grim way, looking forward to that long weekend.

Leroy Menefee was brought in, put in an interview room, and left for Medavoy to question.

It had not been possible, even much later, to satisfactorily explain to himself or anyone else what happened next. Menefee was cursing loudly, crudely. He wanted to talk to a lawyer and

Medavoy went on questioning, his manner growing calmer, ominously colder with each minute.

"You a motherfucker, you got no right, you got nothing. You let me out of here."

"I'm not letting you out," Medavoy said.

"You motherfucker. You let me see my motherfucking lawyer." Menefee was handcuffed through a ring in the wall. He had one free hand.

"You got a lawyer?"

"I don't got a lawyer, fucker. You got to get me one, I ask for him. Get me one." Menefee demanded it curtly.

"Okay." Medavoy felt cold, yet roiling inside. "You got to stay here until I get somebody."

Menefee smirked, waving the free hand, reaching as if to grab Medavoy's coat. "You a chump, man. You nothing but a goddamn motherfucking chump."

"I'm what?" Medavoy asked, knowing at that instant what he was going to do.

"Cocksucker."

Medavoy still had considerable shoulder and arm strength from his baseball days and he played regularly enough with the police league to stay in some shape. He used that talent to punch Menefee in the ribs. One sharp scream came. He hit Menefee again, in the face; the curses stopped and the man began crying.

It was probably, although not definitely, the sight of him crying that jolted Medavoy. Sick, fearful, hating the crying man and himself, Medavoy realized he had just ended his career as a cop. Hitting a handcuffed suspect without provocation was irredeemable. It was, he thought with sick clarity, exactly the kind of thing his father used to do when he rousted bums off railroad cars.

So Medavoy acted. He opened Menefee's handcuffs, wordlessly, trying to ignore the bleeding face, the gradually quieter sobs. Leroy Menefee was only nineteen even if he had a two-page rap sheet. Medavoy knocked over the two chairs in the narrow, cloying interview room. He smelled Menefee's fear sweat and his own.

He shouted for help, bolted from the room. Three other officers rushed in, grabbed Menefee, now crying louder, cursing and fighting, and forced him out and to a holding cell downstairs. Medavoy said someone hadn't handcuffed Menefee properly, he got loose and began fighting to get out. The other cops had seen Menefee, seen the signs of struggle in the interview room, actually wrestled him out themselves. Everyone believed it happened that way.

What he did next was by way of atonement. He worked up the two-eleven on Mrs. Baladarez, checked with the two Santa Maria newspapers to see if Menefee had worked as a paperboy. What Medavoy found out was that Leroy Menefee had two brothers. Daladier was a year older, John a year younger. He remembered staring at the photos of the three young men. Only a mother could really tell them apart, the resemblances were that close. Both Daladier and John had been paperboys. Leroy had not. Medavoy got that assurance over the phone.

So he showed photos of all three Menefee brothers to Mrs. Baladarez. She grew confused and nervous and picked first John, then Leroy as her attacker. "You're not sure, right?" he asked, hoping for that answer.

"I'm sure. It was him. It was him for sure." She pointed decisively at Leroy.

When he went back to the office he put together a package on the case for the DA to review. He wrote his reports as bluntly as he could. This was a weak, untriable case. The woman had seen her attacker on a dark sidewalk, for only a moment, identified her paperboy, which this defendant was not, and picked him out at the scene when she was under medication. No property was recovered on the defendant. The real assailant could have been any of the three brothers.

Medavoy felt Leroy had been paid back for robbing the woman, if he had done it at all. A cracked rib, a broken cheekbone were punishment enough. Medavoy told himself he was helping Leroy Menefee, and the formal complaint of excessive force Menefee had filed against him wasn't part of it at all.

It was the same lie his father repeated at home, the same self-justification. The brutal deception was seamless.

For a week, Medavoy felt righteous and clear. I'm helping him. I got him out of it. The DA dumped the case, no filing at all. The excessive force complaint, without witnesses or supporting evidence, would fade away by itself. Only Menefee's word gave it a brief vitality. His word against cops who said it didn't happen that way.

Mrs. Baladarez had one son, Alphonse. He was twenty-six, out of work, and he brooded for days about the injuries his mother moaned about constantly, her honor assaulted, her attacker now free again.

Alphonse Baladarez owned a .25 caliber pistol, small and blue-gray. He brought it with him when he went to Caroline's, a twenty-four-hour restaurant and card room on Mendota Avenue; tree-shaded and repainted. Caroline's was a landmark of old sin and venality that stretched back to Reconstruction, brothel, funeral home, hotel, brothel again, changing as the city changed around it. Leroy Menefee worked there as a dishwasher.

A week after his mother's robbery, Alphonse Baladarez walked into Caroline's and asked for Leroy Menefee. He found Menefee standing at a great steel sink, hands deep in soapy water, dirty great pots and dishes stacked around him. Cooks, waitresses, the odd drunk wandered through the kitchen so nobody minded Baladarez.

He spoke Menefee's name. Leroy Menefee turned, hands still in soapy water, his face still bandaged, rib taped. From only four feet away, Baladarez shot him, then fired twice more into Leroy Menefee's chest. But Menefee lived.

"I wasn't called as a witness at Alphonse's attempted murder trial," Medavoy said. "The DA said Mom's robbery was weak. The buck stopped there."

Medavoy had not been able to tell Jane about hitting Menefee. Her love might forgive it, and Medavoy didn't want forgiveness for that sin. It was his personal, secret wrong. He was different from his father if he didn't try to beg or buy out of it.

"It was a weak case, Robby. I don't see what's so bad," Jane said.

"See, if I'd looked a little harder, I'd have found Leroy *was* the old lady's paperboy. The newspaper was wrong, they got mixed up or something. The old lady was right when she made the ID. Leroy did it."

"What happened to her son?"

"What do you think, witnesses, he just walks in and shoots Menefee? Jury's out only three hours, they come back with first degree. He's at Folsom, fifteen to life."

"Anybody could've made that mistake."

"I should've done my job better. I should've looked harder. One guy's shot up, one's in the joint for life."

He helped Jane clear the table. "They gave you the Medal of Valor. You did something heroic. It balances out," she said.

"I pulled a truck driver out of the river."

"We pulled him out," she only half-joked.

"Right. We did. Getting the medal makes it worse."

"What?"

"Look, Janie, I'm the department's temporary poster child. I do those pep talks at grade schools. It'll look bad if this stuff gets spread around."

"Can you do anything about it?"

"Like stop it?"

"Yeah."

"I don't think so."

"Then forget it." She was the most practical person he

had ever met. She would work, raise the kid, love him, all on her own terms. It gave gravity to their love.

Medavoy was glad he had told her most of it anyway. It was not a thing he wanted her to find out accidentally.

They watched some of the video, but it was neither peculiar nor dull enough to hold their interest.

There was a screened porch at the back of the house. They stood on it, each with a beer.

"I thought I heard thunder," she said. She looked off into the dark distance, a flash of lightning forking, illuminating, vanishing.

"One one thousand, two one thousand, three one thousand, four . . . ," he paused as the sky rumbled deeply. "Right overhead."

"You going to marry me?" she asked, sipping her beer.

"You mean marry you, have a big wedding or marry you like spend my life with you?"

"Jesus." She looked away.

"I'm sorry." He saw he had hurt her.

They were caught in silence for a moment. Soft rain fell insistently, beading into the tiny rusted spaces of the porch screen. A car honked in the wet, dark night.

"You're not getting younger," she said.

"Yeah. When I'm ninety-seven you'll only be ninety."

"People will talk."

"I'm kind of old-fashioned, I guess. I believe in shacking up, not marriage."

"That's cop bullshit."

"I'm a cop."

"You sure are."

"You'd kick me out if you didn't like it." He held her. "I bet we look like the old farmer and his wife, the painting?"

"Robby," Jane was serious, "we're different from you and Annie. It works with us."

"I want to keep it that way."

"I'm not getting any straight answers tonight, right?" She wasn't angry, only unwilling to replay the conversation once again.

"I tell it like it is."

"Maybe I should kick you out."

"I'd have to leave all this." He pointed at the cluttered porch, unused bicycles, stacked chairs, dusty and rusty metal boxes, and a lawnmower that needed cleaning. "What brought this up? Bad day?"

She pressed closer to him. Behind them was the house, the yellow-lit, warm kitchen, ahead was an impenetrable darkness, lit by flashes.

"I'm tired. It's a long trial. I talk like this when I'm too tired."

He wanted to make himself clear to her.

"I'm really not kidding," he said.

"No?"

"I love you. I love the way things are. You're my future. The kid's my future, too. We'll raise him better because we want to be together. We don't have to be. I don't want to make the mistakes my folks did. Or my own again."

"We won't," she said. "I guarantee it."

Natty's scratching on the door was swallowed in another thunderclap, the land suddenly fired by lightning. Cool and persistent rain fell over them, over the whole city.

TEN

SHADOWS SHOT ALONG the dirty walls, shouts mixed, echoed from room to room, running men burst from door-ways, lurched into doorways, chasing and being chased, hide-and-seek played with drawn guns, broken only by the thunder outside.

"He's coming to you! Get him, get him!" Easter yelled, gun out. He ran into another room.

"Your left! Jesus, there he is!"

"I see him!"

Easter followed the other men, four from his Special Weapons Unit. He sweated even in the brightly colored Hawaiian sport shirt. He wiped his face with one hand.

"Who's got him?" he shouted. "Shit," he whispered.

"I don't hear him."

"Ramon. Ra-mon," Easter called out.

"Nothing."

"Okay. Freeze where you are. He's got to move."

Easter pressed against the peeling wall, the half-rotted

floor creaking, groaning under him. He was in the largest room, three big Coleman lanterns hissing, throwing hard white light and hard black shadows. Scattered over the floor were stained sleeping bags, empty take-out cartons, wine bottles. To his left was a card table with flasks and heaters on it. Small metal scales, neatly folded glassine bags were set near the table. The sharp bite of ammonia hung in the damp air.

"Ramon! Hey. Ra-mon. Where you going?" he shouted.

Thunder rolled overhead again, and he heard his own quick, short breathing, like a diver about to launch himself into space. In front of him was deep shadow, a large darkened doorway. He took a cautious step, shifting a few feet to one side, kicking a skin magazine out of the way. He couldn't even hear his own men, waiting, straining to hear, in the darkness.

Easter stepped to the card table. "Ramon! We got your shit here. We got your car. You can't get out. We're in the middle of no place out here."

The shadows stayed frozen, great hulking shapes moving only when he did, his own black ghosts. The lanterns hissed.

"Ramon! You're pissing me off!"

A voice came from somewhere deep in the house: "We got everything, big guy. Let's move out."

"Nobody moves!" Easter shouted back. He tightened his gun grip. "Shit," he whispered again.

Frantically running feet came immediately off to his right, glass shattered loudly. Easter sprang from the card table and ran into the dark hallway, into a smaller room. Lightning broke across the blue-black bare walls, starkly lighting the man trying to climb through the broken window.

Easter shouted, grabbing the man's waist, pulling him backward. The man's head cracked sharply on the window frame as they fell. He cried out.

The others came running in, their flashlights lancing into the room, shouts filling it. Someone bent and hit the man with the heavy police flashlight. He groaned and went limp in Easter's grip.

"Get Ramon off me," Easter said. Two men lifted the man up. He was bearded, shoeless, wearing beltless green pants and a baggy T-shirt. Someone hit him again with the long, heavy flashlight.

"Don't hit Ramon." Easter straightened his shirt, checking for rips. He picked his gun up off the floor where he had dropped it. Another bright flash burst over them all, the room in tableau, one man held up by two others, three men hovering around them.

"Who you staring at?" one of them demanded.

The man blinked, coughed, lowered his eyes.

Easter said, "You know who I am, Ramon?"

"You all cops," he saw the gold police badges shining on each shirt pocket.

"You know my name, Ramon?"

"How'm I going to know you name?"

"Think it's important?"

"What? I'm busted, okay. Who cares."

"You're right. It's not real important." Easter noticed his breathing, his heartbeat all quickly reverting to a steady rhythm. "Let's take Ramon out where we got some light."

They half-dragged the man back into the living room and dropped him on one of the sleeping bags.

"Your buds left you holding the fort, Ramon," Easter said, sitting down alongside the man. The other men ringed them. They grinned.

"You taking me downtown?" Ramon looked from man to man, some uneasiness forming.

"Sure we're going downtown. First, where's the cash? You got cash here and I don't see it."

"I don't have to give it up." He smirked. "My lawyer says so."

"You don't have to give it up. You want to walk out of here tonight?"

"You take me downtown."

Easter shook his head. "Eddie? Put some handcuffs on Ramon."

The man who had hit Ramon with the flashlight slipped a pair of handcuffs off his belt, knelt, and locked them tightly so that Ramon's flabby arms were bent behind his back. "Goddamn, this guy reeks," Eddie said.

"Where's the warrant?" Ramon asked, eyes going again from man to man.

"We got you on manufacture of methamphetamine for sale, possession for sale, resisting arrest, hell, you got this damn drug lab out in the boonies."

"Who snitched me off?"

"Ramon, you keep missing the important issue here. You been dealing dope, you and your buds. Now, where's the money?"

Ramon struggled to puzzle through some idea. He squirmed a little on the sleeping bag. Thunder startled him and he twitched.

Finally he said, "Am I still busted if you get my money?"

Easter stared at him. "That'll probably depend if I get it in the next five seconds."

"Okay. Okay. See the bag over there? Get underneath, there's a loose board."

One of the men threw back a sleeping bag near the wall. His shadow shot up, wild and angular.

Easter watched, but there was a waning interest in his eyes.

One of the men said, "What's Reilly doing? He getting out? Jesus, he must be burned."

Easter answered calmly, "Don't worry about Reilly. He's okay. He's going to bail tonight."

"We okay?"

"He's solid, bud. We're still tight."

Ramon watched, listened, his toes curling and uncurling.

"We got to do something, Ralph. We got to make sure

we're okay from now on," one of the men said vehemently.

"I'm covering it," Easter said. "Don't worry."

The man by the wall grunted as he raised a board, peered into a space between the floorboards, reached down. "Got a box." He held up a metal box.

"That's it. That's all we got," Ramon said, a smile breaking out. "Open up." He tried to show the handcuffs.

"Maybe a three, four in here." The man counted the money.

"You make a mortgage current with that," one man said.

"Hey. Hey. Open up, open up."

Easter brought his gun from its belt holster. He held it by Ramon's cheek. "Pick up whatever they bagged already," Easter said to the men. "Leave the rest of the shit."

"No more money," Ramon stared at the gun. "I give up somebody. You want somebody?"

"What a buddy, Ramon." Easter shook his head. "Isn't he a guy you'd like to have watching your back?" The men laughed and with practiced ease, scooped up the packaged methamphetamine.

"He's like that asshole Medavoy," one man said.

"You know what kind a gun this is, Ramon?" Easter held it, ready to fire.

Ramon shook his head, his legs rigid, his face trembling and sweating. His breathing hissed like the lanterns.

"We used to have these dinky six-shot police .38s, Ramon. But, you know, everybody worried you'd run out, shooting at some fucker like you who's shooting at you."

"I don't shoot at you. I don't do nothing."

"Don't cry, Ramon."

"This's making me sick, Ralph." The men again stood, ringing the two on the sleeping bag. The rain sounded louder on the old roof and blue-white lightning flashed brightly.

"So last year, Ramon, we got these new guns. They're Sig-Sauers. They're sixteen shot, you got one in the chamber and a whole fifteen more to lay on the bad guy. How's that?"

Ramon swallowed, sweated, his eyes moist, his lips moving slightly.

"The guy who got these great guns for us, his name's Medavoy. He went to the City Council, he said cops need guns that'll stop bad guys. He's a hero, Ramon. They gave him a medal for saving the life of a drunk truck driver who went into the river. You believe it?"

"Come on, let's move out." The men were impatient, as if Ramon had already become unnoticeable.

"I got to finish with Ramon. So, this guy Medavoy is such a hero, the City Council gives him what he wants. Now we all get to carry these great Sig-Sauers. Remember that name? Robby Medavoy."

"Fucking Medavoy," spat Eddie. He was like Easter, dressed in a gaudy sport shirt, his hairless arms white.

Easter smiled. "I made a phone call tonight. I know where he's living now. He can't give it up to the department without getting nailed. He's got no story for tonight that keeps him clean."

"I do whatever you want. I give up anybody you want. What? Tell me. What?" Ramon tried to sit up straighter, but his handcuffed arms made it awkward so he only slumped.

"You just remember the name, Ramon, when anybody asks you. He's the guy who did this to you. Robby. Medavoy. You tell anybody who asks and I won't come after you again. None of these guys will come after you, you do that, okay?" Easter swept his arm around the circle of men.

"What? What'd he do?" Panic, sweaty and deep.

The thunder crashed once more. "He did this."

Easter put down his gun and picked up the flashlight. He swung like a batter and broke Ramon's jaw.

"Take off the cuffs," Easter ordered.

ELEVEN

"**I CLOSED EVERYTHING,**" the Chief said, a little put out. He looked at his cards again. "Now I forgot the bid."

"I thought I heard the bedroom window, Mac," his wife repeated. She looked at the couple they were playing cards with. "It's raining so hard, I hate the idea of it getting in."

"Just before dinner, I closed everything."

"All right." She was dubious. Donna McNeill spoke with a slight twang. She put down a card. "Don't get a hernia."

The Chief did not enjoy bridge night. Three other couples sat at tables in their living room, the talk insipid, the time wasted. Playing a giggly game were Rich and Marian and Todd and Janine, younger civic types. Rich had managed a seat on the Santa Maria Municipal Utility District board. Janine specialized in charity social affairs. The Chief ignored them all as much as he could tonight.

The room itself was furnished with Donna's money, mostly in light, wooden Danish, the chairs and sofa in puffy tan leather.

135

He listened to the rain, the harsh thunder and tried to concentrate on his cards. He disliked games.

"I heard that TGB Properties is going ahead with the port project." He said it casually for effect.

"Who says?" asked the tall, balding man on his right. He was round-shouldered, in an open-collared white shirt.

"A reliable source."

The man chuckled, took a last, ice-clacking swallow from his glass. "Must be Prefach, Mac. He's the only source you got."

"You need another, Ollie?" Donna asked attentively.

"Any gin fizz left? I like Mac's fizz."

"There's about half a blender, I think." The Chief wondered why, in a city of almost half a million people, he still had to play cards with men who had beaten him up in grade school. Probably because they belonged to the Rio Del Oro Country Club with his wife.

"Yeah. I'll take another in a second. I better space them a little."

"You have a few shares with TGB," the Chief said. "Trump or something, I guess." He lowered his cards.

"Not even close. You could learn the game," his wife said, pushing his cards back at him.

"My brother-in-law's the stockholder. I don't own anything." Ollie grinned. "How long do we have to wait on it?"

"After the announcement. It's legal to buy then."

"Costs more, too. Not much of a tip, Mac."

The Chief hated being called Mac and only people who had known him for years did so. His attempt at boasting had failed, too. He still hadn't grasped his inability to play insider games like these people. They were born to it. He only married into it.

Ollie kissed his wife's hand. "Yum, yum," he said.

Donna McNeill watched, looked at the Chief with a little smile. "See? Ollie does it. That didn't hurt, did it, Claire?"

Ollie's wife shook her hand loose. "It gets worse."

"My own true love! Mother of my children!" he said with exaggerated hurt.

Donna still tried to play her cards, but everyone else at the table had given up. The other table went on burbling, dealing, tossing down cards.

Self-consciously, the Chief leaned over and pecked his wife on the cheek. He was embarrassed no one noticed. Donna sighed.

"One of your boys was in my courtroom today," Ollie said. "He wouldn't surrender his gun."

"He's right."

"I've got standing instructions. No weapons in my court-room. Your boy wouldn't do it." Ollie snorted at his wife.

"What was his name?"

"He's a detective. Medavoy."

"I remember him," said Claire.

"Medavoy?" the Chief asked. The name was familiar, but a little remote.

"You pinned a medal on him, Mac. About a week after you made Chief." Donna prompted from long practice. "Mac still doesn't do too well with names or faces."

"I remember, just didn't have all the details." The Chief felt his thin lips dry. He must be pink, too. He would never do this again, no matter how much Donna insisted or coaxed. He was never going to be humiliated by these people again.

"Anyway, I said to my bailiff, you take that officer's gun when he comes in here to testify. My bailiff's John Lytle. You know John?"

"No." The Chief had a warning glance from Donna.

"He's a rock. But he's got it, you know, here," Ollie said, touching his throat. "They can't operate."

Claire finished her own drink. "Tell me why a policeman can't bring a gun into court, Ollie. I mean, a policeman."

"I'm not talking about that now."

"He's going to start and we'll be sitting here when the sun comes up." She held her glass tightly.

"So, the PJ wanted to send John home. I said, hell no. John wants to work in my courtroom for as long as he can." Ollie made it sound like a good deed.

"The Presiding Judge's anorexic, honey. I see her in leotards at aerobics," Claire said.

"I can't even finish my damn story."

"Talk, talk, talk, you think he'd be tired hearing himself all day," Claire said. "Mac's nice. He doesn't say a lot."

"He does his share." Donna always stuck up for him in public. After all, his estimation was now her own.

Ollie grumped, "So your boy Medavoy wouldn't give poor sick old John Lytle his gun. He says he's going to take it to the Police Officers Association if I make him hand it over."

"A good cop doesn't give up his gun, Ollie."

"You sound like a little old lady." Ollie glared at his wife, banged his glass on the table. "I'm ready now."

Donna rose, but the Chief snatched up the glass. "I'll do it." He was flushed and angry.

As he went into the kitchen, he heard Ollie, "Give me a full one this time, Mac."

The Chief counted his steps over to the stainless steel counter, gleaming under fluorescent lights, expensive knives, copper pots and pans hanging from the wall, all from some magazine Donna had seen. Or what one of the communal interior decorators everyone in this end of town passed around thought the house should have. The thunder boomed more distantly now, receding and leaving the spattering rain. With cold, rigid calm, he emptied the blender of frothy gin fizz into the glass. He was astounded at how angry Ollie Knudsen could still make him after all these years, as if the taunts in the sixth grade were still fresh, their lives still to be lived.

He turned; Donna stood quietly beside him.

"Mac," she said softly.

"Never again. We are never doing this again."

"You don't have to sulk. You don't have to listen to him."

"I mean it. This is the last time."

And someday, he thought, he'd tell her how much he disliked the blue pants she wore, the bracelets.

"These are our friends, Mac."

"I don't like them."

Her face toughened. "They're important people. Ollie's a judge, Rich and Marian are in the Chamber, Claire's father . . . "

"I know them." He held the glass tightly with two hands. "I know what they can do for me."

"For me, too," she said. "I'm thinking of the family, Mac."

He struggled to contain himself, to let it pass as so many other slights and wounds had gone by. But tonight, for some reason, he could not. He had reached the edge of the river and started to wade in.

"I want some respect, Donna," he said. "I'm the Chief of Police now."

She looked at his face closely. "And we've worked very hard to get here." She soothed, patted, flattered, the twang almost exotic. "Nothing's going to spoil things for us. Isn't that right? We can see good things ahead."

A honk, Ollie's hard laugh, floated in. Somebody clapped. The Chief put the glass on the steel counter, his wife appeared interested, but not concerned. Several people were laughing.

"I have done everything," the Chief said. "I have put up with everything. And now I want respect. I deserve it."

"Yes, you do. I respect you, Mac. You know that."

He said nothing.

"I know your men respect you." She smiled at him. "All right?"

He found himself suddenly aware of their thirty years together, two children grown and gone, a daughter working in Texas in community planning, a son with dental offices. Donna was lovely, in spite of her efforts to remain young. Thirty years of pickled vanity, exercise, diet, tanning, skin care, hair care, minor cosmetic surgery and the Chief could still make out the beautiful girl who had married him. When had making love to her become like falling onto crushed cellophane?

"The men call me Stevie Wonder. That's my nickname."

"It's not offensive."

"They are going to respect me. No more nicknames." He was thinking of decisive action about the bad cops. The department would see he was a leader by the way he took command.

"You're always a little cranky after lunch with Vin." She was gently steering him back to their guests.

He picked up the glass. "I'm not staying Prefach's boy forever, either."

"Remember that Vin's going to be mayor. He's a good friend to keep. He's been a good friend."

The Chief tried to think of clever arguments, some articulate way of telling Donna what had been coming on him for months. Why it chose this night and this moment to reveal itself, he didn't know or understand. He searched his mind. He had years of facts and graphs locked in memory. But only one thing came to him.

"I've had enough," he said to her.

She was puzzled, but showed it only for an instant when they came back into the living room.

"You all made up?" Ollie cried, hand out for the glass.

"Made up what?" The Chief sat down on the sofa, the heavy fabric skinlike.

"You two always fight." Ollie drank. Claire sighed loudly, looking away. "Mac's lip starts quivering. It's a tip-off."

"We never fight," Donna said. "Is that it for cards?"

In the brief time she'd been gone, the bridge games had dissolved and the chairs formed into a semicircle with Ollie in the center, Claire at his right.

"I was just telling them about the plea I took this morning." Ollie had dumped down half his drink. "This burglar, big white kid. Pled out to fourteen years."

"Why'd you have to say he's a white kid?" asked Rich. He kept knocking Marian's knee with his. She squirmed.

"So nobody would think he's a racist," Claire explained.

"I'm only being accurate."

The Chief listened, arms folded. Donna came and sat by him. She grew protective when there was a hint he was straying. He had given her more than a hint tonight.

"Fourteen years? That's a long time," Rich spoke again. Marian banged his knee hard and he squeaked.

Ollie nodded impatiently. "Hell of a long time in prison. He didn't want to plead. He was being tough when he first came in." He started grinning. "He changed his mind."

"Ollie's such a yawn," Claire said to Donna.

"I'm going to finish one damn story tonight."

"Go ahead, Ollie," the Chief said.

"Oh, well thanks, Mac. I guess I will." He cleared his throat. "Anyway, I have these Finnish air force pilots in the jury box. They're training out at Parmeter. All in uniform. Gray and gold uniforms." Parmeter was an air force base just outside of the city.

"Speaking of planes," Claire said, "we're selling yours this summer. You never use it anymore."

Ollie's stare was hard. "So I said to the kid, you have a right to a jury trial. He looks at me, he looks at the jury box with these guys in funny uniforms, and he says, I'll plead right now. I don't want no jury trial."

Ollie laughed a little harder than anyone else. The Chief didn't want to upset Donna, but he had to claim some dignity from the evening.

"Ollie," he said. "We arrested Reilly this afternoon."

Ollie the judge leaned back in his chair. The rain fell in a sigh outside. "I heard that going out the door. Jesus, Mac. It's about time."

"Jeff Reilly?" Claire asked in alarm.

"Brian," Ollie answered.

"Do I know him?"

"No. I do. Anybody who does criminal law in this town knows the little weasel."

"Oh, somebody from work," Claire said. She whispered loudly to Donna, "Aren't these guys a couple of yawns?"

"It's part of the housecleaning I've started," the Chief said firmly.

"Don't clean the town up, Mac. We've got it just right now." Rich and Marian stood up. "It's an early night for us. Thanks for the game. Our turn next week."

Donna saw them out, hugs and kisses exchanged. The cool night air blew through the house, stirring papers and the curtains, brushing over them.

Ollie said, "You going to be able to hold Reilly?"

"If some judge doesn't lower his bail. It'll be a good case."

"Hey, Mac, everyone's going to disqualify himself for that trial. Everybody's touched Reilly somewhere," Ollie stretched.

"Why don't you set a brave example?" the Chief needled with a wintry smile. He recalled that Ollie had fallen asleep on the bench several years before during the very long and tiresome jury selection in a sex discrimination case against an air-conditioning company. It was after lunch and he simply nodded off. The Women Lawyers, County Bar, Equal Opportunity Commission all weighed in with critical jabs at him. From then on, Ollie determined to stay awake after lunch, no matter how dull the case. He put ice cubes in his shoes.

He has no courage at all, thought the Chief.

"Don't be snide," Ollie said, glancing around to see where Claire had wandered off to. "Brave judges don't stay judges."

"She was headed for the bathroom."

Ollie stopped looking for her. "You know what I mean. I make my share of tough decisions."

Donna shut the front door heavily. She came back pleased that everyone was still engaged in polite conversation. "The rain's almost stopped," she said. "Would anybody like coffee?"

Ollie yawned. "I'll take any unclaimed liqueur."

"Claire'll be back in a minute," the Chief said.

Donna asked the other couple, Todd and Janine, who had barely spoken all evening. They both wore thick glasses and looked, the Chief thought, like groupers.

"What bugs me about cops," Ollie yawned again, frowned, and hooked his thumbs into his pants, "is they think it's all easy. Black and white choices out there. Good guys, bad guys and you're always one of the good guys. I know that's how you think. I see it whenever you guys come into court."

"You haven't the slightest idea how a policeman thinks."

"Mac, I know what I see and hear in my own courtroom. Cops have come in and lied on the stand."

"Give me their names."

"I can't remember right now."

"Then don't say it. It's a stupid slander."

"I don't hold it against them." Ollie unhooked his thumbs and pointed at the Chief. His old eyelid tic was going. "There are a lot of fuzzy lines in this world and cops should realize that."

"They see more wickedness and pain and suffering than you have, Ollie. Every one of them."

"You haven't been on patrol in what, twenty years? Ever go on a raid?"

"Not yet. I know what goes on in this city."

"I bet I know a hell of a lot more than you do. I've been a judge ten years, I practiced law sixteen." Ollie had worked himself into anger because McNeill challenged him. It wasn't permitted when they were kids and that hadn't changed.

"Murder's up twenty-two percent over last year, burglaries up forty percent, violent assaults about thirty. It is black and white out there," the Chief said heatedly.

Ollie leaned back in his chair. "You spent your whole career in the Bureau of Criminal Statistics. You're going to be the worst cop of all, Mac. It's not just numbers and rules."

Before the Chief could blurt out his anger, Donna came in with a small silver tray of drinks and coffee. She set out coasters everywhere. "Is somebody being didactic? I thought I heard lecturing."

"Ollie and I are debating the good life," the Chief said frostily.

"Where are Todd and Janine?" She looked around.

"I think they headed out," Ollie said. Claire flopped into her chair, grabbing a coffee cup with two hands as though trying to warm herself.

"The squids left," she said, sipping.

They chatted for an hour, Claire growing more restless until she took Ollie by the arm. "Say night, night."

"Thanks again, Donna." He kissed her. They all walked to the door.

The Chief peered out across his large, square lawn. A misting drizzle fell over it, and at the edge of the horizon, a few faint stars were appearing as the clouds moved on.

Up and down the street, in other large, imposing homes, the lights shone out as the city's masters relaxed. The Chief inhaled deeply.

"Sorry I got out of hand," Ollie said.

"I liked it."

"Pals?"

"Always pals, Ollie."

Ollie inhaled too and for a second the Chief was afraid he'd put his arm around him. Ollie apologetic was maudlin.

"Talk to your guy Medavoy, will you? It's my courtroom."

"I won't order him to surrender his gun."

"Talk to him. I mean, I want the Police Association endorsement again. Smooth it over for me."

"That's why I'm here," the Chief said. "They'll endorse you."

"Good old Mac," Ollie said contentedly.

Claire gave the Chief a small wave. "Night. I've got a big day tomorrow."

"Something fun?" Donna asked.

"You know, places to go, things . . ." Claire faded off vaguely, took Ollie, and they wobbled slightly to their car.

Donna rolled her eyes. "It went all right," she said as the guests drove away.

"And it's over." He turned to the house.

"It's a pretty evening, Mac. The air smells fresh, doesn't it? Rain always makes the honeysuckle sweeter. You can taste it." She stood just on the threshold of the flagstone path to the door.

"I've got a big day, too."

Wordlessly, she turned and followed him inside.

The Chief carried a police baton in one hand and flashlight in the other as he made his nightly rounds of the grounds. He put plastic covers on his slippers and a bright yellow raincoat over his pajamas. He walked briskly, flashing the beam, poking the baton into the shrubbery. Away, rising dreamlike, came a police siren and he wondered if he'd ever know why. Reports of most crimes never reached him when he compiled and analyzed criminal stats and now, as Chief, he saw even less directly.

His feet squished along the damp soil and the mist clung to him like cold sweat.

He checked his watch. It was twelve-fifteen exactly, five minutes off his usual schedule. Damn useless company and annoying chatter from Ollie. He felt good about telling Donna what he wanted.

The siren was joined by another, night harmonies, and he stopped to listen. The men thought he was a little ridiculous. They always had. He was the man with the numbers hurrying down hallways. But he was going to build up the department, fight for them, clean out the bad cops.

He considered going on a patrol ride-along some night. It would be too affected, though. Any unit he was with would never act normal or handle street problems the way they usually did. He didn't like the bowing and scraping that came with his title. The Chief was surprised to discover he craved to know what his men really thought, how they acted during the long hours of a shift.

He swept through the rest of the backyard, planted with decorative fruit trees, a wooden swing left from the kids. Even by the diminished streetlight, he saw his black-green grass was perfectly trim, every flower bed marked off strictly.

He bounced the light around a final time. A neighbor thought he had hired a night watchman, seeing that light make its regular rounds. The Chief was smug about how well he patrolled his property.

Back in the house, he made certain the kitchen door was locked, the connecting door with the garage locked, all lights on outside, all lights inside off. Then he went to his study.

It was on the first floor. It had been his son's room. When he gave it up for college, the Chief inherited it. Two computer terminals sat on his desk. He checked his schedule, noting that every appointment had been kept today. He ran tomorrow's on the computer screen. A large hole gaped where the City Council was meeting. They were always untidy, running overtime, throwing his timetable off.

The Chief set the computer to wake him at six so he'd have a chance to do some work at the department.

As he was leaving his study, he counted the model ships arrayed on shelves around the room. He had told Prefach a small lie. The models didn't come in kits. Each was hand carved, every mast and hull, all the rigging strung, some taking hundreds of hours. Galleons, battleships, cruisers, and carriers reproduced in complex detail.

Sixty-three of the models. About two for every year of his marriage.

Donna was in bed upstairs. She was propped in a cushion recliner with armrests, two books open, the TV braying.

"We secure, Mac?" she asked without looking up.

"All locked in."

"What time for lights out?"

He took off his slippers and got into bed beside her.

"I have to be up at six."

She still hadn't looked at him. Donna had a contrapuntal mind. It worked on two tracks at once. Reading and TV. Family and career. City and family. Him and her.

"I have to read a few more pages. That's all."

He rolled over, turning his face toward the darkened wall on which her shadow faintly showed, moving when she bent forward or flipped a page. He lay with his eyes open.

"What we talked about earlier, Mac?" she asked coolly.

"What?"

"I want you to remember that respect is earned. It doesn't come to you automatically."

"I know that."

"If you're going to make changes, things that could cause trouble for people we know, check with me, please."

"If that's what you want."

"I think it's a good idea. I'm almost through." He heard the spark in her voice when she'd stood at the front door. The spark wasn't in her voice now and the Chief knew he had put it out. He wondered, over the years, how many sparks he had extinguished and felt regret.

Over the gabbling voices from the TV, he listened to Donna turn pages, and the beckoning siren crying somewhere in his city.

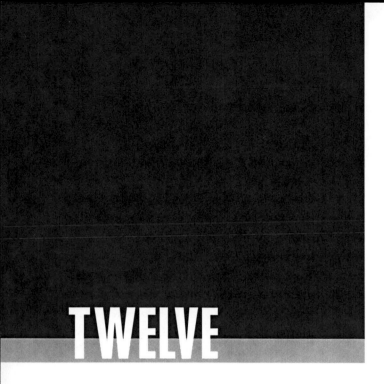

TWELVE

EVEN THOUGH THE RAIN had nearly stopped, Lisio had the windshield wipers on high. They snapped back and forth, making a grating squeal that set Carol's teeth on edge.

I'm okay so far, she thought. I'm wide awake and I've still got a chance.

They were parked outside the Vergennes Lumber warehouse and across the street from a busy McDonald's. They were alone in the warehouse parking lot late at night, windows rolled up and foggy, the car stinking of grease and wet clothes from Kenny's dash to the McDonald's to bring back their dinner.

"You sure you don't want anything?" Lisio sat taller at the steering wheel, boosted up by a telephone book Kenny had swiped from the restaurant.

Carol shook her head. Kenny smacked as he ate beside her.

"Turn off the windshield wipers," she said.

"Bother you?"

"Yes. They're very irritating."

"Can't have that," Lisio said, snapping them off. "Not even a bite?" He waved the partly eaten cheeseburger in front of her.

Kenny slapped the cheeseburger away. "She ain't hungry. She don't want yours anyway."

Carol looked into Lisio's inquisitive, cold eyes. "No, I'm not hungry."

"I was only being polite."

"Yeah, yeah," Kenny belched. He took out the lunch box and put the .45 inside his Raiders jacket. "I'm all ready," he announced, rubbing his hand over his mouth to clean it.

I'm waiting, Carol thought. After the way Kenny acted at the river, I don't doubt his loyalty, how he feels. He's only with Lisio for the moment. Convenience. What about me? She was embarrassed and exultant about using Kenny's feelings for her to bind him closer. But, she admitted, it wasn't all manipulation and show. His raw danger, her own danger, were exciting. It's not simply one thing or the other, she thought.

What I have to do, she analyzed like it was a mundane legal problem, is get Kenny away from Lisio. Kenny is my alibi. Convince him this whole thing is dead and he could free her from most of the entanglements, the threat of criminal prosecution for aiding in a jail escape, assault, robbery. That still left trying to preserve her license to practice law after becoming so involved, unethically, with a client. It was the lesser of all the evils.

Get Kenny somehow to the cops, to the DA, to someone who could make a decision and free her. The two mountainous obstacles were how to get him away from Lisio and how to make an approach to the cops that wouldn't result in her instant arrest.

So I'm waiting for the right moment tonight.

She deliberately hadn't eaten, even though she was hungry after a foodless, frightening day. The hunger emptiness gave her an edgy awareness.

"We'll take a little drive down the street," Lisio said,

wiping each of his little fingers with a napkin, then starting the car. "Look around. Anybody parked out here now isn't moving before morning."

They were poised at the intersection of Interstate 5 and West Isleton, cars rushing north and south just beyond them. It was a neighborhood of warehouses and industrial businesses.

Kenny watched the street as they cruised slowly. "I let you know when I see something."

The anticipation rose in the car. Carol could feel Kenny getting alert, like his antennae were out, feeling along the dark buildings, the fragile streetlights' gloomy glow.

"I thought of using rental cars," Lisio said. He drove self-consciously, steering stiffly.

"Rent cars for bank robberies?" She was startled unwillingly.

"Why not? Too much trouble, though. Use an out-of-town license address and they check you. Too many drug dealers rent cars now."

"Slow down, Dave. I see a couple." Kenny tapped him on the shoulder.

"I see." Lisio slowed. "Then I thought of using your license, your credit card," he shrugged toward Carol.

"I wouldn't have let you."

Kenny nudged her jokingly. "Sure you would."

"Well, it's too much of a paper trail anyway. This is much simpler."

Kenny said to her, "See what I got? Couple older models, no fucking alarms, you get in, couple moves and you drive away."

"I'm pulling up here then you follow me out when you're ready," Lisio said. He maneuvered Carol's station wagon to the curb like a kid taking a driving lesson.

"You never told me about stealing cars," Carol said to Kenny. He had the door open. He carried a Swiss Army knife and a screwdriver in the jacket.

"Shit, honey, I didn't tell you everything." Kenny winked.

He was pumping himself up, she saw, bragging to get his juices going. "I got maybe twenty cars. They was easy. What I really liked was doing electric typewriters, adding machines, radios, TV, anything you carry. That's when I was really sailing high. I get wired up, I walk into some guy's place at lunch hour, walk out with whatever I wanted. I go down to my man on Deeble Street, he gives me whatever and I'm happy again. But, cars. Shit. They no trick."

He hopped out of the car with a jaunty wave. He moved quickly, without looking unnatural, into the parking lot across the street. Two cars sat there, just inside the streetlights' cone on the wet pavement.

She saw Kenny stroll to one, suddenly bend low at the driver's door. A Ford sedan, older, dark colored.

"This is the only really labor-intensive part of the project," Lisio said, watching Kenny. "Most lawyers don't get a chance to see their clients in action."

"I don't want to see it. It's not my choice."

"No," Lisio said tightly, still facing forward, a little black shape, white skinned, his suit smelling slightly of camphor. "You think you're way above it. Lawyers always do. So much better, much smarter." Kenny had the driver's door open.

That took a fast thirty seconds, she thought. Lisio did seem to have everything planned out and Kenny had a few surprises, too.

Maybe I can come up with one for them, she thought. She smoothed her skirt unconsciously. My God, like I'm on a date.

"I could've been a lawyer. It doesn't take anything. No imagination." When Lisio spoke, Carol again noticed the defensive, nervous bite. He doesn't like being alone with me. With a woman, she thought.

"What have you done?" she asked. He might say something useful.

Kenny ducked into the sedan. He must be hot-wiring it. All so smooth, so fast. Even so, Carol found herself anxiously looking to make sure the traffic stayed back near the intersection.

"Are you really interested?" Lisio asked.

"No."

"I've done everything," Lisio went on, as if her denial prodded him. "Librarian. At a medical school. A famous Eastern medical school. Bookkeeper. Actually, accountant at a major brokerage. You'd know the name."

"Try me."

"Why should I? I was even a short-order cook. Master of anything I turn my hand to," the voice was cold, arrogant, and yet unsteady. "And I've kept lists, I've made notes on everybody's who's been shitty. You'd be amazed how long the lists are. Things people have done to me. My half of the money," he nodded slowly. "With my half I'm going to settle things."

"You don't want to enjoy yourself? Have a great dinner? Wine, women, and song?"

He swiveled back to stare at her, skin white, waxy in the faint light. "Things like that don't matter to me. It's what makes me superior. I could make a real bomb, for example. If I wanted to."

"You don't want to?" she asked. It was like talking to a snake that could strike. It was foolish and fascinating.

Lisio laughed curtly. "Imagine Kenny with a real bomb. Imagine how long he'd stay in one piece."

"I see your point," she said.

"He's got it," Lisio looked at the sedan in the parking lot.

She looked and saw the sedan's headlights come on, the engine cough once, twice, then settle into a rumble. Kenny popped up behind the wheel, grinning. The sedan swung into the street. Lisio put her station wagon in gear and they drove a mile or so. Kenny parked, locked the driver's door again. He could get into it in a minute, Carol realized. With the engine already hot-wired, the exchange of cars after each robbery could go as speedily as Lisio claimed.

Kenny slid in beside her, breathless. "Easy. Ain't no big deal when folks won't protect they property." He shook drops of cold rainwater off.

Lisio checked the street name on the city map beside him.

"See, Carol honey? Leave it to old Kenny." He poked Lisio's seat. "Let's go."

One down, two to go, Carol thought. Kenny bubbled along on his own. Lisio drove carefully on the slick streets.

Prisoner in my own car. But maybe I'll get lucky.

In the next half hour they drove downtown, to a nearly empty municipal parking lot beside a block of Chinese restaurants. Only five cars remained in the lot, their bodies heavily beaded with water so it was clear they had been there all night.

Kenny repeated his swift performance, getting into a four-door Mercury in moments. She and Lisio stayed on the street, the engine running. She moved into the front seat because it made it easier for Kenny to slide in and out of the backseat alone.

Kenny drove the Mercury out of the lot, playfully honking its horn.

"That idiot," Lisio muttered. Carol stared at the statue of Sun Yat-sen, a single spotlight playing on it, as they passed by.

She grew tenser. Her mind raced, trying to think of some place or point to throw a stone into the clockwork Lisio had set in motion. But there was virtually no one on the streets. And she needed Kenny. Corroboration, she thought. I tell my story and Kenny has to agree or I'm alone. Just like Lisio threatened this morning.

She tried to sit naturally, but Lisio had cramped the front seat very close to the dashboard so he could reach the pedals easily. She felt pinned to her own car.

Kenny parked the Mercury where Lisio directed, under a broad-branched pine, on a street of single-story little houses built before World War II. Like mine, she thought, with a pang.

"Are we going back to my house after you get the last car?" she asked Lisio.

Kenny trotted up and got in. He yawned often and shook his head as if to clear it. Probably hadn't slept in a day.

"No arguments about that," Lisio snapped.

"Hey, don't jump on her," Kenny interjected.

"I only want to know," Carol began.

"I'm tired to death of her attitude," Lisio complained. "I mean, she's getting a hundred thousand dollars tomorrow. What's she complaining about?"

"She's just asking, Dave. You get so bent about it."

"All right. Yes," Lisio said. "We're all spending a cozy night at your house."

"Thank you," she said.

The clockwork wasn't running as smoothly as it appeared. They were overtired and irritable. So maybe I'll get a chance, she thought. I'll get Kenny and me away from Lisio. First step.

Kenny leaned his head toward her, brushing her with his damp hair.

They ended up about five miles from her house, just over the widest river bridge and its garland of newly installed lights glittering in the misty air.

Lisio pulled into the Cabana Motel, a wedding-cake tiered expanse of rooms with a shining neon sign. He drove slowly until they were deep in the parking lot. It was dead quiet.

"Pick one, Kenny," Lisio said shortly. "The owner's got to be asleep."

"Or getting laid."

"If it makes you happy."

Kenny sighed, yawned, and hopped out of the car. "Keep the seat warm," he said to Carol.

She watched him walk casually across the parking lot, past the dark rooms and sleeping people. He had his hands in his pockets. He paused at another station wagon, shook his head. He got smaller, hazier in the dark. Stop at a van, walk on. Like he's out for some air before bed, she thought. How can they act like that, the ones she defended? Careless about other people and their property. Like it's all part of some vast showroom arranged solely for their benefit.

"Where is he going?" Lisio wondered aloud.

"I can see him."

"I didn't ask you."

Her heart beat quickly again. She felt the return of the early headache. Only a day since the debauch at the marina and she almost longed for its familiar sights and sounds.

Carol looked hard at the little man, perched on the telephone book, her captor. Jesus. Someone had a sense of humor. So she said, "Take a giant-size fuck off. How about it? Just a big fucking fuck off." It felt very good to say that.

Lisio's face twisted angrily. "You don't know what I'd like to do to you right now."

"Bet I do. You can't with Kenny out there, busy, busy, busy."

Her snideness steadied him. He regained his control. She cursed herself. At least making threats he wasn't thinking and she might have spotted some opening, some way out.

"You're right," he told her, icily. "Not now. Later we can talk more about it. When Kenny's asleep." He dabbed at his lips. Sweating again. Like he's asked me to the prom instead of threatened to kill me.

Kenny stopped at a big car. He waved his arms toward her, then vanished and she knew he was working on the door.

"Not a Cadillac," Lisio said disgustedly. "We don't need a car that big. What's he thinking of?"

Carol, though, knew immediately. Its artlessness broke through even her tension. "He wants to do the last bank in style," she said.

Murray Bowler, president of Bowler Building, turned one way, then the other, then back again, finally cramping a muscle in his side as he lay on the fifty-five-dollar-a-night bed in his room at the Cabana Motel.

He was worried about tomorrow and couldn't sleep. First the thunder and drumming rain had kept him awake. Then he had eaten that steak, potato with sour cream, coconut cream pie, washing the whole meal down with three martinis and a half carafe of house red, forgetting in his worry and nervousness how badly liquor hit him on such rich food before bed.

So he tossed and turned sleeplessly. He heard Betsy's proud voice. "You'll get a good deal, Murray. If they give one-half of one chance, you'll come back with the best deal." And she'd given him one of those generous, wet smacks on the lips that showed how sincerely she believed it.

So he'd said back to her, "Honey bear, I will go in there and pitch, pitch, pitch and make that damn Planning Commission take Rio Blanco Estates. I'm going to build it my way," and he kissed her back. He enjoyed kissing her. She was a good kisser over and above being his staunchest, most loyal supporter and wife of eighteen years. Hell, she was as much a part of the business as he was. From the first day until right now, as this big damn Rio Blanco Estates was giving him heartburn.

Murray groaned frustratedly. He wished his wife was with him. He was nearly fifty and about thirty pounds too heavy. He didn't smoke and rarely drank. He ate anything sweet. If he couldn't have Betsy, he wanted a Hershey's with almonds very badly. Lying in this strange bed, in the strange and unfriendly city of Santa Maria, a candy bar would be comforting.

His feet were cold. Even though he was president of Bowler Building and had developments going in four cities up and down California, Murray disliked ostentation, expensive hotels. He liked to live simply. He was frankly embarrassed by hotel employees dogging his steps everywhere. Do this for you, sir? Get you a cocktail? How about another TV for your bathroom? Refill your bar?

He always stayed in places like the Cabana, if possible. Middle of the road, they left you alone and were comfortable enough. But, damn, this place was stinting on the blankets. He never could get the room thermostat to work right and he had on the heavy orange blanket and a thin blue cover and his feet were still cold. Like his doctor said, so much worry about the business, so little exercise, the weight. He was priming himself for a nifty heart attack.

He sat up and reached down to rub his cold feet. Okay, doctor, you keep two kids in college, one at Harvey Mudd in Engineering, the other at USC in Pharmacy. You see how many houses and apartments you have to throw up to make that trick work.

He glanced at the glowing face of the clock on the nightstand. So late and he had to be up early to fight those preppy bright kids on the Planning Commission who wanted to tell him all there was to know about building.

Murray sighed and got up, putting on his wife's coffee-colored robe. It was the most comfortable garment he'd ever worn. He took it everywhere. And he wanted to be comfortable when he went to check the damn Cadillac again. That was another thing. He slipped on his black shoes, feeling funny without socks. So worked up this morning he forgot to pack slippers.

He didn't own any kind of show-off car himself, getting back to the damn Cadillac. Plain simple Chevy or a Honda, anything. Big showy cars were like big showy hotels. They were embarrassing and people stared at you.

He wiggled his toes and went out, making sure he had the room key. That's all he'd need, getting locked out at this hour, on a cold wet night, in his wife's bathrobe, in a strange city.

So since he's coming to Santa Maria to impress everybody with the success and importance of Bowler Building, his wife says, why not borrow her cousin Neal's Cadillac? Which one? Neal has three of them. He likes them.

Neal is typical, Murray thought, of the kind of guy who owns a Cadillac, cigars, big belly, very loud, white shoes. Also in the construction business and always butting in on my business. But, Betsy had a point. There was a slight edge to driving around Santa Maria in one of Neal's Cadillacs, looking like what he was, a very good builder.

Murray looked around the motel parking lot. This was the third time tonight his nervousness about Neal's precious damn Caddy had made him check it. Checked it when he registered and they parked it, checked it after dinner. And now again. No marks, no scratches, no cars too close, Neal barked, that cigar going up and down in his mouth. Neal treated his Cadillacs like children.

Murray slopped along, hands deep in the robe, shoes plopping on the asphalt. If he didn't want this deal so badly, so that any little extra would help, he wouldn't have borrowed the Cadillac. He wouldn't be so worried about it. Worried about what Neal would say or do if he found one microscopic, minute, infinitesimal blemish on the buffed blue paint. A blue Cadillac. The thing looked like a tour bus.

Murray saw the Cadillac now, in a cone of shadow between two high arc lights illuminating part of the parking lot. And he saw someone inside the driver's door.

If Murray hadn't been so churned up from dinner, worry, and not being able to sleep, he never would have shouted and run toward Neal's Caddy. He would have called for help.

He wouldn't have tried to protect the damn priceless Cadillac himself.

Kenny was so intent on separating the ignition wires that he didn't notice the guy bearing down on him at once. The car impressed him, so well maintained and clean smelling, like it had just come from the dealership.

He was about to twist the ignition leads together, the last thing before starting the car, when someone grabbed his jacket collar and dragged him backward.

It was a pudgy guy, yelling at him, trying to smack him with an open hand. Dressed like a bear, all brown and fluffy. "Get out, get out!" the guy yelled.

Kenny shouted back and struck out, connecting with the flabby middle. The guy released his collar and doubled up, then, astoundingly raised both fists like he was going to start pummeling a door.

Kenny didn't think. He reacted by snatching the .45 from inside his jacket, pushing it forward and firing once.

The pudgy guy, fists up, was jerked back hard by the shot. It sounded, Kenny thought in a flash, like a steel bubble in the quiet night air.

He kept low and ran back toward Carol's car. He was afraid she would think less of him and Lisio would call him a fuckup.

"They're fighting," Carol said. "Kenny needs help."

Then she heard the sharp sound. It is different from a car backfire, she thought. The abrupt crack at the end makes it quite unmistakable as a gunshot.

"Somebody's shooting." Lisio strained to see through the windshield.

Carol instantly made a decision and acted. She jumped out of her door and started toward Kenny, who was crouching and running for them.

Lisio shouted at her, flung open his door. She didn't stop to see if he had his gun out. He was instinctively trying to block her.

As she rounded the car, Carol came up on him. She seized his left arm and yanked him from the car. He was small enough and her leverage great enough that he spun five or six feet across the glistening pavement, a dark little bundle that cried out in pain.

She swung into the car. Her own car, hers again. She put it in gear and screeched the tires, driving toward Kenny. How's that for a farmer's woman? she thought. Strong as an ox.

Kenny was at the side of the car and she slowed enough to let him bounce in, gasping, slamming the door. "Go, go, go!" he shouted, staring ahead of them.

Carol turned a sharp left coming out of the Cabana Motel lot, sped up, and missed a yellow light heading onto the bridge again, the festive lights hung on it gleaming past her.

"What happened, Kenny?" she demanded loudly, driving south, past the downtown towers and her own green office building.

"Some dude came up and grabbed me, honey. He's going to beat the shit out of me, I don't know what." He breathed huskily.

"You shot him?"

"I ain't getting beat up."

"How badly was he hurt?"

"Hey," Kenny calmed down enough to look around the car, "where's Dave at?"

"How badly was he hurt?" she barked. I got Kenny up here by taking him in hand and I can get out of this by taking him in hand again. Don't give him any choices. It was one of her lessons from dealing with cons. Direct commands work best.

He shouted back at her, "I don't know. You get hit with this fucking thing, it's bad." He half-drew the .45 from his jacket.

"Are you going to shoot me, Kenny? Like your pal said he would?"

"No, Carol honey. I'm just all confused here. Where's Dave? Where's he at?"

"He's back there. Listen to me, Kenny."

"Back there? What the fuck's going on?" He hit the dashboard in frustration.

She strained to sound calm. "I'm going to get us both clear of this, Kenny. You do what I tell you. That is our one and only hope."

"You dumped him back there?" He was incredulous, staring at her.

She wondered briefly if Lisio could manage to get away before someone came out to see what had happened. If he didn't, what kind of story would he tell to explain himself, his gun?

As long as I've got Kenny, I've got a way out. She held tight to that thought.

"It's over," she told him. "Everything's off."

"We got to go back for him. Dumping a cripple's mighty cold, Carol honey." He was bewildered and upset. His hair was slick on his forehead and he mopped sweat and mist from his face. Shooting that man had disoriented Kenny. It was not part of the plan.

"We're not going back," she said. She wished she had a coat on. It was cold enough to make her shiver. "At the river you said you loved me. You cared for me."

"I do. Why'm I doing all this if I don't?"

"You've got to trust me again, Kenny. You're in my hands just like at Chino."

"Oh, Jesus, Carol honey, it's not going like I wanted. Dave back there, that guy. I don't know what we're doing." He peered back into the darkness, then ahead, then at her almost beseechingly. "I don't know what to do, honey."

"I do," she said.

She couldn't take them back to her house. Lisio knew her address and she didn't want to find him showing up suddenly or the police either.

It was essential to stay away from the police for a while, at least until she had laid the groundwork first. A way had to be found to approach them, a safe way, to bring Kenny and her out of hiding. She was amazed at her ability to think logically even now. She had an idea of how an arm's-length deal could be made with the police tomorrow.

She parked and checked them into the Ramona Hotel on South C Street, a formerly impressive neighborhood of homes and hotels that had come undone in the last twenty years. The Ramona, adorned with plaster cupids and satyrs, pink and decaying, was close enough downtown to Reilly's office that they could walk there tomorrow if they had to.

Kenny followed her, watching warily around them. He viewed the hotel with sullen, angry distaste.

As she and Kenny went through the lobby, four old men sat on a dun-colored lounge watching a black-and-white TV. The whole place was thick with old smoke and sweat. Sand-filled ashtrays stood everywhere. One man, blinking his watering eyes, leered at her as she took Kenny's arm at the elevator.

"Man, honey, I been in enough places like this," Kenny said sourly as they got to their room. "My stepdad, he moves us around, sticks us in shitholes like this. I seen these places so I know them with my eyes closed."

He opened the bathroom door. "Yeah. Old tub, a little hot water. Oh, yeah, I know this place."

"Nobody knows we're here. It's downtown," she said. "I don't pretend to be an expert on hiding out."

"You doing just fine." He pulled off the Raiders jacket, flipped off his wet sneakers and sank into a gray chair. "Same old shit. Here I am, thinking it's going to be different, I got some moves, and it ain't. Back at the same hotel."

"It's only for tonight. I'm taking us to see my boss tomorrow." She debated calling Reilly tonight, but didn't know where he'd be. "Take your clothes off, Kenny. Dry off." She pointed at the chipped tiled bathroom.

"First night together, I see it a lot different from this." He shrugged off his shirt. He had goosebumps. He put the .45 on the single bed.

"I better keep that." She put out her hand.

"Yeah, that's me. Go all the way." He handed her the gun.

She was surprised at how heavy it was. Like most lawyers who deal with criminals, she had little notion of what their weapons felt like. How can you hold this thing to shoot it, she wondered.

Kenny wandered into the bathroom. Pale skinned, hard and lean. He may have just killed a man. She slipped the gun under the side of the bed where she would sleep. The shooting complicated the situation she'd have to lay before Reilly. I don't know where I fall, either, she thought, slipping off her shoes. It depends on whether I'm pegged as an accomplice or victim.

The room was small, a bureau, heavily scored with cigarette burns and carvings, two gray chairs, and a bed stiff and squeaky. The windows looked down on South C and its endless traffic, people out for a good time at the bars and two video arcades, a strip joint, and a Korean storefront advertising massage flexology.

She went into the bathroom. Kenny sat in his underwear on the edge of the old-fashioned bathtub, carefully drying his feet, toe by toe. She was puzzled at her reaction to him now. Not fear. Even if he was a killer. It was hard to pin down.

He loves me, she thought. My first real love affair. It nearly made her laugh. This is what our steamy letters and fantasies turned into. Some joke.

"Give me the towel," she said gently. "I'll do your head and back."

He grinned halfheartedly and turned his back to her. He sighed as she rubbed. "Feels really good. I can't figure where I fucked up, honey. Dave's got this thing all laid out so neat, it don't have any problems."

"Any time you start using force, threats," I sound like a pompous law book, she thought in dismay, "unpredictable things happen. You didn't know someone would come out." She rubbed his hair briskly.

"That don't matter, right? Like what you said at the river, someone dies, we all eat it, right?"

"I don't know yet. He might only be wounded."

Her reddish hands fluffed Kenny's blond hair. Maybe she felt pity for him. Lame, she said to herself. But there was some tenderness and some lust she had to admit.

"I always been ready before, you know, whatever's going down." Kenny bent his head forward slightly. "Not tonight. I blew it."

"You're tired," she patted his back.

"I never been so tired. Even strung out, wasted, never so fucking tired."

It was characteristic, she thought with detachment, for Kenny to care about his own fatigue rather than the man he shot or even Lisio. I'm probably his only link to the real world of human feelings outside himself.

It was very late. Kenny crawled into bed, groaning with pleasure. She undressed in the dark. He's watching me, she thought.

"Real nice," he whispered.

"What?"

"You. There, just like that. Just like what I used to dream about."

She got into bed, and Kenny hopped out.

"What's wrong?" she asked. He pushed the bureau in front of the door and then stacked the two chairs on it.

"This kind of place, you don't want some asshole poking in sometime. I know this place, honey." He got back into bed, drawing his body close to hers.

Or maybe it's to keep me inside, she thought.

"You think Dave's okay? He got hurt?"

"I don't honestly care," Carol replied.

"I hope he's okay."

So maybe it's me and Lisio he thinks about, she thought, his hands draped over her loosely. They lay face to face.

"Don't worry about him. Tomorrow I'll call my boss first thing."

"He got any dopers?" Kenny's voice was sleepy.

"A few. He owes me some favors. He'll help us."

"How come?"

"How come what?"

"He owes you?"

Carol felt Kenny's firmness against her. She didn't know if he wanted to make love or if she wanted him to. "I delivered briefcases for him. Payoffs, I guess. I never asked. He has clients who need extra service."

"He can help?"

"He knows a lot of people. He's had a lot of experience."

Kenny slid his face so close she felt his breath. "You been bad, Carol honey." His voice was faint, almost mocking.

"I know."

Suddenly he gently kissed her. "I feel real bad. I wanted a lot better than this." He drew a deep, heavy breath in the darkness.

"I know you did."

"Got so much to think about tomorrow. So much to do."

She listened, hearing the cars on the street below, muffled laughter and cursing somewhere in the hotel. "You don't have to do anything more. I'll take the responsibility."

The minimum for Kenny out of this was back to prison with at least five years added on for a violent escape. The minimum for her was back to Reilly, the daily round of researching motions, interviewing clients, keeping the flow of legal papers smooth.

The worst for them both was much worse no matter how you looked at it.

"Stay with me," he said. It was a question, two children in the dark.

"I'll be with you."

She whispered his name, then stroked his hair. He had fallen asleep. After a while, she tried to sleep, too.

THIRTEEN

MEDAVOY WAS UNDERWATER AGAIN, tugged forward by
the river's invisible, inexorable current, trying to force open
the truck cab's door. He gasped again, head shooting up
into the curling, whitish foam, into the dancing halo of light
from the helicopter hovering maternally above him, dangling
a white life preserver that kept slipping, sliding off the slick
skin of the truck's trailer, which stuck out of the river like a
sword. He couldn't hear anything in the river's roar—not the
cars on the bridge with engines still revved, or the helicopter.
The fire engines had just arrived, in a chorus of sirens, and
he saw the blush of flame from the burning station wagon
the truck had hit just before jackknifing into the river. Four
people dead in the station wagon, he found out later.

Jane. Where was Jane? He had seen her for an instant,
on the bridge pointing downward, directing the cops who
showed up.

Medavoy was underwater again. And again. The truck
door yielding up its treasure reluctantly. He was sober now,

the angry confusion from Zaragoza's party burned off. He and Jane had quarreled about who would drive home. He was too drunk, she said. She was right. But he was in his prove-something mood and took the car keys.

Then they were on Daley Bridge, connecting the south area of Santa Maria with the rest of the city. Night mist was torn by the burning station wagon. Medavoy never knew, Jane couldn't explain, why he had stopped the car, and almost without hesitation, jumped into the river, searching for the truck driver beneath the dark, furious water.

It was like hitting Leroy Menefee. It happened because a lifetime of ideas and impulses collided with a moment's events. He didn't think of Jane, or the newborn kid, or his job, or even himself. He stood at the bridge railing, like a cut-out against the flaming station wagon, Jane later said, and jumped. People were gaping, shouting, rushing back and forth, and he was gone.

That choking, terrified sense of the air being drained from your lungs. He wanted to scream underwater, tearing open the truck door. He found the driver, half-wedged under the dashboard, and yanked him out, the two of them forced along by the river current like corks.

He burst upward, arm cradling the truck driver's head above the water, gasping, swimming with awkward fearful slowness toward the distant bank whitely shining in the helicopter's beckoning halo. The huge life preserver lowered gently to him again, and he slipped his free arm into it, and like departed souls rising heavenward, he and the truck driver drifted up, the helicopter taking them to the sandy bank.

Burning rubber, gasoline, the scum of the river, he smelled it all at once, hanging there a few feet over the black water. It was a short time, suspended with the truck driver. He panted from the exertion and felt a calm detachment from the world. Surrounded by the cacophony from the bridge, high and to his right, fire trucks, police cars, the grinding motors and cries, he experienced, for a second, a complete indifferent serenity.

It was horrible and wonderful.

There was Jane, on the bank, he heard her shouts, pointing at the helicopter, telling the cops on the river's edge to catch them. Medavoy felt himself and the truck driver settle to earth again, bound down by gravity.

Jane was with him, ordering the paramedics over, bending over him, smoothing hair from his eyes with sure, brusque hands. She was angelic. She kissed him even as rougher hands bundled him in blankets, lifted him to his feet, shook the truck driver from his iron grip.

A wall of absolute blackness, filled with the roar of engines and shouting people, inexplicably lit by phosphorescent whiteness suddenly, blew up over him.

"Robby," Jane said.

He rolled over in bed. "What?" he sighed the sleepy shock of returning to dim wakefulness.

"Somebody's honking outside."

"So?"

"Johnathan's going to start yelling."

"I was dreaming about the river." He smiled at her, where she lay close to him, their breaths intermingled. The bedroom was dark except for a thick wedge of streetlight dappled with branches.

"Again?" she whispered.

"You were in it, don't worry."

A car honked twice, short and peremptory, like a summons.

"Tell them to knock it off," Jane said, pushing him toward the edge of the bed.

"Why don't you?"

"You're the cop."

He snorted, groaned, and got out of bed, padding to the window. He pushed aside the soft blue curtain. The street was empty up and down, all the cars in their driveways except one directly across from him. Its headlights were out, the driver in shadow. The horn sounded again.

"Just kids," he said, trying to get back into bed.

"If Johnathan wakes up, we're up for good."

He went back to the window, raising it slightly.

"No," Jane whispered hoarsely. "Don't shout. You have to go out."

"I was having a good dream, too." He swore quietly when the horn honked. Medavoy was at the bedroom door.

"Robby. You don't have anything on."

He waved it away. "It's four in the morning and anybody wants to see me in my shorts, hey, they're welcome."

"I better check Johnathan, make sure he's asleep." Jane tiptoed behind him.

"I'll scream next time you do that, Janie. You got cold hands."

The lawn was wet and cool on his bare feet as he stepped gingerly over it, to the sidewalk. The street glistened in the pearly light. He squinted, shivered a little in the night air. The car across the street was a blue or silver T-bird, shiny and waxed fiercely enough to almost glow in the dark. Medavoy knew who was in the car.

He splashed in a puddle crossing the street. He stopped at the driver's door. A flashlight beam shot out, blinding him.

"Hi, bud," he heard Easter say.

"Shut the fucking light off." He put up his hand. The light snapped off. Everything was momentarily fringed with violet. "Get the fuck out of here."

"Don't give me an attitude right off, bud."

"What do you want?" Medavoy could see him now, aging surfer in a Hawaiian sport shirt, arm nonchalantly hanging off the steering wheel. Easter was smiling at him.

"I wanted to bring you some news. Reilly bailed about two hours ago. He's pissed."

"Don't give me your bullshit, Easter. What are you doing here?"

"No, really. I wanted to tell you Reilly's out, he wants to find out how far you're going to take this thing with him."

"He's going to the joint."

"I don't think he wants to hear that, bud. He wouldn't do too well in the joint, you know?"

"Well, that's kind of tough. We pulled one of your tear gas grenades from his safe."

Easter grimaced, shook his head. "Hey, bud, he wanted some real protection, made a big-ass deal about it. Like a teddy bear. He had to have it."

"He's dead. You gave him a grenade. What's he going to do?"

"Hell if I know."

"Gas his waiting room or something?"

"He's a lawyer. You know these guys."

They both momentarily united at the stupidity and foolishness of civilians and lawyers particularly. Medavoy stood back. It was odd how streets of solid houses, cars, trees, and lawns could sound so hollow and flimsy in the middle of the night, like stage sets about to be struck.

"Yeah, it's late for me. Great news about Mr. Reilly." He felt his skin cringe.

"I haven't slept a whole night in ten years. Talk to Gef about it."

"Get the hell out of here, okay? No more bullshit." He turned from the ghostly T-bird.

"Okay, bud. This's for me. How far you going to take this Reilly deal?"

"Far as it goes."

"That's a long, long way, bud."

"He's dirty and you're dirty and that's how it goes."

Easter nodded, head out the window. "So you're telling me you don't want to come in with us? Offer's still open, like

I told Gef this afternoon. We've got a lot of openings, it's a big, big town all of sudden. We could get some teamwork going with your guys."

"I'll be too busy in court."

"So I thought. I said that to Gef couple of days ago. I said you're one of these crusader rabbits. Guys never been in the service, never been in a real fight. I see you as the kind of guy who's got to make it up. He says no. He says Robby doesn't shit on everybody."

Medavoy leaned closer to Easter. He could see the wrinkles and bloodshot eyes, smell the minty breath. Easter had been drinking decently before he drove up. Medavoy was tempted to let whoever was on patrol know it. A drunk driving charge would put Easter on suspension instantly.

"Stay away from me. Stay away from my unit," he said slowly. "Stay away from Gef or we'll have a real fight."

"Right, bud. He tell you his war stories?"

"You heard me."

"No? I'm surprised. Gef's got great stories about Vietnam. I guess he figures you wouldn't understand."

Easter's hand was on the ignition key. He seemed to have lost interest in Medavoy. He had scraped a nerve, though, that old nagging feeling vets spoke a language all their own. Something I'll never learn, Medavoy thought. I'll always wonder.

Like he wondered what had happened to Easter. Years upon years of good service, even if he got rough too often. Medavoy did understand that. What happened then? Was it the last baby, dead in its crib, mother screaming? Or the last big dope dealer who drove a car better than you ever could hope to? Or the last robbery victim, painfully scratching out a description of his shooter because he was now partly paralyzed?

I saw all of that, too. I never wanted the money, the dope like Easter. I never started spreading the corruption to other cops. Maybe he wants more and that's all there is to it. Maybe he's just a greedy, vicious son of a bitch.

The car started, a throaty, well-tended motor that probably gleamed. The sound echoed along the hollow street.

"You got a chance to go now." Medavoy's arms tensed.

"I better take it. This is where you're shacking up?" Easter glanced at Jane's house, unlit, small, and sheltered under its oaks. "Divorce's a bitch, isn't it? I did it twice and I said never, never again boy. Nice neighborhood."

Medavoy assumed Easter had his gun nearby, by the side of the car door, on the seat beside him. He suddenly felt naked in the street.

"This isn't a kosher shack up, right bud? Don't worry about me. Turning in other cops isn't my style." He ground out the words. "I just like knowing where you live."

"Anything happens here," Medavoy was frightened and angry, "I'm not waiting for any goddamn case to go through court. I'll nail you myself."

Easter put the car in gear and hiccupped with a grin. "All I said is it's a nice neighborhood, bud."

Medavoy stood in the street until the car was out of sight, the sound of its perfect motor fading.

He shut and locked the kitchen door. In the darkness near the hot-water heater, Natty raised her pointy snout and growled briefly from her wicker bed. The last time he tried to pet her, she snapped at him. "Thanks, wonder dog," he whispered going past her.

It was still throughout the house. Jane had the covers pulled to her chin.

"Okay?" she whispered.

"Yeah. Great." He stood at the window, curtain aside, looking out, listening, waiting for the anger to leach out of him.

"You took a long time."

"They're gone. It's all quiet." He sat on the edge of the

bed, hands between his legs. He felt Jane scootch over to him.

"Back's all tight, Robby. Feels like little bumps." She began gently massaging, loosening, warming him. She paused when there was a brief false cry from Johnathan. They waited to see if any more followed. She went on, her touch calming him.

"I owe you a little something," she said, pinching him lightly.

"Maybe I just want to go to sleep."

"Do you?"

He groaned, his muscles relaxing, Easter's taunts and threats evaporating. Easter was the one in trouble. His accomplice had been arrested with stolen property, police equipment in his possession. It was Easter who must be frightened tonight.

"No," he said, reaching for her.

"You like that?"

"God, yes. Just like that."

"Pretty noisy."

"It's your fault. Do that again."

"Was it kids?"

"Where?"

"Just now. Was it kids out there?"

"Wrong house. I don't care if I don't sleep at all."

"We got to be quieter."

"He's a big boy. He knows what we're doing."

She laughed, low but delighted. "You're crazy, Medavoy."

"Right. It's me."

"I'll get a sitter for tonight. We'll go out to dinner, like we used to. It's your turn to make it anyway."

"I'm not so bad."

"You're good at this. You can't cook."

He nuzzled her neck. "I'm Superman."

"What'd you tell them outside? I like your cop talk."

"Forget it."

"You're tense again. You feel all tight. Come on, relax."

"I said forget it. We're safe."

"Safe? That's a weird thing to say, Robby."

PART TWO

FOURTEEN

THE NEXT MORNING, while Jane finished dressing, Medavoy took Johnathan across the street and left him for the day with the Cabrals. The Cabrals had eight children and one more didn't seem to significantly alter the household rhythms. Medavoy liked visiting there anyway. Innocencia Cabral made desserts for three Mexican restaurants in Santa Maria and her house always smelled richly of cooking sugar and cream.

It was only six-thirty, but already one of those northern California days to brag about. The storm had cleared the air, freshened it, and the tingle of a spring morning was strong. Stark blue sky. Green hills ringing the city. Best of all, Medavoy hadn't heard of any new crisis on the radio as he cleared away the breakfast dishes. A fair amount on the Pacific Security robbery, a jittery Alice recounting her experience, but it vanished into the welter of a flood in Oregon, various upheavals, and the possibility of a transit strike in the county.

So far so good, Medavoy thought cheerfully. Most of his bad news had come over the radio as he got ready for work

over the years. He found out about the robberies or assaults
or burglaries that would occupy him for days or weeks in
between chirpy ads for cars and rock concerts.

He took care of a few other minor chores, tying Natty
up to a used croquet stake in the backyard, giving her water,
checking the back door to make sure it was locked.

Jane had changed into her work clothes, the demure
impostor he first met, outfitted in a blouse with a small
blue bow, pale gray skirt and jacket, briefcase. She was sipping
from her second Dr. Pepper of the morning. It was all she had
for breakfast.

It was about a quarter to seven when Medavoy drove
them downtown, taking a slightly longer route to miss the
bumper-to-bumper aggravation on the freeway. He glanced
frequently at Jane, briefcase on her lap, drinking the Dr. Pepper,
the fresh morning sunlight glimmering in her dark hair. She
was very beautiful.

"I have something on my face?" she asked him.

"No. You look great."

"You're staring at me. I thought something's wrong."

"You look good, that's all."

He knew he sounded jaunty, careless. Maybe it was the
fine morning, the absence of any emergency waiting for him.
The only nagging worry he had was Easter. He hadn't told Jane
about it and decided to wait until he sounded things out at
the department a little. There was no point in bothering her yet.

"You are so damn jolly in the morning, Medavoy," she
said, closing her eyes.

"I feel good."

He noticed her tone changed. "Have you seen any cars
coming by the house the last couple of days?"

"What cars? When?"

Jane shrugged. "Compact, something bigger sometimes.
They don't stay. They stop, drive away. I saw them a couple
of times in the afternoon when I was back early."

"Like police cars?"

She shook her head. "No. New cars. Not the old crap you guys drive."

They passed trailer parks and a Boy Scout campground, huge powerlines set in green fields and Medavoy turned right onto North Eighth Street heading toward the darker, more crowded downtown.

"Could be anything," he said. "House hunters maybe."

"No one's got a house for sale."

He didn't want to alarm her. "It could be somebody downtown."

"The department can't be that interested in us. It's too petty."

Medavoy thought it could also be tied to Easter. But he knew it might be less sinister, even though threatening. "Listen, Janie, Stevie Wonder's got us filling out forms on how many hours we sit at our desks, how our investigations rate on a point scale. You got to tell your supervisor every week how many points you racked up. We got the department turning into a factory. Believe me, they could be that petty to check up on me."

"Can you find out?"

"I'll ask around."

"If you took the lieutenant's exam, you could set your own rating, Robby."

"Not me. Not with this crew in charge. Jesus, that's why my supervisor's a drunk. That's why I get to play acting-super again today probably."

"If I see these cars again, I'll go over and ask what's going on."

"No," he said too sharply, "I'll check it out first."

She played with the strap on the briefcase. Jane was more than a little frustrated about their partly concealed relationship. She also wanted him to advance in the department, use his notoriety. She didn't understand the nonsense, tedium, and irritation anybody in authority had to handle under Stevie Wonder's middle managers.

He tried to change the subject, get back the upbeat mood of the morning. "You hear my robbery on the news this morning?"

"Sure I did. It doesn't make any sense to me."

"Like what?"

"Who uses a bomb to rob a bank?"

"Lots of assholes."

"They don't carry it. They don't walk around with it." Jane was blunt. "That's crazy."

He hadn't thought of it so directly before, but she was right. "Yeah, they blow the vault, they blackmail somebody."

Jane nodded. "I think that bomb's a phony. I mean, I know that poor kid was scared, but that doesn't mean it's real."

"These guys or women or whatever don't have to be mental giants, Janie."

"Even an idiot isn't knowingly going to carry a real bomb."

Medavoy grinned over at her. "It's a different angle. Maybe you're right."

"I should take the lieutenant's exam."

"You're the only one who will," he immediately regretted the flippant reply when he saw her flash of annoyance. Okay, he thought, so your family worked selling insurance, wholesale dairy, furniture, anything to make ends meet and you can't get it why I'd pass up extra money and a new title. "Sorry," he said sincerely. "How about we drop it."

"It's dropped," she said. She obviously wanted to say more, but for harmony, held back.

We both work at keeping this thing going, he thought.

Even at six-fifty-five, the street in front of the Santa Maria County Courthouse was crowded with yellow school buses, Metro buses, and cars letting people off when Medavoy pulled up. The new courthouse took up a whole long block with its white, featureless stone and steel bulk. It was still called new even though it had been there for ten years, a broad plaza with skinny trees and an abstract design fountain leading to it from the street.

Jane opened her door, got one leg out. "Damn. We forgot that videotape. It should go back."

She winced with the noise. It was hard to be heard over the clank, bang, and thud from jackhammers and bulldozers toiling on either side of the courthouse, driving two more great office buildings into the sky.

"Forget it. It's a gift. Guy gave it to me."

"Why'd he do that?"

"People always give cops things. Lunch, doughnuts, car wash, little things."

Jane smirked. "So it's a bribe."

"Hell. It's nothing. It makes a guy feel good to give a cop a little gift. I know guys who haven't paid for lunch in years." He was amused by her apparent innocence.

"Robby," Jane said, both hands on her briefcase, "the bad cops you're after, they take things, too."

A car hit its horn behind them and a Metro bus rumbled into the far lane, waiting for him to move. "They take big things. This is little."

She leaned over to kiss him. "Little bribes don't count."

"Right. There's always going to be little bribes."

She shook her head. "You're such a case. Can you come back at noon? My judge's got us on a half day and I'll go get the car."

"You want to meet out here?"

"Fine." Then as she was about to close the door, Jane said, "I got a terrific idea. How about a picnic? We go out to Miller's Point for lunch?"

Medavoy nodded happily. That would be a pleasant break in the day, by the river with the boats gliding by. "Be here at twelve. I like it."

"No excuses, Robby." She knew his tendency to beg off because of some witness or investigation.

"Word of honor," he said. He watched her wade into a roiling mass of schoolchildren on their way to a tour of the courthouse. A picnic would be ideal. All he had to do now was make the seven A.M. supervisors' meeting and find out who had taken an interest in Jane's house. And mine, too, he thought automatically.

Medavoy cut in front of the Metro bus and sped to the Police Department five blocks away.

FIFTEEN

THE LITTLE MAN on the chaotic bed stretched, groaned, and sat up abruptly, as if from a bad dream. But Lisio had no bad dreams or any dreams that he could remember. He used to dream as a child, but that stopped. He believed he stopped dreaming during the long convalescence in the hospital after he broke his pelvis and right leg.

He trembled. An awful night, another change in his plans. All because of her, the great dumb love of Trask's life. Tall, gawky, dangerous woman, Lisio judged contemptuously. She would be dealt with today.

The sheets and covers of his motel bed were piled in the center of the room. The lights still burned from his work through most of the night. On the glass-topped desk he used as a workbench were the results of his long labor, a corsetlike contrivance with thin red wires looped around pockets set along its outside. Small tools, more wires, bits of plastic and tape and batteries lay scattered on the desk.

Lisio's next-door neighbors were arguing again. He listened

avidly for a few minutes to the bright excitement of anger and promised violence.

He sniffed his armpits. He needed a shower this morning after such a long, tiring night. Reluctantly, he got out of bed. It was a rare pleasure to throw things around the room in the Best Western motel, the spindly chairs jammed together, five days of newspapers, the *Wall Street Journal, Scientific American*, chemical and technical magazines where he dropped them. In Chino such behavior would have meant punishment. But since he got to this ridiculous city, he acted as he wished.

Until last night. Until that woman threw him from the car like he was garbage. Throwing his plan into turmoil.

She would have some surprises of her own today.

He didn't open the room's heavy curtains. He liked the secret, cavelike feeling. Lisio walked awkwardly, his deformed hip making him waddle. He stripped off his lime-green shorts and got into the shower.

It was such a simple plan. It required Trask, who could move quickly, thoughtlessly, who was utterly disposable when the time came. And then this revolting complication. Who would have imagined Trask would act this way? Because of that woman, insisting on this city, on her participation?

Lisio hated her. Much more since a few hours ago, but he always hated her. It was one emotion he understood. She took advantage of his deformity. Thought she was superior.

He had long since stopped thinking of himself as repulsive. He adored his deformity. It made him unique. He stood under the shower's hot water, feeling the rage at her.

Lisio soaped himself and tried to sing a little. It was not his fault he had fallen from the fourth-floor fire escape of the apartment building his parents lived in. The flames were rising higher and higher, the men below shouting at him to jump. He was only six years old. He was terrified and he jumped.

He rubbed gentle hands over the monstrous collision of bone, tendon, and muscle. The break never healed well.

Months in the ward with dozens of poor children, the gasping, gagging all day and night. The smells. The doctors whose clumsy fingers left him broken.

As a result, he never grew tall, either because of the broken bones or because it was a judgment on him. His mother thought so. She was so like Trask's mother, substituting religious fervor and hallucination for everything. This was his punishment for setting the fire, she said again and again. "You are marked for your wicked crime."

He stepped from the shower into the steamy bathroom. In all of the other fires, other hotels and warehouses, his grade school, he never again made the childish mistake of being inside the building when it burned.

Burning. Fire. Hellfire. Damnation. A possible link deep in the brain, where all those missing dreams are lurking.

He dried himself. The Best Western towels were beautiful, thick, white and heavy. The most beautiful towels he'd ever seen. He gathered three towels and added them to the piled sheets in the middle of the room. Four years at Chino, sometimes with Trask as his faithful guardian, and all because of bad checks. Comical.

Last night had been very unpleasant. In the motel mirror he saw the green-blue splotches on his side and arm where he'd struck the pavement. The shock, humiliation, and pain of that was unbearable. Lisio shut his eyes. He saw the car driving away again, knew he was abandoned and in danger. It was necessary to will himself upright, damp from the pavement, and hurry toward the motel, from which people were even then emerging to see what the noise was about. He'd lost his walking stick. He moved comically. Shame, shame.

He called a cab in the Cabana lobby. Everyone was far too busy with Trask's gunshot victim to even glance at this little, harmless, obviously insignificant man at the telephone.

It was a wise policy, he learned years ago, to maintain one safe haven everywhere he went, just on the chance something like the disaster in the Cabana parking lot took place. He came back to his motel room, in pain, raging at Trask and the woman. Knowing even then that he would have the money today or die.

Knowing that Trask and the woman would pay.

As he dressed, Lisio carefully wrapped the corset around his upper body. It covered from his collarbone to his navel but didn't bind at all. When he had everything except his shirt on, he took eight sticks of dynamite from a gym bag beside the desk. He had stolen them three days before. Each stick went into one of the special pockets in the corset, each was connected to a thin red wire until Lisio looked like a lumpy brown sausage.

On went a very loose yellow shirt. Lisio liked his reflection. He was powerful. He was in absolute control of anything he saw.

Seven in the morning. Time to leave. He unfolded a sharp pocketknife and scraped some of the fluffy white cloth off the towels—a dry snow flurry onto the sheets; wet it all down with a small can of gasoline. He set a candle in one of the Best Western glass ashtrays, filling it with an inch of gasoline; he quickly finished dressing.

With a windbreaker added last and zipped up, Lisio looked only stout. He lit the candle in its bath of gasoline, a half-inch of wax from which a stiff little flame rose in the stuffy air of his room. About ten minutes to burn into the gasoline.

All he carried when he left the room a moment later was the marked map of the city in his pants pocket. In his room was a strange birthday cake, piled sheets and towels, an ashtray on top with a single candle.

During the last week in Santa Maria, Lisio had gotten around by bus as he made his observations and false calls to the police to test their reactions. He ate his breakfast every day a block away at the New California Cafe. He walked there now and sat down, third booth on the left as always.

"Hi again," said Elaine, forty and cheery in the busy morning rush. "Usual okay?"

Lisio nodded, keeping one hand unconsciously in his pocket. "I'd like the eggs fried today."

"Big change," said Elaine, grinning. Someone called for coffee. "Coming. Black or did you change that?" She poured from a dull aluminum pot.

"Still black." Lisio didn't like casual chat. He already felt sweat pearling on his upper lip. He tried to think of the corset to regain his calm.

Lisio grinned badly. She left to put in his order. He had sweated. Not nerves. Talking to her. He thought again of the corset. It was not like Trask's shoe box. It was real. Lisio knew Trask would require powerful incentives to go on with the plan after what was about to happen to the love of his life.

Elaine brought his eggs and bacon. There was much hurrying in the cafe, off the counter stools, off to work. Lisio started to eat.

"Another bus of them old folks came in at your place." She pointed back at the Best Western.

"Oh, yes?" He couldn't think of anything.

"Bus says it's the Jolly Wanderers. You should see them, about sixty guys and gals can't get one foot in front of them." She shook her head. "Every damn tour bus of them old folks doesn't give us one dollar's business. They got a deal with the House of Pancakes three blocks over. We get zip."

Lisio couldn't resist. "Maybe they'll skip breakfast today," he said.

"I'd like that," Elaine agreed, brushing a loose brown hair off her eyes. "Kind of make my day they didn't get that business."

Lisio was happy, in a small way, to have granted her wish. As he finished his toast there was a *whomp* sound, as though in the earth, and he saw a column of rapidly climbing gray-black smoke rise from the Best Western motel. It pleased and excited him as always. While he waited for his check, he took out a length of silver photographer's coil and carefully connected it to the corset. He threaded the shutter button through a hole he'd made in the windbreaker's right pocket.

Only a definite act of will was needed now, squeeze the shutter and the mechanism around him would explode, enough force to lift a good-size house off its foundations, so many pounds of pressure per square inch, as though he possessed the strength of a giant.

Everyone in the cafe was up—at the window, on the sidewalk—as the smoke from the motel rose, spreading outward and dissipating almost gorgeously like a great gray flower.

He paid his bill. Elaine, distracted, took the money. "I never seen such smoke. I never seen a fire like that. Where's the fire department? That's just up the block."

"I don't think you should worry."

"Look at that. The whole side of the motel's going," she said fearfully. People stood or ran back and forth for a better view on the street outside.

"Believe me, the city fire department has a much better record of getting to emergencies than the police."

"They better get here fast."

"They will." He opened the door.

"You think so?" She watched the smoke and a thin wail came from the motel. Perhaps the Jolly Wanderers.

"I'm absolutely certain," Lisio said. He felt in charge again. "Good-bye, and thank you."

He walked past people making absurd comments on the fire, found himself entranced by its size and color, the raw smell of burning wood, plaster, plastic flavoring the air.

Lisio walked another block and sat down on the blue bench at the Metro bus stop. He had a wonderful view of the commotion and beauty of the fire. He waited for the number 43 bus that would take him to the intersection of Eugene and Claremont, one block from Carol Beaufort's home.

SIXTEEN

MEDAVOY LEFT HIS CAR in the space reserved for his supervisor, Lieutenant Gordon Ornelas. It was hard to get parking near the police department without paying an enormous monthly charge, so he partly welcomed Gordo's growing number of absences.

The department's parking lot was filled with almost two hundred squad cars, blue-white, blue-white in the morning sunshine. He stopped by the combination gas pumps and car wash. A thin, stooped man with a sniffle was splashing soapy water on a black four-door.

"Hey, Mutt," Medavoy said.

"Yo, Robby. They make you supervisor yet?"

"I don't want it."

Mutt wiped his nose on his overall sleeve. He wore a baggy pair of department-green overalls, grease-marked and dirty. He had been a line patrolman ten years before, but partial disability from being stabbed during a fight between a very angry husband and wife left him the choice of early retirement or a change of assignment to something he could still handle. Mutt was always a cop, he said. He didn't care if all he did now was make sure the squad cars ran well and looked sparkling clean.

"I thought you'd be king of the mountain today," Mutt went on soaping the car, "because you said so much in the paper this morning."

Medavoy recognized the car getting the thorough wash and wax as belonging to the captain who ran Investigations.

"I didn't see the paper," he said irritably. "I must have been shooting my mouth off."

"Oh, yeah, yeah. We got this Pacific Security Bank deal covered nine miles from Sunday. We got descriptions of the pukes. We got their car. Sounds like a real good piece of work, Robby." He sniffled and chuckled.

"Mutt, the media dickheads didn't even show up until I was driving out. I haven't seen the fucking car. Somebody downtown's been putting my name out on this."

"Stevie Wonder's press widget. Always got to show the department moving. We don't stand still."

"Shit." Medavoy moved to avoid getting a sudden splash of water as Mutt vigorously worked the car's hood. "Hey, I got a favor—"

"You know who's car this is?" Mutt interrupted.

"Yeah."

"They're all here, bright and early. Stevie came in about half hour ago. Assistant Chief's up there, Operations, Administration, Investigation, everybody's up on the fourth floor." Mutt sniffed and shook his head. "I got bad sinus today."

"Wonder what's going on," Medavoy again sidestepped Mutt's sponge action. "You worry when those guys get up early, don't you?"

"I told you, they're making you supervisor right now. You took care of the bank thing so fast."

"They're doing something. Can I ask a favor?"

"I don't do dope, I don't give loans, I don't snitch. Anything else?"

"Friend of mine's got trouble with her transmission." Medavoy paused briefly, unsure of what to call Jane. There was nothing permanent about their lives together. He had no token of their connection beyond his love and there wasn't any simple descriptive word. She meant so much to him and there was so little way for him easily to pin it down. "She's got her car with some flake. Can you take a look for me?"

"Sure. Tell her to bring the car in."

It was forbidden by departmental regulations to use staff for private work. But Mutt was washing a captain's car for him. These were the small frauds that made life run.

"She'll come in this afternoon, Mutt. It's a VW Rabbit."

"I'll be here." He sniffed very loudly, almost snorting. He slapped his soapy sponge across the car's windshield. "Tell me what the brains are up to, okay?"

Medavoy nodded, held up a hand. "I got to see how I solved this bank deal."

He crossed the street to the Police Department. Behind him, beyond the parking lot, were the tracks of the Southern Pacific, and a little farther, the expanse of the rail yard itself where his father had worked. Each day he went to work, Medavoy was reminded of his father and his years as an SP cop with a measure of sadness and sometimes envy. Simpler days, he imagined, simpler choices.

Strung across the street, from the rooftop of the Police Department to a tall oak, was an electric wire on which hung a blue globe the size of a big toy balloon that said POLICE DEPARTMENT at night. Two detectives from Auto Burg, both in shirt-sleeves, happily gave him grief as he went up the marble steps to the building.

The Police Department building was an early twentieth-century gesture, a granite-faced four-story block ornamented in a Romanesque style, now mottled with leaf sap and weathered in its palisade of old trees.

Alonzo Patterson was the Chief who built it, too big for the city at the time, said his critics, too expensive. Patterson argued every chance he could that Santa Maria would grow and the police department should retire the horse-drawn paddy wagons; the rattling cars that were starting to appear frequently were the wave of the future. Someday, he said, Santa Maria would even have to build a bigger city jail. The department's new building was denounced as "Alonzo's Folly" and Chief Patterson retired only two years later. He moved to Mendocino to raise roses.

Medavoy didn't like the look of the building—gray, dour, and embattled. The exuberant, high windows that broke the front's severity had been grilled over during the riotous Sixties in preparation for upheavals that struck the courthouse. The city-county jail lay directly behind the building, connected by walkways and security fences topped by cameras, the whole construction having a harried, disjointed appearance.

The morning shift was starting to dribble in, the graveyard to yawn its way out, when Medavoy strode quickly up the marble stairs that wound in a sinuous curve from the cramped lobby. The center of the stairs was slightly depressed, worn down over the three-quarters of a century by crime and criminals. Besides the current exhortative posters from the city, the lobby also held a display case of trophies for the public to admire. In the middle was a brown plaque of brass nameplates, which, from a distance, looked like a country club golfing award without a shiny golfer figurine. Closer up, the nameplates held each Santa Maria police officer killed on duty since 1904, beginning with Harry Albright, shot breaking up a gambling game on the river, to Mark Bagdasarian who served a failure-to-provide-child-support warrant on a man who didn't want to be served. Medavoy had gone through rookie training with Bagdasarian. He felt a tie to every name on the plaque.

He went through a glass door into the Robbery Detail, which shared the second floor with Auto Burg. Easter and Special Weapons were housed in dark, machine-oil-ripe quarters in the basement. The walls in Robbery were imitation brown veneer that had started to buckle away from the plaster. It was musty and slightly medicinal. Only one of the six closely grouped desks was in use. Two telephones rang on other desks.

"How," Medavoy said to the detective flipping through a thick stack of papers on a clipboard, then passing it to him.

"How," answered Stanley Masuda, hand raised in Tonto's greeting.

"Gordo call in sick? I used his spot and I don't want to get towed."

"The wife called. So you get to be our acting honcho again," Masuda drawled.

"Anything I got to take with me?" Medavoy filled his mug from the dented coffee maker gurgling on top of a short file cabinet.

"Quiet night for us. Twelve new reports, couple contact cards on local pukes, couple incident reports."

Medavoy nodded, taking a quick look through the early-bird roster of reports Masuda had handed him. As acting supervisor, he assigned them to the detectives on the detail. Twelve new robberies wasn't unusual for Santa Maria overnight. In the summer, with good weather and people leaving windows open, it could jump to twenty. Twelve was reasonable for the spring.

"Anything here you don't want?" He held up the clipboard.

"All of it."

Medavoy glanced at his own desk. He picked up the hand-written report pages in his basket. "You got to take potluck like everybody, Stanley. Hey, here's my Pacific Security supp. Patrol guys found the car about five blocks away." He read, sipped, and checked the time. "Peanut shells inside, lots of prints. Whoops."

"What?"

"Car was stolen day before yesterday in a Chino escape. Could be fun. I love it when cons start running around."

"Who got out?"

"It's in here someplace. I don't have time now." He dropped the supplemental report back on his desk. A bank robbery with a fugitive involved was distinctly out of the normal run of fast-food shakedowns, domestic strongarms, and gas station cash register thefts. It might even be fun.

Medavoy made a scan of the clipboard hanging on the wall near a dusty collection of wanted circulars and reports from state police agencies and the FBI. Nothing else had come in since yesterday.

"You talk to Gef last night?" he asked Masuda.

"Yeah." Masuda crumpled page after page of a report and neatly tossed them into Zaragoza's wastebasket.

"So what's going on?" Medavoy asked.

"We went out for a while. He said the Reilly bust went great, you had a good time breaking things."

"He tell you what his problem is?"

Masuda shook his head. "Midlife heebie-jeebies."

Medavoy knew Masuda wouldn't cover up any serious problem he noticed among the Robbery Detail detectives. He was trustworthy. But he genuinely might have missed something from Geffen.

Masuda was about Medavoy's age, a weight lifter and very heavy, squarely solid. He filled his T-shirt, stamped with a greeting to a local killer on Death Row. "Adios, José" it said over a gallows. Masuda would put on his coat and tie when he officially went on duty at seven-thirty. He wore thick glasses and was the sentimental member of the detail, remembering every anniversary and birthday, wives and children included. On Mondays he brought doughy

Japanese sweet rolls his wife made and Medavoy found inedible. The two of them had joined the department together.

"Yeah," Masuda reluctantly agreed. "I think the job's getting him down."

"I don't know. That asshole Easter made some cracks at the bank yesterday. Gef blew up." He didn't mention the other conversations Easter and Geffen must have had, the ones Easter talked about last night.

Masuda croaked, bounced out of his chair. "He hates that guy. So do I."

"I get nervous when I don't know what's going on with you guys," Medavoy said. He was running a little late for the morning supervisors' meeting.

"He's on a hump. He'll get over it. Gef is solid." Masuda didn't seem fazed by whatever he and Geffen had talked about. Maybe it was all trivial. He rolled his head and pointed at the clipboard under Medavoy's arm. "I got fifteen active investigations, Robby. How about going light on assigning me anything else?"

"Kiss my ass, motherfucker," Medavoy grinned. "You bend over and take it like everybody." He started for the door.

Masuda tossed a wadded up report page at him.

"Before everyone heads out, I want to talk to them about the fallout coming from the Reilly bust," Medavoy said.

"That's rocking the boat," Masuda chuckled. He reached for his ringing telephone. His wife usually wished him a good day before his shift started.

Medavoy didn't wait to hear them cooing and murmuring. He carried the robbery report roster and his coffee up another flight of marble stairs to the meeting. He had the new information on the Pacific Security investigation to read, had to find out about this prison escapee, find out who was watching Jane's house, and what was wrong with Gef.

And sit through listening to the other supervisors complain

and weave and dart from any criticism. It was already looking like a tough day.

In another meeting were four men and the Chief, plastic cups of coffee, half-filled ashtrays in front of them on the small round conference table in his office. The drapes were wide open, the room hazy and shimmering with sunlight.

"I haven't announced the Second Coming," the Chief said sarcastically. "This is simply a necessary organizational restructuring."

"Well, it seems sudden," white-haired, jowled McMurray in Operations said. "Kind of drastic."

The Chief had a glass of water and he emptied it. "I want more day-to-day control over the department. I sit up here and all I ever see is Bart." He pointed at the burly cigar smoker on his right, the Assistant Chief, the man people usually assumed was the Chief of Police when they first met him.

"It's going to be complicated to draw up a new chain of command," Druliner in Administration didn't look up.

"Then get busy on it today."

"How about we all consider it and come back with some ideas in, like, a week?" McMurray got a nod from everyone but Bart and the Chief.

The Chief had gotten this revelation as he lay sleeplessly in bed last night. He was cut off on the fourth floor, separated from his men and their work. He needed to hear what was happening directly from the heads of the three branches of the department every day. Already the pleasant task of producing new directives and a whole organizational diagram lay ahead.

"No. I want this plan in place within the week. I want your specifics on my desk by Monday."

"Two days? I can't swing that." Druliner was sharp.

"You better do it."

No one mistook the threat. There was a silent surrender. The three captains, all twenty-year-plus veterans, gave each other furtive, perplexed glances.

"If that's what you want." McMurray was on his feet.

"That's exactly what I want."

The Chief remained seated until the three men had left. He strolled to his large oak desk, so old and stained it was nearly black. It had belonged to Alonzo Patterson and like his fortress building, successors could only add on or repaint.

"What are you pouting about, Bart?" The Chief paused in tapping out new commands on the two computer terminals on the desk.

"You have to ask."

"I am not cutting you out."

"They think so. I think so."

"You're still Assistant Chief."

"Big deal."

The Chief felt very sure of himself this morning. He put his hand on Bart's flabby shoulder. "Old friend, we spent two decades in Criminal Statistics and I'd take your advice over anyone else."

"Seriously?"

"On my honor. You feel better?"

Bart nodded with a rueful smile. "It just came out of nowhere and I thought I was being shut out."

The Chief was back at the computers, tapping with assurance on one, then the other. "It's time for a shake-up. I heard Druliner going out just now."

"What'd he say, the son of a bitch?" Bart relit the black cigar, puffing on it fiercely.

"He said, 'What's happened to Stevie Wonder?' The answer is that things are going to be different around here. I want to go on a raid, I don't care if it's narcotics or vice or what. I want to get back on the street."

"Wow," Bart said, as thick smoke curled around him. He

was overweight and red-faced.

"This is my department and it's time I acted like it was."

"And you got City Council this morning."

"I know that, I remember." The Chief didn't like to be reminded he still had to beg. "Get Schroeder from Internal Affairs up here in ten minutes." He tapped faster, numbers and graphs forming and vanishing on the computer screens.

"Internal Affairs?"

"We're cleaning out the bad apples today, Bart."

"Wow."

"Get me Medavoy's personnel file, too. Now." He recalled the cop Ollie Knudsen had complained about.

"Right away, Mac," said the Assistant Chief, happy to be useful still. He glanced out the window behind the Chief, past the blue ball hanging outside.

"Something's burning."

"What?" the Chief asked absentmindedly.

"Over there, see the smoke? Some kind of big fire." He pointed at the lazy, thick gray column of smoke to the west, several miles away. The smoke had flattened, spread, giving it a flowerlike appearance.

"Get me Schroeder and Medavoy's file." The Chief didn't look up.

SEVENTEEN

"**I'LL DO ALL THE TALKING,**" Carol cautioned Kenny a final time. She had one hand on Reilly's door. The heavy brass knob was frozen and hard. In her other hand was a paper bag and the .45.

Neither she nor Kenny had slept very well and holding the gun and standing in the muffled richness of the hallway, at the door to the office where she normally worked, disoriented her. It was too early for the other people—bankers and lawyers, real estate giants—to be at work.

The frosty light from shiny gold holders on the polished walls made her and Kenny look midnight pale. She didn't like seeing Reilly so early. And even though she'd taken a tepid shower, she still had on the same clothes from yesterday and she felt gritty.

But, I know what to say now and I've got a plan, she thought.

"Yeah, go ahead. Great. You tell him the whole deal." Kenny nodded curtly. He bounced a little from foot to foot.

"What's the matter?" She fiddled uselessly with the doorknob. The tall sturdy doors stayed closed.

"Nothing's wrong. You the jumpy one. I say, do it. Get it over with."

"Relax. Calm down," she said. He was oddly up after such a bad night, facing the end of the bank scheme. Carol wasn't sure, but she had a vague impression of Kenny getting out of bed in the middle of the night and using the telephone. He denied it. She was dreaming, he said. Who would he call anyway? She was the only one who could do anything for him.

He protested enough about it as they were dressing that she wondered whether it was a dream or not. Still, when she first woke up, Kenny was sitting in one of the chairs, taken from his barricade. He was watching her while she slept. Devotion? Fear? It was spooky.

There hadn't been any trouble getting out of the Ramona. Her car was parked where she left it. In the confusion and thrashing around last night, she'd forgotten entirely about the shopping bag of bundled cash and wigs in the trunk. There was a heart-stopping moment to check and make sure it was all still there. It was.

The only real problem this morning was getting into Reilly's office.

She hit the door with her open palm. It made a tiny splatting sound. "Brian's expecting us. I talked to him a half hour ago." She didn't add that Reilly wasn't wildly enthusiastic.

"Let me, honey." Kenny shouldered by her and pounded on the door. "Hey, hey! Open the goddamn door!"

He stepped back, hands on his hips. "Give it up, babe. They ain't in or they don't want you."

She put her ear to the door. Like sounds from the ocean floor, faint clicking came to her. I've got to get in, she vowed. Brian is the one path to safety through all of his contacts around town. "I hear typing. Someone's got to be in there," she said fiercely. I sound a little panicked, she realized.

"You want to break it?"

"Let me try once more. They've got to let me in." She beat on the door again.

In midarc, as Carol was about to land a solid one, the door opened slightly. A red-eyed, flabby face came partway into the wedge.

"Nielda," Carol said with relief. "We've been banging on the door for hours."

The opening widened; Reilly's secretary let them in. "I had the earplugs in. Rush, rush dictation. I didn't hear."

She said it sullenly to Carol. They didn't get along and Carol believed Nielda resented her freedom. Nielda had two high-schoolers to brood over.

"What happened?" Carol looked around the reception room and into Reilly's outer office.

"We got searched."

"Hey, Carol honey, I don't think this's the guy we need." Kenny squeezed her arm.

"Be quiet. Who searched you?"

"Who's he?" Nielda looked suspiciously at Kenny.

Before Carol could answer, he shoved an enthusiastic hand out. "I'm Waylon Jennings."

"He is not. It doesn't matter who he is, Nielda."

Kenny thrust out his lower lip as though insulted. He seemed to like the ramshackle appearance of the office. The chairs were overturned, stacks of files laid randomly on the floor, spilling to one side, law books, appellate decision reports, stacked, dropped open, file cabinet drawers pulled out like long metal tongues, one metal cabinet dented and burst wide, cushions piled on each other. In the middle of the room was a black plastic trash bag and Carol saw yellow file folders dumped into it.

"Look what they did. Look at my desk. What am I supposed to have? They took everything out." She pointed indignantly.

"Who did it?"

"Who do you think?" She asked as if Carol was feeble-minded. "Cops. A ton of cops."

"City police? Sheriff? Feds?"

"City cops. They left this." She sarcastically showed a copy of the search warrant to Carol. "Don't touch anything," she snapped at Kenny.

He looked up from poking among the books and papers. "You think I might mess this stuff up?"

Carol tried to read the warrant. Something terrible had happened to Reilly and she was immediately worried her own connection to the other side of his practice was known. But the warrant seemed concerned with other things, stolen property, drugs; all she had ever done, she was certain, was make illegal payoffs to builders and the planning commission. It was worrisome that Santa Maria cops had executed the warrant. That meant the investigation was about local matters, not countywide or federal.

"Brian didn't mention this over the phone. Stop that, Kenny."

Nielda rubbed her nose. She might have been crying. "Who is he?" she asked loudly.

Kenny was whistling jauntily and punching the piled sofa cushions like they were a speed bag. He was very fast and very hard. He didn't stop, only looked over and grinned at her.

"He's a friend," Carol said, dropping the search warrant. "We have to talk to Brian."

From the inner office came a cry, "Nielda! Nielda!"

"What?" she yelled back.

"Where's my Rolodex?"

"How should I know?"

"Did they take it?"

Nielda looked sullenly at Carol. "He stayed on the floor the whole time. He says it makes it look like they were walking all over him and he wasn't doing anything. My God. They smashed the safe, the file cabinet. And he just lies there and lets me get it."

"Nielda!"

"What?"

"Who's out there?"

"It's Carol," Carol answered. "Come on, Kenny." She put out her hand. She thought he needed some reassurance in the face of this turmoil and she certainly did.

"You brought your lunch?" Nielda pointed at the paper bag in Carol's hand.

"It's something else," she said. Kenny took her hand.

"It's a .45," he said with a gaping smile.

"Of course it is, Waylon," Nielda snapped. "I got to finish this dictation for him. He's got restraining orders, return of illegally seized property, malicious prosecution, pages of it. He was in jail most of yesterday and all he did was write these damn motions for me to type."

"Like your dress," Kenny said.

Carol pulled him toward Reilly's inner office.

"He's pretty mad at you," Nielda said to Carol's back. "He wanted you here and he couldn't find you. I called and called."

"I was out," Carol said.

"She's so cute," Kenny said to Nielda, winking.

Carol was startled, again, when she went into Reilly's office. He stood behind his desk, the drapes drawn, the room sepulchral and confining. Reilly had a cigarette angled in his mouth, puffing out smoke regularly, reading rapidly over papers, then dropping them into the wastebasket, his open briefcase on the desk, or another black trash bag. Every file he had was piled on his desk. His safe, broken, empty, like a metal scream, was raggedly open. The furniture in here too was thrown around, upended and disordered, as though a willful and malicious child had been at play.

Reilly had his tie loosened. His phone rang, but he waited until Nielda picked it up or it stopped.

"You look like you're leaving." Carol let go of Kenny's

hand. He whistled, low and cheery, and looked around the office.

"Call this weeding, Carol. I'm weeding out any little problems still lurking here." He dropped more pages into the briefcase.

"I have to talk to you. It's important."

"Well, I do have a few problems of my own. But I thought since we've shared a few things over the last couple of months, we better understand each other."

Carol set the paper bag on Reilly's desk. He gave it a quick glance. "I need your help, Brian. I need any influence you have in town."

Reilly sorted through the sheaf of papers in his hand very fast, most falling, like discarded wings, into the trash bag. He ground out the cigarette in a marble ashtray. He yawned suddenly and involuntarily. "Sorry. I haven't been to bed all night. Got to clean this place up in case I get another visit. They didn't get everything. They didn't know where to look." He grinned at his cleverness.

"Am I involved?"

Reilly shook his head. "Peripherally."

"Then you owe me a favor."

Reilly stepped from behind the desk, a fat, clumsy man. He patted her arm paternally. "I wouldn't let anything happen to you, Carol. Now. Who is the friend?" He pointed at Kenny, now perched on top of four sofa cushions.

"He's why I need the favor."

"Well, there're favors and favors. Something you can do for me. Maybe something I can do for you."

Kenny popped off the cushions, his hand stuck out again like a glad salesman. "Pleased to meet you. I'm Wayne Newton."

"Who's the clown?" Reilly asked Carol without smiling.

"This is Kenny Trask. I told you about him several times."

Reilly drew the drapes back, the heavy blue sliding away to reveal the brighter blue of the sky, white-clouded. The Santa

Maria downtown lay below, gray-black buildings, other high office towers glittering in the sun. Reilly rubbed his eyes.

"Oh, yeah. He's the appeal you wanted me to pick up. Armed robbery? Doing time at Chino? When'd you get out?"

Kenny started to answer, but she cut him off. "Shut up," she said. His attempts at humor got on her nerves. She'd only had strong black coffee to face this interview. It was nothing compared to the pills and drinks for a regular morning. While the sensation of clarity was unfamiliar, she didn't like it enough to be cool and collected. There was too much at stake.

"I ain't here to cause trouble." Kenny frowned, raised his hands in surrender.

"He escaped two days ago," Carol said to Reilly. Lay it out like any case. "There's one injury. That's part of the problem I mentioned over the phone."

Reilly looked more closely at Kenny, sitting and grinning on the cushions. Then to Carol, "One injury? Are we talking about GBI?"

"Kenny?" she asked. "Did you do enough damage to cause that man great bodily injury?"

He vigorously shook his head. "No way, honey. I bet he's up and frisky right now. I just hit him."

"Just hit him," Reilly repeated slowly. "Get him out of here."

Carol snapped back emphatically, "Brian, you're going to help me. I'd like you to do it out of friendship."

"I'm not talking to you while he's here."

She was ready to play on terms Reilly appreciated, especially considering the developments since yesterday. "He knows everything that's going on. I told him about you. I've told him what I've done for you." She found two matching cushions, shoved them into the sofa and sat down. Reilly sat behind his desk, slouching, looking very tired and very grim.

"I wish you hadn't done that, Carol. I've been very good to you. I've kept our arrangements quiet for both of us."

"I need all the help I can get, Brian. Kenny is going to turn himself in. He was forced into robbing a bank yesterday." She hesitated, looked at the wrinkled skirt and soiled shoes from the river. I must look like a refugee, she thought. Even at this moment, I hate that as much as anything.

Reilly didn't take his eyes from her. She went on, "I was also forced into going along during that robbery. I didn't participate, but I was there."

"What kind of force? Specifically?"

"A gun. The principal figure in all of this, he had a bomb."

Reilly raised his eyebrows. "A bomb?"

"Hell, no," Kenny chuckled. "It ain't real. Just for show. Scare the shit out of them."

Reilly ignored Kenny and Carol could tell he was furious. "And there's another player, too? Someone you haven't told me about?"

"Carol honey, I don't think we got to say no more," Kenny interrupted.

"There is another party," she said, "but the initial problem has to do with a follow-up, Brian. Last night, Kenny shot a man. We don't know his name or where he is or how badly he's hurt. Now, Kenny was attacked. It was self-defense."

"Damn straight," Kenny agreed.

Reilly smiled thinly. "Self-defense. What were you doing?" he asked Kenny directly for the first time.

"I got this car, got it ready to move out, and this dude jumps me. Just jumps me," Kenny said indignantly.

"Was it his car?"

"Hell if I know."

Carol knew the thing was getting away from her. She had to bring it back to something simple, concrete, something that Reilly alone could do for her. "Brian, as I said, Kenny's going to turn himself in. I need help because of my involvement. Who can you talk to?"

"Carol," Reilly inhaled deeply, blinked his red-rimmed

eyes, "you have a bank robbery, one assault, and one shooting. You might even have a homicide."

"I know that."

Reilly shut his eyes. For a moment, she was afraid he'd fallen asleep. He seemed to be talking to himself.

"I must have been very bad in another life," Reilly said, eyes closed, "I must have royally fucked up." He opened his eyes, his head sunk almost to his chest. "Carol, when I said I'd talk to you, I only wanted to discuss our own upcoming problems."

"As you can see, there's a lot more," she said.

"There sure is. You can look forward to the cops talking to you."

"Man. Oh, man." Kenny snapped his head back, snorted. He paced beside her.

"You'll get a call. In a day. Maybe today. Medavoy from Robbery will ask you about me. Do you have something to tell him?"

Carol twisted her head to bark, "You're making me nervous doing that, Kenny." He slowed his pacing, but didn't stop. He put his hands into the pockets of the ridiculously short Raiders jacket.

She said to Reilly carefully, "If you help us now, I don't have anything to say to Medavoy, do I?"

"I suppose not."

"Man," Kenny pointed, "this guy can't help himself, Carol honey. He can't do shit for us. Right? You can't do shit for yourself. Can you?"

Reilly smiled very tightly, a scarlet-veined cheek twitching. "We've got a deal, Carol. You have a very complex set of entanglements to unravel. I'm always here to help you."

"I was sure you would be," she said, feeling a bolt of tension leave her. Kenny clapped his hands several times and muttered epithets she couldn't make out. She tried to organize her thoughts. Reilly was a powerful man, no matter what had happened yesterday. He had friends and dependents all over the city. All she had to do was simply and clearly lay the whole bank scheme, the police-response wrinkle as Lisio explained it yesterday, before him. Reilly would know where to buy the best deal for her.

The phone rang with sharp, abrupt insistence. She jumped a little. Kenny reached forward fluidly, seized the phone, tore it toward himself, and tossed it to the thick carpeting. It landed with a soft, cross thud. It vanished into the heaped confusion on the floor. He opened the paper bag and held the .45 loosely, limbered.

"No," Carol said harshly. "Put it down, Kenny. Everything's all right."

"Let me handle it, babe." He held his hand up soothingly. "How much money you got here, right now?" He asked Reilly genially.

Reilly sank deeper into his chair, sinking into himself as well. "What's the deal here, Carol?"

"You go to court for dopers? You know anybody who deals?" Kenny asked loudly.

"I'm warning you," she said, reaching for the gun, "put that down now."

"Hey, don't butt in!" and for the first time, she saw a feral intensity in his expression, like a dog with a piece of meat growling menacingly even at an owner it loves. He would hurt her. She was certain of that.

"Look around. There's no money. You think there's any money left? You see any?" Reilly glowered at Kenny.

Kenny took a few steps until he was right between Reilly's fat thighs. The man's bloodshot eyes were wide; he said something pleading to Carol.

"Put your hand on the desk," Kenny shouted.

"My hand?"

"Spread your fingers. Now. Do it." Kenny pointed the gun at Reilly's left eye.

"Carol, do something."

She shook slightly, an outward sign of the fear that came mixed with anger and frustration. What could she do? I'm a leaf trying to stop a river, she thought.

Kenny grabbed Reilly's slowly moving hand, slapped it on the desk, holding the wrist. "Money?" Kenny asked.

Reilly mumbled, tugged his hand and Kenny swung the .45 by its thick barrel and whacked down on the outstretched fingers as though hammering nails into tough wood.

Carol cried out, jumped back, hands to her face, as Reilly screamed; Kenny struck again and again, then let go of the hand. Reilly jerked backward, curled up in his chair. He was doubled over in his big chair, holding the hand. A drip, drip of blood began onto the stylish carpet.

"Carol says you got dopers. They pay cash, they give you something like gold or something. I know. She says you got all kinds of shit going on here. So, you got some stashed right now?" Kenny had his face very close to the moaning man.

"Don't hurt him, please, no more." Carol took little steps back and forth. "Nielda will hear."

"She's got those fucking things in her ears. She won't hear anything." He bent to Reilly again. "I got to know right now what you got here."

Reilly said something painful, his head rolling back on his shoulders. He cupped his broken, bloody hand, trembling. He didn't seem able to speak very well.

"What?" Kenny impatiently demanded.

"He said his hand hurts, his hand, his hand," Carol said.

"Sure it does. That hand's busted ten ways."

"He can help me," she said savagely, and Kenny didn't catch the singular. "He's the only one who can do anything."

Kenny swung the .45 again with greater force, hitting Reilly on the side of the head, knocking him out of the chair. The chair spun on its rollers and fell over, Reilly going down on his back. He screamed twice and a bloody mist spumed up.

"Leave him alone, Kenny," she yelled, grabbing on his shirt back. Like I can really tear him away, she thought. I can handle that little freak Lisio, but Kenny's another story. She went on futilely pulling at him.

"You think I'm having a good time? Think this's for fun?"

She rocked back, out of his way. The man who could have opened doors at the police department lay bleeding on the floor, Kenny panting over him.

"What are you looking for?" she asked as calmly as possible.

He knelt, threw Reilly's coat open. Most of Reilly's sharply ironed white shirt had come up when he fell, and a mound of pale fat belly jiggled. It had a vulnerable, mortifying indecency to her. "He's got to have something." Kenny wasn't really talking to her, she realized. Reilly went on coughing and gargling as Kenny tore through the coat's inner pockets, pulled out a wallet, and from another pocket, neatly folded fifty dollar bills. "Okay, see? That's all I wanted. We're square, okay?" He spoke into Reilly's uncomprehending face.

"What do you think you've just accomplished?" she asked, standing beside the wide window. I wish I could fly out of here. She looked out onto the city's tall buildings and streets.

"I got my fucking confidence back, honey. I mean, I was pretty out of it last night." He yanked open the drawers on Reilly's desk, spilling out papers, small pill bottles, bourbon samplers, paper clips, all sorts of junk onto Reilly, who appeared content to lie there, feebly moving his head, his eyes sometimes open, mostly closed, mouth angled oddly open and bloody. "But, you know, Carol honey, I really think it's only being so tired. Like I wasn't myself, you know," he shrugged.

"Now you are."

"You bet. Ready and raring. Tell you what. Go get the bitch outside, bring her in here."

"No, Kenny." Carol looked around the mess on the floor, trying to see the telephone. "What I'm going to do is call the police. Take my chances."

Kenny's eyes went wide in a comical expression of bafflement and irritability. Like a cartoon, she thought, some Tom and Jerry thing he saw a hundred times and the whole world has the plasticity of a cartoon to him. Hit a man and he'll snap back. Break his hand and it heals tomorrow. Nobody has pain but you.

"We ain't got time to mess around," he said. "We got a tight schedule. Go get the bitch."

She reached for the telephone. What am I doing? She was stricken. He'd ripped it out.

"Okay," Kenny said, "we'll both go get the bitch. We got to put these guys someplace so they don't run around."

"I'm going outside and use Nielda's phone," Carol said. "I'll be right back."

Kenny pointed the .45 at her and sighed in annoyance. "Come on. Let's go. Time's wasting."

She looked at the gun, dark, quiet, senseless. Like magic, the scene cleared for her. It was so plain she had missed it, like forgetting just now that he had destroyed the telephone.

"You talked to Lisio last night at the hotel," she said.

"Yep. And he ain't mad at you. He understands."

"Jesus Christ, Kenny. Stop it."

He waved the gun, motioning her toward the clattering sound of Nielda typing. "You going to thank me later," Kenny said.

EIGHTEEN

THE FIFTH-FLOOR CORRIDOR in the county courthouse was roused for a new day. As Jane walked down it, past the ten courtrooms, some with their doors open, she saw the daily crowd. Always the same, she thought, and always different. Jurors waiting in tight bunches beside the courtrooms or along the walls, women with babies in strollers, lawyers whispering, gesturing to men, eyes hard on them, who braced themselves against the walls. Bailiffs, the easygoing side of Santa Maria's law enforcement, waved at her from their courtroom doorways.

She waved back. She carried her steno machine like a mace, holding the tripod legs together. Even when she didn't know the cops waiting to testify, she could tell who they were in the crowd. The men in suits, usually too sporty or too dour, reading the newspaper and sighing. They were cops.

She was a little put out with Robby just now. His casual dismissal of her hopes for moving up in the department, the little digs about bribes, the whole sidestep he did last night to avoid talking about marriage. *Like I don't know what a bad one is like,* she thought. *That's why I didn't marry Johnathan's father and get into a bad one.*

She was nearing Department 24, the courtroom doors open. The jurors sitting outside had formed a few friendships and were broken into little groups of two or three.

She had just started wondering whether it was right to impose on the Cabrals to take care of Johnathan, even if the day-care places she'd tried lately were so lousy, when a short, shock-haired man in a poplin suit came up beside her.

"Ready for another exciting day of testimony, young lady?" the white-haired man asked.

"Morning, Smitty," she said, slowing a little. He couldn't move very quickly anymore. "I figure it's going to be more of the same," she lowered her voice so the jurors wouldn't hear, "lying jackasses and lying lawyers."

"Hard to tell the difference."

"I don't think there is one." She was very fond of Smitty. He was the senior court reporter, due to retire in a year. He was also the last reporter who took down testimony without a steno machine. On his table in a courtroom were pens, steno pads, ink bottles, and blotting paper. Every judge deferred to Smitty when he looked up and said sternly, "I didn't hear that last answer." The witness would always be asked to repeat it loudly.

"No. Probably not." Smitty smiled at her. He had a tiny cigarette butt clamped tightly in his mouth, like he had sucked the whole thing into a point. He said, "You have a minute or two?"

"Not really. Righteous Ron's got a half day and he always starts on time." Her judge liked to run his courtroom as though it were a punctual commuter express.

"He'll wait for me," Smitty said, taking her arm. "I need to talk to you."

Jane was curious about his insistence as he led her into
Department 21, which was dark that day. Judge Gilmore was
having his gallbladder out. Smitty closed the high doors.

"I have to hurry," Jane said. There was something sad
about an empty courtroom, like an unused rocking horse.

"I want a little privacy," he said and she was afraid he
was again going to ask her to go into partnership with him
when he retired. Smitty thought they could both make a grand
living as reporters on their own. He had twenty-five years'
experience and knew every lawyer in the city.

"I don't want to talk business today, Smitty."

"No, no, young lady. This is personal. I just heard something about your friend Medavoy."

Jane lowered her steno machine to the clerk's desk. "What
about him?"

Smitty frowned, spit out the cigarette fragment. He
scratched his chin. His shaving was a little erratic, so he had
white stubbled patches. "You know Earl Schroeder over at
SMPD? He's in Internal Affairs?"

"No. Never heard of him. Robby's never mentioned him."
She felt a spike of dread. Smitty was one of the very few people
who knew completely about her and Robby. He was one of
the people she trusted.

"He's a lieutenant, twenty-year man. He's due out in a
couple of years. We've known each other since high school.
He's a cold fish if you don't know him. But, we've stayed
friends over the years. Go up to Clear Lake every September
for trout. Wonderful fishing up there."

"Cut to the point, Smitty. I want to hear what he had to
say," Jane broke in.

Smitty shook his head in apology. "What I meant was that
Earl's a straight guy. He's never lied to me. He doesn't tell me
every scandal or rotten deal he finds out about, but he doesn't
keep many of them secret, either."

"Scandal? What are you talking about?" she said sharply,

hoping it wasn't her. The strange cars, the strange calls, Robby's paranoia about the new administration in the department cracking the whip on regulations and propriety. "What's Internal Affairs saying about Robby?"

Smitty took a breath. "It's very bad, young lady."

"Then I want to hear it."

NINETEEN

MEDAVOY STOPPED DOODLING on his clipboard. He tried to listen to Hollenbeck, because he was up next and after that he could sneak out of the supervisors' meeting and actually get to work.

He looked around the brown table in the former storage room on the third floor. Stevie Wonder demanded that the supervisors have their own conference room complete with a framed color photo of him looking like a car backfired beside him, easel for charts nobody ever brought, coffeepot for coffee everybody brought himself.

The table was so big in the little room it made the six men around it sit almost with their backs against the wall.

Medavoy knew he wasn't wrong when he told Jane it was impossible for him to go after higher rank. Look at these guys, the top of the department, under the deputy chiefs, and they all seemed as wiped out as a guy with a bad hangover. I'm not planning to look that way after I've been a cop twenty years, he thought.

At the head of the table, Lieutenant Pesce ran the meeting with his stopwatch beside him. Stevie Wonder decreed that no staff meeting go longer than forty minutes without advance permission. So Pesce's got to keep everybody babbling pretty fast, Medavoy thought.

Medavoy glanced at John Hollenbeck, the former British bobby who headed Homicide-Assaults. He was finishing his tale of overnight woes in a flat Midlands accent.

"And last, I've got a shooting at the Cabana Motel on Comstock Avenue," half-glasses half-perched on his thin nose as he read, "in the parking lot. Victim's in critical at Santa Maria Community. White male adult, shot once in the upper torso. Large caliber bullet, maybe a .45," he peered out, "nobody's had a good look at the thing since the quacks took it out."

"Drug deal?" asked Samuelian in Narcotics. Big man who nearly took up two chairs.

Hollenbeck sucked air. "Victim was wearing his bathrobe. Out by a Cadillac Coup de Ville belonging to his cousin or wife's cousin."

"So he wanted a toot before bed," Samuelian said.

"That wouldn't be my guess," Hollenbeck answered quietly.

Medavoy looked down the table. "Am I going to get this one, John? Any kind of theft involved?"

"Well, all we have so far is the car. Hot-wired. Victim surprised the asshole and the asshole shot him. Now, if the victim goes bad, well it's a homicide so I'll certainly keep it. For your information, gentlemen, that would make number seventy-two for the year. We've beat last year by ten so far."

Another supervisor, beside Medavoy, clapped sarcastically.

"Hold it down," Pesce said briskly. He was tan, with only a fringe of gray hair left. His white shirt had as many wrinkles as his face. "Tell them the special angle, John. Hurry it up."

"Sorry. Victim's from San Jose. Murray Bowler, a construction company president. There's a small amount of publicity expected."

Medavoy grinned. That was an understatement.

At the other end of the table, Easter looked up. He had been resting his head on his hands. "Maybe Medavoy should take it. He's getting the attention on everything else."

"Fuck off," he replied automatically.

"On your own time, not mine," Pesce admonished swiftly. "Okay. You're up, Robby."

Medavoy put his clipboard squarely in front of him. The others went on with their coffee or smoking. Pesce fooled with a paperclip. The only supervisor missing was Schroeder from Internal Affairs, but nobody really liked having him nearby anyway. So Medavoy worked at ignoring Easter's frequent derision and tried to put out of his mind that any of these men might be involved in the corruption eating at the department.

"Two major items. The Pacific Security branch in the Del Paso Shopping Center got nailed yesterday. They got two suspects, and it looks like we got one in a wig. Driver's wearing a wig probably. I got to look at the security video this morning."

"What kind of descriptions do you have?" Pesce asked, noting it for his daily meeting with Stevie Wonder later. The other men paused too. Bank robberies were not that common.

"Middle-aged white female for the passenger. For the driver, the guy in the wig, we got a good description from a witness and a sheet from Chino. He's Kenneth James Trask, twenty-eight, blond on brown, about one-fifty to one-sixty. Five-nine. We can put that out now. I'm getting hold of control at Chino and getting his nine-six-nine-bee package up here."

"Medavoy left out the bomb." Easter sat forward in his seat. He still had on the same Hawaiian shirt from the night before and he was curt. "The pukes used a bomb in a shoe box to get the drive-up teller to give up the money."

Pesce pointed his mechanical pencil at Medavoy. "You know what kind of explosive?"

Medavoy shook his head. "Maybe it wasn't a bomb."

"When we catch up to these pukes, you grab the shoe

box," Easter snorted. "You let us know what it is."

"Look, I talked to the witnesses. I know how this guy Trask handled the shoe box. I don't know if he can make a bomb. I'll find out."

"You don't need to be a fucking genius, Medavoy."

"I don't want to put it out that this guy's got an explosive if he doesn't," Medavoy flared. "I don't want to scare the shit out of everybody."

"Hey, I told you once, on your time, guys." Pesce rapped the pencil on the table. "Anything else on your suspect?"

Medavoy avoided Easter's mocking grin. "Yeah. He's doing seven years at Chino off an armed two-eleven and he escaped from work furlough day before yesterday. Beat up a store manager, stole a car that got used at the bank, and he's got a .45," Medavoy glanced at Easter. "And the gun's definite."

Hollenbeck cleared his throat. "My auto burg victim is a .45 slug. Why don't you let me have a copy of your reports. For safety sake."

"I'll give you the damn investigation if you want."

"Copy of the reports is fine."

Samuelian spoke up, "Why did your Chino asshole come all the way up here, Robby?" Unlike the rest of the men, he had a Diet Coke in front of him.

Medavoy shook his head. "Don't know yet."

Pesce pointed. "Find out right away. I don't like cons with guns or bombs running around town." He made another note for his own meeting with Stevie Wonder. Medavoy wanted to say he'd just gotten the reports, the case was only about seventeen hours old, he was doing double duty as acting supervisor. But in the new regime, those explanations didn't count. When Stevie Wonder wanted something to happen, he wanted it at once. People and investigations were like chess pieces, as movable or useful. The Pacific Security investigation was now past due apparently because Pesce exhibited the reflected will of the Chief.

"I got one other item," Medavoy said.

"Everybody listen," Pesce said coolly. "Go ahead, Robby."

"You all probably heard we busted Brian Reilly yesterday and he was real dirty. He's dead on possession, extortion, receiving, and he had a tear gas grenade in his office safe." Medavoy spoke directly and looked at Easter when he stopped.

Easter still rested his head on one hand. He half-smiled. The other supervisors wouldn't look at him. They knew what the tear gas grenade meant and where it had come from.

"What does this bust mean to me, Robby?" Hollenbeck asked the question they all had on their minds.

Medavoy couldn't gloss over it for any of them. The whole stinking problem was going to boil over with Reilly arrested. "Reilly might roll over on some cops who've been helping him. Guys in your details might be named. Even if Reilly doesn't roll over, the DA's got to make his case by naming cops."

"You have names, Robby?" Pesce asked gently, tapping his pencil.

Medavoy took a breath. The question was bound to come. He slid his clipboard toward himself. "Yeah, I do," he admitted. "But I'm not giving them up here."

"If IAD orders you?"

"Is Schroeder going to order me?" Medavoy demanded of Pesce.

At that, Easter snorted, pushing back against the wall in his chair loudly. "I don't believe this fucking act. Medavoy's pissing in his pants to run upstairs and give up every goddamn cop in the department. He's going to make himself a big fucking hero by shooting down all his buddies."

"Motherfucking son of a bitch!" Medavoy was on his feet in rage. "I'm not taking any more bullshit from you!" He pushed toward Easter.

Pesce shot to his feet, the wrinkled tan face broken in anger. "Sit down! Both of you, that's it. Sit down and shut the fuck up!"

Easter was standing, beckoning, the half-smile fixed on his face. The other men shrank back as far as they could to the wall.

Hollenbeck waved Medavoy down, as though a guest had upset dinner.

Medavoy knew he was only an instant away from jumping across the table. He would be justified, with witnesses, nothing dirty or vile like Menefee's secret blows. But Pesce had given him a direct order and there was no telling who Stevie Wonder would back. He slowly sat down. Easter stayed up.

"You guys jerk off here with Medavoy. You listen to his shit. I got better things to do," he announced, striding from the room. "Later, Robby. Okay?"

Pesce called after him, then threw his pencil at the door as it slammed shut. "Shit! Okay, now everybody get this once and get it good. Not one goddamn word about Reilly and any bad cops. No memos, no leaks, no comments, nothing to anybody. Not to any asshole drinking-buddy reporters you know. I'm speaking for the Chief and he's the only one speaking for the department. I don't care who's a son of a bitch." He stared at Medavoy. "You're handling this on your own. Clear?"

Medavoy didn't blink.

"Clear, goddamnit?" Pesce repeated.

"I got it," Medavoy said whitely. It was like battling your own arms and legs to keep this thing in control, not strike out. He sat back in his chair, arms folded.

"You keep a lid on your detail, Robby. I swear to God, your guys are going to eat shit for the next ten years if I hear anything about Reilly or bad cops coming from them."

"Don't worry about my guys." Medavoy's stare was hard. "My guys are okay. My guys took Reilly."

Pesce sat down, breathing heavily. He brusquely brushed his hair back. "Pencil," he stuck his hand out to Samuelian, who hastily put one in it. "You've got to brief the Chief on this today. Clear?"

"When?"

Pesce scribbled. "Right after he gets out of the City Council meeting. Maybe ten, ten-thirty."

"How about right now? I don't want to wait."

Pesce bore down on the pencil, glancing irritatedly at the relentless stopwatch. Time gone because of people's emotions. "The Chief's in a meeting now. Important meeting."

Medavoy swallowed slowly, took the clipboard up. He didn't know who to rely on in this room. He didn't know if there was one man who would back him up when the time came.

"I've got important things to do, too," he said. He left without looking back.

Cold water on the face, hands cupped, bringing it up, washing off the grit and sourness of the supervisors' meeting, Medavoy splashed water in his eyes again, then shook his head with dissipating anger, and wiped his face with a paper towel. Somewhere, down the hall from the second floor men's room, he heard a high-pitched, agitated male voice, "No, no, the jeans are my brother's, dude. The smack's mine. I want my smack back, Jack," then cops' voices rising over it.

When he looked up, Zaragoza stood by the men's room door. He was in the shirt-sleeves, a thin black tie, like a bandit or pit boss at a casino.

"What's up, Jimmy?" Medavoy finished drying his face. He felt badly about losing control at the meeting. Someday, he thought, you'll let it out only when you want to. Not lash out like the old man did, not let somebody provoke you.

"Nothing much. You out of your meeting?" Zaragoza was craning his head around, looking everywhere.

"I'm out. Easter and I're going a few rounds."

"Yeah, right." Zaragoza had started looking into each stall, banging the doors open.

Medavoy picked up his clipboard. He needed to get hold of the VCR and watch the security tape right away, then see what the Crime Lab had done with the peanut shells and tire marks.

"How'd the Reilly cleanup go after I left?" Medavoy came over to Zaragoza, checking the last stall.

"Oh, good, good. You got a report. He didn't cop out to anything, went quiet. I booked all the evidence except the grenade, sent that over to the Sheriff's Department. They got that bomb-proof evidence locker, we don't."

Medavoy walked toward the door, amused at Zaragoza's odd behavior. The men's room was old, with rusted pipes and ancient porcelain fixtures green-stained and cracked. The window was permanently painted shut and the pipes rattled abruptly.

"Reilly's not talking unless the DA cuts some deal."

"They don't have to deal."

"I bet you everybody wants dirty cops more than a dirty lawyer, Jimmy."

"Hey, wait a second, Robby."

Medavoy paused. Zaragoza turned the old lock on the door. "Something going on?" Medavoy asked.

"Yeah. You ever know a crank dealer named Ramon Trebayo?"

"He have any other names?"

"I haven't seen his rap yet."

"Never heard of him." Medavoy dangled the clipboard.

"Okay, Robby, this Ramon guy's over at Santa Maria Community. He's got like a really bad busted jaw. He gets dumped off at the hospital late last night, nobody gets any good look at the car."

"So?"

"Soon as they wire up his fucking jaw, this Ramon guy's making noises for paper and pen, he got to write something. He's still kind of out of it, but he's writing out that a cop named Medavoy broke his jaw."

Medavoy chuckled. "What? I don't even know the guy."

"He's said it again this morning. Now he's really specific. Robby Medavoy, Santa Maria city cop, tried to shake him down, get his crank money. Then Robby Medavoy broke his jaw." Zaragoza bit his lower lip. "You know what it sounds like."

"Like Baladarez." Medavoy was sharp, cold at the implication. "Like a repeat. Anybody have any cases with this guy?"

"Narcotics doesn't. I asked just now. I don't know about anybody else." Zaragoza chewed his lip worriedly. "This asshole's setting you up, Robby."

Medavoy shook his head, leaned against the old sink. Overhead, the rows of rusty pipes rattled furiously as someone used water upstairs. "Not this guy, Jimmy. Who's he? Who am I? Somebody else's rigging this."

"Maybe because of Reilly?"

"I think so. We got Easter and his jackasses asking about me, we take Reilly yesterday, Easter shows up outside Jane's place last night."

"Jesus Christ," Zaragoza said. "That son of a bitch. You going to have to say where you were. You got to lay that out."

Medavoy knew he could only provide himself with an alibi by involving Jane directly in a department scandal. In order to clear himself of an extortion and assault charge, he would have to admit he was violating department regulations by living with Jane. If the whole thing became public, and Reilly's continuing legal course made that almost unavoidable, she would face ridicule at least. Unwed mother and brutal cop. She might not be able to work at the courthouse.

"I'm not bringing her in," he said. "No way."

"Ask her, Jesus, Robby. You got to ask her."

"How'd you find out about this bullshit so fast?"

Zaragoza half-grinned. "Nikitas in IAD told me. We're old pals. We fucked up cases together in Auto Burg."

"Tell him thanks," Medavoy said gratefully. "I don't want to burn him by doing it." It was a tremendous favor Zaragoza's

friend had done by revealing a complaint, made in strict confidence, to Internal Affairs. It was a dismissible offense, but
like the car wash Mutt did, the department functioned less
by rules than their breach.

"I got more bad news." Zaragoza was utterly serious. He
lowered his voice.

Medavoy stepped from the sink. "What else?"

"IAD not only has the complaint, some tight asshole at
the hospital phoned it in this morning. Right now Schroeder's
in with Stevie Wonder."

"He wasn't at the supervisors' meeting."

"Yeah. And Stevie Wonder's asked for your personnel file,
Robby. He's meeting with Schroeder and he wants your sheet."

Medavoy tried to think it through quickly. It sounded as
though the Chief was personally taking an interest in this crank
dealer's complaint. Maybe Pesce's dramatic command to brief
Stevie Wonder on the Reilly bust was no more than a trick to put
him before an impromptu review board of the Chief and IAD.
Maybe they hoped he'd confess right away and settle the issue
cleanly for them. Medavoy couldn't think of any reason why
Stevie Wonder would suddenly want his personnel file except
this complaint. They had only met a few times over the years,
casual conversations in the hall, Stevie weighted with computer
printouts, sometimes in a razor-sharp creased uniform, off to
pander to the City Council. Then once at length last year, Stevie
Wonder asking him detailed questions about the river rescue.
Were you scared? Did you think about it first or just do it? What
happened in the water? Would you do it again? The questions
posed with professional indifference, a copy's ready stock in trade,
but Stevie Wonder looked just like people in the supermarket
or on the street who stopped him because they'd seen the story
on TV. Medavoy thought it was hero worship.

But Medavoy didn't know what went on in Stevie Wonder's
mind beyond that he had a sole ambition to be Chief of Police
and probably wished the world was a clock.

Medavoy didn't even know if Stevie Wonder remembered pinning a medal on him a year ago.

Someone tugged at the men's room door. The old wooden door and its frosted glass shook.

"Let's get out of here, Jimmy," Medavoy said.

"What're you going to do?"

"Wait for IAD to come and get me." He grinned without meaning it.

"Jesus, Robby, you got to ask Jane. She's neat. She'll go with you all the way."

"That's why I won't ask her."

Zaragoza smoothed back his slick black hair. He was deeply sensitive to any changes in the department's equilibrium, especially since his own roasting at the hands of the Supreme Court. He hated unresolved stress problems.

Medavoy unlocked the door. "I'm taking Jane on a picnic today. I'll talk to her." He only said it to relax Zaragoza a little.

A detective from Burglary barged past Medavoy, eyeing him and Zaragoza with annoyance. "We all got to use this place, fellas," he said tartly, heading for a urinal.

The hall forked, on one side was Auto Burg, Robbery the other. From the lobby below came catcalls and whistles, echoing up the marble stairwell. Two teenage girls in dingy white blouses and jeans sat outside Auto Burg. They smoked and kicked their feet.

Zaragoza tugged Medavoy's coat lightly. Ahead was the public window in Robbery, like a cheap doctor's office, with a sliding frosted-glass partition hiding a civilian clerk and metal chairs on the linoleum floor.

"You got two visitors, Robby. I'm warning you."

"This day's got to get better. Who's waiting?"

Zaragoza pointed. "Little Lynell. She's hot about something she left out of her robbery report. She's got to see you."

Medavoy groaned. The young woman called him three or four times a day, for a week now, about recovering property stolen from her when three men, who she claimed were strangers, burst into her apartment. She wore star-shaped earrings and smoked clove cigarettes. She said she was a witch.

Medavoy knew he couldn't avoid anything today. He walked on. "Who else?" he asked.

"A guy from Chino. He's got a bunch of records on their fugitive for your bank deal."

"He got up here fast. He must've been driving since three in the morning," Medavoy said admiringly. At least he could plunge into the bank robbery investigation before somebody came tramping down from the fourth floor and summoned him to Stevie Wonder's presence.

"He's not only got records you're going to love, he's got letters. They got letters from this guy's cell. Some woman was writing to him. They're porno."

Medavoy had already seen Lynell, dressed in a floor-length earthen-colored robe, legs crossed, clove-scented smoke mephitically coiled around her from the cigarette she held.

"You round up a TV and the VCR for me, would you, Jimmy? Get Gef, too. I want him and this Chino guy to watch the bank security tape with me."

Lynell looked up, eyes slightly unfocused. She smiled at him.

"Easter ain't getting away with it," Zaragoza said, the unresolved setup bothering him obviously.

Medavoy walked by Lynell, past the other people waiting.

"I tell you what it comes down to, Jimmy. I'm going to have to get him before he gets me."

TWENTY

MEDAVOY, GEFFEN, ZARAGOZA, and the deputy assistant warden from Chino stood around a stolen TV on its padlocked cart in the Property Room in the basement. There were no windows in the room, except for slits cut in the stone walls at six feet high, which gave a perfect and useless glimpse of shoes and ankles on the sidewalk outside.

"Is it Trask?" Medavoy asked. He rewound the Pacific Security Bank security videotape for a second look and coughed slightly when the deputy assistant warden shot an agitated cloud of cigar smoke by him.

"That is the little asshole. For sure," said Bud Corrigan, the deputy assistant warden. He bit down on his cigar. He had a gray crew cut and wore khaki work clothes. "I'm going to bust his butt when I get him back."

"Okay. Watch it once more. Tell me anything you see."

To one side of them, Zaragoza whooped. He had been reading the letters Corrigan brought from Trask's cell. "Wait till you read this, Robby. This lady's great, she wants to ball this guy until his dick falls off."

Corrigan grunted at the news. "They're all like that, pal. She and the little asshole been writing porno back and forth for about a year now."

"Watch the TV," Medavoy directed. The ghostly, streaked black-and-white images twisted and flowed again.

"It looks like a bomb to me," Geffen said. He stood separate from them, near the door, arms folded and tense.

"Me, too. Problem is, I don't know beans about explosives." Medavoy stared at the shoe box, coiled wires, intricate mechanism shoved up toward the camera. In the right-hand corner of the picture, a digital display flicked off seconds. The whole robbery took about forty-five seconds. Very smooth. Very focused, he thought. No unnecessary running around, shouting, waving guns. Right to the point.

"You can make a bomb out of anything," Corrigan said. "You come down to Chino with me, I show you bombs made out of film emulsion, match heads, lighter fluid, one from a damn magazine's shiny paper."

Medavoy nodded. "Trask smart enough to do that? Could he put one together like that?"

"Trask's a little asshole thinks he's a big asshole." Corrigan rummaged through a thick stack of papers he'd brought, laid on the metal shelf beside him. "See this here evaluation they did at Vacaville? The shrinks gave him an MMPI; say he's 'dull-normal intelligence.' You like this one. The shrink at Vacaville says there's only one mitigating factor for this asshole. He's got 'soft, doelike eyes.' We made copies of that," he puffed furiously, "they got it on bulletin boards in every police department in Riverside County."

"Maybe he got one from somebody," Medavoy said. "He didn't make it himself."

"He could've made a fake," Geffen added. "How smart's

he got to be for that?"

Corrigan shook his head, held out his cigar. "That little sucker he's holding there looks damn real to me. Trask couldn't do that to save his life. That's what I'm telling you."

"He dumb enough to carry a real bomb around?" Medavoy pointed out what Jane had suggested in the car. He rewound the tape again.

"He's dumb enough," Corrigan said.

Medavoy didn't add that Trask had been clever about getting himself put into the work furlough program. He knew how to work the system and make it easier to escape.

Medavoy stared at the brief tape again, hoping answers would miraculously appear. "Who's that with him?" He pointed at the TV.

"Can't make her out. Little asshole keeps getting in the way."

"Don't know her at all?"

"Looks a little like his lawyer, this gal Beaufort. The one's been writing him." Corrigan gestured at Zaragoza, still entranced by the letters he read.

"Some lawyer," Zaragoza said appreciatively.

"You have anything about her in the package?" Medavoy asked Corrigan, pointing at the stack of files.

"Don't think so. Look, I come up here with this nine-six-nine-bee bullshit myself so you'd have it all right away. I want to get him back like yesterday. I get a real black eye when someone walks away from my work furlough detail." He flipped through the papers. "All I got is about Trask. Juvenile ADW, two of them, knife fights in high school, grand theft person, purse snatch, then that Sambo's armed. He had couple beefs at Vacaville before we got him. Two guys jumped him. One's the Archangel Gabriel, he thinks Trask's Satan. The other one," Corrigan shook his head amazed, "likes him. Trask beat the shit out of both of them."

"This is not a guy who comes up with any kind of bank robbery," Medavoy said. "Gef? That right?"

Geffen, back against the door, nodded. He watched the snow on the TV after the tape. "He's a basic puke. No brainer."

Corrigan apparently had gotten excited by the reports. He started reading aloud abruptly. "He's moderately antisocial, got some sexual difficulties. I love this shit. He's never going to 'in all probability form meaningful relationships with women or contribute productively to the community.' You believe they get paid for writing that crap?"

"Jimmy, you got an address for that lawyer?" Medavoy asked.

Zaragoza checked several of the envelopes he held. "Lemon Street, Riverside."

"Well, I'll tell you, Bud, Trask's got some relationship with some woman here in town," Medavoy said. He knew Corrigan meant well and the long drive north to bring these documents was quite a sacrifice. He didn't, though, think much of Corrigan's judgment or counsel. "What bugs me is why Trask came here to rob a bank. Our banks aren't special."

He rewound and played the tape a fourth time, freezing a frame of Trask, mouth distorted, hand out, taking money from the teller.

"He's got a wife. Got a kid, too," Corrigan said.

"Where?"

"Sacramento. Trask's from there back a while. But, he don't care about them."

"The wife care about him? That her on the tape?"

"Nah. She never visited. Never wrote. I called her soon's I knew he's gone and she just told me to tell him to go to hell and stay there."

Geffen strolled to the TV. "He could be passing through to Sacramento to see his kid. I could see a guy doing that."

Corrigan shook his head, puffed heavily on the fat cigar. "He's been keeping it a real secret. I talk to Trask, you know, shoot the shit when he comes back from the plumbing store, ask how's the job going. Never talked about his family. Period. He's not what you'd call a family man." He grinned at the gag.

Medavoy shut off the TV, took the tape out of the VCR and boxed it. "He's not going for his kid, Gef. He came here specifically."

"How come?" Geffen asked.

"He wants something here. He and this woman, whoever she is, they dump a car after the robbery. They had another car. He's got some moves laid out."

"Or somebody did it for him."

"We got to find his Santa Maria connection or we're in big trouble," Medavoy said. He waved to the civilian clerk, solitary in the midst of metal storage cabinets packed with jumbled tagged evidence, cases alive and dead. Stained clothes, guns, knives, bats, batteries, radios, TVs, wallets, purses in disorder as if washed up.

"We're done," Medavoy said to the clerk. "Thanks for the room." He grunted, hefting Trask's bulky prison files.

Zaragoza, still holding the letters, muttered, "That little shit. He wouldn't let me take a TV out of here. Said there's no sign-out form submitted in advance."

"We all got our paper," Medavoy said, leading them out. He noticed Geffen trailing, preoccupied, behind them. He turned to Corrigan. "You staying in town?"

"Got to go right back, my friend. You got everything you need from me."

"The connection's somebody here Trask wanted to see." Medavoy turned to Zaragoza, still poring over the letters and shaking his head in amusement. "Jimmy, you want to call the lawyer and find out when she last heard from Trask? She might have a line on where he's going."

"Lawyer's not going to talk to me," Zaragoza said.

"Ask her anyway. She can surrender him, tell her. We won't come get him."

Going up the stairs, past the double-doors that hid the Special Weapons Unit from view, Medavoy asked Corrigan, "Trask have many friends? Anybody you'd watch?"

"Usual asshole crowd. Nobody I'd rate higher than him."

"How about cell mates?"

Corrigan dropped his cigar and ground it out on the steel stairs, pausing to let Zaragoza and Geffen go by. "He had three. One transferred. Made it to Mule Creek, the new prison. One moved to another tier. One released."

"Who got released?"

"Weird little guy, David Lisio. He's in on some forgery. Lot of shit about him making weapons. He and Trask were kind of pals."

"When'd Lisio get out?"

"Week ago, I don't remember exactly. That sure wasn't him on the videotape." Corrigan started up the stairs again.

Medavoy awkwardly shifted the files and reports under his arm. Drop it and Trask would be spread all over the concrete floor.

"How about Lisio making a bomb?"

Corrigan nodded. "Sure as hell could. Smart little guy. Very weird, hardly talked to anybody."

"Give me somebody who knows where Lisio got released," Medavoy said when they were on the landing.

Corrigan was effusive. "I do whatever I can for you, Robby. I know he's got a parole agent assigned in LA. He's supposed to report there. How about I get his PA to call you?"

"Thanks. I'd be kind of interested to see what this little guy's been doing the last week." Medavoy huffed as Corrigan held the door open for him.

"She moved," Zaragoza told Medavoy when he came back to Robbery after seeing Corrigan off.

"Where?"

"I called the State Bar. They gave me an address here. She's working for Reilly."

Medavoy snorted. "Give me a fucking break."

"Swear to God, Robby. Carol Beaufort left Riverside about four months ago and came up here and Reilly hired her. She's a criminal law specialist."

Geffen, at his desk, finished his one cup of coffee for the day. He was still a little in training. "What other kind of lawyer's a crook like Reilly going to hire?"

Only Masuda, head down and studying reports on his desk, ignored the chatter. He sat under a clownish picture of dancing pigs advertising the annual police football game.

Medavoy felt a surge of excitement. "She's in on it. Trask didn't end up in the same city as his lawyer by accident."

"You want to bet Reilly's started into bank robbery?" Geffen said, slipping his cup into a desk drawer. Medavoy thought he looked worse than yesterday and wished there was some time soon to find out why.

"Jesus," he slapped his hands, "wouldn't that be great? Nail his ass on a bank robbery and he goes away for ten years, no questions."

"We missed her yesterday," Zaragoza pointed out. "Remember Reilly making all that noise about her?"

"Yeah, I do. You get a home address for her?" Medavoy asked.

"They wouldn't give it out."

Geffen groaned. "You don't let them think they have a choice, Jimmy."

"I'll call Reilly's office," Medavoy grinned. "They'll love to hear from me again."

He went to his desk behind Masuda. Zaragoza and Geffen started to argue about who sounded tougher on the phone. Masuda raised his head, as if coming up for air and gently asked them to be quiet.

Medavoy was glad civilians didn't get to hear this kind of thing. It did sound like a boys' clubhouse instead of a major crime detail. He rapped his desk. "Before I forget, there's going to be some strong fallout from the Reilly bust." He briefly told them about the scene at the supervisors' meeting.

Masuda puffed out his cheeks. He looked like he was trying to flex them. Geffen and Zaragoza frowned.

"So watch yourselves," Medavoy went on. "Somebody wants you to do something, check it out with me. Check it out with the bureau captain."

"How about IAD? Check with them?" Geffen said softly, glancing at the posters of men with machine guns on the walls.

"Anybody wants anything out of the ordinary, come to me."

Masuda emptied his cheeks. He was solemn, formidable. "Are they trying to nail us for nailing Reilly?"

"Yeah," Medavoy acknowledged, "they might be."

Geffen rolled up his shirt-sleeves. In disgust he said, "Great loyalty around here. Great department we have now."

"Gef, it's the way the world goes," Medavoy said.

Zaragoza, with a conspiratorial wink said, "We look out for you, too, Robby."

"I appreciate it, Jimmy. We all watch each other, it'll be okay. Stevie Wonder's got to do something to clean it up soon."

"He's got to clean up the Special Weapons guys," Geffen said. "We know where it stinks around here."

"It won't be Easter's guys alone. You get a funny request, looks too good, back off." Medavoy got himself another cup of coffee. The others sat for a moment, thinking, then went back to work. Future problems were always put to one side. The immediate ones, the reports and investigations requests, calls that had to be made, were too demanding for anything else.

Like my problems, he thought. Like what Easter might be doing and what IAD is doing right now, the captain upstairs with my file.

So he turned to the one problem he could do something about. He sat down at his desk, splashing a little coffee onto the plastic cover on his blotter. A brown pool formed on pictures of Jane and Johnathan blowing out candles on a birthday cake, a formal studio portrait of Jane. He swabbed the coffee off with a paper napkin.

The department was fully alive at that hour, typewriters clicking, phones ringing, the teletype chattering and stopping.

Medavoy got Reilly's number off the arrest report and started to dial.

"You can't avoid me."

He looked up in surprise.

"I've been sitting outside for hours and hours." Lynell the witch tapped her foot and glared frostily at him and he thought she was silently hexing him.

"I'm not avoiding you. I forgot you."

"Well, I got some important stuff to tell you."

Medavoy knew the others were watching, and he'd probably start laughing if he saw any of them. He kept his eyes down. "Tell me what?"

She gathered her robe up and flopped into the pastel-green city chair by Medavoy's desk. Medavoy briefly looked up, saw Geffen's shoulders shaking and Masuda made a noise like escaping steam.

"I have to add something to my report."

"What?"

"Something else they took from my apartment." She brought out a clove cigarette.

"Don't smoke that thing."

"You're into health?" she asked, amazed.

"I ate five pounds of clove-spiked ham when I was a kid. What got taken you didn't tell me in your first report?"

She traced a finger on his desk. Medavoy was having a very hard time keeping a straight face. "I know I told you about the TV, my stereo, the chairs, my money in the coffee can. But, they also took a box." She used her hands, "About so big, so high, okay? It's black. It's got this lock and it's got my name painted on the side."

"About the size of a foot locker?"

"It is a foot locker."

"Anything distinctive about it?"

Medavoy wrote. She cleared her throat. "My name's on it. My star sign. Pisces."

"Okay. What's in the box?"

"Does it matter?"

"It'll help me find who took it."

"You got to find it right away," Lynell's voice was panicky.

"Why's that?"

"It's my devil box."

Another explosive sound came from Masuda. He coughed rapidly and left the room. Zaragoza stared at Lynell.

"Your devil box." Medavoy, after the upheaval with Easter and everything else, tried to write this down on the contact report form, failed and tried again not to laugh. "What is your devil box?"

"It's got like animal hair, my book of chants, some mirrors, things I found in the woods." She avoided his stare. "Private things. It's really, really important I get it back in three days."

"You keep any dope in it, Lynell? I got to know, you know, I'm a cop."

"I do not use artificial drugs."

Zaragoza interrupted, "Can't you sort of fly around and find the box? Don't witches fly?"

"I do not need this prejudice," Lynell said. "This is my property and I have to have it in three days."

Medavoy knew he'd hate himself for asking. He held his pen over the report form. "What happens in three days?"

She inhaled deeply, letting it out in a malodorous gust. "The vernal equinox comes in three days. There are certain forces you don't understand. If I don't have my devil box back for it," she threw up her arms, the robe sliding down over white, skinny arms, "we might all just forget it. Forget the whole world."

He nodded slowly. He picked up a red pen. He circled a date three times on his wall calendar. "You see what I just did?"

She watched, wary. "Does that mean something?"

"The triple red circle is the most heavy symbol for a cop. I can't say yes, I can't say no, but maybe you'll get the box back now."

She nodded. Zaragoza nodded and Geffen shook his head.

"We all have forces to command," she said, getting up. "Thank you."

"And thank you for not smoking, Lynell," Medavoy said as she left, robe swirling around her thin body.

"You are some bullshitter, Robby," Zaragoza said admiringly.

"I get a lot of practice around here," Medavoy said. He could get back to the business at hand. He dialed Reilly's office.

He spoke, listened, his face set, then momentarily surprised. Zaragoza and Geffen argued again and Masuda returned, giggling and asking if the witch was gone.

So now things get interesting, Medavoy thought, hanging up. He got his coat from the hangers by the coffee machine. "Gef, you got an hour?"

"If you want."

"We're taking a drive to Reilly's office."

"Talk to the Beaufort gal? Or maybe Reilly's got a civil suit against us?" Masuda asked. He and Zaragoza could read nothing else in Medavoy's still-surprised expression.

"Nope. Somebody just beat the shit out of him. I want to have a witness along when I see him."

TWENTY-ONE

PARKED OUTSIDE of the emerald tower where Brian Reilly had his office were SMPD squad cars, a fire truck, and an ambulance. When Medavoy and Geffen arrived, a harried cop was trying to keep the downtown traffic moving briskly past the building. Everybody wanted to see what was going on.

The ambulance, lights still flashing, pleased Medavoy. It hadn't left yet, which meant Emergency Services in the city didn't have a much better response time than the cops.

"Why the fire truck?" Geffen asked as they went inside.

"I don't know."

"They always dispatch a fire truck. I never knew why."

"Cover all your bases."

"So you could send a garbage truck, too."

"I would."

The corridor outside Reilly's office was crowded as Medavoy and Geffen shouldered their way through. Every other office had emptied out. Three TV camera crews pushed everyone

239

else aside with snapped, flat commands. Two cops stood at the closed doors of the office.

"I got nothing. I just got here." Medavoy raised his hands to the cameras and microphones that sought him out. He smiled because he had learned it was best. They took anything else as blood in the water and fought over it. A smile was nothing.

"What a bunch of assholes," Geffen muttered.

Even though he tried to get past them, shrugged away their questions, they persisted, pressing closer. "Does this have something to do with his arrest?" a woman yelled.

"Let me talk to him."

"He's unconscious, Robby." He didn't know a lot of reporters, but since he had achieved some celebrity, they all called him by his first name; he was used to that.

He motioned for the cops, who held the doors open. The camera crews strained forward, people pressed to the walls, complaining.

"You think it was one his clients?"

"We heard it's a dope deal. True?"

"Is Reilly in a corruption investigation?"

Then, a voice shouted, "Was it crooked cops, Robby?"

He turned suddenly, trying to see who asked the question in the confusion. Only a gallery of faces, like they were stacked on each other. Geffen had gone inside the office and waited for him, the room cluttered with trash bags, books, files on the floor. Cops worked amid the disorder without excitement or perplexity. It's our one strength, Medavoy thought, pushing his way into the door and having it closed again and guarded.

Geffen disgustedly gestured at the stirred babble outside. "I hate that bullshit."

He looked around for the on-scene supervisor. Someone was directing the investigation. He tried to calm Geffen down, too. He was flying off the handle far too quickly. Perhaps it was what Masuda said, the job had finally gotten to him.

He went to the inner office. Hollenbeck fastidiously put cushions back on the sofa while two ambulance attendants cinched Reilly—torn shirt, swollen bandaged face—onto a stretcher.

"What're you doing here?" Medavoy asked, stepping out of the way of the busy attendants.

"Hello, Robert. Hello, Gef. I got the call first."

"The call went to Homicide?"

"My first word said he's dead and gone." He pointed at the noisily breathing Reilly being bounced a little on the stretcher.

Medavoy looked at Reilly. He was unconscious, pallid, as inert and battered as dough before baking. The attendants were a small woman and a short man. Medavoy reckoned them against the bulk of the fat man.

"Can you get him out?"

"Sure we can," the woman answered. "Lift. Lift. Lift," she ordered the other attendant.

Medavoy and Hollenbeck pressed back as the two grunted, raising the stretcher up and forcing it at an angle through the inner-office doorway. The woman began to dip, the fat man groaning from his bloody and bandaged face. "Catch it, catch it," the woman called frantically.

The attendant at Reilly's feet swore, the stretcher thudded to the carpet. "Let's stand him up," he suggested.

"You want a hand?" Medavoy offered.

Geffen started forward, always ready to go the extra step.

"We got him," the woman waved Geffen back.

"They got him," Geffen folded his arms.

Medavoy heard Hollenbeck grunt as the stretcher was upended, Reilly's head dropping to his chest. Then, with shuffling little steps, much pushing and huffing, the two attendants forced the stretcher sideways through the doorway, banging its upper grips on the top of the door frame.

"There's another lawyer and secretary who work here,"

Medavoy said to Hollenbeck. The stretcher disappeared into the reception room.

"Only one here, Robert," Hollenbeck stepped gingerly over a bowl of mints spilled over the carpet.

"Who?"

"His secretary. She's back in the supply room. Very talkative." He turned to Geffen. "You're very quiet."

"I'm in shock," he joked badly. He looked away, embarrassed.

"I'm looking for the other lawyer," Medavoy said. "Got another case and she's in it."

They walked back to the supply room, passing fingerprint dusters, a photographer, and several cops who seemed to have nothing much to do, but wandered back and forth cackling to each other. It was not a neat crime scene, but Medavoy had never known Hollenbeck to run a clean, tidy scene.

"You put in the call for me, didn't you?" Medavoy asked.

"Yes. I didn't think anybody else would notify you."

"It's my case. Reilly's mine."

"Oh, Robert, we both know what's happening in the department under the great leader. Suspicion. Paranoia. Printouts."

Geffen laughed. "She's in there." The sight struck him funny.

Medavoy paused. Nielda sat on a pile of accordion files, pointing again and again at the incident report sheet a cop was writing on. He knelt beside her. She was disheveled, hair tangled, blouse shifted halfway around her waist. "R as in Roy, R. R. I spelled it for you. Beaufort. Beaufort."

"Are you all right, ma'am?" Medavoy stood in front of her.

"All right? All right? How could I be all right?"

"Are you hurt?"

The cop shook his head, stopped when he saw her dumb hate.

"They tied me up, they kicked me, they threw me in here on top of poor Brian." She shook. "My God. Poor, poor Brian."

Geffen asked, "You want anything?"

"You bet I do," she blazed.

Hollenbeck cleared his throat and whispered to Medavoy, "I'll leave this with you now. It is your case. Don't let the few bad ones in the department get you down."

"Thanks. I know it isn't everybody, John."

"Enough said." Hollenbeck patted Geffen and marched out.

"There has been trouble, trouble ever since you came here yesterday. Do you know that?" She snapped at Medavoy.

"Was that Carol Beaufort you were just talking about?"

"My God. Who else?"

"Where is she now? Did she come in today?"

"Come in? Come in?" Nielda was wild-eyed, from the cop beside her, up to Medavoy and Geffen. "What do you think I was telling him?"

"Tell me."

"She came in here with that little pal of hers and beat the hell out of poor Brian and tied me up and kicked me in here and why aren't you doing something?" She rose partway off the accordion files. Stacked around her on shelves were legal pads, ribbons, pens, legal forms. Medavoy noticed that her wrists were red and he hoped whoever found her hadn't cut the cord or rope so as to destroy the knots. They were instructive about their makers.

Geffen made notes on a small notepad. "You want to move out of here?" he politely asked Nielda.

"Is it safe?"

"What do you mean?"

She looked fearful. "Is he gone? Have they taken him away?"

Medavoy asked, "The guy who was with Beaufort?"

"No. Brian. I don't want to see him again." She shuddered, pointed at a pinkish patch on her leg. "That's him."

"He's gone. They took him to the hospital." Medavoy held out a hand. "Come on out. We'll clean you off."

"I don't think so."

He recognized the signs of delayed shock, much worse than the teller at Pacific Security. Nielda was about ready to go completely over the edge. He saw that Geffen knew too.

"The longer you stay there, the harder it gets to get that off," he pointed at her leg and wouldn't say "blood." "Believe me. We can do something about it right now."

"Harder?"

"Almost impossible. It sets."

She shuddered again and slowly got off the files, mincingly, as if stepping in something unpleasant. "Wash it off. Wash it off."

Medavoy took her hand and led her to Reilly's bathroom. The aftershave, electric razor, electric toothbrush waiting to freshen their master for his next court appearance. It struck Medavoy as poignantly futile.

"See? I have had experience with things like this," he said casually to Nielda as he used a washcloth to gently sponge off the dried foamy blood. She watched intently, like he was performing surgery on her. "Comes right off. No problem."

"It does," she said wonderingly. "I thought it wouldn't ever."

"There. It's gone. Feel it? Like it was never there."

She smiled at him gratefully, patting her leg. "It tingled before. Now it doesn't."

Geffen helped her sit down on the sofa. She coughed, flushed, stared at the cops who walked in, were waved out by Medavoy.

"Do you know why Beaufort brought this guy with her today?"

Nielda shook her head. "He came out with a gun. He shouted, my God, so loud, made me come back to Brian's office." She looked around her, the upturned chair behind his desk, the blood spots on the carpet and the wall.

"What did Beaufort say?"

"He was her little friend. One of her little friends, typical for her, some guy she'd picked up and brought over here and they beat us and tied us up." She shuddered again.

Medavoy patted her hand like he was an old friend. "Take

it easy. It's fine now. Who told you what to do?"

"He did. Always shouting."

"How'd you get Brian back to the supply room?"

"Her little friend shouted at me, I picked up his shoulders."
She looked at her hands, twisting her face. "Carol took his
feet. We dragged him and he kept moaning."

"Tell me what he looked like." He kept his hand on hers.
Geffen stood guard at the door, keeping it open enough to
see what was going on in the next room, but making sure no
one disturbed them.

"Younger than her. Always younger for her. Twenty or
thirty, I think. She likes that."

Medavoy had a two-year-old picture of Trask from the file
Corrigan had left. He held it out to the woman. Her mouth
whitened.

"Do you recognize him?"

"Her little friend."

"She call him by name?"

"He would've shot us. I could see that."

"Did she call him any name? Tell me." He soothed.

"Kenny. She's complaining how heavy Brian was. Kenny, he's
too heavy. Let's go," Nielda mimicked bitterly. "Then he used
the extension cord in the supply room to tie me to Brian," she
looked at her leg again, "and he lay on me and I couldn't move."

Medavoy put the picture back in his pocket and nodded
to Geffen. "Do you have an address for Carol? You know
where she lives?"

"You bet I do." The old hatred flared again, bursting
past her fear and shock. She wobbled off the sofa and went
to Reilly's devastated desk. "It's in the book. I put it there.
Brian always said she's the best, she does the best work. Like
I didn't know what was going on here."

"What?" Geffen asked curiously.

"He's sleeping with her!" she said explosively, brandishing
a blue-bound address book. "That's why Brian hired her."

"Oh," Geffen said.

"She's at 5643 Eugene Avenue, you know, across the river. I bet they've gone. She's paying Brian back, getting her little friend to do her dirty work."

Medavoy got up, writing down the address. He smiled at her reassuringly. "Would you like someone to take you home?"

Nielda frowned, looking around. "I can't stay here. No. No."

"I'll get a ride for you."

He spoke to one of the cops in the next room, heard Nielda say something to Geffen behind him and then, "She's got to be punished for this!" starting to sob in great, rough gulps.

"It's no payback, Robby," Geffen said as they went through the lobby. A few hardy reporters trailed after them, but Medavoy's pace and peremptory dismissal kept the rest waiting for something better back at Reilly's office.

"It's no payback for screwing her. Maybe it's for the Pacific Security deal."

"Reilly and Beaufort set it up with the puke from Chino?"

"It works for me right now."

"You got to read some of her letters to Trask, Robby. They're like what you write in high school at your horniest."

"Not my high school." He nudged Geffen. "I forgot. You went to Holy Martyrs."

"The first wife was more frustrating."

"Shit, this makes my life a lot easier. Either she or Reilly came up with this bomb scam," he said wonderingly to Geffen, even though they had lived in Santa Maria all their lives. "This is a damn small town."

He was astonished, even after twelve years as a cop, how a bank robbery, phony bomb, prison fugitive, crooked cops and lawyers had gotten confounded together and drawn him in. It was possible that Trask's former cell mate was involved or someone unknown, but it was certain Carol Beaufort united them all and getting to her would simplify things.

He checked his watch. Only ninety minutes, maybe a little more, before he had to see Stevie Wonder and find out what kind of snare had been laid for him with the crank dealer and Easter.

Call Jane, he thought. Beg off on the picnic, beg off on picking her up, too. She'd have to get a ride from somebody. Make sure to tell her Mutt would look at her car. Medavoy didn't enjoy the convolutions his day had suddenly developed. Maybe he could take her to dinner, something special downtown, to make it up.

They were at the car. "Call in and see if we got anybody closer to Eugene Avenue. Get a lid on that address," Medavoy said, getting behind the wheel, starting their lights on the unmarked police car.

The Emergency Services ambulance was still parked in front of the emerald tower, lights revolving, the two attendants jerking the stretcher with Reilly on it back and forth, trying to get it into the ambulance. A crowd watched, traffic slowed, the cop in the street energetically waved Medavoy into traffic.

Geffen picked up the radio mike as Medavoy angled swiftly past the construction sites banging and booming, the skyscrapers arcing overhead in the business district.

"You handled Reilly's secretary. She was spooked," Geffen said gravely.

"We do the same things over and over, Gef. I had a fifty-one-fifty couple years ago. Woman's in the supermarket, goes nuts. I show up, she won't leave, she's out of it. Says her arms are getting longer. Everybody's trying to get her into the ambulance."

"Downtown's checking to see if we got any units on Eugene," he held down the mike button, spoke again, listened.

"So I look at her," Medavoy said, "I tell her, yeah, your arms are getting longer. We got to get you to the hospital right away. She says, that's where they gave me the poison that's making them get longer. I look at her, like I did Reilly's secretary, I tell her, yeah, but who do you think's got the antidote? Oh, she says, the antidote. And she follows me right into the ambulance."

"Two units available, Robby."

"Get them over there now. Nobody in or out."

Geffen spoke. Then, "They'll cover 5643 until we arrive."

"My mission today is to bag this asshole Trask. And his girlfriend." He breathed deeply. "That sounds good."

Geffen replaced the mike, leaned forward, wound tightly. "Bag him, yeah. We do the same things over and over."

"Don't crap out on me. That's the job."

"I'm sick to fucking death of it."

Medavoy couldn't mistake the despair, worse than yesterday, as bad as what Masuda had alluded to. He tried distraction. "Let's have some fun for part of the ride." He hit the sirens and parted traffic around the car like a sharp wind through sand. He glanced at Geffen, perturbed, lonely. "You with me on this?"

"All the way. You know it, Robby."

"Okay. You were fading out."

Geffen shifted in his seat. "You got the fifty-one-fifty into the ambulance. Maybe you can help me," he chuckled faintly.

"Name it," Medavoy said without looking at him.

TWENTY-TWO

ABOUT A HALF HOUR EARLIER, Carol and Kenny had gotten back to her house. She was not surprised to see Lisio waiting for them. He stood beside the front door like a shy solicitor.

During the drive back from Reilly's Kenny worked to soothe her, calm her, cajole her. He'd protect her from Lisio if there were any trouble and there wouldn't be because Dave wasn't mad. He said so. The plan mattered Dave said, not him, not anything done to him. "So Carol honey," he'd said, "you take it easy, you slow down. You got me and nothing bad's happening while I'm with you."

Carol didn't really believe Kenny could protect her entirely from Lisio. She did believe Lisio valued this long evolved scheme above all and since Kenny was indispensable would curb any revenge he planned against her. So while they've got banks to rob, Lisio won't hurt me. And Kenny's here, too.

And Kenny won't let me go.

She thought about making a break while Kenny and Lisio were occupied during one of the robberies. It could be done.

After what had happened in Reilly's office, only physical survival made any sense, not fear of going to jail, or being humiliated in public or disbarred or anything else that could happen to her. Stay alive, get away, and worry about the future later.

Carol, until that morning, realized she had never actually felt real terror.

It's different, she thought, getting out of the car, it's not at all like simple fear. She found her legs worked slower, her mouth had constricted so that even breathing was harder. It was as though she were buried in mud, trying to run, to even think of running.

Real terror wasn't like the short, painful stab of fear everybody gets. This went on and on. It was the terror of Kenny and Lisio taking her back into her own house, one at each arm like escorts. She wondered why Lisio looked much fatter this morning, wearing that tight windbreaker, his hand rooted in its pocket.

So here I am, back in my own living room. The dust and clutter astoundingly unchanged. Like nothing had happened to her over the last twenty-four hours. She understood something now, trying to force the image of Reilly's blood-wetted face from her mind. Until she actually saw Kenny tear a man up, she'd only conceived of his violence in remote, analytical terms, not even very imaginative. His rap sheet was faceless, it didn't scream or bleed like Reilly had.

I don't even like Brian that much, she thought, but it's something different when someone you know, work with, talk to every day gets beaten up before your eyes. She tried swallowing and couldn't. That was terror. Knowing that Kenny loved her and was doing all this because he did. Even that poor man last night, she'd only heard the gunshot, never been close enough to get splattered with his blood.

Since he escaped from Chino, Kenny's savagely beaten two men and shot a third, she thought. And now what? Now he's back with Lisio to rob banks.

She discovered she couldn't move her legs at all now. I just stand here. Why is he so stiff with his hand in his pocket?

Lisio said to Kenny, "Go back to the bedroom and bring two empty suitcases out to the car. When you come back, I'd like you to bring about a gallon of gas. Get it out of her car."

Kenny frowned. "What'd you need the gas for?"

Carol wanted to shout. To burn something. He likes fires. Her mouth wouldn't function. She felt her thoughts grow heavy, soggy.

Lisio snapped back, "I've had to change plans since she made us miss the last car, Kenny. I want the gas."

"Okay, okay, don't get so grouchy. Look, we all here now. We back on track." He headed to her bedroom.

Carol tried working on each breath. It helped a little. She stared at Lisio. He called out, "We're on a schedule. We've got to leave soon." Then he said to her, "You look awful. You look like you haven't slept in a week."

"I'm all right," she gasped. Kenny bustled and banged through the living room, two matching suitcases with straps in each hand, a large empty water jug clutched in his teeth. He mumbled something to her.

"What?" she gasped again.

Lisio translated. "Do you have a hose outside? So he can siphon some gas from the tank?"

Kenny nodded. She nodded and he thumped, grinning out the door in a hurry.

Lisio glanced around the room with distaste. Carol saw, for the first time, that he was shiny with sweat. It must be hot in the windbreaker. No, it was something else. He looked at his watch with a twitch. Jesus, she thought, he's all tense, too.

Maybe there was a chance. Carol cursed herself, the rigidity of her jaw, the flabby way her thoughts lumbered, collapsed. There was an opportunity now and she had to take it. She struggled and spoke.

"I'll stay here," she said slowly, working on each word. "You've got me boxed in. I can't go to the police. I can't go to my boss anymore," don't think of the man and his pain, his blood, "I'll take a cab and meet you at the airport. I'll be there at ten. You said the reservations are for about ten?"

Lisio didn't answer. He simply looked at her. She repeated it. Lisio's right hand, buried in the windbreaker's pocket, fumbled. He won't answer, she thought in growing alarm. He's going to do something.

Kenny thumped back inside, the water jug full of yellowish gasoline. "Loaded up and ready to go," he said. He said something bland, soothing again to her.

"Put the gas down, Kenny," Lisio said. He unzipped the windbreaker and spread it. "I've got eight sticks of dynamite wrapped around myself. It's enough to blow three tons of concrete into the air." He held a silver wire and silver plunger in his right hand. "This is a photographic shutter. I put my hand in my pocket. I press the shutter."

Kenny peered in bewilderment at the wires and sausagelike sticks around Lisio's body. "You're shitting me, right? You got dynamite on you?"

Carol had no doubt it was real. He wanted to feel strong, powerful, in control of whatever he saw, even if it meant destruction. She had heard enough from him in the last day to understand that.

So he isn't going to let me stay here if he's wearing a bomb, she realized, standing rocklike. He's got other things in mind.

"I said that we'd have the money today," Lisio spoke huskily, from his own emotion. "I'm either going to have that money and get a new start or there's going to be nothing, Kenny. This is my day."

Kenny smiled crookedly. He thinks it's a gag; she felt her own sweat dripping down her back, on her sides. What can I say to Lisio? There's got to be something. But the words weren't there.

"I think it's fucking dangerous," Kenny said, poking at the corset, "unless you playing a big joke. It's another phony, right? You got it all set to scare them shitless?"

"It's real. All I do is press the shutter."

Kenny frowned. "Jeez, Dave. You better be careful. Maybe you better take it off."

Carol moved her feet, trying to slip to one side. Anything to break this grip. How far can I get, she wondered? Where do I run from them?

Then Lisio said breathlessly, "I am not joking. You have to choose now. We leave now."

"Thought that's the plan."

"You kill her." Lisio jerked his left hand toward her and flinched, as if he'd thrown something.

So there it is, plainly spoken, right out in the open, she thought. Jesus, if I only had a little courage. I could break his neck. I could do something.

She looked at Kenny. His eyes were wide.

"Kill her?" he repeated.

"You have to choose. Right now." Lisio zipped the windbreaker. Fat and deadly he spoke to Kenny.

Kenny looked at her. She looked at him.

"Okay," he said slowly, unwillingly, "I choose."

She heard herself, a distant voice, say "Kenny," then saw him reach for the .45 in his jacket. Saw the look of triumph on Lisio, understood that something in Lisio's attitude, tone, his ultimatum convinced Kenny. Maybe threats that had been delivered and carried out in Chino and there was no way to deflect Lisio's purpose.

"He means it, Carol honey." Kenny had drawn the gun. "I sure ain't going to get killed." He rocked a little with tension.

"My God," she managed to say, the words bursting out, "let me go, Kenny. I'll just drive away. I'll go away."

Lisio snapped. "Shoot her now."

Kenny turned to the sound of Lisio's voice and Carol

broke, running spontaneously, driven by the terror that had immobilized her a moment before. Get to the side door, get out the kitchen, the idea flashed in her mind. She blundered into the dining room, sharply hitting the table, knocking over the cheap candle holders, barking her shins on the chairs. Behind her, Lisio yelled and Kenny shouted at her.

She thrust out, banging the swinging kitchen door open. Cross the kitchen, then through the small alcove, out the door. Kenny came around the door from the dining room, Lisio yelling again and again.

Like a game of tag, she thought. Just a game.

Halfway across the kitchen, her shoes clacking on the floor. Go to the Ramirezes. Go to anybody. Get out, get out. Kenny banged through the door, lunging toward her. She was rejoicing, a few feet ahead of him. Then outside, her neighbors would see and hear.

Hands out, ready to seize the side door. A quick impression of the house across the driveway, curtains shut. Carol felt Kenny's hard arm around her waist, his other arm around her throat like a garrote, the .45 banging her head. She choked and strained forward.

She twisted, but he was much stronger. He dragged her back, through the kitchen, across the living-room carpet leaving tracks. And always, the whispers in her ear to be calm, it was okay, it was just Kenny.

She couldn't slow him down much and Lisio trailed them.

"Where're you going?" he barked.

"Stay back, Dave." There was a catch in Kenny's voice. "I do this my way."

"Remember what I've got here." Lisio's hand moved again in his pocket.

Kenny shouted back at him, then she was in the bedroom, things scattered around from his search for suitcases. She felt the rush as he violently flung her to the bed. The door slammed shut.

She started pleading in a rush of silly, horribly pathetic cries. Make him pity, she thought wildly, anything.

He gleamed with sweat. She cringed back against the wall, on the bed, listening to her own stammering, terrified voice.

Kenny looked like he was going to cry. He held the .45 toward the floor.

"I wouldn't hurt you, I wouldn't touch you, swear to God," he babbled, pleading back at her. "He's nuts. He'd do it to both of us."

"We can get out of here," she said, slipping on the bed covers. Kenny shook his head.

"He's right there. He's got that shit. We only got a second here, he's going to start making noise."

Carol turned, frantically trying to see a way from the room. Lisio indeed began speaking from the other side of the bedroom door.

"What's going on? What's happening? There's no time," Lisio called out.

Carol grabbed Kenny. "Shoot him through the door!"

"That thing'd blow up, honey. I got to do this my own self, my way."

She reached for the gun, he snatched it back, pushing her off the bed, to the floor on the far side away from the door.

This is what it comes to, she thought, hitting the floor hard. All the years of waiting and feeling life going by, the stupid nights with men I didn't like, all the schemes to get away.

Kenny knelt beside her. "Trust me, Carol honey. I get something going, I get him looking the other way. Maybe we just finish the banks. Remember I be at the Citizens Savings, wherever the fuck that is. Or I meet you at the airport, ten sharp." He touched her face. "You be there. I come for you, but we stay together."

Before she could say anything, he aimed the .45 downward and fired three times to her left a few feet. Lisio's questions from the other side of the door stopped.

Kenny headed for the door and she squeezed down to the floor, smelling the tang of gun smoke in the airless room. She tried to make out what was going on, to slow her shallow, gasping breaths. In the awful terror was a wild euphoria starting. I'm still alive, she thought.

There was movement in the living room, something crashed to the floor, Kenny and Lisio speaking hoarsely, rapidly. The front door banged closed.

Carol slid quickly along the floor into the bathroom, climbing into the shower, burrowing down into the tub, hidden by the shower curtain. Soap and shampoo, damp, she lay there, in a tight ball.

Then there was the faint sound of her car starting, revving and fading again.

She lay in the shower, exhausted, fearful of the door flung back, Lisio appearing or Kenny with the gun pointed at her for real. Like what he did to Brian or those other men. What he could have done to me, she thought.

Carol didn't know how long she stayed in the shower before an acrid scent stung the air. She inhaled and her heart beat so fast she felt the artery throb in her neck. Get out of the shower, see what's happening, get out of the house. Get out of Santa Maria.

When she climbed out of the shower and went cautiously into the bedroom, she saw the haze distinctly. It was smoke slipping under the bedroom door. She touched the door. It was warm. My house is burning, she thought with stunned certainty.

Which also meant Kenny and Lisio were long gone. She steeled herself, hand over her nose and mouth in a vain attempt to close off the stinging smoke, and hurried through the living room, bright and filled with flame, the front door blocked. Here it goes, she thought, all the memories and treasures carefully trucked from Riverside, photo albums of Mom and Dad, law books, rented furniture, everything black and hazy like a shadow in the fire.

Someone was pounding and shouting on the front door. She crouched and ran through the kitchen, past the burning dining room. When she went through the side door, neighbors were already there reaching for her, old ones and youngsters, appalled and thrilled. Two men in sport shirts seized her, and she recognized one of the Ramirez kids. There was much confused chatter—Was she hurt? What happened?—as they pulled her away from the house.

The whole block was out on the sidewalk. They pointed and cried when smoke burst out of the roof.

"I'm fine, I'm not hurt, thank you," she said as they hastily passed her back to safety. "There's no one else, just me."

One man, holding her arm painfully, a striped shirt thrown on, stared at her with dark, intense concern. "My wife hears gunshots. Somebody shooting?"

"There were no shots."

"Those guys, they got out of there fast. How come they leave you?"

Carol felt suddenly that she would vomit. "I think I'm in shock," she managed to say.

"Hey, lie down here, get a coat, get a blanket, she's falling down."

She was eased to the ground, onto someone's lawn. "I'm sorry, so sorry, I just have to lie down."

"Lie down, you feel better. Here comes the fire trucks, see? Gee, they bring the whole department. Get back!" the man shouted at people about to step on her as the trucks drew up. "Maybe they save you house. Look at all those hoses, all those guys."

"Look at them all," she repeated, her mind running over another thought as the fire engines keened loudly and men began running to her house, dragging hoses, shouting instructions. Carol thought of Kenny. He could have killed me. But he saved me. Someone pushed a folded coat under her head.

Kenny didn't talk to Lisio as they drove toward Merchants Savings. Lisio was making excuses, the same bullshit he would do for hours in the cell when something bad happened. A couple of times Kenny got so mad as he was driving, he nearly hit cars on either side of him.

He kept thinking of Carol, how frightened she looked. He hated feeling so dumb, thinking Lisio wouldn't pull something. The guy couldn't walk straight, how's he going to act straight?

So they drove along, right at the speed limit, sun out, skyline rising ahead, great day to hit a bank. Lisio kept checking the street names, telling him where to turn. He had his watch out, looking at the time. Had to hit this place right at nine, right as it opened.

I got to be such a dumb fucker, Kenny thought, I let Lisio make me scare the hell out of my girl and get me to sit next to him and he's got all that fucking dynamite. Kenny wasn't frightened as much as angry with himself. Fool-proof plans. Shit. Lisio always plans and this one didn't seem to be working out too great.

"Are you going to talk to me at all?" Lisio said.

Kenny, white-lipped, stared ahead. He felt as pent up as when Trask beat him up. He wanted to feel the way he did when he knocked Trask down, clubbing him with a chair.

"I know how you feel." Lisio went on looking at his map. "Make a left at the next signal. But there was no choice."

That did it. "You don't feel nothing for nobody. You just a little asshole, Dave."

Lisio glanced up, fat sweat drops on his forehead. "Kenny, she would have gone to the police. She proved she was willing to risk us both last night."

"Risk you."

"And you. She was going to make you give yourself up. What would have happened? Back to the joint, no good time, no work time. Straight bad time." Lisio sat crookedly against the door.

"Don't make it sound like you're looking out for me. I seen how you loved messing with that gas in her house." Kenny thought of Lisio's delight splashing the gasoline over furniture, lighting it and the burst of flame. "You having a great time. And you tell me, how smart's it to make a fire like that, man? Everybody sees it."

Lisio sighed tensely, wiping his forehead. "It takes care of evidence for a while. It makes it harder for them to figure who did what. It gives us time."

Kenny snorted in disbelief. Sure, great idea, Lisio. He wanted to kick himself around the whole damn city for calling Lisio from that hotel Carol took them to.

Lisio gave him an emergency number to phone, just in case they got separated or something went wrong. So last night, Lisio says, *you did exactly the right thing calling me, Kenny. I'm not hurt. I'm not mad. I understand she must have been startled by the gunshot and reacted badly.* And Lisio says, *this all doesn't change anything for tomorrow. We go ahead like we planned. I'll be waiting for you at her place. All you have to do is short-circuit this crazy scheme of hers to screw our deal tomorrow.*

I believed him, Kenny raged. Nothing changed, go ahead like we planned. Dumb. Dumb.

He turned left onto a straight, heavily-traveled street, slowed at a light. Lisio pointed ahead. There was another shopping mall—this whole damn city's one damn mall—and a single-story bank like yesterday, this time done up with nautical insignia in gray and blue, like a beached riverboat. Everybody wants to look like a fast-food joint, he thought.

"Are you all right now? Can you go through with it?" Lisio stammered as he asked. "Because there aren't any choices left. This is it. Our clock's running."

Kenny shot an evil eye at the little man. "Shit, don't do

anything, Dave," he snapped, seeing the hand jammed in the windbreaker pocket. "I'm okay."

He had already decided that once they were through, he'd still have over a hundred thousand dollars. Carol was safe and knew where he'd be. Get rid of Lisio, put him on a plane or shoot him or something, if there was a chance, and he and Carol could go on with their plans.

Kenny thought again. A light seemed to go on in his head. Without Lisio, of course, he'd have the whole thing. Two hundred thousand. He would definitely look for some opening to take care of Lisio now. Especially after what the little fucker had just done to him and Carol. Look at that dynamite. Little fucker's probably been thinking about dumping Carol since he got here. Never was going to let her and me go away.

Just needed me. Kenny's light burned more brightly. Used me.

Dumb, dumb, he thought again. You are so dumb.

That would change today. Surprise the little fucker.

He drove into the shopping mall encircling Merchants Savings, slowing the car.

"We're at the starting line. We're going to get everything we want today." Lisio psyched himself, dabbing at his sweat.

"Let's do it," Kenny said grimly.

TWENTY-THREE

WHEN THEY GOT RIGHT UP to the bank, the problem was obvious. "The drive-up window's closed," Kenny said angrily, gripping the steering wheel.

"It can't be," Lisio refused to accept what was in front of him. "It's never been closed, not all week when I checked it."

They were pulled up beside a decorative hedge, the car's engine roaring when Kenny nervously hit the gas.

"Well, sure as shit, they got it closed now," Kenny retorted. There was an orange-and-white barricade blocking the drive-up lane and the teller's window was dark.

"You'll just have to go inside," Lisio said, the familiar click in his voice whenever he got scared. Even with that dynamite on, he's still a coward, Kenny thought.

"That's a fucking great idea. Go inside. Maybe they got a guard in there, okay? Maybe he's got a gun, okay?"

"I checked it. There is no guard."

"You checked the fucking drive-up window, too."

Lisio bent down and handed him the shoe box and empty shopping bag. Kenny had gotten everything ready when he put the suitcases in the trunk, dumping the cash from yesterday into one. It looked so beautiful.

"Kenny, we're already two minutes behind schedule. We can't leave here so early."

"How about we sit in the parking lot, Dave? I go for that."

"Get the money," Lisio ordered. "Go inside and get it." He whispered anxiously. "I'm waiting here."

Kenny grabbed the shoe box and bag. "Okay. I go inside. Fucking stupid shoe box. I still got my gun." He patted the .45 underneath his jacket. He was not exactly sure how many bullets were left in it.

Kenny recalled what Carol used to tell him when she came to visit. Seize your advantage. Use your boldness and courage and no one can stop you. He'd march in, first teller by the door, and do whatever it took to get the money. Lisio was really building up a very bad time for himself.

When Kenny got out, Lisio clumsily slid over to the driver's side, the engine still running. Kenny kept repeating Carol's exhortations. A woman with a baby swaddled in a stroller struggled with the glass front door of the bank, the stroller going in first.

He pressed by her roughly and she said something snappish, but Kenny had turned on the old automatic pilot, like when he was riding high on crank or smack or whatever happened to be handy that day.

A quick scan of the bank lobby, low ceiling, vault open at one end behind a friendly white railing, ship's binnacle, anchors, and a lot of heavy rope all over to give that seafaring effect. Three people in line at four teller windows, all women. Two men at the little captain's tables making out slips. Two more women behind another railing. Low voices, lilting strings playing faintly on the muzak.

No one shouted in a bank.

So the first thing Kenny did was shout, run to the teller, knocking down the woman standing in front of her. Show her the box, and get the right reaction. All the money into a pile and into the bag, which he handed to her.

It was dead quiet in the bank suddenly, only the strings playing on obliviously. Everyone stared in shock and amazement and someone whimpered. No one around who looked like a guard. Kenny noticed the cameras on the walls, little red eyes. Fuck them.

The teller, a slender black woman, was trembling, bringing up these great stacks of money, dropping them in the bag. He obeyed another old habit, don't think about the time. Time didn't matter at that point, it was elastic and played tricks. Just do your thing like it was your only job on earth.

He did shout again that he didn't want any booby-trapped cash or dye-marker stuff put in there, because then he'd blow the whole damn bank up. The teller, looking much worse than the little babe yesterday, hadn't even thought of obstructing him it seemed.

The shopping bag was coming back, shoved quickly, and he seized it, becoming aware at the same moment of a car's horn blaring and a woman shouting outside. He ran toward the glass door, box and bag in hand. Outside was the woman with the stroller, rushing away; she had the stroller going like she's in a race and her mouth was going as fast. Someone would be coming.

It was Carol's car, Lisio working the horn, that made so much racket when he came out of the bank. Couple more feet and he'd be inside and away they'd go.

Then he saw the two kids in blue security-guard uniforms beside one of the stores in the mall, the woman running to them and shouting.

Lisio moved the car toward him, the passenger door open. Kenny was momentarily shocked when one of the guards pointed a small gun at him. I ain't pointing anything at him, he thought in hurt perplexity. I just got this money.

His next thought was stark terror that Lisio would send them all blasting twenty feet in the air. Got to get in the car and get out.

With only a few feet separating him and the car, Kenny awkwardly, violently reached for his gun in the jacket. One of the security guards, even more astoundingly, was running to him while the other pointed the gun. Kenny shouted back and fired at the man coming at him.

The guard tripped, fell, and Kenny realized he'd hit him. The other guard vanished behind an arcade pillar.

Kenny swung himself gymnastically into the car so hard he banged into Lisio, slamming his door, and they bounced, sped out of the shopping mall. He heard himself cursing, Lisio replying, but at the same time, Kenny had one of those out-of-body experiences he used to have when he was a kid. Like he was looking at the picture of the Kennedys, lighter than air. It always happened when his mother was drunk, passed out, and Trask was beating him. It left his body on earth to feel the pain while he soared away.

He was soaring again as Lisio careened into traffic, settled down, badgered him about what happened, asked was he hurt. It took a few minutes for him to come back to the ground.

"It went about as good as a fucked plan can go," Kenny said, feeling the anger rising, holding it down only because he was afraid of Lisio's dynamite. He watched Lisio driving, arms straight, hands on the wheel, following the map beside him, barely seeing over the dashboard.

"But you got it, you got it and we're on schedule, right now." Lisio was excited, revving up like a little motor himself. "Caldwell, College Green, left, then a right."

Kenny opened the shopping bag. "Shit. Whole pile in there. Looks good, no dye or shit on it. Hey, they shot at me," Kenny said furiously. "They shooting at me."

"It won't happen again. Everything's right on track here,"

Lisio promised, steering into a street Kenny half-recalled from the night before. "See? The car's there. We make the change and it's nine-oh-five. Cops are rolling back there. They arrive," Lisio shook his head when some sweat stung his eyes, "nine-ten. We're on our way to Central Valley Savings."

"I don't want no more trouble, Dave. I swear, I don't want no surprises anymore." He dared to point threateningly at Lisio, like they were back in the cell at Chino and he could call the shots.

"But consider how beautifully everything's going." Lisio pulled Carol's car right behind the Ford sedan. "Even with these new developments, we're on our way right on time."

Like trying to kill me. Kill Carol, Kenny thought in bitter anger. He felt for his knife to open the Ford's door again. He had been wrong, he realized, at the river yesterday. Lisio was part of his old life, not the new one. He had to be cut away.

"Let's make the damn change and get going," Kenny said, getting out, looking around the quiet street, the homes watching him under that blue sky and galleonlike clouds. "The faster we go, the better."

With Lisio's frequent urging to hurry, they switched cars in about a minute, suitcases, shopping bag, and shoe box. All that held them back was Lisio's slow, clumsy movement. He would drive, he said and Kenny made sure he knew not to disturb the hot-wired ignition system.

Kenny had learned one valuable thing from the dash from that bank. When Lisio drove, he used both hands. No hand in that damn pocket on the shutter. Get him to slow down enough, and you had your opening before he could do anything about it.

Shit, he thought, the day I got to take second place to this little shit, ain't come yet. And today ain't his day. It's mine.

"Come on, come on, come on," Lisio said, twisting at the wheel. "Nine-seven. Got to move, hurry Kenny."

Kenny had paused, leaned out to snatch something yellow stuck under a windshield wiper.

Kenny chuckled, reading it, Lisio driving down the street, turning right onto a big boulevard, Sunrise Avenue, and asking what the joke was.

Kenny held out the yellow paper. "We got a parking ticket."

TWENTY-FOUR

JANE WAS IN THE COURT reporters' office on the second floor of the courthouse. She had the phone to one ear. It was after nine, she saw by a quick look at the clock. Smitty stood beside her, working on another cigarette. Two Vietnamese interpreters were in heated argument while the Spanish and Chinese interpreters played gin rummy at a small table in the corner. It was a crowded arrangement to have the interpreters and reporters sharing space.

"Some quiet? I'd appreciate it," she said. The noisy argument dimmed but didn't go out.

She was waiting for Masuda to come on the line. This was the first chance to use the phone she'd had since Smitty told her about Robby's impending internal affairs investigation. Luckily for her, the one witness scheduled in the trial that morning had gotten a sore throat at the last minute, so the judge excused the jury and sent everybody home until tomorrow at nine.

Jane rubbed her temple. It was quite a nasty burden to have dumped on you, but she was thankful Smitty had done it.

"Stan?" she said when Masuda finally picked up his phone.

"Jane? Hiya. What's up?"

"Robby there?"

"He's out in the field," Masuda answered a little carefully.

She imagined him using the handgrip, squeezing it as he talked. Masuda always had something, a rubber ball, those steel handgrips, to play with when he worked.

"Can you get hold of him?"

"Do I have to?"

Jane didn't want to say anything over the phone, because she was unsure who listened at the police department or what Masuda knew. "It's very important, Stan. I need to talk to him right away."

"I can leave word if he calls in."

"I have to talk to him."

"Things are busting out," Masuda said. "He's going to be tied up, I can tell you."

"So I better go to him. Where is he?" Don't let it get too blown up, she thought, but Masuda's got to understand the urgency.

"I shouldn't tell you."

"This is important," she said. "It's about his future. In the department."

"His future? Like what?"

"Look, Stan, you know me a little. I wouldn't disturb Robby about anything unless it was important he know about it."

"It can't wait?"

Jane glanced at Smitty, standing by in case she needed anything. She felt a twinge of guilt for not giving his dream of a business any real thought. He idly looked through a steno pad of black-ink notes. "It's coming down on him now. Right now and that's why I've got to talk to him."

A pause at the other end. "Okay. Maybe I've got some idea what you're talking about," Masuda said. "He's going to 5643 Eugene Avenue. He's with Gef. You know where it is?"

"I'll find it."

"Anything I can do to help out?"

"I don't know yet."

"You tell me if there's anything. I like you guys. Let me tell you, he's got the bank deal, a major assault, some other stuff cooking so he's going to be real busy there."

"What's at that address?"

"A suspect. On all of this shit."

"I'll stay out of the way. Thanks, Stan." She hung up, thinking that Masuda was one of the allies Robby had when the department turned its machinery on him. It was incredible they could seriously believe he'd be involved in stealing from drug dealers.

Then she thought of what he'd told her last night, the sloppy investigation. Jesus, Robby, she thought, you sure leave them a lot of ways to get at you.

As soon as she got off the phone, the Vietnamese interpreters raised their volume, gesturing extravagantly. "I need a car, Smitty. Mine's nonfunctional," she said.

He dug around in the tan poplin suit and gave her the keys to his car. "It's down in the courthouse garage. Space five."

Jane took the keys gratefully. "Thanks. Robby and I need a lot of luck right now."

TWENTY-FIVE

AT NINE-TEN THAT MORNING, the Chief was in his office, in his stocking feet, a legal pad in his hand. Outside his window, the blue globe swayed gently in a slight breeze and an SP freight rolling through the nearby yard faintly whistled.

He was coming to the end of what he judged to be a successful meeting with Schroeder from Internal Affairs. Schroeder sat at the conference table and slowly polished his glasses. He wore his gray suit buttoned.

"So we agree there are eight," said the Chief, looking at the pad with dismay and delight. Dismay at the corruption in his department, delight that he was going to take decisive action about it.

"I wouldn't swear that's all." Schroeder went on polishing. He was fair, tending to ruddiness, middle-aged, and careful.

"How many others?"

"There are some rumors about four more," he said, settling his glasses back on his nose.

"I want to go ahead against the eight dead-solid ones."

270

"First off? How do you want it?" Schroeder asked calmly.

The Chief pulled a chair beside Schroeder. His fleshless hands were on his knees. "Notices of suspension today. Set up departmental disciplinary hearings for Monday."

"They'll bring their lawyers."

"We'll say it'll make things tougher for them. God. Do they expect to disgrace their uniforms and have me sit by?"

"Suspend them all and you stop my investigations. Anybody else is probably going to skate."

The Chief glanced at the legal pad. Bribery, assault, extortion, out-and-out robbery, and probably much more IAD hadn't been able to sufficiently uncover. He would like to tell Prefach in a few minutes the bad apples were on their way out. It could sway some of the Council that he was firmly, ruthlessly in charge. Under their direction, of course. Prefach would never let him forget that, he frowned. Breaking that umbilical cord was next on the agenda.

"I want them suspended as of five P.M. today," the Chief said, still frowning, scuffing his black-stockinged feet on the carpet. "Get your reports together and walk them over to the DA. I'll call him now."

Schroeder nodded. He was the Chief's man, just as the Chief was Prefach's man, each dependent on his sponsor for the vitality he enjoyed and the position he occupied. Arguments had to be subtle or discreet, never blunt. The Chief saw Schroeder forming such an indirect argument.

"Very bad publicity, Chief. Eight cops, six on our Special Weapons Unit, one a supervisor with a commendation. Have you thought about it?"

"Of course I have."

"Well. Suspending six Special Weapons men means the Blue Team is about broken in two. We better not have a crisis in the next couple of weeks while we build that unit up again."

"We still got the Green Team. They can handle an emergency."

"I'm thinking of the spin, Chief. Are you going to leave the city unprotected? That's how they'll ask it."

"The worst thing is to dribble out these cases, Earl," the Chief snapped, noting that Schroeder hadn't endorsed the action. "It has to be a bold, single stroke." He stood up, pacing, then went to his desk.

Look at the time. The seconds ticked off on his computer display. He was irritated the meeting had gone on so long; he was violating his own efficiency guidelines.

"I don't want you to look bad." Schroeder started for a cup of coffee in the kitchenette at the back of the office.

"I'll handle the PR. You're not very happy about this," the Chief said.

Schroeder's jowly face was blank. "We agreed when I took on IAD it was best to have somebody who didn't like the job very much."

"I can't have reservations on this one, Earl. You've got to be completely with me."

"You know I am."

The Chief nodded, having gotten his formal declaration of support. "Their badges, on your desk, by five. All set?"

Schroeder paused. "One thing. Ralph Easter's a department vet, Chief. He's done good work. Do you want to tell him yourself?"

The Chief pushed his feet into his shoes, bent to tie the stiff black laces, the highly shined black shoes glistening as if wet. "No. He used up any special consideration by his conduct."

Bent over, the Chief didn't see Schroeder's momentary look of disapproval. It wouldn't have mattered, though. The Chief, as Schroeder knew, once set on course, didn't waver. Or have any signs of weakness about who might be hurt. No signs he showed anyway.

The Chief spotted another file on his desk. The detective Ollie had complained about, Medavoy. He'd quickly reviewed the file and found much he liked. He tapped out another series of numbers on the computer.

"What do you have on Medavoy in Robbery, Earl?" he asked.

"That bum purse snatch. Some excessive force complaints that folded."

"You'd say a good record?"

Schroeder paused. "Something else just came in."

"How bad?"

"As bad as what we've just been talking about."

"Can you check it out immediately?"

"It's already in the works. I've got a guy on it."

The Chief didn't want to know more at the moment. Too much information was as bad as too little. It made for clutter and muddy thinking. "Well, I've got Ornelas's absence record here. I'd like a new supervisor in Robbery. I see Medavoy got an MOV," Medal of Valor.

"You gave it to him." Schroeder made it sound like a mistake.

"I'd like to make him supervisor. If this new problem dissolves."

"I'll be working on it. Along with the suspensions," Schroeder said and he left, leaving the Chief with a nebulous dissatisfaction. Schroeder was perhaps too sensitive and secretive for IAD.

The Chief saw on the computer that Pesce had just scheduled a ten-thirty meeting with Medavoy. Impossible. He'd still be tied up with the City Council. Besides, he wanted to hear what Schroeder found before meeting with Medavoy himself.

Bart opened the side door without knocking. It was normal after so many years working together. The heavy face was a reminder.

"I know it's time," the Chief said.

"You don't want to rush into the City Council meeting. You want to come in confident."

Bart looked out for him like an alarm clock, better here at work than the computer.

"What do you think, should I wear the gold or the suit?" The Chief went to the small closet near his bathroom. He had a suit coat hung beside his blue, gold-sprinkled uniform. As Chief he was entitled to a dress uniform with four gold stripes on the sleeve and four gold stars at his shoulders.

"In the blues you look like Omar Bradley, Chief."

"I liked Bradley."

"Maybe the blues're too intimidating."

"I'm trying to get a substation and more men. I want to be intimidating." He took down the dress uniform and changed in the bathroom.

He and Bart were like an old married couple in some ways, quarrelsome but minutely sensitive. Bart was now telling him what a good idea the blues were. It wasn't sycophancy as much as a desire to make him feel good about the choice, to make the Chief feel secure.

Besides, the Chief knew Donna liked him to wear his dress uniform whenever he could. It was an outward and visible sign of their successful efforts at his career. He would wear it to the City Council for her, too.

"Schroeder thinks I'm being too harsh, Bart. Not in so many words. He wants to go slow with the suspensions." He buckled his belt tight against his thin waist, adjusted his dark tie tight against his thin neck. I do look like Omar Bradley, he thought, gray hair, weak eyes and mouth. The uniform will save the day for me.

"Schroeder doesn't know what's right. He's an old lady," Bart snapped.

"Maybe he's right. I sometimes wonder what my father would have said. I imagine going into his study, Sunday morning, right after he's preached and blessed everybody. Sent everybody home from church with a clear idea of right and wrong and what to do." The Chief pulled on his uniform coat, straightening it, almost feeling Donna's hands lovingly smoothing the deep-blue fabric, aligning his padded shoulders. He began buttoning, thin fingers over gold.

"I hated going into his study. There he was, sitting under

this God-awful painting of Christ entering Jerusalem. And that's where he'd let me have it for some mistake. Something done or undone," the Chief ruefully chuckled. There were always mistakes in that house.

"He whip you?" Bart watched the ritual dressing.

"Never. I just found out, in plain, brutal language how far I'd strayed from the Truth."

"Boss, don't worry about it today. Go in there like that, you're going to get every vote."

The Chief wasn't listening entirely. He was still remembering. "My father would have told me, when you see your duty, do it. If I asked him about these corrupt officers, that's what he'd tell me. That's why I'm right and Schroeder's wrong."

Bart handed him his hat as he came out of the bathroom and filled his black briefcase with the studies, graphs, projections of population and crime stats he'd prepared.

"You want the car?" Bart asked. It meant rousing his driver, a bright-eyed patrolman without ambition.

"I'll walk. It's four blocks and a lovely day." He gave the computer a final tap. "My dad had all the answers, no bend, no give. Today our sins and successes are all numbers. In computers. They don't bend, either."

Bart nodded. He was used to this. He was not expected to understand or even answer. The Chief sometimes liked to talk without fearing it would go further.

The Chief fussed with the gold threads on his hat, making sure they weren't tangled. "The numbers don't tell me why a cop like Easter goes bad. Or why the others do."

"Boss, today all you got is the City Council and you're going to make those bastards do the right thing."

The Chief grinned at Bart's pep talk. "Damn right. I may look like Omar Bradley, but damn, I feel like George Patton."

The walk to the Administration Building took only a few minutes and was very pleasant. The Chief strode purposefully, greeted people, breathed the storm-cleaned air, and knew everyone saw him as the embodiment of their safety. He was realistic enough to know he didn't have many acts of defiance in him. Whether it was Donna or Prefach or the City Council or his own department, he had to strike now while the spirit was in him, before he went back to the regular pattern of his life.

The City Council sat in its chambers in a semicircle like a row of judges. Behind them hung the great city seal. There were only a few people in the audience for a morning meeting, and a few reporters who whispered when he came in. The Chief tried to catch Prefach's eye. The Council listened to a man, gesturing angrily with a pencil, standing at the podium before them.

Prefach whispered to the mayor, beside him, and left the semicircle. He bent down to the Chief, sitting to one side.

"We're a little late. I'll cut off Mason's fucking airport ordinance."

"I'd like to keep to some timetable, Vin."

"They're in a bad mood. We may have to delay the substation."

The Chief stiffened. "You said they'd agree. What's the problem all of a sudden?"

"Four of those idiots think we can wait. So you've got to give them some horror stories. Babies full of crack, old ladies beaten up. Scare them into it." Prefach wasn't joking. He knew the Council, the Chief realized. It was demeaning to pander to them this way.

"I do have some numbers." He tapped his briefcase. "I can announce eight suspensions for criminal conduct."

"They'll love it. The firm hand at the tiller, Steve." Prefach looked up when the council's clerk called his name for a vote.

Prefach squeezed his shoulder and bounded back to his seat. Another session of tooth pulling, the Chief thought.

He got ready to testify.

TWENTY-SIX

EASTER WAS ON A CONFERENCE call in the Special Weapons office in the basement. He had three other men with him, all working on their own cases. He hated conference calls.

"Say again," he shouted to the DEA agent.

The FBI agent on the line answered. So did the Bureau of Narcotics Enforcement agent in Sacramento. Easter missed the DEA agent in the blabbering.

"I can deploy up to twelve men," he repeated. "We bring our own equipment, you don't have to supply anything," he tried shouting over the BNE agent. They were all trying to plan a joint raid on several large methamphetamine labs in the northern corner of the county. He hadn't worked with these three clowns before, so it was time to reinvent the wheel and explain who could do what. His guys would provide the majority of the firepower. As usual.

The babble came over the speaker phone on his desk. "Don't bring flashbangers, we got them. Anyone hear me?" He picked up another blue stinger capsule, popped it down with a gulp of coffee, and waited for the crack to hit his head. How else do you stay up for almost twenty-four hours straight? He felt pleasantly light.

"I don't believe these guys," he said to his men. They looked up.

The office was more like an armory, flak jackets, assault rifles, pistols in steel cabinets, chained and bolted. Boxes of flashbangs, to explode with sound and light and scare the hell out of everyone without blowing them up, tear gas grenades, the thin musk of machine and gun oil in the air. Easter was in his black uniform.

On his desk, the red light and the beeper went off together.

"Got a call, fellas, got to go. Bye." He hit the phone, the other men alert, too.

The dueling narcotics agents were replaced by the bass voice of their dispatcher, loudly echoing through the office. A bank robbery, shots fired, possible explosives, one man down, and Easter broke into a smile. He bounced up, acknowledged the call.

The others were up, too, already gathering their gear. The Command Post van was parked directly outside, filled with their radio and portable communications, even a small kitchen.

"It's our good bud from yesterday," Easter said. "What's our rolling time?"

"Ten minutes from here," someone answered.

"Get the rest of the Blue Team in. I don't care what they're out on, who's got them assigned." He was strapping on a black, lightweight pistol.

They were all old hands together and knew this drill. Radio calls were already going out.

"More fun than real work, right?" a man unlocking the heavy assault rifles called out.

"Damn straight."

The room was moving, Easter overseeing with bright-eyed, sharp commands. "Get the Green Team on standby. Get them at the five-minute mark." Meaning they would have to be able to drop whatever they were doing—assisting an arrest, serving a warrant, chasing gangs around town—on five minutes notice.

His black uniform rustled as he dropped the flak jacket around it, pushing the Velcro snaps closed. "Another bud of mine's going to show up."

"Who's coming?"

"Medavoy's coming." Easter finished fastening the sides of the flak jacket, the others also bulky, encased in black arrogance. Zippers sighed, clasps clicked, bolts were shot home. "My bud Robby."

"Keep him away from me," someone growled.

Easter smiled hard, fatigue melting like wax. These men had been with him last night, running after Ramon. They shared secrets from everyone but a few other select members of the department.

"He's got to come. He's looking for this guy." Easter heard the first hiss and spit from the handy-talkies being switched on.

"We'll all be there. We can settle some things right maybe."

TWENTY-SEVEN

WITH THEIR LIGHTS and siren pumping them up, forcing other traffic away like they were a bullet, Medavoy drove toward Eugene Avenue. Sometimes the artificial rush made things seem unclear, ambiguous, others were sharpened. Maybe, he thought, it's the excitement of chasing down a suspect.

Whatever the reason, Geffen told him what was disturbing his nights and days. Medavoy drove and listened and discovered there was not as much of a gulf between him and the vets as he assumed. Everyone had accidents best forgotten, events that were unquiet and upset lives.

Geffen had told Easter, whom he thought might understand better than Masuda who never got out of Saigon during his tour. Geffen didn't want to talk even now to Medavoy because it all became real with words. Like when I told Jane about Baladarez last night, Medavoy thought, the city streets flashing by. Talking brought it all back.

Geffen's unit had ended up off Highway 13, not far from Binh Duong, but far enough that they were filthy and tired and the steamy mornings began like hot baths day after day.

They made camp in the brush, he told Medavoy. It was August, bright-colored skies and humid days trailing off into humid nights. The area was secure and they built a fire. There was a shallow, sluggish stream running nearby and they washed off some of the day's sweat. Off the dirt track they had come over was a small cluster of huts, not even a named village, some temporary place five or six families had stopped.

Geffen relived the pleasure of that stream. The liberating, exhilarating pleasure of feeling safe for a moment.

You could talk loud, your voices raised after days of whispers and fear, he said. They laughed aloud, the ten men he was with. They got ready to cook over the fire.

One of the last to wash in the stream was Harry Weisman, a lean sharpshooter who had a subscription to *Playboy* that somehow managed to find him wherever he was sent. Weisman was laughing, buttoning his still stiff, dirty fatigues as he passed the fire. They were all loud, letting off steam.

"He got about ten paces, he said something, I didn't get it, and we heard this bang, real loud, real sharp," Geffen said, staring out the windshield, the siren over him. "Not like a shot. I never heard a round like that, but we all went down. Got real quiet around camp right away. I was lying down when it happened. Weisman, he kind of grabbed his side, he fell over."

"Sniper?"

Geffen turned a hard, almost imploring glance on him. "You got to get into the place, Robby, into our heads. We didn't know. We just see Weisman go down and man, he is bleeding. He's got this big damn hole in his side. You remember how surprised you were, first one-eighty-seven by gunshot or knife you saw? How much blood comes of a body sometimes?"

Medavoy nodded. "I thought I'd throw up."

"It's worse when you know the guy."

"Any more shots?"

"There weren't any shots," Geffen said, shaking his head.

"You said there were."

"No, no, Robby, get into the mood. You got to be there with me. Try it," Geffen said intensely. "All the shit we'd been through, we think, damn great, pressure's off a little. All we're doing is jumping in this fucking warm stream. Glad to be alive."

"What happened to Weisman?"

"Somebody threw an aerosol can into the fire. Spray can of bug repellent. I mean, why keep it? It's no good. The bugs ate you anyway."

"The can blew up and hit the guy, right? So?"

"Listen, Robby. Okay? You hear me now?"

"I got it so far. Don't get bent out of shape."

Geffen laughed effortlessly, emptily, his long legs pushed to the floor. "I wish you'd been there. Maybe you could've done something."

"Me?"

"You got a way of seeing things sometimes. It might've been different. It got so quiet, stayed like that. Then this kid and his mother, they come out of the rat huts, they didn't know we were down in the bush. They're doing something out there in the fucking dirt and somebody started shooting at them."

Medavoy had an idea where Geffen's accident went from there, as his own twisted back on him, too. You couldn't evade it forever. Jane was right about his medal balancing things a little in his favor. Gef didn't sound like he'd ever had a chance to strike his own balance since then.

"It was an accident, Gef," he said, spinning the wheel so they were on Madison heading west, traveling toward the river and the older, cheaper homes built before World War II.

"Just listen to me," Gef was sharp. "We just kept shooting, tore that little shithole up. Some people came running out, mostly kids. Couple went down, the rest kept running down the road. Someone yelled, it was like magic, we all stopped.

That's all there was. Didn't go on for more than twenty, thirty seconds because we were scared and mad, Robby."

"Who yelled?"

"Me."

"So you stopped it. You do any of the shooting?" It had to be asked, he knew. It was the reason for Geffen's confession.

"Sure. I wasn't different from anybody else." Geffen sat forward, long arms between his legs. "I hit at least one. Saw one go down when I was firing."

Medavoy interrupted, "You got a whole line of guys shooting. You don't know who hit who. You don't know. And you didn't do anything afterward, right? That was all?"

He nodded. "They ran, the ones who were down, old lady, couple of kids, they're dead. It wasn't on the map, they're wandering probably, so it's like it never happened. We didn't report it."

Weisman, Geffen said, was dead. They buried him and left the others. Medavoy asked the last question. "You know who chucked the can in the fire?"

Geffen touched his chest. "That's pretty fucking obvious."

You assume it's all over and done with, Medavoy thought, as they crossed the Madison Street Bridge and he turned right onto Crossland. Then the memory comes back, vital and searing when you least expect it. He wondered why he never dreamt of Leroy Menefee, only those terrifying moments in the river. Maybe the river washed the bad away and that's all I want to remember.

"Why's it getting to you now, Gef? Been a long time."

The siren rose and fell and Medavoy thought he heard other sirens approaching, too. "Beats me, Robby. That's why I'm kind of scared. I never thought about it, never mentioned it. But I kind of always tried to do a little better on the job, every day, to make it up. I think so anyway. Like I was trying to get it right. Now I don't think I can." He shook his head. "Makes me scared."

"You want my advice? You want to hear what's it like from my side?"

"I'll take whatever you got."

"This is all I know, Gef." Medavoy sped down Arroyo Verde, a small street of white-and-green little wooden homes and high trees, "You can't do it over. You can't wipe it away. That's what I found out. You go crazy trying to fix things that happened yesterday."

"So what's the answer?"

"Beats the flaming fucking shit out of me. I just know you try to make sure it doesn't happen again."

"That was a war," Geffen said, slumping back.

"We got the same thing. Same things are right and wrong," Medavoy knew it wasn't completely true. He couldn't join Geffen in that place years before. But they had the choices to come to worry about.

He neared the intersection of Arroyo Verde and Eugene Avenue and saw the dispersing smoke rising over it. Fire trucks were bearing down on them.

They both immediately forgot about the past. Geffen swore at the pandemonium engulfing the street.

"Jesus, what happened down here?" Medavoy demanded, turning onto Eugene.

A very young patrolman, setting up barricades, sweating, the radio clipped to his shoulder buzzing, tried to hold Medavoy's car.

"Fire battalion chief says nobody goes in, sergeant," he shouted, pulled aside one sawhorse barricade and let two roaring fire trucks speed by. The kid kept waving his arms constantly.

"You don't take orders from the fucking fire department," Medavoy said. "I'm the supervisor of the Robbery Detail so open that fucking barricade and let me through."

The kid hesitated, yelled at cars trying to creep by and people running along the sidewalk. "You sure you want to go in there?"

"Positive. Open up," Medavoy said. Geffen expelled a loud breath. A home in the middle of the block burned feverishly, with red and black ferocity, spitting smoke and sparks into the blue sky. Fire and ladder trucks packed around it. Neighbors clotted along the sidewalk.

The kid moved the barricade and Medavoy slowly drove through. It was wild, the fire spreading apparently, and yet in the shifting colors and shapes there was beauty, too.

"Goddamn, Robby, look at this place. The whole block could go up," Geffen said, startled. "You think that's 5643 in there?"

Medavoy got close to the yellow, pythonlike tangle of fire hoses and trucks, the men in bulky yellow slickers running, standing in a wavering line before the fire that seemed to move with them. A fine black soot fell over them.

"That's 5643," Medavoy said, counting the house numbers on either side of the fire. "We got some major fuckup here. You go see if you can find Beaufort. I got to find out what's going on."

"Meet you back here in five minutes," Geffen shouted, getting out of the car. He headed for the people crowded against the barricades in the street, held back by SMPD cops, all looking over their shoulders whenever the fire gave out a loud crack or rumble.

Medavoy went to an older fireman, standing beside the loud water truck. The fireman pointed, shouted. His gray hair was slick.

Perhaps Trask's bomb had been real after all. This might be the beginning and end of the investigation. It would not be the first time a bomb had been clumsily handled and blown its maker to hell, starting a fire. Beaufort and Trask could be in there now. It would straighten his day out neatly.

"Anybody in there?" he shouted to the older fireman, a

battalion chief, who squinted briefly at Medavoy's gold badge pinned to his coat pocket.

"One got out. Don't know about anybody else. We just got here."

"Who got out?"

"Don't ask me. Got my hands full this morning. She's over there someplace." He pointed generally behind him, the fire truck's engine straining, a mist from the high-power water hoses' jets falling back over them with the soot. Medavoy already saw he was getting a sticky black coating.

He stepped back as the battalion chief jumped in front of him, ordering men forward toward a rich orange-red spout of flame that roared up only a hundred feet away.

"You got an arson here?" Medavoy shouted again.

"Can't tell yet. It's either deliberate or a gas line. Got a motel burning, too about three miles away. We got half the city units fighting that one. Interstate's blocked off. We didn't need this one."

"Motel an arson?"

The battalion chief nodded vigorously. "Definite. Some son of a bitch didn't want to pay his bill," he snorted, never looking at Medavoy, only at the fire playing before him. "I hate these damn little cracker boxes," he pointed around them at the homes, "they go up like excelsior and you lose a block before you know it."

Medavoy didn't believe in coincidence. People tended to make their own accidents and collisions and he thought there was some link between this fire and the motel. "You think a bomb did either of these things?"

"Bomb?" The battalion chief looked at him now. "Something going on here? Something going to blow?"

"There may be a bomb involved in a case I'm working."

"Jesus, Mary, and Joseph." The battalion chief snatched up an older-model walkie-talkie and started shouting warnings to posts around the fire.

"I'm ordering everybody back," Medavoy said.

"Goddamn right you are. Get them all back to the end of the block."

Medavoy yelled for one of the cops at the barricade, who trotted up. He gave instructions to move people quickly without scaring them. The man didn't blink but sprinted back to the barricade and the word was passed.

"It might be a false alarm," Medavoy said. "These assholes showed some kind of plastic explosive. Maybe phony."

"That's real," the battalion chief pointed at the fire, his men only retreating a few feet, water arcing in gray, rainbowed blasts onto the fiery house, the ones on either side starting to burn. "I can't take my men out. This place would go for sure."

It was like the bridge a year ago, Medavoy thought, soot falling, shouting men and rumbling engines, the same tension and confusion. Maybe something was in the works for me, he thought. I don't want it with Jane and Johnathan to worry about now.

Something cracked, crashed inside the house; Medavoy's head jerked toward the sound as a plume of red sparks flew up like wasps released from a broken nest. He spotted Geffen waving and a woman beside him.

"I got to go. Hope you get it under control," he said.

"Two arsons in one day," the battalion chief snapped. "The whole damn city's going to hell today."

"You can always let it burn," Medavoy said, leaving.

"Don't tempt me," the battalion chief answered.

There was a ritual to go through, Medavoy knew, like hunters with a catch. So when he got to Geffen, Geffen said to him, "Here she is."

He held onto a tall woman, older, maybe midforties, even fifty, with a blanket on her shoulders. She watched the fire dully.

"Are you Carol Beaufort?" he asked her. The ritual demanded it, even though they were three people against a concrete lawn divider, the rest of the crowd moving away down the block, held back by cops and barricades. The fire lurched and bellowed in front of them.

"I'm Carol Beaufort." She looked at her flat shoes.

It was hard to see her as one of the duo causing so much trouble around the city. But she resembled the passenger in the videotape and Reilly's secretary had named her a few minutes before in a brutal robbery. What's missing, Medavoy thought, are all the whys. Why the motel, this fire, why Reilly? And where Trask and his shoe box were.

"I got to talk to you right now. Over at my car." Medavoy took her other arm.

She looked into his face. "Do I know you?"

"Not yet," he said.

Medavoy sat her in the front seat, stood beside her, and had Geffen keep everyone else away. He debated taking her downtown first but decided she might answer questions better here with the image of her burning house in front of her.

He didn't want to waste time, either. He had to find out where Trask was and cancel the bomb.

"Okay, Carol, I'm just jumping right in," he said calmly. "You know Kenneth Trask?"

She acted almost elderly, slow, deliberate, pulling the custard-colored blanket around her. But she didn't sound elderly. The voice was cool, hard. "Am I under arrest?"

"For what?"

She smiled, coldly. "You're supposed to tell me."

"Should I arrest you? You done something?"

"I know the games. I don't want to play. I want to go if I'm not under arrest."

"Okay. Where do you want to go?"

She paused then, shivered and retreated a little and Medavoy knew she had what he wanted. She was tougher than she first seemed, but whatever Trask had done was unnerving. "I don't know now. I don't know where to go."

"No more games, Carol. Tell me where Trask is."

"I honestly don't know."

"I don't have a lot of time to stand around here. I have to find him."

"Listen, detective," she huddled under the blankets, "what's your name?"

"Detective Robert Medavoy. See my badge? Robbery Detail. I been to Reilly's office, seen what you and Trask did. So tell me what you can." The firemen nearby gave out a cry followed instantly by a slow, terrible creaking collapse as the blackened shell of Beaufort's house dissolved into itself. Jesus, it went up like nothing, he thought.

She looked at him. "Brian said you'd want to talk to me. I guess it's destiny."

"Talk about what?"

"Detective Medavoy, you know I'm a lawyer. If I start answering questions about this man you're looking for, you can say I was an accomplice."

"Okay, tell me if Trask's in there." He pointed at the black, burning house. "Is he dead?"

The car's radio squawked and Geffen answered it. The breeze shifted and began dropping wet soot on them and the car.

"There are some conditions if I answer."

"Christ, Carol," Medavoy jabbed his finger at her, "you're helping yourself if you answer me, you give me a reason to like you."

"Can you deal?" she asked. "Do you have the authority?"

"It's my case."

Geffen slapped the car roof to get his attention. The acrid smoky air was hazy. "Robby, they got a hot two-eleven at the

Merchants Savings, same deal with a bomb, two guys. One man down."

Beaufort snapped up on that, jerking to her feet. "Kenny? Has Kenny been hurt?"

"Two guys got out," Geffen said over her repeated questions. "We got a couple of units in pursuit."

At least that answered the immediate question. Trask was alive and causing trouble. "We're moving on it, Gef. Call us in, tell them we're rolling."

"What about her?"

Medavoy saw that Beaufort seemed to care very much about what happened to Trask. "She's coming with us. Wherever Trask is, she's going to be there."

"You'd better hurry," she said. "There isn't much time."

"Thanks for warning me," he said, taking her thick, freckled wrists and carefully putting handcuffs on them. "Maybe you'll talk to me on our way, Carol. You're under arrest now."

They got into the car, Geffen driving, using the windshield wipers to move the black mush begrimed on the glass. He flicked on their lights, siren blaring. Medavoy sat with Beaufort in the back; she rocked and grew agitated.

"Who's the other guy? The one's with him?" Medavoy asked as they sped down Eugene Avenue toward the crowd and barricades.

"He's a little freak named David Lisio and he's very dangerous. That's all I'm going to say now. That's all until I find out what's happened."

"You don't have anything to deal with, Carol," Medavoy said.

"You better believe I can deal," she said harshly.

He let it go for now. She looked away, reflective and inward. Get to the scene first, Medavoy figured, find out if Trask and Lisio were still in the vicinity. The car's radio spat and crackled the so-far fruitless chase for the two of them.

The crowd was pushed from the barricades so they could

go through, the young patrolman on guard sweating and still waving his arms too energetically.

"Special Weapons probably beats us there," Medavoy said, leaning toward Geffen. "Son of a bitch Easter's been driving around Jane's house, spooking her."

Geffen turned the radio chatter down slightly. He shook his head. "Maybe it was him. Probably me, Robby. I been trying to figure how to knock on your door."

"You? Just come on up."

"What was I going to say? Strange shit with some gooks a long time ago? No way. Thanks for listening. Forget I bothered you with it."

"Didn't bother me. I'll do what I can, help you out."

"Forget it."

Medavoy sat back, Beaufort apparently deaf to the conversation, thinking and looking out the window. Some things, he knew, could never be forgotten.

TWENTY-EIGHT

NOW THAT SECOND BANK, Central Valley Savings, was how the thing was supposed to go, Kenny thought.

Lisio had rolled up through the drive-up window, just like he and Carol did yesterday. Flash the box at the teller, and scoot out with the money.

At the second, and last change car, Kenny dumped the shopping bag's cash into the pile in one of the suitcases. Lisio stood beside him. It was about nine-seventeen and so far they hadn't seen any cops even cruising nearby.

"Look at that," Kenny enthused, smoothing the bundles of cash so they'd fit more easily into the suitcase. "Filled this one, already filled the fucker up." He snapped the suitcase shut. Tied the straps tightly on it. He and Lisio were shielded from the street by hedges and overhanging branches. The whole street was about as quiet as last night. Everybody in this town went to work, he thought happily.

"Get it loaded, we're getting close again," Lisio said, still staring at his watch. He was so sweaty now he rarely put his hand into the windbreaker pocket, as if the sight of all the cash they were effortlessly collecting surprised even him.

"There's like nearly a hundred," Kenny said, grabbing the very wrinkled shopping bag, slamming the trunk on the four-door Mercury. "I bet we clear two hundred easy."

Lisio lumbered into the driver's side, urging, "Come on, get in, no more time," and Kenny slipped in.

Sure enough, Lisio had to fool with the seat, bend the steering wheel, adjust everything so he could just manage to drive because of his height.

They hadn't spoken much during the second bank, and Kenny had been bothered by a couple of things. He cleared his throat as Lisio signaled, turned widely into the street, and started down another residential street toward the west end of the city.

"Dave, how come I ain't seen no luggage? You been in town a couple of days and you don't have any clothes?"

Lisio shook his head. He took shallow, gurgly breaths because he was nervous. "I checked my baggage at the airport before I met you. I didn't intend to be held up by my luggage or worry if I lost it."

Kenny nodded. Typical Lisio, always making plans for things he probably wouldn't have thought of. "Okay. So how about all that shit you're wearing now? What're doing with it after we finish? I ain't riding around with it."

"Of course you're not. I couldn't even get into the airport with this on." Lisio now dropped his hand into the pocket, found the car was hard to control, and put both hands back on the wheel. "I'll dump it before we get to the airport. I won't need it."

"Maybe you don't need it now," Kenny said, hoping he was being sly. Put Lisio off the scene a little, think he was completely in with the program.

But Lisio shook his head, hair damp on his forehead. "No, I prefer having it as insurance until we're finished, Kenny."

"Hurts my feelings."

Lisio grunted. "Read the map off to me. I know it, but I'd like to verify things."

Kenny picked up the map. He had the time, and the moment would come when Lisio would relax and assume everything was over and done with. Then that's it for Lisio. He thought contentedly, excitedly of the suitcases in the car's trunk.

"What gets me," he said, reading the street names off to Lisio, "is these fuckers almost act like they want us to have the money. They make it so easy."

Jane slowed Smitty's car, shocked by the smoke and flames in front of her. The entire block on Eugene Avenue was closed off. Several houses burned and a dark, roiling smoke cloud moved over them.

TV cameras had arrived and were setting up. The crowd pressed back against barricades watched the cameras with as much interest as the fire. She edged the car up to the nearest barricade and a frantically gesturing young cop.

"I'm looking for Detective Medavoy," she said loudly.

"Never heard of him. You have to back up. Clear the lane."

"He's here with Robbery."

She knew it would be impossible to find Robby in the rush of men and equipment beyond the barricades, in all the black smoke, rising into the blue sky and white clouds, the firemen and hoses looped and stretched along the wet street. What was going on? What kind of case was Robby working on?

She had to find him, the news was too important. She started badgering the young cop. He darted from side to side, shouting at people, very worked up.

"Are there any detectives here?" she called out to him.

"You from downtown?"

He had looked at Smitty's Ford, then gone back to berating people.

"Yeah, I'm from downtown," she said. It was true, even if his perception about the meaning was different from hers.

He began pointing north. "Okay, okay. You missed him by a couple of minutes. They all got out of here."

"Where's he going?"

"Okay, the word I got is anybody who asks from downtown, they've gone to Merchants Savings Bank."

"Any address?"

"I missed it."

"You have a lot to worry about. I can find it." She tried to sound sympathetic. The address would be in the phone book.

"It's crazy here. Tell them to get some more guys out here."

"Take it easy," she said, making a wide turn and driving away from the fire. Something important enough had happened to yank Robby away from this. If her information wasn't as fresh, she'd let it wait until she saw Robby at noon. But he wouldn't make the picnic, she knew that. He had to hear this information now.

Frankly, there was a definite rush, excitement in chasing him down, following along through the craziness. I hear about it in court, Robby tells me about his experience, but it's different doing it yourself, she thought. Everything, that fire, the hurried drive, had a sharp-edged vividness, as if charged up.

Thank God for Smitty's Santa Maria city car, the one he was entitled to from the motor pool as senior court reporter. The old Ford was decorated with Santa Maria parking permits, city seal, even seat-belt safety campaign stickers the city was running.

Of course the young patrolman took a look and figured she was doing something official.

In a way, she thought, I really am. I'm going to help a good cop keep his job.

TWENTY-NINE

MEDAVOY SPENT THE FIRST few minutes at Merchants Savings Bank learning that they had missed Trask and Lisio. Patrol units flooding the nearby streets had lost track of them entirely.

He had no idea where they were going or what they had in mind next. There was one person who did and he was going to find out from her in the next five minutes. Without a doubt, he thought.

He had Geffen take Carol into the bank's conference room and put a cop on the door.

The Special Weapons Unit Command Post van was parked outside, the men in black uniforms seeming to absorb light. Easter watched sardonically while Medavoy ordered yellow-ribbon cordons put up around the parking lot, and set the techs to work on the spent bullet shells, markers placed beside them. More patrol cars kept arriving and he set them to work on the restive crowd of shoppers bottlenecked in the arcade and parking lot. This crowd, unlike the stunned people at the fire, was angry.

Easter followed him into the bank. Medavoy said, "They dumped the car someplace around here. They're in a different car."

"Maybe they flew away."

Some of Easter's Blue Team had come into the bank and thought the crack was funny. Medavoy hated the idea he had to watch men in his own department, but these were the same guys who were setting him up.

"So if you want to do something, go look for the Ford sedan, light blue these chumps dumped." News of the second bank had come in.

"My men aren't moving," Easter said. "I give them orders."

"Okay," Medavoy said evenly, "tell them they can stand around here with their thumbs up their asses. I'm not releasing them."

Easter and the Blue Team took the news lightly. The bank's nautical lobby was animated with cops and civilians in clusters, a few sobs, and questions being asked. Faint string music drifted down over them. "You're not releasing us?" Easter asked sarcastically. "What gives you the authority, bud? I don't see any."

Medavoy paused, nodding to the cop on duty at the conference room. "It's my case. So the chain of command runs through me."

"I don't know if you want it, bud," Easter said. He stood in black, half-taunting, half-angry. "What're you going to be doing now while we stand around?"

Medavoy was glad Geffen had gone out to supervise the cops in the parking lot and avoided a second run-in with Easter. I don't need to keep cops from going after each other right now, he thought.

"I got Trask's girlfriend," he said to Easter, opening the conference room door. "I'm going to make a deal."

Carol waited until the detective closed the door. All the drapes had been closed so the room was swathed in beige.

He's got kind eyes, she thought. Almost shy.

But that could be a trick. She had been fooled too often in the last twenty-four hours to take any observation at face value.

"Do you want me to read your rights again?" Medavoy asked her gently. They had gone through the exercise on the wild ride to the bank.

"I think I know them," she said. She sat up straight in one of the bank's thickly cushioned chairs. There was hard bargaining coming up and she thought the setting appropriate.

"You'll talk to me?"

"Isn't that what we're doing?"

"You know the drill and we're going to get real serious. I want you to do this freely."

She pushed aside one of the drapes near her. The bank was oddly busy, people moving around with papers, talking. But no one seemed very excited. Strange behavior. She let the drape fall back.

"How is the guard?" she asked. Best to know all the facts against you.

Medavoy shrugged. "Got hit in the leg. He'll probably lose it."

Carol grimaced in genuine pain herself. "I'm very sorry. I'm sure Kenny didn't shoot first."

"Like the guy he nailed last night? He's critical. You know how that can change things if he dies."

"Yes, I do."

Medavoy seemed to be trying to relax and startle her at the same time, the soft voice, the implied threats. He pulled up a chair beside her, like they were old friends, the kind eyes watching her.

Can't let him know just yet how little time there is, she thought. I can use that to pry myself loose. It was all, she realized, coming down to a matter of exquisite timing.

"Okay, Carol, I don't have a lot of time, you know that. I'm going to talk straight. Probably straighter than anybody except your folks ever have to you."

"You don't know my folks."

He smiled a little. "After twelve years as I cop, I bet I do. I bet I know what they'd think of all you've done lately."

The only way she could tell he was anxious was the drumming fingers on the conference table. The voice and eyes stayed calm.

"What time is it?" she asked.

"About nine-twenty," he said. He was alert. "What does that mean?"

"If you want Kenny and Lisio, you've got about forty minutes."

"For what?"

"First, I want some absolute understandings. Can you do that?"

"Can you give me Trask and Lisio?"

"Yes," she said firmly. An involuntary shudder passed over her, a reaction from the morning's exertions. Her red-knuckled hands knit together tightly. "I can tell you where they're going."

"Okay." Medavoy leaned forward a little, a big man, confident in his quiet way. "Here's what you don't get. Every second we fuck around in here, Trask and Lisio can do something. You probably know that better than me. The second they kill someone or blow something up, you're dead. You're an accomplice and you didn't give me shit to stop them. That's first degree."

"I do know the law better than you, Medavoy."

"Okay, if that doesn't bother you, how about Trask? We see him, he's not getting a chance to shoot anybody else."

The shyness was a pose, she decided, ruthless bullying son of a bitch hiding beneath it. He had caught her exclamation when it sounded like Kenny was shot. *I've got to keep Kenny alive. He's my alibi and he risked his life for me.*

"What's your offer?" she asked coldly.

"You give me their location, I go to the DA and make sure you get a lid of no more than five years total, for everything that's happened."

"No good."

"I'm throwing in robbery, assault, harboring a fugitive," he used his fingers to count the charges.

"Stop it. I want two things from you and that's all. I want immunity. I want your absolute promise that Kenny will not be hurt."

"I can't give you that. He's shooting at people."

"It's one of my conditions. You've got to broadcast it to all your units."

Medavoy got up. He's going to bend, she thought, I can see it. He wants what I've got very badly. His face grew angry.

"I don't understand how a woman like you, smart lawyer, could hook up with a dipshit like Trask. I do not get it."

"You don't have to. Time is running out, Medavoy. We both can't afford to waste it."

He jammed his hands in his pockets. "We can make an effort to take Trask without shooting him. He's got to surrender. You cooperate in taking him, I get you a sentence lid of five years."

"He won't shoot first."

"So we've got a deal?"

"I want immunity."

"That's too much."

"I will help you take Kenny. I want him alive," she said. "But, I'm a bystander. I haven't done anything and I will not," she heard her voice rise unnaturally, "be punished."

"Immunity's a tough sale to the DA," Medavoy said. "You've got to deliver."

"Write it out," she said.

He sat down instantly, took out a small notepad and began scrawling. When he was done, he handed the page to her and they both signed it. She thought it was faintly comical, her whole life reduced to a page from a cheap notepad.

"All right," she said, shivering again, folding the page and putting it in her pocket. "Ask a question."

He had her give a short, very concise summary of Kenny's abrupt arrival, Lisio and the scam based on police-response time. When he heard that, Medavoy shook his head in dismay. She told him about the dynamite corset, the way Kenny had protected her. She noticed the tiny soot particles on Medavoy's coat, like black dandruff.

"What's the name of the next bank?" he asked swiftly.

"I don't remember if it's Santa Maria something or Valley Savings. I wasn't paying much attention then. I heard it, but I wasn't listening."

Medavoy slammed a fist on the conference table. "You've got my word written out what you'll get if you live up to this deal, Carol. But, if you screw it up, I give you my word, you're going to look at every charge I can pile on you."

He had his handy-talkie out, a streamlined walkie-talkie, the volume up so that a raucous scritch and hissing voices filled the muffled room explosively. Trying to startle me again, she thought. She gathered her thoughts.

"Don't threaten, Medavoy. It's stupid. I know the tactics. There were four banks. The last thing Kenny told me was to meet him at the Citizens Savings Bank. I don't know where. They don't have another car to switch, so they'll be using the one from the third bank. Get that description and you can follow them."

"Okay," he calmed down. "Citizens Savings. What time?" he was repeating it into the handy-talkie for whoever was listening.

"Lisio said about nine-forty-eight. Then they drive to the airport. Then they fly away. But Kenny won't. He'll try to find me."

"You can't remember the next bank? Nothing? You sure?"

She shook her head. "I am goddamn sorry I don't. I only know the last one for certain."

"Okay, we're moving out of here, Carol, and you keep telling me anything you think of, okay? We're partners now. Don't let me down," he spoke to the handy-talkie.

The conference room door opened, two cops coming in, a woman between them. Carol assumed she was another detective, but the demure, soberly dressed woman looked with concern at Medavoy. Real emotion, like she cared for him.

It was Medavoy's sudden, automatic amazement that changed Carol's mind about the woman.

"Jesus Christ, Jane. What're you doing here?" his hands went out to her. He lost interest in the handy-talkie, still hissing.

"Something's going on, Robby. I had to see you right away."

"Who's she?" Carol demanded.

"This's nothing to do with you, Carol," Medavoy snapped, ordering the handcuffs back on her. "We're moving. Bring her along," he said to the cops.

Carol watched with envy, irritation, and curiosity, as Medavoy bent toward the woman, kissed her, and hurriedly escorted her from the conference room and the bank.

Think about yourself, she said sternly, think about what's going to happen if they catch up with Kenny and Lisio.

Jane slowed down when Medavoy did outside the bank. A large man, like an aging surfer dressed in black, called out, "You see who's here, Medavoy? You want to do something about them?"

She looked. Arrayed along the sidewalk around the shopping mall parking lot was a colorful caravan of TV news trucks. Two cops chased after a man who jumped between them and ran toward the bank.

"The area's sealed," Medavoy said. Jane didn't know this

voice, it was commanding and abrupt. His cop voice. "Put a couple of your guys in front. That'll scare everybody."

The man in black saluted. Without meaning it, she saw. The snide look he had gave it away. She wondered who he was and why he apparently disliked Robby.

She wanted to talk to him, but something thrust itself forward before she could say anything. Her head turned suddenly at the sound of helicopters.

"Gef! Get them out of here! That son of a bitch thinks he's supposed to land! Tell him to stay up!" Medavoy threw his hands up.

Geffen had appeared near the side of the crowd, he ducked quickly into the dark glowing interior of the black Command Post van. Three men in black uniforms, police written on their backs, holding black, complex weapons, trotted toward the line of news trucks and the crowd that grew even as she watched it.

Two helicopters overhead stopped lowering, rose again, their deep deafening call reminding her of that other night, when she thought Robby was drowned. These helicopters swung off to the east, like obedient servants.

The woman Robby had been talking to was brought out, head forced down as she went into an unmarked police car in front of the bank. She sat in backseat, staring at Jane. It was disconcerting to have a stranger watching, examining you like that.

"You can't stay with me, Janie. I'm moving very fast and it's dangerous."

"I've got to talk to you. Something's come up and you could be in a hell of a lot of trouble," she said emphatically.

"You came all the way to tell me?"

"Of course I did. I heard it at the courthouse," she started to go on, but he stopped her.

"It's about IAD, right? I know about it. You went to a lot of trouble for me."

"Don't make it sound like I was making a damn delivery," she said tartly. "You know how important you are to me."

He softened. "Forgive me, okay? I just got through with a rough session in there, I got worse coming up, and I can't turn it off."

"Who's she?" Jane asked, nodding toward Carol in the car. They were both running on glass, she thought, and neither of us can slow down or look down. I shouldn't be hard on him now.

"One of my problems. You got to stay here."

"I'm along for this trip, Robby," she said decisively. "I've seen it so far, I want to go the whole way."

"I could keep you here."

"You know you couldn't. You don't want to." He was checking his watch every few seconds. He was in some kind of danger and she intended to be close by, to hold out a saving hand, like the night by the river, if needed.

He was angry, uncertain. "I got to explain why you're here. Somebody might ask."

"Tell them I'm a civilian ride-along. I work at the courthouse."

He made up his mind quickly. "Okay. There's no time. Stay by the car now, then you got to stay behind the line where we're going."

"I'll stay out of the way," she promised.

"This isn't the one to come on, Janie."

Geffen appeared at the van doorway, the line from a headset linking him to the equipment inside. "Robby. We started the sweeps for their car."

The large man in black appeared and nimbly heaved himself into the van.

Medavoy gave her a quick, almost cold peck on the cheek, then climbed into the van, too.

She heard sirens again. The whirling, churning tenor of the helicopters overhead again as she walked to the police car. The river was unseen, Jane thought, rushing beside you,

carrying you along faster. She avoided the eyes of the woman
in the car's backseat.

Medavoy and Easter stood beside a map of Santa Maria on the
van's center table as Geffen called out the intersections overflown
by helicopters searching for Trask and Lisio's abandoned car, a
Ford Fairlane, blue body. It was close inside the van, two Special
Weapons men standing by a rack of assault rifles.

"They're heading for number three," Medavoy said. He
looked bleakly at the maze of streets, blocks, numbers on the
dense map. "The question is, which fucking bank? Which
one's number three?"

"Just passing Atlantic, Robby. Negative. Nothing below,"
Geffen spoke flatly, he was good enough to do that, but couldn't
hide the tightness underneath his words.

Easter was propped on his knuckled fists. "What're you
doing, Medavoy? We should be all over that area now."

"Doing what? We don't know what kind of car they're in,
where they're going." He glanced at his watch. "We got five
minutes before they get to the third bank and hit it."

"We got to be ready to drop down on them like a fucking
ton of bricks," Easter glared at him.

"Then what? You got one guy wearing a hell of a lot of
dynamite. You got a guy who shoots at anything that gets too
close. They're going to be moving through residential streets
here," he swept his hand over the map, "no matter which
way they go."

"You get a sniper close by, bud, you can take care of
the dynamite."

Geffen spoke again. "Over Glen Ellen. Negative."

Medavoy knew he had to make a decision very quickly.
The timetable Trask and Lisio forced on him allowed for no
calm decisions, no clear calls. It had to be fast. Nothing more
was possible.

"There's no time to get a sniper anyplace safe," he said to Easter. "We'd have to catch them on the run from the third bank and they're going to be right in the middle of city streets."

"My guys can take them."

Medavoy glanced at the stored grenades and rifles, lights and heavy rope. Somewhere a bank was about to be robbed and he couldn't stop it. All he could do was try to get one step ahead of these guys. Beaufort had given him that much.

"I'm not going to risk it. Gef, get on the air to Santa Maria Airport. Tell them to have their security out on the approach roads." He traced on the map. "There're like two roads in. Get our units out there. The airport's got a buffer of a mile of fields around it, so we can keep these assholes from getting close to it. If something happens, at least it's out in the open."

"How you going to know which one's them?" Easter demanded truculently. "Thought that's why you're dicking around here now."

"After the third bank, we'll have a description of the car. They won't get out of Santa Maria at the airport."

"So what're you saying, bud? You just going to let them hit a bank and do nothing about it?"

Medavoy nodded. "It's got to be."

"I do not fucking believe you said that, bud."

Medavoy realized there was no one else taking responsibility for what was about to happen, good or bad. He could call downtown, get the bureau captain or the head of Operations to oversee, but it would be time consuming. Beaufort said the Citizens Savings on El Camino Grande was the fourth and last bank. That would have to be where he stopped Trask and Lisio.

Geffen said, "Still negative over Sunrise, Robby. You want the sweeps to come back in this direction?"

"Tell the helicopters to stand by. Put out the description of Beaufort's station wagon, too. Maybe they didn't change cars. Maybe they're still riding around in it."

"Suppose these assholes start shooting like they did here?"

Easter said, twisting away from the map, pointing out the van's front windshield. "Suppose they just shoot up this next bank?"

Geffen broke in, "One of the copters got the car they dumped. On the thirteen hundred block of Mayfield. You want them to sit on it?"

Medavoy shook his head. "Get a patrol unit on it. I want the copters ready to move when Trask and Lisio hit the road after the next one." What about Easter's bitter question? He looked from the map. "All of this's a crapshoot. I'm taking the risk."

"You sure as hell are, bud." Easter looked incredulously at his men. "You're risking everyone in that bank."

"Look, Trask and Lisio are going to be at number four, last on their hit parade, at nine-forty-five," he checked his watch. "So we're going to set up there, Citizens Savings. Get everybody out of that bank."

"We should bottle them up, cut them off on a surface street. We can control that."

"They'll see us. They'll see the roadblocks."

"They'll see the damn roadblocks at this other bank, bud."

"But they won't have time to do anything about it. We did this gag before. Remember, Gef?" he traced on the map. "We got this tip about some pukes who were going into a jewelry store. We didn't want to spook them, so we set up an accident in the street outside. They came right in, figured the cops were up to taking care of the accident. We didn't look hostile. They figured we're supposed to be there."

"You just lucked out with some really stupid guys, Medavoy," Easter said. "These guys aren't coming right into your arms."

Medavoy shook his head. "Gef? What'd they do?"

Geffen twisted the headset a little so he could hear. "We just wanted them close enough, trying to decide what's going on. Then they kind of gave up. Nowhere to go."

Voices from the communication gear crackled faintly. Medavoy said to Easter, "Okay? You put your snipers around the accident, keep them low. We slow them down enough, get them into a crossfire and you take them out if we can't get them to surrender."

This seemed to agree with Easter, partway. "In the street?"

"All the action will be in the street, no civilians at risk. The bank's empty."

"They don't go any further?"

"That's the end of the line."

"What kind of accident?"

Medavoy didn't think Easter would play completely straight with him, the guy was too wired up and angry to do that. But they might make it successfully through the next half hour. After that, the two of them could settle everything.

"I don't give a shit what kind of accident. Get a couple of cars, ram them together so it looks like a fender bender. Use your Blue Team, then get them out of sight. I figure we can put three units, six guys around the cars. It'll look like an investigation."

"Uniform guys?" Geffen asked quietly. They would be exposed.

"Has to be. I don't want the Weapons guys anywhere Trask and Lisio can see them. Keep them hidden," he said to Easter.

"I think I know how to set that up, bud." Easter barely turned and started giving orders to one of the men in the front of the van. Another voice barked out over the radio.

Medavoy looked at his watch again. Right now Trask and Lisio had arrived at some unsuspecting bank somewhere in the city. Events he couldn't control now would determine what happened to his career and other peoples' lives. He grinned slightly at Geffen's serious, tight expression. If you don't want the responsibility, you're in the wrong job, he thought.

"Gef, get hold of units around Citizens Savings. Evacuate the place, get everybody into the shopping center. Make sure they stay clear, stay down. It's got to be done fast, and don't scare the shit out of everybody."

Geffen nodded and began talking through the van's

communications to downtown and then to the patrol cars. Easter was talking to his own men. "I want the Greens alerted. Tell everybody we're rolling to the scene."

Nine-thirty, Medavoy thought. On a clear Friday morning. He wondered what he'd be thinking about at ten.

He said, "Gef, copters holding?"

"Ready when you are, Robby."

"Okay, when the word comes on this next bank," he took a deep breath, "tell all our units on the street, no hot pursuit. They are to leave the car alone. Do not pursue."

Easter turned from the separate dialogue he had with his teams. His lined face was bemused. "You want to let them waltz right through the city, bud? These bad guys?"

"I don't want them to do anything before they get to us. I don't want some patrol unit to jinx everything."

Easter half-grinned, as if he thought Medavoy's predicament were amusing. "Coming with us, bud?"

"We'll go in my car. I got Trask's girlfriend."

"You really got a lot out of her, bud," Easter said sarcastically. "Made a hell of a deal."

Medavoy ignored it. This wasn't the time or place. The van's engines rumbled. "Come on, Gef. Let's go." He jumped out of the van, Geffen landing right after him.

Easter was at the van's door, pulling it closed. "You don't know if the pukes are going to kill somebody right now. What're you going to do if they pull the pin and there's no cop car around to stop them?"

"I'll have to get another job," Medavoy said. He sprinted the few feet to his car. Jane stood beside it; Beaufort stared out at him.

He took Jane's arm, steered her to the front seat. "I'll ride with Beaufort. You drive, Gef. Let's beat these mothers to the damn bank."

There had to be a problem, he decided, when he didn't know if he meant Trask and Lisio or Easter and his men.

THIRTY

THE CHIEF PAUSED in his testimony, waiting until old Lindow stopped wheezing and checking his handkerchief. Over each red plush councilmember's chair was a spotlight and Lindow's face was moist. The Chief thought it was ridiculous to televise these meetings when the council looked so awful.

He resumed, hoping to keep their attention. "So our total available sworn personnel to date number six hundred twenty-two," he said, pushing his glasses back up his nose. "And as you can see from the graphs I've distributed, I'm proposing a budget increase to permit a deployment of our officers in three overlapping ten-hour shifts every day rather than four overlapping shifts."

He glanced up, annoyed to see Prefach whispering excitedly to one of the innumerable staff kids he always seemed to have around. The rest of the City Council appeared stuporous. To the right of the podium where he stood, the Chief had up his charts of patrol strength in each councilmanic district and response times for emergency calls. It helped to show how more officers improved things in the district.

310

He cleared his throat, wondering why Prefach stared at him. "With additional officers and this shift manipulation, I project a reduction of waiting on calls. Officers will not have to wait for backup if they can be deployed in two-man cars rather than one. And, of course, this will save gas and wear and tear on the patrol cars."

He stepped from the podium to the chart. Prefach scribbled something and the kid, in coat and tie from one of the local colleges, scurried away with it.

The Chief got as far as raising his pointer to the chart when Prefach broke in. "I request a short recess. I apologize to the Chief of Police, but I have to attend to something."

The mayor nodded, banged her gavel and out went the TV spotlights as the council shambled out through doors on either side of the great city seal.

Prefach, at his usual trot, came over. He had a sour look and he took the Chief's arm, convoying him out of the chambers to a conference room reserved for the council. People smoking and gossiping in the hall watched with mild interest.

Prefach slammed the door. "You've got a priority problem, Steve."

The Chief complained, "What's the urgency? You interrupted me."

"Your staff isn't getting emergency communications to you," Prefach said sourly.

"They're not supposed to disturb me when I'm here."

It didn't impress Prefach that the council was given such preference. "Look, Steve, there is a man running around this city with dynamite strapped to his body. He's just held up two banks and shot a security guard. He probably torched a motel. You've got another giant fire in the eighth district. You've got nearly the entire fire department tied up on these fires."

The Chief did not like the way Prefach intimated these were solely his problems.

"Calm down," he said. "I'm sure Metro patrol is on top

of it. The Special Weapons Unit is mobilized, too. That's what they're trained for."

Prefach stood by the conference table. "Who gives a shit, Steve? In about fifteen minutes, this is going to be the biggest story in the city."

"My men can handle it." Suddenly the Chief was aware of his uniform.

"They better. I'm getting this hearing tabled."

"What about the money for the department?"

"You don't appreciate the situation, Steve. You've got a major, major crisis out in this city's streets. My information is that things are crazy out there. There won't be any money, any construction okayed, until this situation is resolved."

"I said my men are on top of it. If it will make you feel better, I can verify what's going on." The Chief disliked Prefach's habit of standing within six inches of him. The boyish charm was gone. Only the ambition and hunger remained.

"You're not going to verify anything," Prefach said, pointing at him. "You're getting your ass into the field. You head up this goddamn thing personally."

"Personally?"

"The Chief of Police takes personal charge of the hunt for this nut with the dynamite. The Chief stands up for his city."

The Chief was queasy. I could do it, he thought, but it's pointless. It's all for show, one of Prefach's publicity gimmicks.

"There's no need for me to be out there, Vin," he said hotly. "My men are trained, and I've got confidence in them."

Prefach came to within a few inches of his face. He was softly sinister. "See, Steve, you and I are tied together. People think of me, they see you. They think of you, they see me."

"It's good teamwork this year, Vin."

"So I'm not going to have people think I failed because you didn't do your job."

"I'm Chief of Police," he shot back. "I am doing my job."

"This is the biggest damn disaster to hit Santa Maria in

twenty years. If you're not out there saving this city, I'm going to bust you right out of the department."

"Go to hell. You couldn't do it."

Prefach was stern, an angry parent. "I sure can. You can keep your doorman's uniform, Steve. Just get out there." Prefach almost pushed him. "Now."

The Chief saw that he meant it.

It was a terrible rush back to the department and the Chief loathed fighting his way through the crowd of reporters and TV cameras that seemed to have sprouted, funguslike, in front of the building. He marched furiously to his office.

Bart had the TV on. He half-rose when the Chief came in. "You let me down," the Chief snapped at him. "Prefach just gave me my battle orders."

"Mac!" Bart said in horror. "I'm sorry!"

The Chief threw his briefcase across the room so that it landed partly on his desk, scattering papers onto the floor.

"Oh, for Christ sake!" the Chief shouted when he saw Prefach come on the TV, speaking from the council chambers. *"Chief McNeill felt so strongly about this developing situation, he said he had to be there himself."* Prefach's face was intermittently visible behind a wavering line of microphones. *"So I asked for an immediate adjournment as he wanted me to."*

Bart helped him pick up the fallen papers. "You looked okay just now, Mac. You sounded fine."

The Chief straightened, an ache in his back. "Prefach's got more stooges leaking to him in this department. That's my next project, shut down Prefach's sources."

"I tried to get hold of you. He must've got everything faster."

The Chief tossed the papers to his desk, feeling hot and angry and fearful. *I can't say no to this one. I've got to go out.*

"Well, you let me down," he repeated. "Where's my gun?"

"You need it?"

"For this, I've got to have the whole nine yards, Bart."

"Okay, okay, don't get upset. I'll get it." He lumbered to the credenza and came up with a shiny black automatic and a shiny brown-leather apparatus.

"Now what you're going to do, Bart," the Chief thought he sounded depressingly excited, "is call down and get my car ready."

"Right. Right. Right. Go in style. Show them you're boss."

"Shut up." He couldn't stand still in his anxiety as Bart worked on trying to gird him in the gun and holster. He gestured, arms waving. "Get my car ready. I want it to leave this building with every damn light on and the siren going."

"Great, Mac."

"And at the same time I want an unmarked car to get me out of here as quietly as possible."

"Where's your car going?"

"Anyplace far away from where I'm going."

"How come?"

The Chief patted the holster, checked the gun. At least I qualify every year. I know what the damn thing feels like. He took out his handkerchief, wiping his hands and mouth. He dried the moist bridge of his glasses.

"I don't want that clan of TV jackasses running after me," he said waspishly. "Let them follow my damn car into the next county."

"They been doing this story live for the last ten minutes." Bart pointed at the TV where a map of small red dots appeared. Then a jumpy picture of firemen and smoke, then Prefach again. Then the Chief in front of the department, waylaid by the troupe of cameras.

Watching it, the Chief shut his eyes. Like a gnome in a costume, he thought.

"Damn Prefach threatened me," he said furiously to Bart. "Get the cars and let's get going."

Bart swore at Prefach as he dialed on the intricate telephone console between the computer terminals on the desk. "You want me to get my gun?"

"En. Oh. You stay here. I need somebody marginally reliable to keep track of things."

Bart's face fell into canine sorrow. He spoke into the phone, with reflected anger.

The Chief winced at his own form on TV, the shouted, repellent questions, the whole sideshow performance. Donna should be here. She'd have some suggestions, some way to get me out of this. No time to call her. No time at all.

"Turn that junk off!" he shouted at his own image, Bart wide-eyed. "And tell me where I'm supposed to go!"

Masuda offered Zaragoza one of the spongy brown sweet cakes his wife had made. They were alone in the Robbery Detail office.

"They make me sick, I'm sorry, Stan. Like ten packs of sugar in my coffee."

"Look at me. You think it's bad for you?" He flexed one thick arm and his white shirt rose.

"Sugar makes you supertense, man."

Masuda licked his fingers and looked at the stack of investigation requests dumped on him from the DA office. Always the new deputies did that, the ones who hadn't figured out what they needed and didn't need to make a case fly. Like the kid DA who wanted him to go out and bring in an assortment of dildoes for a victim to look at in a rape case. Sometimes he didn't think law schools taught common sense. "I try to bribe you, Jimmy," he said. "Now I just ask. You want to take some of my interviews here?"

"I got my own caseload, man. I'm snowed under."

"You're bullshitting. You ain't done anything all morning."

"I get to it."

"I'll buy you lunch."

Zaragoza's phone rang. He held up his hand to Masuda and answered it. Masuda got up, not wanting to look at the horrible pile of silly requests, and switched off the coffee machine. Zaragoza was talking on the phone.

"Yeah, Gef," Jimmy frowned deeply. "Sure, Gef. You sure? No shit? Jesus. Jeezus. Okay. Okay. Give it to me." He started writing on the back of a file folder, not bothering to find a piece of paper.

Masuda had seen Jimmy with that same, sickly expression when that state Supreme Court nailed him. He hung up.

"What's Gef want?" Masuda asked.

"We got to meet him. He's heading to some bank with Robby. I got it here."

"What's the big deal?"

Zaragoza roughly snatched his coat from the back of the door. "The whole town's going to fucking blow up. He says Easter's going to waste Robby."

THIRTY-ONE

LISIO, FROWNING, SWEATING heavily and trying to drive at the same time, glanced at Kenny. "Did the car act funny at all last night?"

Kenny shook his head. He kept an eye on traffic around them, little places in the street where cops could hide and jump out at you. The sort of dirt-colored Mercury he'd swiped last night would shake, then sputter every so often. "Ran fine when I moved it. You bump the ignition wires or anything?"

Lisio frowned worse, peered under the steering wheel a little. "I don't think so. They might've come loose."

"I'll check it before we head for the airport. I ain't stopping after we finish." Kenny had half-lowered the zipper on his jacket. The .45 was easily reachable. He felt limbered, loosely at ease. The third bank, Santa Maria Federal, had gone so silkily it was weird. It really was like these people couldn't do enough to pass over their cash. Both suitcases were nearly full and he wondered if the last bank would be too much. What a thing to worry about, too much money sticking out of your suitcase.

"What time, Kenny?" Lisio didn't dare look away from the street. They drove by camper dealerships and office buildings.

"Nine-thirty-five."

"No cops?"

"I ain't seen one."

Lisio allowed a small smile, hunched forward as he was to drive, the thick body and its dynamite looking soft and vulnerable. "It's working as I imagined. Just as I imagined. The cops are all running around the last couple of banks; they can't keep up with us."

Kenny had to admit that Lisio had done a fine job of thinking this one out. The few glitches that had arisen were unforseeable, part of the risk of doing business you might say.

"Okay, so we do this last one," Kenny said, "we get out to the airport. When you going to get rid of that dynamite 'cause it's worrying me."

"Don't think about it. I'll drop it someplace before we head for the airport."

"Sure?"

"I said I would."

Kenny sat back, happy he could feel the .45 against his belly. Lisio was lying, he was certain. Look how he played the whole thing with Carol, lies all the way. Sure he'd take off the dynamite, give up the one fucking thing that kept Kenny at bay.

He's going to fuck me sometime after we're done, Kenny decided. So I got to take care of him first.

The Mercury lurched slightly, Kenny jerking a bit in his seat.

"Something's wrong, Kenny. The damn car's not in gear or something," Lisio snapped.

"Want to pull over?"

"No time now. Citizens Savings is the furthest distance we've got to cover. I'll stop if something really seems out of whack."

"Drives okay. Only got to make it another twenty, thirty minutes and who gives a shit after that."

Lisio wiped his sweating forehead. "No, you're right. I'm too jumpy. I hadn't counted on being so nervous. Even though it's going so well."

Kenny patted him genially on the shoulder. Like tweaking the dragon's nose, he thought. Lying little fucker. "Way I do it, you kind of float along, you know what's going down, but it don't get to you."

"I'll try that."

"Sure. Just float. Like it's all a movie."

Lisio inhaled deeply, anxiously. "Only a few more minutes."

"That's it, man. Go with it."

Lisio braced himself against the steering wheel, concentrating on the cars around them. "I was thinking just now, there's no reason a man couldn't do this several times, get a million in a couple of cities."

Kenny played along, thinking about the payback after this last bank, someplace on the road out to the airport, got to be some deserted side street or something with all these fields and shit he'd seen driving into town yesterday. Someplace you could drop a misshapen little liar so it'd take a while for him to be found. Then go find Carol and take two suitcases and fly off into the sunset.

"Yeah, man," he said to Lisio, "I like it. Maybe we can talk about it."

Medavoy had Geffen running the siren full blast, clearing the cars ahead of them. Between him and the front seat was a wire grille, sturdy enough, he knew, that a .20 drunk couldn't bend it or an irate wife beater break it.

Geffen and Jane sat up front, Carol Beaufort with him in the back. They seemed to be flying as Geffen pushed the car, but sometimes slowed when traffic didn't move out of the way.

It was agonizing to think they'd miss Trask and Lisio.

If that happened, the last fallback was on the road to Santa Maria Airport.

Medavoy didn't think much about the problems he faced in the department. He thought, and dismissed it for now, of the weight that would crash upon him, leaving a bank open to robbery, letting the culprits have a free ride.

The word had been pouring from the radio about the third bank, Santa Maria Federal on Watson Avenue. No injuries, no damage and the car Trask and Lisio were in was succinctly described, a brown Mercury, California plates, probably a four-door model.

Geffen drove with the negligent intensity only a cop in hot pursuit manages, arm draped over the wheel, body back against the seat, eyes roving across the rapidly changing roadway ahead.

"We're running parallel and ahead of them, Robby," he said. "They won't even know we're coming."

"Speed it up, Gef," he said without thinking. They must be pushing eighty now on four-lane surface streets.

Over the radio came steady progress reports from other patrol units and the helicopters, charting the movement of Trask and Lisio toward Citizens Savings. Everybody was obeying orders and staying well back, just keeping them in sight.

"Easter's going to beat us by a couple minutes," Geffen said. They heard the raw, disembodied voice of the Special Weapons supervisor giving orders for the phony accident in the middle of El Camino Grande, about a half block down from the bank itself. The evacuation of the bank was underway, and people were being moved away from the stores closest to it.

When Medavoy glanced out the window at the streets and buildings, restaurants, bars, churches, and parking lots slipping by, he found he couldn't keep up the old cop game of recognizing places where some offense had been committed you investigated or knew about. Like there's Andy's Lounge. Shoot-out two years ago, one dead. Camper World rushed past. Bunch of auto thefts, one camper set afire last year. Street names, Birch, Walden, Brewerton, places where there'd been beatings, burglaries, dope deals, and murders. A cop's tour of the city wouldn't impress the Chamber of Commerce favorably, but it was part of the city's life, too.

"Hear that, Robby?" Geffen asked.

"What?"

"Easter's got a perimeter set. We got a box for them."

Jane turned to look back at him through the grille. "They won't be able to get out now, right?"

Medavoy nodded. "They drive in, they stay in, one way or the other."

Beaufort twisted her hands uncomfortably in the cuffs. "Remember our deal. I've got your written promise."

"I know what I promised."

He wanted to reach out and touch Jane, but held back because Beaufort was there. He didn't want her to see him express affection, any soft emotion. Jane turned back, looking ahead as they drove. Jesus, that was stupid to let her come, he thought. You made one stupid mistake already putting her out in this thing.

Beaufort said, "I mean it, Medavoy. I intend to hold you to the agreement. No matter what happens." There was desperation in her voice. She was way out in the middle of that river and he was the only lifeline she had to get back.

"I haven't given you any bullshit so far, okay? I'm playing this as fairly as everybody lets me," Medavoy said. The siren seemed louder, shooting through the blue morning, toward the city skyline.

THIRTY-TWO

IT WAS A GOOD TRAP, Medavoy decided, once they arrived and got the thing set. There was no margin for error. If Trask and Lisio decided to go directly to the airport now, there would be hell to pay.

He looked around the area. Citizens Savings Bank sat alone on a deeply green swatch of grass, a brown-and-white building with a flag drooping in front of it. A four-lane street, El Camino Grande, ran in front of it, and behind it was a vast parking lot, glass-fronted stores in uniform ranks shielded from the sun by a salmon-pink arcade roof.

The parking lot was filled but there were no people walking through it to cars or stores. If you paused to study it, this absence would look strange, out of place. Medavoy hoped that neither Trask or Lisio would have enough time to notice that all the shoppers had been cleared back and that just inside every store stood a cop.

In the middle of El Camino Grande, cutting off the center lanes, were two cars, a station wagon and a compact, their frames touching and the compact's windshield shattered, a glittering spray of green glass shining on the black asphalt. Easter had commandeered the cars from unwilling shoppers, promising the city would reimburse them.

Medavoy, Geffen, and four cops busied themselves around the cars, and cops at either end of the block diverted or slowed traffic. When Trask and Lisio's Mercury drew near, all other traffic would be sent onto other streets.

Citizens Savings was an empty building. On its low roof, below the rim of the brown-stucco front were three Special Weapons snipers, all armed with .308 rifles. Medavoy made the choice. The heavier bullets wouldn't deflect through windows or buildings and a .223 rifle might. Medavoy wanted to be sure of hitting Lisio particularly, if it came to shooting at them. The risk was that the heavier bullet would punch through a surrounding building and strike someone unintended.

On the opposite side of El Camino Grande were a gas station—EZ Service—and brick apartments. Two more snipers, the entire sharpshooter team in Special Weapons, were on the apartment building's third-floor roof and inside the gas station. Easter was with the sniper in the gas station, closest to the possible action, Medavoy noted. The Command Post van was parked out of sight on Black River Road, a nearby side street. Carol Beaufort remained handcuffed in his car beside the van, a cop watching her.

Jane turned to look back at him, raising her arm as she crossed El Camino Grande. It was almost a jaunty wave. He told her to cross the parking lot and wait inside Longs Drugs on the other side. It was farthest from the staged accident and two cops at the store's doorway waited for her.

He watched her walk, solitary and purposeful, past the Citizens Savings building without a glance.

The sky cleared of the white, stolid clouds, the air growing stiff and windless.

Geffen, handy-talkie always at his mouth, kept up a

constant back and forth with the helicopters monitoring the Mercury's path.

Medavoy, hiding his own tension, his wish to be away with Jane at home, smiled at the cops who pretended to work on the cars with him.

"Okay, guys?"

"Like a couple of vests," one of them said—Frost, the guy with five kids.

"Can't do it," Medavoy said. "The pukes might see."

"I'd feel okay if I had a vest on, like the Weapons guys," Frost jerked a thumb around at the hidden snipers. "Or our guys who aren't in the line of fire."

Medavoy shot a glance at Geffen who only raised his eyebrows. "We won't need them," he said to the cops. "They won't get near us."

He held his own handy-talkie tightly. Pray to God they won't get near us. It had been unsettling to watch with Gef as the Special Weapons men slipped on bullet-proof vests and so did the other cops, closing the Velcro fasteners. Into each vest, just over the heart, went a porcelain plate for more protection.

No armor for us, he thought. Trask and Lisio would wonder why cops checking a car crash are wearing bullet-proof vests. So we stay out here bareback. No protection.

"Gef? What's up?" he asked sharply.

"Closing dead on, Robby. Passing Elmira now. We got about a minute."

The tenseness was gone from Geffen's voice, for the first time in days. As if he's welcoming Trask and Lisio, Medavoy thought.

Zaragoza and Masuda, who'd been busy with the evacuation, trotted across the street to him.

"It's all nailed down, Robby," Masuda said. "Everybody's down and ready."

"When they coming?" Zaragoza worriedly chewed his lip.

"Less than a minute."

"We're going back to the apartment." Masuda pointed behind them. "We got a line of fire from the lobby."

Medavoy nodded. His watch said nine-forty-nine, Lisio was off by only a minute. He was one smart con, saw right to our soft spot and worked it, he thought. He would've gotten away with it except for Carol Beaufort.

"Okay," he said to Zaragoza and Masuda, "get out of sight now. Keep your handy-talkies ready."

Masuda gave him a thumbs up, pulled Zaragoza by the coat sleeve, and the two loped across El Camino Grande, over the sidewalk, into the apartment building.

Medavoy checked Jane again. She threaded her way through the thickest section of parked cars. Jesus, he thought, this's cutting it close. Hurry up, get out of there.

He spoke into his handy-talkie. "We should have contact real soon. Do not move toward the vehicle. Let them pass through. We'll slow them, flag them down about fifty yards from the accident. We got the snipers on the apartments, the bank, the gas station and we got a cross fire."

"At a stoplight," Geffen interrupted. "Just northwest. They're at the intersection of Del Norte and Riverside."

"Last time, everybody," Medavoy said quickly. "I order Trask and Lisio out of the car. They got five seconds. We'll be covered by these cars. If they aren't out, then you blow them out."

Easter's voice rasped brightly, "I hear you."

Medavoy felt alone, even with Geffen beside him; the other cops nervously looking around. He did a last check with all the posts, got all clears. The street was unearthly and still, like last night with Easter.

Except I got Masuda and Zaragoza on the side of the street with Easter and Geffen with me. I'm not alone like last night.

"Talk to you after the fun," Easter rasped over the radio.

Medavoy put his handy-talkie on the compact's front fender. His shoes crunched on the broken windshield glass.

He looked for Jane, but didn't see her in the parking lot.

We can do it, he thought, we got a lot going for us. It was a faint, inner cheer. "Get over on the other side of the wagon, Gef," he ordered.

Geffen moved so that he was shielded by the station wagon's bulk from the oncoming lanes of El Camino Grande.

"They just passed the perimeter, Robby. They're inside now."

Medavoy stared down the long, normally heavily traveled street. He saw a ruby glow from flares fifty yards away, thin smoke trails rising from them. Soon I'll see them, he thought. They'll see the flares and the cars and there'll be no turning back. His breath rushed in and out.

He saw Geffen crouch. He felt for his gun and the cops near him froze.

Jane bumped her leg on a low-slung fender. She swore, sucked in a breath.

It was so quiet suddenly, like a covering of mattress ticking had fallen over the shopping mall and parking lot. The cars appeared bright, vibrant under the morning sun.

She looked at the staged accident. Robby didn't move. The men with him were immobile.

An awning covering the patio of the Mandarin Emperor restaurant creaked, rustled, sighed. In the Longs Drugs doorway, two cops silently, madly waved her toward them.

She looked farther along El Camino Grande and a brown, insignificant Mercury came toward her.

THIRTY-THREE

KENNY SAW THE OBSTRUCTION ahead first. He made out two cars, like they'd cracked up, stuck right in the middle of the street, making it impossible to get around them. "Some kind of accident," he said, looking forward intently. "Couple cars and some cops, too."

"I can't drive around it. It's in front of the bank." Lisio was trembling, left hand going to his forehead frequently, coming away damp. Just keep that hand out of the windbreaker, Kenny thought. He decided this was not a great idea, to be heading toward a bunch of cops.

"Just keep on going, man. We got enough. We got two fucking suitcases back there, I can't even close one too good," Kenny said.

"It's only a traffic accident," Lisio said.

"Yeah, but what they going to do when we come hauling ass out of the bank, Dave? You got no response problem when they sitting right on top of you."

Lisio sweated, hitched his hip around because it was sore,

and nodded, slowing the Mercury down. "They're just ahead."

"So, I tell what you do, my man," Kenny spoke softly, thinking he'd keep this coward calm and cool, "you just drive by easy, you keep going and we make a run out for the airport, okay? How's that?"

Lisio had passed the guttering flares in the street. He was only doing about twenty-five now, Kenny thought in anger, starting to make the cops wonder why he's slowing down so much maybe.

"Come on, Dave, just keep going. Keep going. Couple guys driving by, that's all."

"That's all," Lisio repeated, his hand dropping into the wind-breaker pocket like he had a rabbit's foot in there for luck. Goddamn, get that hand clear, Kenny thought. Lisio shook a big drop of sweat off the end of his nose. He was whiter than a sheet.

"Hey, man, watch out with that photo thing, okay? We got no worries, we just cruise by," Kenny said.

Lisio brought both hands up to the wheel again. "Yes. We can simply drive by."

"Like nothing."

"It's a shame to miss the last bank," he said. "It's not right."

"Accident happens," Kenny said. "Just take it easy and go with it. Speed it up a little, like we're okay."

Lisio nodded, and the Mercury moved a little faster. Man, you hurrying to you own funeral, Kenny thought. You just lost a couple minutes out of what time you got left and you don't know it.

Lisio spoke nervously. "One of the cops is waving us forward, Kenny."

The Chief sat in the front seat of the unmarked robin's-egg-blue police car. He huffed and grumbled at the priority memo

Schroeder had left on his desk, the last thing he scooped up to take with him. He dashed downstairs to the garage, waited until his official car rushed off in a bawling clangor, drawing the TV trucks and reporters with it. Grim delight in leading them on a goose chase, he thought. Then he ducked into the unmarked car, got out the public exit and into the midmorning traffic. He didn't want to turn on the siren or lights and draw attention again.

He sat in front because anything else looked too aristocratic. Like something one of Donna's childhood friends would do, riding in a coach.

"We're coming up on it, sir," said his young patrolman driver. He didn't know this kid, Kozlowski, at all. Used a strong aftershave, but the Chief couldn't ask its name without feeling funny.

"I didn't hear you," the Chief replied, still reading.

"The bank's ahead. Some accident in the street, too."

The Chief huffed again at the IAD memo. There was, according to Schroeder, sufficient reason to believe Medavoy was involved in a shakedown, the victim badly beaten last night.

"I've got bums all over the department," he said aloud, thoughtlessly.

"Sir?"

"Why are you slowing down?"

"The accident ahead, sir."

"Did I tell you to slow down?"

"No, sir."

"I told you to ignore that traffic officer back there, didn't I? Because I had a reason. I want you to keep driving."

"I think he was trying to say something to us," Kozlowski answered. He hadn't gotten a handle on the Chief as a passenger at all, didn't talk, wanted the radio kept silent while he read, said he'd heard enough about what was going on. He was the Chief after all, but Kozlowski, with only two years as a cop, could see that calling him Stevie Wonder made sense. He was a strange guy.

The Chief, for his part, did not enjoy an argument with a subordinate. "I do not give a damn what he wanted to say." A dirty-colored Mercury, sputtering occasionally, slowed ahead of him. There were cars blocking the middle lanes, a cop beside them waving. The Chief summed up the accident at a glance, a station wagon crossing oncoming traffic or a compact speeding too fast to make an illegal lane-change had collided. Typical poor Santa Maria driving.

"I don't see any crisis," he said aloud, looking around for the catastrophe Prefach had described. "All I see is an accident."

"If I go any faster, I'll hit the Mercury, sir."

"Do you see any crisis? What's the trouble? Where's all the trouble?"

Kozlowski reached for the radio. "You want me to check with dispatch?"

The Chief's face whitened in anger. "I said keep it off. I said I wanted some quiet. Somebody's going to do what I say around here."

Instantly, he felt shame. Kozlowski's face had gone whiter than his. "Sorry, sir."

"Let's go. Hurry up."

"I'll hit the Mercury, sir. I'm nearly climbing up it now."

"Hell, I'm not sitting behind some damn little car while some damn traffic officer decides what to do. Hit the siren. Hit the lights. Go around the damn Mercury, go to the left."

First he had to dump nearly the whole Special Weapons Unit and its supervisor. Now the man he wanted to head Robbery was in on shakedowns. My own driver argues with me. The whole department, the Chief concluded, was a mess.

Carol waited under the shade trees hanging around the car. It was thoughtful, she admitted, for Medavoy to have her handcuffs removed, her window rolled down enough to let in

FUGITIVE CITY 331

some fresh air. Her guardian cop leaned on the hood. From the black van in front of her, men came and went busily, quickly, self-importantly.

She put her head back with fatigue. Medavoy's written agreement crinkled a little in her skirt pocket. Maybe I've repaid Kenny for what he did, she thought, bought him a little extra consideration if things turn ugly around Lisio now.

She didn't want to think about the dynamite or losing Kenny and having to face the aftermath of his escape by herself. That would take some doing. Explaining the lust letters. Explaining the escape, the thefts, the assaults, everything Medavoy had mentioned.

Explaining what she had done for Reilly, too.

Let's face it, she thought, looking again at the busy black van under its shady trees on this secluded street, I need a lot of help to get out of this.

"Ten more yards," Medavoy whispered to Geffen and the others, their eyes fixed on the brown Mercury coming at them. It was nearly in the cross fire he could call down if Trask and Lisio wouldn't surrender. He waved his arms slowly, like a cop flagging down cars.

Geffen's handy-talkie screeched furiously.

Medavoy instinctively looked again toward the shopping mall parking lot, hoping to see Jane. She was there, about halfway across. He cursed. Cut it too close, he should have sent her earlier, she'd be in Longs by now.

Something pale blue, hidden until then, moved quickly up behind the Mercury.

"What the hell's that?" Medavoy said involuntarily.

Resting on the compact's hood was a bullhorn. He reached for it. He would hale Trask and Lisio, stop their car, cut this short immediately.

"It's a car, some fucking car's coming," Frost said hoarsely.

Medavoy raised the bullhorn, counting the diminishing yards. There was a second car on El Camino Grande and he had to stop the Mercury before it came farther, before Lisio's dynamite endangered them all.

Geffen shouted into his ear, "Robby, it's Stevie Wonder! It's his car!" the handy-talkie wavering in his hand as it spat out the impossible news.

The Mercury had driven nearly up to the shopping mall's entrance, about forty yards from them, and started to swing out to right, as if to pass by the accident in the street.

"What the fuck is he doing here?" Medavoy said. Geffen brushed by him, hands upraised, signaling wildly up and down.

The pale-blue car swung quickly from behind Trask and Lisio, trying to speed by them, cut ahead, and turn left into the shopping mall. From the blue car came a startling, sickening siren, then red-blue lights winked on.

"Get down! Get down!" Medavoy shouted. It was unbelievable that exactly what he had worked to prevent was happening, a cop car bearing down on Trask and Lisio. The blue car moved up arrogantly, closing the last few yards between it and the Mercury, still moving to the right, and the shopping mall entrance. In a second, the blue car would be alongside the Mercury.

Over the imperious siren, Medavoy had time to shout once more.

From the EZ Service opposite Citizens Savings, Easter and his sniper, the heavy .308 rifle balanced on boxes, pointing out through grimy fly-specked windows at the path the Mercury would take along El Camino Grande, heard the sirens start, saw the blue car speeding up to pass the target car.

Easter had just gotten that adrenaline surge before an operation, cleaner and harsher than any drug. He held his handy-talkie and binoculars and watched the crazy blue car in astonishment. Some fucking idiot hadn't gotten the word, he thought.

He saw Medavoy waving, Geffen waving more frantically. The Mercury was speeding up now, would be going much too fast for the cross fire, perhaps even get out of the trap entirely.

Somebody had just blown the whole deal, he thought, the surge bursting through him. He didn't even look at his sniper, the .308 tightened to fire. He made a decision instantly as he saw Medavoy crouch, hiding away on the side of the station wagon and the two cars about to slide by each other.

He blinked away a lone drop of sweat in his right eye, spoke into the handy-talkie to his snipers.

"Fire," he said.

Kenny and Lisio had started shouting at each other the moment the sirens began and now, Lisio seemed to go into a convulsion, twisting his head around to see what was happening, shaking with rage and fear.

Loud metallic thumps started on the car. Kenny didn't know what they were for a split second, then the windshield shattered into fragments, peppering him and Lisio with glass. Lisio screamed at him, foot still on the accelerator, driving them forward. "They're shooting at us!" and his face was white, already speckled with blood where glass spray had hit him. His hand was fumbling into the windbreaker.

Kenny drew his gun. "It's okay, Dave." He had no intention of letting the little creep turn him into a firecracker. Something thumped into the rear seat, the car shuddered, grinding loudly, and Kenny shot Lisio point blank in his screaming mouth.

The concussion was terrific, not like in the open last night, and Kenny didn't stop to see what happened. Lisio's head had blown back and filled the seat with pieces of blood and bone.

It was like someone was tossing hard pebbles against the

car, but the impact was greater. Like rifles, Kenny thought. He pushed open the passenger door, fell out onto the asphalt and intended to run toward the nearest shelter he could find, anything to get away from the cops who must be all over, everywhere shooting at him. He heard the little thuds of bullets striking the asphalt. Everybody's down on me, he thought in bewilderment, like I done something so bad they got to take all this trouble to nail me. He assumed there was some way these cops should have known the shoe box bomb was fake, he only shot the guy last night because he was startled, and beat up Reilly and the guy near Chino because they obstinately obstructed him.

Kenny still had the .45 in hand, had gotten just to the rear fender of the still-rolling Mercury, much slowed because Lisio wasn't on the gas and something had given out in the motor, intending to make a run for the parking lot across the street. He couldn't tell exactly where all this heavy gunfire was coming from, but it seemed to be off to his right mostly. The parking lot looked safest.

Man, Kenny thought to himself in the few seconds since the shots began and he fell out of the car, I done it this time. I have done it up just fine. He wailed inwardly, like when Trask started one of the long, painful beatings.

He managed to get parallel to the other side of the Mercury, thinking he'd have to risk the dash across the remaining lanes of the street, open to the gunfire, when something very heavy struck his left leg and knocked it from under him. He spilled facedown to the asphalt, thinking he'd caught his leg on something. He started dragging himself, then decided the best thing, under the circumstances, was to simply stop, stay facedown on the ground, and maybe the cops wouldn't shoot at him anymore.

Medavoy had thrown himself behind the protection of the station wagon, yelling for Geffen to get down because some of the sniper fire, deliberately or not, was landing close by them. The Mercury had slowed, but still came on. Frost and the other cops were shouting, on their feet, running in panic for the apartment building across the street.

You can't hear one single shot, he thought, the snap and boom of heavy arms fire was so dense it was a chorus. He could see the Mercury quake slightly every time it was hit, first the windshield blown apart, then the headlights, one tire suddenly flopping down, the car stopping about twenty yards from the staged accident.

Where was the guy who bailed out? Medavoy had seen someone, black jacket, same build as Trask, get to the rear of the Mercury, then lost sight of him. The blue car had abruptly tried to make the shopping mall entrance at high speed, to get away from the gunfire. Its sirens and lights added to the confusion.

Medavoy had turned to Geffen, to get him to raise Easter on the handy-talkie, his own was left back on the compact's fender. As he did so, the Mercury's brown skin burst outward, upward like an angry boil, a ball of light and noise and concussive thrust that pushed him to the asphalt. Lisio's dynamite, he thought, scraping his jaw on the ground painfully. He blew it.

He imagined even the gunfire stopped. He thought so because the clanking, arhythmic sounds of the Mercury's pieces falling back to the ground sounded absolutely clear and tonal.

▉▉▉▉▉

Kenny was low enough that he felt the whoosh of the cop car pass by him within inches, felt the lift and buck of the ground as it heaved with the explosion. He wanted to dig himself right through the sharp-smelling asphalt, right into the safety of the earth.

Fucking Lisio was dead, brains all over the car so he didn't do it. Kenny tried to stand, couldn't, and decided to make a break for the parking lot after all, in the smoky, stinging dimness after the car went up so spectacularly.

Maybe one of those damn shots the cops were getting off, he thought, hit Lisio's body, set it off. Had to be something like that, something the cops did. Sure as hell wasn't Lisio doing it.

He discovered his left leg was twisted, numb, and very bloody. Like somebody had whacked it with a great hammer. He felt like crying when he saw that. He couldn't see that he was dirty, smoking where hot metal had caught in the Raiders jacket, smoldering. No pain yet, but he was sure it would hurt like a son of a bitch sooner or later.

The air was filled with the smell of gasoline and oil, burning paint. Kenny groaned because an electric ache thrust up his left leg. He had to get out, get to the parking lot, find someone to get him out. Get back to Carol, she'd know what to do now.

He crossed the last lanes of El Camino Grande at an awkward lope, unmolested, the gunfire suspended. The cops were probably ducked down for a moment, frozen by the explosion, waiting a second for an all clear. Lisio had saved him. Kenny moved quickly in spite of the pain. He had a few moments grace in this smoky confusion.

Amazingly, he had held onto the .45, almost a reflex, his fingers locked around it. He loped into the thickly parked cars, sliding along their cool metal bodies. He heard shouting behind him, back toward the street, the cops up again, a few solitary shots. His leg dragged uselessly and he knew it was broken. The cops had shot him and broken his leg. He cursed, gasping, face hollowed with effort. Stay down, stay hidden behind these cars. Then, just ahead, crouching, startled by the explosion, the bits of metal and paper blown into the air, was a woman between the cars.

It was like she was waiting for him, like she'd been put there for him. She's got a car, he thought. She's going to get me out. If he stayed low, it would be hard for the cops to see him, the smoke was fuzzing everything, they still hadn't gotten their bearings again, probably still frightened something else would explode.

He hurried toward the woman, his breath husky, eager and scared as he grunted along, leg dragging, drawn forward in desperate hope. He didn't notice the singed, irregular bits of paper, like confetti, whirling wildly in the heated air, tiny scraps of green, the accumulation from four banks.

Medavoy was on his feet first, trying to raise the snipers on his borrowed handy-talkie, checking in with the other posts. One of his cops lay in the gutter just before the apartment, unmoving. The roof of Citizens Savings had a circlet of fire, ignited by hot metal from the Mercury. Palms along the street and lining the shopping mall entrance popped and crackled, like huge torches and the whole place was hazy, dim, and stinking.

He gave another cease-fire order. He didn't want anybody shooting in this smoke. He called in ambulances and told the helicopters to stay overhead.

"Goddamn," Geffen said breathlessly, wiping his eyes, and coughing, "took the whole thing up."

There was nothing left of the Mercury but a black under-carriage on wheelless rims, smoking and burning.

"Somebody got out. You see somebody bail out and take off?" Medavoy asked. "It looked like Trask."

Geffen shook his head. "I didn't see anything."

Medavoy wondered if it had been an illusion, something that came close on the explosion. This was one fine disaster. "I can't get anybody. I can't get Easter or any of his guys."

"Maybe they switched frequencies, I don't know," Geffen said.

"Somebody's got to find them, tell them to hold position until I find out what's happened. No shooting except on my order."

"I'll check for you, Robby," Geffen coughed.

Medavoy said, "Let the fire trucks come through with the ambulances, but keep the perimeter up. Nobody else comes in."

Geffen nodded and turned toward the other side of the street. Medavoy started across El Camino Grande, coughing, hearing the multitude of sirens that grew louder each instant. The snipers who had been on Citizens Savings ran past him, ignoring him. He shouted after them. Cops ran from the apartment, the side streets, but he didn't see Masuda or Zaragoza either.

He ran to the overturned blue car. The force of the blast lifted the car into the air or spun it with such violence that it rested on its roof in the grass border around the shopping mall, crushing hedges and a palm. The windows were shattered, the grass and sidewalk nearby thick with leaking fluids and glass.

Cops had started prying the doors, shouting to each other. Medavoy directed them. He didn't think of Stevie Wonder or what a colossal blunder he'd made. Just get whoever was inside free. That was enough. Finger pointing was bound to come later.

He reached in through the upside-down passenger window, slashing his coat on the broken edges, grabbing the man crumpled onto the roof, still buckled into his seat. His uniform was torn and the gold braid dim in the smoky air.

Medavoy fumbled hastily with the seat belt. There was flame and gasoline and no way to tell how long it was taking the fire trucks to get through. He heard the helicopters hovering as he tugged.

Without the glasses, hair and face dirt and grease spattered, Stevie Wonder looked like he was sleeping off a long drunk.

Medavoy shouted for help and another cop began working to unfasten the seat belt.

Stevie Wonder stared at Medavoy. "Get my driver," he hesitated at the name.

"He's dead," Medavoy said. Just a foot away, the car had come down hard on that side of the roof, crushing the driver's head. Cops had gotten his body partway clear.

Medavoy reeled back at Stevie Wonder's weight, pulling him free of the car, another cop helping. Stevie Wonder coughed loudly, limply, almost dead weight, was laid on the grass border, about thirty feet from the car. He looked at Medavoy. "Who are you?" he asked.

"Medavoy. Robbery, Chief," he grunted, letting go of the weight.

"I need to talk to you," Stevie Wonder said solemnly.

In mechanical succession, two shots splatted into the grass beside them, the cop who had been helping Medavoy, cried out and fell. Medavoy covered Stevie Wonder, eyes darting around to see where the shots had come from. Lisio was dead, probably Trask too. So who was shooting? He looked around fiercely, his own Sig out now, ready. The cops nearby had flattened to the ground, yelling at each other.

He saw Easter, in a stiff armed pose, drawing down on him from the protection of Stevie Wonder's wrecked car. Easter held an assault rifle and Medavoy, in that passing instant, knew his own gun would never respond fast enough.

Missed with single shots, Easter'll go to automatic fire, Medavoy thought, he doesn't care now who he hits—me, Stevie Wonder, other cops. He was sick with the idea another cop hated him enough to shoot him. How could Easter think he'd get away? It's not like last night, the two of them alone on the deserted street. There are all kinds of witnesses here, cops, and the firemen who'll come roaring up in a minute.

Then Medavoy saw the distorted face, eyes past fatigue, and realized Easter didn't care anymore. In the great bang of the car going up, he saw his chance, Medavoy exposed. Medavoy recalled the drawn, yet artificially energized man last night. This was Easter's flash. So many people, so much confusion, everyone numb, ears ringing from the explosion, he could say he thought he saw the gunman. Maybe he'd get away with it in the smoke and noise.

Maybe he doesn't care if he gets away, Medavoy thought instantly.

Stevie Wonder moved under Medavoy. Can't get away, can't even call for help.

He heard Geffen shout, "Behind you, Easter," saw Easter swing instinctively toward the sound.

Easter fired the rifle, a burst of fire. Medavoy didn't see Geffen, but in the second Easter turned, Medavoy rose up, aimed the Sig and fired at the bulky, black shape.

The Special Weapons supervisor jerked violently to the right, as if pulled by a strong hand, then toppled forward, rifle hitting the ground. "Hold your fire! Hold your fire!" Medavoy yelled, getting clear of Stevie Wonder and running toward the wrecked car. Two palm trees burst suddenly into flame, catching fire like their neighbors.

He got to Easter first, saw the ragged neck wound, the surprised look on the tired, lined face, then ran on, searching for Geffen. The cops had gotten off the ground, and were checking out the scene. The first ambulance rolled through, coming down El Camino Grande, red lights spectral in the hazy air. He found Geffen, two cops huddled by him, near the shopping mall entrance. He was unconscious, bleeding in the chest. Medavoy felt a fierce agony himself, seeing that. He knelt down briefly, as if by sight and touch he could do something. But the ambulance had slowed; he stood, shouted, and waved it over. Another came behind it, looking for other victims.

Medavoy stood aside while the cops helped the attendants work on Geffen. Nothing else to do.

It was an old trick Geffen had used on Easter. When you were tailing a really bad puke everybody agreed shouldn't or wouldn't be brought in, you waited until the puke got into a store or gas station, had some poor civilian at gunpoint or knife point. Then you popped up from behind the puke, yelled for him to freeze or drop his weapon and the normal reaction everybody counted on was for the puke to turn toward the sudden noise. Then you put him down and nobody could call the shooting unjustified, except the poor civilian who probably had a heart attack or shit in his pants thinking he was going to die.

And Easter went for the old gag, drawing his fire toward Geffen.

He had started trembling; delayed reaction, he thought, and coughed, wiping his eyes. He had his handy-talkie up. "Masuda? Zaragoza? Somebody answer me on this goddamn thing."

Fire trucks moved down El Camino Grande, too, a line of trucks rolling up in front of the apartments, into the parking lot, disgorging men and hoses.

"I hear you, Robby," Masuda answered, crackling. A second later, Zaragoza responded, "Go ahead."

"Where are you?"

"In the apartments. I got some cops and couple Special Weapons guys in here, everybody's waiting for Easter or you or somebody to tell them what to do."

"Jimmy? Where're you?"

"Gas station. I'm alone in here."

"Get over and help Stan." Medavoy had trouble keeping his voice steady. The ambulance attendants had torn open Geffen's shirt, shoved needles into him, so much haste, brisk orders. He doesn't move, Medavoy thought. Like a sack of flour. Then the next thought struck him. I shot a cop. I killed another cop. He saw the other ambulance near Easter and Stevie Wonder.

"Robby? You still there?" Masuda asked, urgent and worried.

"Yeah." He got control again. Too much to do right now for anything else. "Jimmy, Stan, listen up. Keep this real quiet, but you do it now. Tell the Special Weapons guys to give up their weapons. And you watch them after that, you hear me?"

"Take their weapons?" Masuda asked dubiously.

"Affirmative. If you can, get them out of here and back to the Command Post, okay?"

"What's up, Robby?"

"We got an open channel," he said, knowing his words were being overheard in the Command Post van and anywhere else cops were tuned in. "Just let them know the operation's over and they got to give up their weapons." He didn't want snipers with high-powered rifles and exotic equipment finding out that their super had just been killed by another cop.

"You got it, Robby," Masuda answered. "Somebody said that's Stevie Wonder out there. That true?"

Medavoy turned from the frantic work being done on Geffen, hoisting him tipsily into the ambulance on a stretcher. "Yeah, he's out here. He's hurt."

"Jesus," Zaragoza breathed over the air.

"Get on it," Medavoy signed off. Cops no longer ran across the street, but more patrol units were driving up, filling the cluttered lanes of El Camino Grande and the sun overhead had a red, distended appearance through the drifting smoke. The firemen worked on the burning Citizens Savings Bank and the scattered fires set by the exploding Mercury. He wiped his eyes again. He spoke into his handy-talkie, giving instructions about the civilians still in the stores and Longs Drugs: Keep them back. Water droplets drifted through the air like sweat and the asphalt was shiny with it.

He walked back to Stevie Wonder, ambulance attendants hoarsely talking back and forth. Nobody at Easter's body was so excited, the men covering him, already starting to make out the reports. This was going to be a tough one to clean up, he thought.

Stevie Wonder stared up at him as an IV went into his arm, three cops jittering around him, trying to look purposeful by keeping people back, barking commands too loudly at them, running for whatever the ambulance attendants called for. Red and blue lights from so many patrol cars and ambulances gave the whole dim scene a partylike atmosphere. Medavoy didn't know what to say to Masuda or Zaragoza, how to tell them what Geffen had done for him.

Stevie Wonder was lifted onto a stretcher, the attendants calling out, "Clear, clear, clear," to themselves and the cops around them. Stevie Wonder looked at Medavoy. "Did I hear shooting?"

"Yes, sir. We had a problem."

"What kind of problem?" asked as if he really knew where he was now or what had happened to him.

Medavoy wiped his tearing eyes. Just the smoke, nothing else, he told himself. "I shot Easter. The Special Weapons super."

Stevie Wonder frowned deeply, his head falling back on the stretcher as he was hoisted into the ambulance, the attendants brusquely pushing the cops away. Stevie Wonder said aloud, "My boys fighting? No. I'll have to tell Donna."

Medavoy stepped back, the ambulance swinging wide, getting around the real and false wrecked cars in the street, twisting around the maze of patrol cars. He couldn't bear to see why it was taking so long for Geffen's ambulance to get under way, why so much work had to be done on him at the scene.

It was only then, with a sense of belated guilt, that he thought of Janie. She must be going crazy wondering what's happening, how he was.

He coughed, swatted away some flying embers that danced in the air like fireflies. Get over to Longs Drugs. He had to do that now. He didn't want to be out, alone, when the feelings about what he'd done and what had happened hit him. Like Alice yesterday in the bank, he thought. It just gets you all of a sudden.

He started toward the huge drug and household store at the other side of the shopping mall parking lot. Two cops ran by him. "Somebody's yelling for you," one said. They had their guns drawn.

"Where?" he asked immediately.

"Up ahead. In the parking lot."

He ran with them. Who could be shouting? Another injured cop? He refused to consider the other possibility, Jane being hurt or in trouble. It couldn't be her. She made it into the store before anything went up.

They halted in the middle of the parking lot, the cops unsure where to go. The stores around them were indistinct, vague impressions in the smoke. "Over here someplace," one cop said.

Medavoy listened, hand up to keep the others quiet. He heard a male, throaty voice, bellowing from someplace to his left, in the dense pack of parked cars. Thank God. It wasn't Jane at all.

"Medavoy?"

"Right here. What's wrong?"

"I got a woman."

"Tell me where you are, we got ambulances, cops to give you a hand."

"Fuck you, fuck the cops. I ain't talking about getting no hand," the voice was raging, "I want a car. I want you to drive us away."

"You hurt?" Medavoy felt his gut tighten. It could be any woman, anybody in the whole world.

"I'm fucking fine, Medavoy. She says she knows you, you can take care of business here, get me out of here. That's all I want, get the fuck out of this city."

He closed his eyes. Okay, face it. Do what you have to, treat this like any other bad call. Except he couldn't do that. It was Jane and it must be Trask. Lisio had the dynamite that blew up. One of the cops started to move. "I'll get around his right," he whispered.

"Stay here," Medavoy snapped. The cop stopped, gun ready. He had disarmed the snipers and couldn't rely on them. He had about a dozen cops he could call in, the helicopters overhead. That was all. He had a nearly fully loaded Sig. "I want to hear from the woman. Trask, right? Let me hear from the woman."

Another short lull, Medavoy strained to hear, the cops stood poised beside him.

"Robby? I'm all right. I'm sorry." Jane's voice was firm, normal. She coughed at the last word. Seemed to be coming about a hundred feet to his left. They must be near the ground, Trask using the cars as bulwarks.

"Get a car over here now, Medavoy. I see any cops but you near me, I shoot her. I shoot anybody I see except you. You know me, man? You know how I take care of things."

"I know, don't get excited. Keep cool. I'll get your car."

It wasn't like my old man, Medavoy thought, trying now to figure out how he'd get Trask away from Jane. He held his handy-talkie. The old man would get a bum out of a railcar, couple of quick jabs with the stick to know who he had the bad luck to meet. Duck walk him across the tracks, maybe some pals would join the old man, a quartet of SP cops having a good time with a bum.

And the bum was alone and had nothing and the old man had his gun and a stick.

And Trask's got Jane. He's got everything. Medavoy didn't wait any longer. Trask called out for him again. He got on the handy-talkie to the car near the Command Post.

"This is Medavoy," he said, quite calmly, very quietly. "Bring the car and the suspect up to the mall entrance, I'll have somebody direct you to me. Real slow, okay. We've got a hostage situation."

THIRTY-FOUR

CAROL BEAUFORT WAS HAGGARD and sharp-eyed when she got out of the squad car. Two cops flanked her and behind her fire trucks spewed water on the burning foliage. Medavoy quickly told her that Trask had a woman hostage, demanded a car.

"I can't get cops near enough for a shot at him because I don't know where he is. I don't know how he's holding his hostage."

"Who is it?" Beaufort asked, rubbing her upper arms slowly as if cold. Her lean face was dark-circled with fatigue.

"The woman in the car with us," Medavoy said.

"What do you want me to do?"

Medavoy had three cars drawn up inside the parking lot. "You tell him the car's here, but you don't want him to go. Tell him to come out, hands on his head, leave the gun. I'll be able to see if he does."

Beaufort glanced at the cops, nervous and fine-strung by the events of the last few minutes. "You can't shoot him if he puts the gun down."

346

Jesus, he thought, she's bargaining again. Like that stupid piece of paper means anything at this moment. "Look, Carol, you get him clear of his hostage and you get him to lay the gun down. He's staying here. This is it. You got to convince him to stay alive."

Bluff, he thought. I have a fifty-fifty chance of nailing Trask the way things stand. He's got a hundred percent chance of hurting Jane. Medavoy wiped that possibility away. Focus on the thing you can control, Beaufort and getting him and the gun separated.

She took the ultimatum stiffly. Though it was still only near ten A.M., she shivered. He took off his jacket and she put it on, holding it tightly. "All right. Tell me what to say."

"Okay. Tell him the woman walks behind him. He goes first. Tell him to keep talking when he comes out. He's got to have his hands locked on the top of his head. Leave the gun on the ground."

She nodded. "All right. All right. I'll bring him out."

Medavoy handed her the bullhorn from one of the cars. "He doesn't know you're here. Use it."

She nodded again. She raised the bullhorn. Tough woman, he thought, holding his handy-talkie. She better come through for all of us.

"Kenny? Can you hear me? It's me, Kenny?" her voice bounced, rolled across the parking lot, punctuated by the emergency sounds behind them, trucks, men, and equipment.

"Carol honey? Jesus. Jesus."

She hesitated. Medavoy was cold. "Go on." He knew why she paused. It was impossible to miss the childlike surprise, the hurt and lost tone in Trask's voice.

"Kenny, you've got to come out now. I'll tell you exactly what to do," and she shouted out the instructions slowly. Because he's dull-normal intelligence, Medavoy grimaced, hand hard on his handy-talkie, and he'll never form a meaningful relationship with a woman. Beaufort looked over at him when she finished.

Medavoy strained for Trask's answer. Nothing. Only the men crying out, trying to get the street under control. Then, the hoarse bellow, "Carol honey, I don't care what they told you, I ain't leaving you. I ain't going back. So you get that car up here or I just say fuck it and shoot this gal here."

"Don't do that, Kenny. There's no need. I have promises from the police that you will be taken into custody. Nobody has been killed."

"Lisio. I shot old Dave."

She tightened her mouth. "I'm sure that was excusable, Kenny. You must come out now. Please. For me. I'm here."

Medavoy whispered to the cops waiting for his commands. Six men carefully set themselves around the parking lot, blocking the three entrances. He hoped Jane was being sensible and not planning any wild rush or independent action. It was too uncertain for everyone, hard to see, to think, and she'd be hurt.

"Okay, Carol honey, listen. You got them cops with you?"

"Yes, Kenny."

"So you get that car here. You bring that Medavoy and you come over here."

"They swear you'll be taken unharmed, Kenny and I believe them. They will not, repeat, not let you leave this parking lot."

Trask yelled, almost gaily, "We see about that. Now, you come on, honey. Start real slow in a car like you're coming in, do some shopping. You honk couple times and we take it from there."

She started to speak again, but Medavoy took the bullhorn.

"Trask, this is Medavoy," the voice loud, hard. No give or argument even inferable. "You come out now and you can make it all right. We go any longer with this, you're going to get killed. I'll give you thirty seconds to come out, hands on the top of your head."

Beaufort shivered. "He doesn't sound right."

"Like what?"

"I think he's hurt. Or in shock. I don't know."

Medavoy heard Trask yell. "Fuck you, you got ten seconds, I better hear that car coming, you driving and Carol with you."

He lowered the bullhorn. Into the handy-talkie he said, "I'm taking a car into the parking lot. Nobody is to move, all right? Do not interfere until the hostage is clear." He said to Beaufort, "You coming?"

"I don't have to, of course."

"It's your choice." He started for one of the cars.

She came up beside him, slipping around to the passenger side. "Not really. Very little of this has been my choice."

Medavoy rolled the squad car forward, slowly, as though made of oil, his eyes roving the cars around them for some movement. He had the handy-talkie between his legs, his Sig by his right hand. Beaufort breathed heavily, arms together, also watching. They had gotten to the middle of the parking lot. His handy-talkie crackled.

"Robby? It's Stan. You want some help?" Masuda hissed.

He grabbed the handy-talkie. "Stay put. Keep the channel clear."

The handy-talkie hissed emptily in his hand. He slowed more, row upon row of boxy cars silent and dark in the haze. An auto graveyard. There was dust and ash in the air still. He looked at Beaufort. He didn't know if he'd have come along in her place.

"Okay. Let's see where he is," he said into the handy-talkie. "Everybody watch and get the best shot you can. But don't open fire."

Beaufort rolled down her window. "I can't see him. If I talk to him more, I can persuade him." Although when she thought about it, Kenny had acted pretty much the way he wished for the last forty-eight hours.

"Let's bring him out," Medavoy said, honking the horn long and deliberately. He stopped the car, its engine idling softly.

For his part, Kenny had just finished a detailed, although short explanation of the Convicts' Code to the woman this cop Medavoy seemed so worried about. The woman, nicely dressed, nice little legs on her, sat against a car wheel and listened. The Code came down to, don't mess with somebody unless you want to get messed with, don't fuck anybody until you want to get fucked, and don't snitch on your friends. The woman nodded, little delicate face, almost like fine china. She seemed as fragile as a glass doll and he was sorry he'd knocked her to the ground when he came into the parking lot and spotted her.

"So," he said at last, "the Code means I ain't going to hurt you, I treated you okay, right?" She nodded. Dark hair, cute little mouth, eyes on him deep and dark, too. Kenny was almost protective toward her. He could see why the cop liked her. "You understand," he asked, "I ain't going to hurt you unless they make me?" She understood.

The car honked, Kenny cautiously raised his head and Medavoy saw him. "I got the car. I got Carol here, Trask. Come out, leave the gun."

Kenny shouted back, "You get out of the car. Carol honey, you get ready to drive, okay? I got my gun on this little gal here so just be cool."

Cool, Medavoy thought. Where'd he get that antique admonition? He put the car in neutral, stepped out so Trask could see him. The handy-talkie gabbled annoyingly.

Carol reluctantly got out of the car. She stayed beside the passenger side because no matter what happened, she was not going anywhere more with Kenny. The borrowed sport coat smelled faintly of dog.

Medavoy's heart rose in a hard lump when he saw Trask come from behind a pickup and a camper. Jane was in the crook of his left arm, the .45 against her cheek firmly. He was smudged and dirty and the two of them shuffled oddly, Trask half-hopping and pushing Jane.

She stared at Medavoy, scared but alert. Look at me, he thought. Just keep looking at me.

"Let her go," Medavoy said. "Jane, you start walking toward me.

She jerked a little in Trask's arm. "I can't," she said.

"Where's Carol? I don't see her," Trask groaned, stopped his sluggish half-hopping. Carol, hiding behind the car's hood, saw that he was injured, his leg dragging behind him.

"Here I am, Kenny," she called out.

"I want you to let the woman go, Trask. Let her walk to me," Medavoy said.

Kenny, the gun heavy in his hand, didn't like this tall cop in shirt-sleeves, hands out like he was asking for a favor. His leg had begun to feel quite unusual in the last few moments, little flashes of heat and electricity racing up it. He didn't feel at all like standing there.

"Carol honey, I'm coming over to that car. You get in the driver's side, okay honey? You just do it now." He started forward again, hopping and pausing. "You get back. I tell you, man, you put your fucking gun down, okay? How's that? You drop that gun now."

Kenny had spotted the waist holster and the small black automatic in it. He wished he knew more about guns, but he assumed if cops had it, there was some good reason.

"Okay. Okay. Very slowly." Medavoy kept his eyes on Jane, looking at her intently. He reached for his gun carefully.

"I can't go with you, Kenny," Beaufort said, still ducked behind the hood. "I really can't do it anymore. You just have to give up. I'll be with you."

There was something in her voice that captured him at that instant, as if, like the unearthly promise of the Kennedy picture, he saw how silly any attempt to get out of this parking lot would be. I can't just float away, even if I got this gal and

Carol and a car. The .45 seemed to bend his hand downward with its weight. I ain't doing so good, he thought. Maybe I just go with Carol, like she says, I'm all in now anyway. I got no fight.

He drooped, the arm leaving Jane's neck. She twisted in his loosening grip. "You mean it, Carol honey? You stay with me?"

"Wherever you go. I promise."

Medavoy had his own gun out, raising it. Trask didn't seem to notice. "Put your gun down, Trask. Step away from the woman. Right now," he barked harshly.

Like those scary little metal bolts of lightning running up and down his leg, Kenny felt his mood change. If he gave up now, what about everything Carol had told him in prison, standing up for himself, taking no grief from anybody? She loved him because he was a rebel nobody could put down. So how would she stand by him if he gave up now, let this cop and a woman take him into custody.

He fumbled, bringing the .45 toward Medavoy's chest. "Fuck you," he started to yell.

Jane swung her foot back sharply, into the injured left leg, driving her elbow into Trask's middle at the same time. He screamed, tottered, the .45 going up, firing wild. She threw herself to the ground.

Medavoy bent, aimed in a classic V and fired the Sig four times at the clear and unobstructed target Trask presented, balanced on his good leg, crying out. The Sig jumped four times, a moderate kick.

At least two of the bullets hit Trask, one perhaps going wide. Trask fell to his side and Medavoy ran to him, kicking the hand still clamped around the .45 until the gun skittered across the asphalt. He held his own gun ready to fire again, but it was unnecessary; Trask had started slow, final convulsions and a thick stream of blood flowed downward along the asphalt from him, gravity-drawn toward the drains for rainwater. Like that kid Geffen and me found, Medavoy thought, breathing hard, lowering his gun finally. The same pathetic sight.

He was unutterably glad it was Trask bleeding away on the ground and not him. He went back and got his handy-talkie, calling in the shooting, calling for an ambulance.

Jane got up, not bothering to brush the dirt and ash from herself, staring at the man dying in the parking lot and Carol who slowly walked to Kenny.

"You okay, Janie?" Medavoy holstered his gun and touched her tentatively, then more urgently, her mouth, arms.

"I feel a little rocky," she answered, touching him, too.

"Sure, sure. He didn't hurt you? You didn't get hurt?"

"No, I'm okay." She let out a long, horrified breath. "I'm shaking. I can't stop. Is that right?"

He held her closely, feeling his own trembling, trying to soothe them both. "That's the way it goes. Nothing you can do about it."

For the second time that morning he had killed a man. It was hard to grasp. In twelve years as a cop, he had only fired his gun once on duty and missed. Now he had fired and killed. This was going to take some getting used to, he thought. He held Jane, then stepped back. Carol knelt beside Trask, trying to smooth his hair. It looked odd, seeing someone in his coat, Medavoy thought, kneeling over the man he'd just shot. He said gently, "Ambulance is coming. Should be right here," and they all heard the *whoop-whoop* siren as the ambulance bustled into the parking lot.

Carol nodded without looking at him. "It just didn't work out, did it? I couldn't get it to come out right."

"His choice. He was going to shoot."

She staggered to her feet and Medavoy held her arm to steady her. "I don't mean this exactly. It's everything. Poor Kenny." She shook her head, looking very weary, stooped. "What a mess I made."

The cops nearby had run in to see the kill, say they'd been

there when the last puke was brought down. They stood in a ragged circle while the ambulance attendants came through and began working on Trask.

Masuda and Zaragoza ran up, too. "Robby, you all right? Everybody okay?" Masuda blurted out.

Medavoy nodded. "Take her downtown," he pointed at Carol. "You don't have to cuff her."

Jane stood beside him. Twenty or more people were crowded into the space between the rows of cars and where Trask lay. He wondered what the whole thing looked like from one of the helicopters still loudly circling above them. Probably a lot more manageable, less untidy.

Zaragoza said the Special Weapons guys were being loosely watched by other cops. "They take Gef away yet?" Medavoy asked, holding tight to Jane's hand.

Masuda nodded. "Just now. I don't know how bad, either."

"Anybody from downtown shown up?"

Zaragoza, hands on his hips, turned from the others still watching the work on Trask. "I don't think anybody's left downtown, Robby. The whole fourth floor's coming here or to the hospital."

Medavoy had to smile slightly at that. That guy Lisio had managed to drag the whole police department out when he finished. In one morning, he turned the city upside down.

"You better go downtown, too," he said to Jane. "They're going to want triple statements from everybody and it'll be easier for you downtown, okay?"

"What about you, Robby?"

"I got a lot more to do here." Then he lowered his voice, looked at her. "I was scared shitless I lost you."

"We're okay. We made it," she said. "I don't care about anything else."

"Yeah," he said gently. Then to Masuda he added, "Take Jane with you. I'll catch up with you downtown or at the hospital. Where'd they take Gef?"

"The new one, NorCal Receiving. They got the best trauma unit."

Medavoy hugged Jane, then she walked with Masuda and Beaufort back across El Camino Grande to a patrol car. It took a great deal of effort not to go with Jane, just to be with her, reassure himself every second that she was safe and he was all right, too.

He had gotten his coat back from Beaufort, awkwardly slipped it back on, and broke up the clot of cops who had better things to do than watch the ambulance attendants or crack jokes about what had just happened.

It took two more hours to secure the scene enough so that he could leave. More ambulances came and went, the fire trucks finally ending the siege of the blazes around the street and on the bank, the whole area now damp, blackened, and stale smelling.

All of the Special Weapons men were driven downtown, too. The Command Post van remained, and Medavoy sat on the bumper. The two fat men from Ballistics, Perry and Merriman, came hauling through, taking his gun and everyone else's, tagging them with names and badge numbers. Every gun would have to be test fired for the most monumental shooting review the department had ever conducted.

"Handle this one special," Merriman said to Perry, taking Medavoy's Sig, dropping it into a plastic bag, giving him a small receipt slip. "Two homicides on this one."

Perry, who rarely spoke, laid Medavoy's Sig reverently in the large evidence bag.

Medavoy's stomach rumbled and he realized it was about noon, like any other day in that regard, and he hadn't eaten since early morning. Nobody could give him any conclusive word on the injured men. Everybody was in surgery or under the blackout the Assistant Chief had dropped over medical news.

Pesce, who had taken over the scene from Medavoy, jumped down from the van. He chewed gum rapidly.

"You want to let me go?" Medavoy asked him. "I want to check at the hospital. You don't need me for anything else here."

"Yeah. Why don't you go straight to the hospital," Pesce said carefully. "Then go downtown, give your statement, do your reports, okay? Take a little time, Medavoy. Think about what you're going to say."

"Just what happened."

Pesce spat out his gum. "I'm not one of your fans. I don't think you're a bad guy either. I'm just saying you should think about what you put down on paper. How you answer what you get asked."

"Okay. I'll think about it," Medavoy said.

"You got a lot of exposure here," Pesce said, low. "Lot of things can happen. I got some advice for you."

"What is it?" Medavoy asked, listening with concern. Pesce was in the crew upstairs. He had a sense of their thinking.

"You get over to the hospital, you'll run into Druliner, all the deputy chiefs. They're all hanging around to see how things go. Watch yourself."

"Are you saying they're looking for someone to blame?" Medavoy was certain he was clear on everything he had done to take Trask and Lisio. He could stand up if he had to.

Pesce shook his head. "I know these guys, Medavoy. They're looking for someone *not* to blame. They want to save somebody's ass."

"Like who?"

Pesce snorted, wrinkled tan face cynically grinning. "How about the Chief?"

The annex at NorCal Receiving was jammed with cops and reporters and Medavoy had to be escorted through the crush outside into the building. He was given a lot of deference, like visiting nobility in a village. The cops wanted to smooth the way for him.

He ignored the questions reporters shouted at him, the press of bodies that seemed to be all around. He stared ahead, was briskly taken through the pastel-green corridor, boisterous and sweaty and excited, through doors guarded by two enormous cops.

It was quiet in this part of the corridor. Men in suits whispered to each other. A few sat on aluminum and leather couches. It was a new hospital, without the reek of antiseptic or body smells.

Medavoy spotted them immediately—the captains who all had the title of deputy chief, Operations, Administration, and Investigation. All together in a huddle, all looking up as one when he came escorted in.

On the telephone, jabbering loudly, was that burly Assistant Chief, his cigar dead in his mouth. The three deputies didn't seem particularly attentive to him.

"Medavoy?" barked a white-haired deputy chief, Mc-Murray, his superior in the chain of command below the Assistant Chief and Stevie Wonder, a normally remote and unseen figure.

"Yes, sir," Medavoy answered. He looked around for a nurse or doctor, someone to talk to, the buzz and distraction from the reporters filtering through the glass doors.

"Over here," McMurray ordered. "I want to talk to you."

"I want to find out about one of my men, sir."

"Which one? We've got four wounded officers and two DOA in the basement."

"Detective Geffen, sir," Medavoy said tightly.

McMurray had a reddish face, like so many of the long termers upstairs, and his white hair made him almost benign. He rocked on his heels, impatiently. "Still in surgery."

"How is he?"

"How the hell should I know? I'm not the doctor." He

softened. "Everybody's a little bent, Medavoy. Come over here."

He put his arm on Medavoy's shoulder and guided him to one of the couches farthest from everyone. The hospital intercom softly beeped or called out to doctors. On the pale walls were abstract flowers and stark lines, like the yellow brick road.

The other deputy chiefs wandered over to the Assistant Chief, as though guarding him. Or keeping an eye on him.

"What's the deal, sir? I got a lot of work and I'd like to get home." He sat forward, trying to shake off that arm on his shoulder.

McMurray leaned close, smelling of aftershave and coffee. "Sure you do, Medavoy. There're a few things I've got have crystal clear first."

"Okay, sir. Anything you want."

"First, I think you did a fucking great job out there. I think you could've been more careful, let Pesce or your supervisor know what's happening, but you got the job done."

"Sir, my supervisor's off," he began, but McMurray had only spoken for effect. He tightened his grip on Medavoy's shoulder.

"Now, there are a hell of a lot of questions coming up, Medavoy. Who authorized what? What about the shooting?—a lot of questions. You ready to answer them?"

"Damn right."

"Okay. You mind going on the lie box?"

Medavoy recoiled slightly. A deputy chief wanted him to take a polygraph exam? About what? The shooting of Easter or the setup that still hung over him? "Why's that necessary? I just give a statement."

"Medavoy, this is a very special investigation we're into now. Nothing like it's ever hit the department. There'll be a lot of oversight, a lot of second guessing, a lot of people pointing fingers. For your protection, and the department's protection, I want to be able to wave this fucking lie-box exam and say, he's telling the absolute goddamn truth and the fucking machine proves it. End of second guessing."

"I don't mind taking one," he said. His stomach rumbled again. "Can I get some coffee or a sandwich or something here?"

McMurray snapped his finger. "Some coffee, okay? Something to eat." One of the cops jumped as though prodded and disappeared at a trot.

"How's the Chief? He didn't look good when I got him out of the car." Medavoy thought it wise to remind McMurray who did that.

The deputy chief shook his head, pushed his white hair back roughly. "He's upstairs, beautiful room. He's got some kind of concussion, busted leg, cracked rib. But he's not bad. Not like a couple of others."

The cop reappeared with paper cups of hot coffee that burned and fluffy white chicken sandwiches. Medavoy ate his in three gulps. The deputy chief handed him his, too. "I'm worried about Geffen. I'm glad to hear the Chief's pretty good."

McMurray watched him eat. "What are you going to say about him? In your report?"

"He spooked the two pukes. I think he made a major mistake." He blew on his coffee. McMurray stood up, hands in his pockets, sucking his teeth even though he hadn't eaten. Medavoy wondered where the families of the injured and dead men were. This place was reserved obviously for department brass only.

"I don't think you should say that," McMurray said.

"It's all I can say, sir. It's what happened."

"Medavoy, maybe you just write your report simply for now, okay? Until we sort things out better? I don't want you putting anything down you can't live with later. You understand?"

"No. I don't." He did not like the direction of the conversation or the way the other deputy chiefs kept checking him out.

But McMurray wasn't going to say anything flat. "Just do a bare bones report, Medavoy. We can add to it later, all right?"

"All right, sir."

He got up and started for the door, the cameras and crowd outside. The Assistant Chief dropped the phone, and grabbed his hand. "Thanks. Thanks for what you did." He picked up the phone again.

McMurray said, "I want you to turn your badge in, Medavoy. I've got to put you on suspension until after the review. Just formality."

Medavoy stopped dead. "Suspended? You suspending me?"

Druliner, the deputy chief, Administration, said sourly, "With pay. Don't worry about it, Medavoy. Everybody who fired a weapon is on suspension."

"Which is one reason for us to wrap up the investigation and review right away," McMurray said. He held out his hand.

Medavoy slowly took out his badge, in its folding black case. He removed his driver's license. It always helped to carry it with your badge if you got stopped. You flashed the license and badge at a cop at the same time and no one could accuse you of using your job for a favor. It stung him to pass the badge to McMurray. "I'm going downtown to do my report," he said.

McMurray looked at the other men. "He's going on the lie box. He's writing a simple report."

"That's wonderful," Druliner said. "You better get to it, Medavoy."

"What happened to Trask? I didn't find out," Medavoy asked. The other men had turned from him and started whispering.

McMurray glanced up. "DOA an hour ago. Good shooting."

It was perfunctory but sincere, the department's typically laconic compliment for grace under fire. Medavoy nodded, unsure how he felt about it himself yet.

As he pushed past the two cops guarding the doors, he almost collided with that councilman, Prefach, bulling his way in to see the deputy chiefs. Prefach's face was set, determined, and he simply swept Medavoy aside. Squeezing through the loud, frenzied crush of reporters and civilians, Medavoy briefly looked behind him and saw them together, cops and the politician, in deep conversation. He had an idea who they were talking about.

THIRTY-FIVE

HE DIDN'T GO IMMEDIATELY back to the department. He rode out Anderson Avenue, past the expensive department stores, until he was in a neighborhood more to scale and stopped at a taqueria. He sat on a wooden bench, mechanically ate two tacos and a beer, and listened to the breathless stream of nonsense about the incident pour from a radio balanced in the small outdoor stand over the stove. He wiped his greasy fingers, shutting his ears and mind to the exaggerated account on the radio. On the other side of a mesh fence, kids from the neighborhood played soccer or chased each other in a tree-shaded park.

He watched them for a while, trying to compose his report and dreading what he would face when he walked through the police department's doors.

He had to protect himself. Pesce said as much, and Mc-Murray's direct order meant the hunt for scapegoats had already begun. He heard the word heroic over and over on the radio. Medavoy had no doubt that what was heroic this afternoon could turn cowardly tomorrow. All depends on how they play it, he thought.

He left the temporary sanctuary of the nearly deserted stand reluctantly and drove downtown.

When he parked his car at the department, he got a small taste of the reception to come. Mutt jumped at him and wouldn't stop shaking his hand. Apparently the word about Easter's shooting hadn't gotten clear yet, all they knew downtown was that the pukes had been spectacularly put down, the Chief rescued, and Medavoy was a hero.

It was the same when he went through the marble lobby. Cops going out stopped him. A few walked by, but the incident was bound to cleave the department. Some men had obviously heard more than others, some had a stake in the bad things going on. Some didn't like him. He stared for a moment at the trophy case and the sad memento of fallen officers. It was going to be tough to see that every day and know he'd added a name to it.

Even if Easter deserved his death, he had been a cop for a long time and it wasn't something you could ever think about without some pain. And there were the others, too.

Upstairs, the whole second floor had been emptied out of secretaries and support personnel, all of them sent to the third floor where a temporary interview assembly line had been set up. People waiting to be interviewed—about forty or so, he reckoned by the line against the wall, halfway up the stairs— murmured and chatted. Until a detective in shirt-sleeves came out, someone left, a name was called out, and another witness went in.

He found Masuda and Zaragoza frantically pecking away at their typewriters.

"Looks like a ghost town here," Medavoy said, throwing his coat off. He sat down heavily.

"Jesus, Robby, you finally got here." Masuda looked silly, a big man hunched over an electric typewriter trying to coax words out of it with two fingers. "Place's gone crazy. Fourth floor's gone nuts."

"I just saw the whole bunch at the hospital. No word yet on Gef?"

"Nothing come through," Masuda said. "I check about every fifteen minutes."

Medavoy nodded. That was all there was to do.

Zaragoza sputtered, "That shithead Pomerantz in Investigations, he gets the word here he got to have reports on what happened on his desk by 1400. A whole report." He shook his head in disgust. No wonder he and Masuda were flying. Reports due by two P.M. had only about forty minutes to be completed.

He looked at his own in-basket, a stack of supplementary investigation requests on other cases dropped in, regular as clockwork, like it was an average day. "Jane still here?" he asked, trying not to show how much he hoped she was.

"She got in, got out about half hour ago," Masuda said. "They hardly talked to her."

That was unusual, too, he thought. She had been at the scene and a key participant. A special interview was undoubtedly being readied for her once all the other statements and reports were in hand and could be used for comparison. He didn't like the progress of the investigation at all. "She go home?" he asked quietly.

Masuda nodded, tapping his typewriter from excess energy. "She's pretty tough. A lot of these guys around here look worse than her."

The background noise from the stairway and the third floor was like a baseball game that started late, the fans anxious for it to get going. Scraps of the radio reports drifted through the chattering. Medavoy pulled out some report forms. Bare bones, McMurray said, only the events without the precursors? It was hard to tell. He intended to write a very careful account that couldn't be used against him either way, too barren, too accusatory.

Someone on the fourth floor had ordered the news trucks and reporters to stay a block away from the department, on penalty of interfering with a police investigation. The reporters screamed, Masuda said, but nobody had dared come near the building.

Medavoy began typing. Leave the Chief out, just something spooking Trask and Lisio. Jesus, he thought, this thing isn't going to make any sense. If he wrote it fully, though, maybe McMurray would say he'd disobeyed an order.

No one answered the frequently ringing telephones. Zaragoza didn't think anybody with any good news would be calling them and any news about Gef they'd get themselves.

The typewriters clattered noisily, then Medavoy stopped. "I been suspended until there's a shooting review."

"They can't suspend you," Masuda said indignantly. "It's self-defense. That's the only reason you fired."

"Okay, guys, I'll tell you, I'm worried." He repeated what Pesce and McMurray had said.

Zaragoza grew so agitated he jumped up. "They come after you, Robby, we got a union. We take the whole department out."

"Jimmy, I don't think they know what they want yet, how this is going," he said. "Maybe I'll get another medal. Maybe we all will."

"And the check's in the mail, you know," Masuda said. "We got to find out who else they suspend. They didn't get me or Jimmy."

"Only shooters," Medavoy said. "No, it makes sense so far. I'm just getting a weird feeling. Maybe I'll know what's going on tomorrow."

Zaragoza loosened his thin black tie. "You got us, Robby. We stay with you. We back you up. Whatever those assholes do."

Masuda nodded. "No question."

The support moved him deeply, but he didn't want them to see that. He grinned instead, "Tell me we didn't take care of business. You see the way that place looked? We wiped the two pukes off the map."

Zaragoza hooted loudly. "You shoulda seen the guys I was with, running around, shooting. Man, we took care of it."

Then Masuda jumped up, imitating the frightened, exhilarated, wild-eyed cops and their headlong dash along the street. Medavoy laughed until he bent double, the three of them jockeying to tell more outrageous versions of what had happened. They got so noisy one of the solemn, tense detectives doing the mass interview came down and told them to shut up.

By three o'clock, he had written as much as he could, and took off for NorCal Receiving to wait for word on Gef in person. He brought his report with him. Masuda and Zaragoza said they'd meet him later, as soon as their reports were done. Sooner or later, as Medavoy glanced at what they'd written so far, he knew Stevie Wonder would be pinned down for what happened. Too many people had seen him speed into the ambush, lights and sirens going.

Which made McMurray's order hard to figure out, he thought. You can't keep a lid on this thing. It's got to come out.

He noticed that there were cops, singly and in groups, listening to radios or watching TVs almost everywhere he went from the building on his way to the hospital.

It was possible to imagine the whole city pausing, listening and collecting itself, like a man after a heart attack tensely, intently hearing the rush of his own pulse.

Medavoy couldn't find any of the deputy chiefs when he got to NorCal and navigated his way through the growing crowd of shouting reporters filling every room, underfoot everywhere he went, asking questions of anyone, even people waiting for treatment in the out-patient clinic.

The chiefs were apparently all on a pilgrimage to Stevie Wonder's private room. Medavoy found a detective working for McMurray and gave him the report to pass along, then went to the trauma wing of the hospital. A separate waiting room was set aside for the families of the wounded officers. He found Geffen's wife Sandra and the kids nestled on a thick plastic couch, quiet, not the playful bunch he remembered. He brought them sodas from a machine nearby and they sat drinking, chatting in a desultory, disinterested way. With them was an older man and woman, nervous parents of a young cop.

He sat beside Sandra and the oldest boy, Rudy. "You still got that sofa ready for me?" he asked Sandra. She looked at him in puzzlement and Rudy grinned.

Medavoy, embarrassed, realized he had spent those nights on the sofa when Geffen was married to Robin, his second wife. Mind's going, he thought. He asked Rudy about soccer, the girls about a school play.

"You run out of things to ask about," Sandra, a slight, fairhaired woman said softly. She had dressed hastily, coat over jeans, sandals. Medavoy had seen a lot of people jerked from their lives like this but he never got used to being with them. He couldn't even try now.

"Pretty soon you do, yeah," he admitted. "I think it's good it's taking so long. It means they got something to work with." He wanted to believe that.

Geffen's wife didn't react, eyes raising only when the buzzing sound of the reporters drawing near bothered her. The department was doing an excellent job of keeping the families protected. He wondered why the other two cops didn't have their families at the hospital. You never could tell. It was even barely possible they didn't know what had happened to their sons and husbands.

Geffen's wife thought over how long he'd been in surgery. She counted on her watch. "Going on six hours. My first delivery took twenty-two hours." She sighed and cried softly.

Medavoy put his arm around her and the older couple huddled silently together.

Around four, he grew so restless and pent-up and worried he left the room, enclosed in glass on three sides like one of the bank conference rooms he'd seen in the last twenty-four hours, went out to a public phone and called Jane.

"I'm waiting at the hospital on Gef. Nothing so far."

Jane had Johnathan in the room, he could hear the crying from the kid. "You want me to come down?"

"No, you got the kid. No point in you being here."

"Can you get home soon?"

"I'm going to stay one way or the other, Janie," he said, gripping the receiver, looking across to the glass waiting room and the despairing, desperate people suspended in it. "I can't come home yet."

"I'm with you, Robby. You know that?"

"Yeah, I do. I'll be there when I can. Love you," he said and hung up.

Too much is hanging fire, he thought. He must settle things with Jane tonight, straighten them out at least, and face the next days together.

Masuda and Zaragoza showed up and they all waited until a doctor in a green gown, wrinkled and sweat-rimmed at the arms, came through, blinking with fatigue himself.

He was a young man, tall and limber-looking like Geffen. Medavoy held Sandra's hand as the doctor ran it down quietly, pointing to his own body to illustrate.

"Your husband had four wounds to the upper torso," he said to Geffen's wife. "Two were penetrating, two were through-and-through. The penetrating wounds caused a great deal of tissue damage so he lost a lot of muscle in the back. Well, let me make it simple. He had injuries to his lungs and some bony structures. One of the through-and-through injuries was to the spinal cord. So there is paralysis of the left arm and leg and it may be permanent."

Medavoy felt the hand in his grow limp. Masuda wiped his eyes and Zaragoza breathed deeply. The kids listened silently.

"When can we go to him?" Geffen's wife asked softly.

"I'd prefer in the morning. You could look in on him a little later. Maybe an hour, when he's in a bed." The doctor spoke to her for a few more minutes, then turned and Medavoy followed him out.

"He's going to recover?" Medavoy asked when they were out of earshot of the others. "He can go back to work sometime?"

The doctor, young and old simultaneously, shook his head. "Not a chance. You've got a man with a hundred-percent disability."

The words drove themselves painfully into Medavoy. "He know that?"

"He's still out. Tell me, did you guys go after drug dealers? We're starting to get automatic rifle wounds like that."

Medavoy, shaken, said no. "They didn't have weapons like that."

The doctor was grim. "It's the kind of wound you used to only see in combat."

Medavoy returned to the family, told Sandra Geffen to call him if she needed anything; Masuda gave her every phone number he had, writing them on his business card. Zaragoza said he and Sugar would come over any time. The three of them left her to wait for the chance to see Geffen later. They knew as much as they needed to know about what had happened to Geffen and what was going to happen to him. Medavoy blew Sandra Geffen a kiss, sitting in the glass room with her children.

Wordlessly, he, Masuda, and Zaragoza got out of NorCal Receiving, walking briskly through the cops guarding the doors, past reporters who followed them for a while—through the dense line of people drawn up around the hospital, attracted by the cameras and lights, the high drama and immediacy of the day's events. The day had faded while they waited in the hospital, becoming rosy and blue tinted like a watercolor.

About four blocks away, Medavoy led them into a dark, small bar, dolls with ancient sequined skirts in its window. The TV over the bar was on, broadcasting pictures from the hospital, the cleanup on El Camino Grande.

"Ask him to turn it off," he said to Masuda, pointing at the bartender. There were only four other people in the bar, dim figures with cigarettes hunched over their tables. Masuda usually got a quicker response when he asked for favors because of his bulk.

The bartender shrugged and turned it off. No one protested. They sat at the bar, ordered and drank two rounds before anyone spoke.

"He's alive. That's a hell of a deal," Masuda said.

"You never know what's going to happen. Tomorrow maybe, he sits up in bed. Next day, he gets up, takes a piss on his own," Zaragoza said and bought a third round.

Medavoy drank quickly and without pleasure. He got a fourth round. "I wouldn't be sitting here except for Gef doing that goddamn trick." He was tired enough to sleep for days. "He won't be a cop anymore, and that's a damn fucking price to pay for everything."

Masuda raised his glass, "To Gef."

Medavoy raised his glass, "To the Robbery Detail the way it should've stayed."

On the third floor of the hospital, Geffen's family had come into his room, shared with five other patients, and stood with him even though he was still unconscious.

Above him in a private room, the Chief lay on his back, braced, bandaged a little, sweating and nauseated. Donna arranged her clothes in the modest teak bureau which stood beside the small cot she insisted be brought in. She had started to make the room cheery, adding vases of flowers, a picture of the family from home.

The Chief had never felt so sick, in pain both moral and physical, in his whole life. Even on those terrible Sundays when his father dressed him down, the slap was transient. This lasted, the knowledge of his recklessness and its cost.

His room was protected by two uniformed cops. The deputy chiefs had tried to see him and he had them kept out, even barred Bart and Prefach. Only Donna had been admitted, and she was going to stay with him.

"Did you say something, Mac?" She turned from the bureau. It was a room she had picked. Like a tastefully decorated hotel, it had drapes and thick carpet, heavy sitting chairs.

"I made a noise."

"I thought you said something."

"I feel awful. I'm making noise because I feel terrible." He couldn't even roll away, hide his eyes, turn from the tormenting images.

"It's too early for another pill."

"I don't want another pill. I want to get out of here." He had a brief dream of rising, incorporeal, from his bed, and drifting through the parted cream-colored drapes, over the city, into the growing twilight.

"You don't have to act like a child," Donna said, finishing her unpacking. "You were very lucky." She looked tired, he thought, and frightened. The sharp retorts were part of her relief he was alive.

"I've never had pain like this," he said quietly.

"The others are dead. Some have worse injuries. One's crippled."

The Chief groaned with anguish. "That's what hurts me. I did it."

Donna closed the bureau and sat on his bed carefully. "Now, Mac, you can say things like that with me, but you mustn't do that with anybody else. Especially Vin. Or your deputy chiefs."

"I want to get out of here. I want to go home." He listened to himself with another burst of shame. Like a child, that's how I sound.

She smoothed his covers. "We're going to be together for a week here. Then perhaps we'll go home."

"What have I done, Donna? How am I going to get around it, just get my mind around the thing?"

A triangle of yellowing sunlight, the last of the day, fell over her slender legs. "You've got good people, Mac. They're handling it, and you've got Vin, too."

"But it's my *fault,*" he said, forcefully enough that he had a cold fear something delicate was breaking inside himself. "My men. My responsibility."

"You're medicated now, you don't see things properly. The department is proud of you. You did your job and faced a great danger," she said gently, lulling him. "Accidents happen, but I'm very proud of you."

"Are you? You shouldn't be." He thought again of his driver, crushed to death beside him. He groaned, eyes shut.

"I'm sorry, Mac."

"I've got to do something," he said. "I've got to get around it."

"You won't do anything until we've discussed it. All right?"

"Yes. All right." He faded. "If only it would go away."

"Shall I sing to you?"

He opened his eyes. Her voice was tentative, soft, and the entreaty bolder than he'd heard from her in years.

"Do you want to?"

She nodded, touching him. "I'll do it very quietly, like I used to. I hope I still have my voice."

"You do."

"Any requests?"

"You choose." He held himself motionless. She leaned over, brushed his hair back, touched his lips. Hope, he thought, seeing her face lined but serene, was sometimes terrible. I hope now. I hope I'll forget everything I did.

Donna began singing, almost a lullaby, gentling and sweet. He was not the Chief of Police and she was not the daughter of one of Santa Maria's first families. They had just met. They weren't in the hospital, but in a stand of eucalyptus bordering that cornfield, right after a long lunch. They sat on the grass, then lay together and she started singing.

It was almost possible to blot out his shame, his crushing responsibility for the disaster. I've got to do something, he thought, her voice rolling over him. I've got to make it up somehow.

He would see the deputy chiefs and Bart in the morning. Beg their forgiveness.

Carol Beaufort sat across the table from a reporter named Goodhue in the interview room of the Santa Maria County Jail. He was young and wore dark granny glasses even in the jail's dim lighting. He had on a corduroy jacket and made small notes on the pad in front of him.

She wasn't impressed, even if he was from the city's largest newspaper. She asked about Reilly and found out he was "pretty banged up," according to Goodhue.

"Poor Brian," she said quickly, meaning it. She thought often in the last hours of Kenny, too. He had risked what little he had and lost everything to be with her.

"So why're you talking to me?" Goodhue asked.

"You're not the only one. Since they left me here I've done about three interviews. They won't let TV cameras inside, so it's only newspapers."

"So why're you talking to all of us?"

Carol was dressed in jail jeans and a faded gray sweatshirt with the jail's name on it and a number. She had showered

374 WILLIAM P. WOOD

in a steel room, been fingerprinted, photographed, prodded, inspected, and put in an isolation cell because of the possibility the other inmates would bother her. She was already famous.

"Well," she said, rubbing her chapped hands, "I'm a lawyer. I try to put my side of a story out if I can."

Goodhue scribbled. "Have you been charged yet?"

"Well, technically I don't think I'm under arrest."

He snorted. "You're staying here and you aren't under arrest?"

"It's a legal question." She smiled emptily because it was also absurd. "I mean, they could charge me. I've got an immunity deal." She showed him the agreement Medavoy had written out.

Goodhue read it, raised his eyebrows. "So you could walk right out of here."

Carol stood up. The room was unfinished, cinder blocks and plastic chairs. It was not something to look forward to. And I won't have to, she vowed. "Where would I go? No house. No friends. No boss." She smiled again. "And I don't know what the people of this city think of me."

"Not a lot," Goodhue admitted with understatement.

"So, why not stay here until they straighten out my immunity grant? They even feed you. If you can keep the food on your plate."

"Who takes it? Guards?"

She shook her head. "My fellow political prisoners."

Goodhue flipped a page. "You afraid the cops, Medavoy in particular, will go back on the deal?"

Carol didn't know what she was afraid of at the moment. She had lost Kenny as an alibi, but lost something else. She felt lonely. It was very unpleasant, like a dry pain.

"Mr. Goodhue," she said, pacing a little, then facing him. "I have to look after my own interests. I have to make it hard for the cops to back out of the deal. Medavoy may not always be able to help me."

"You're kidding. He's a hero. I mean, they got an inquiry going, but he's a genuine hero." Goodhue actually sounded startled.

She sat down again, splaying her hand out. He was too young. "My experience with cops and people in power is that they don't always do the right thing."

"So you're just using me to buy some public insurance, tell your story?"

Someone banged a gong or pot in the jail, and there was a chorus of female giggling. "You hit the nail," she said.

"Okay, let's hear your side of this thing. It's a real mess out there now, bulldozers, cranes, fire trucks. Like a war zone."

She had gotten the whole story down to a fair summary after doing the other interviews. A sanitized account of her ties to Kenny, the appearance of Lisio, her own helplessness, coercion, attempts to get free. Kenny, though, kept popping into her mind as she talked, like he was still alive and vital. It was going to be tough tonight, dreaming about him and what happened, she thought, and no way to get through it with drinks or pills.

Goodhue broke into her recital. "Carol, are you saying there's some way they can go after Medavoy? He's got some problem?"

Maybe Goodhue wasn't so young and credulous after all, she thought. Medavoy must have broken a dozen police regulations when he went after Kenny and Lisio, and she had her own suspicions from some of Reilly's references to him. Another bang on that pot somewhere, indicated the jail was readying for dinner. She shuddered. "Look, I'm not going to hurt a man who can help me."

"So there is something wrong." Goodhue wrote in shorthand so she couldn't read it. "Makes a better story. Sorry."

Medavoy got home after five, hesitating at Jane's house for a moment because of the three vans and TV crews parked on her lawn. He gritted his teeth, drove up, and again repeated a dozen times that he had nothing to say pending the department's review of the whole affair. Microphones kept pushing at him. He weaved a little, getting into the house and hoped none of the reporters had noticed where he must have been. Standing on their lawns, spilling into the street, were most of the neighbors, all of the Cabrals waving to him. Spontaneously the people began applauding and calling his name. He waved back.

Jane and Johnathan were in the kitchen, with the lights on and the curtains pulled. Natty raced up and growled at his shoes.

"I'm sorry, Janie. I'll go someplace else tonight if you want."

She looked up from spooning macaroni into a squirming Johnathan. "You crazy? Don't be noble. How about I go and you stay?" She grinned to show it was a joke.

"Forget it. I am crazy," he said and dragged off to the shower, the dog clicking and barking after him. He stood under a hot spray for a while, hoping to clear away the confusion and waves of fatigue. If it was going to be like this, he didn't know how long he could take so much attention. It wasn't that he minded cameras and people applauding. He liked it, he admitted to himself. But not for something like this.

He changed into brown slacks, a new shirt and when he came out again into the kitchen, Jane was finishing with Johnathan. An open milk carton sat on the table.

"You doing okay?" she asked, standing up and putting her arms around him. "You want anything to eat?"

"No. I'm not hungry. How about you?"

"Maybe I shouldn't be all right, but I don't feel badly, Robby. I think about that guy. He was real worried I tell people he didn't hurt me. I never knew someone who was alive, talking, worrying, thinking about today and tomorrow, then dead a minute later. I had an uncle who died when I was a kid," her bare arms showed in the T-shirt she wore, "but it wasn't like this."

"This is how it happens," Medavoy said. "Now you know. We both do."

"You did what had to be done," she said. "I wish it didn't have to go that way, but it did."

"I know that. It just makes everything different," he said, trying to form his feeling into words. Johnathan and the dog played on the floor, indifferent to what was being said. "It all looks the same around here, but it's not."

Jane kissed him, then went to the sink. "You sure? I mean, besides all those reporters outside?"

"Yeah," he said quietly. "We came close to losing each other. One second the world's one way, the next it's changed completely."

"So how's it going to be different for us?" She started washing the dishes. He got a beer from the refrigerator, offered her one and she shook her head. He held the cold metal of the can on his forehead for a moment.

"I don't have it all worked out," he said. "It's part of what I've been thinking about, at the hospital, holding you, in the shower just now. We're sitting here this morning, I'm worrying about crooked cops, office politics, what Stevie Wonder's doing. You and me standing on the porch last night, listening to the rain, thinking today's going to be like yesterday, tomorrow's going to be the same. All the time we're planning, thinking, worrying like that, Trask and Lisio and Beaufort are out there and heading right for us."

"Maybe we were heading for them."

"So it's like every hour it's coming closer and we didn't know it. They were out there getting closer to us and they didn't know it. Easter, he's running around, setting me up, getting it all in a line, ready to take me down, and he's just a couple hours away from me shooting him. He didn't know.

Or Gef. Or Stevie Wonder. The goddamn Chief of Police is making these big moves, he's changing the whole fucking department, he's thinking, planning, and he's got a couple of hours left before he drives right into Trask and Lisio."

Johnathan wailed a little at Medavoy's hard tone, looking up from the floor anxiously. Jane wiped her hands, reached down, lifted him into the high chair, and clapped his small hands together so he laughed.

She looked at Medavoy. He said, "I get back downtown tonight after I been to the hospital, they'll be clearing out Easter's locker. Same for the Chief's driver, anybody else. These guys, the Special Weapons teams, they're pretty hard."

"You all are. You have to be."

"Maybe we do. It doesn't matter how tough they are. They go through Easter's locker, and Internal Affairs is going to be there, you can bet on it. They take out his things, put them in a box for his family, these guys are going to cry. They hate it when other cops do it, they'll hate it with IAD standing there, but it'll happen."

He ran his hands through the kid's fine hair gently, without being aware of it.

Jane held the kid's hands together and he squealed happily. "I was surprised they didn't ask hardly anything downtown," she said. "Just a very quick once-through. You know why?"

He shook his head. "Million possible reasons. They thought you're upset, they wanted more information first, they'll call tomorrow. Could be anything."

"But it is strange."

"Yeah. So's everything that happened today. I got suspended, too." He grinned crookedly at her, sat down in the chair, and fingered the milk carton.

Jane rubbed his leg. "Jesus, Robby. I'm sorry. How can they do that to you?"

"Just part of the investigation. More like a vacation."

"You're bullshitting me," she said sharply. "You think

something's going on downtown, don't you?"

"I'm not sure yet." He looked at her. "I want to get my life straightened out with you. No matter what else happens."

Natty raised her sharp brown head to the sound of motors in the TV vans going on, the hum of voices rising. Probably time for everybody to do a broadcast, right from the lawn of the famous cop who nailed the bad guy, he thought. Jane said, "Right now you know what I want. You know how it should go."

She held Johnathan by one hand, then took Medavoy's. He swallowed with difficulty, not from nervousness but longing for her. "Please marry me," he said.

"All right," she said.

THIRTY-SIX

MEDAVOY WAS AWAKE early the next morning. He expected to look out the bedroom window and see the street empty and the front yard clear of reporters. It was a shock to see that their numbers had grown overnight. Five TV vans now crowded the street and reporters, in thick coats against the spring morning chill, clustered along the sidewalk, taking pictures of the front of the house, of passing cars, of each other.

It was their muted conversations, the trucks' engines, that had awakened him. Usually the kid does that, he thought. He slipped carefully out of bed. Jane had the uncanny ability to sleep through anything. He pulled the covers over her. She sighed in her sleep, hair partly covering her face.

Might as well face them and find out what's going on. Reporters didn't start showing up in such numbers unless something had happened.

Medavoy dressed quickly in old jeans and his old Police Baseball League sweatshirt and went outside.

The reporters jumped to life, lights on, shouting at him, ten or twelve pushing microphones. What did he think about the charges? Was he taking money? Did he shoot a fellow officer because they were taking bribes together?

"Hey," he said loudly, "I haven't seen anything. I haven't heard anything since yesterday."

"Did you really let armed felons go after a bank?"

"How many crooked cops do you know personally?"

"Do you think the DA is going to charge you?"

Medavoy was outraged at first, then realized it didn't matter what he felt. They'd yell questions at him if he opened his mouth at all. So he decided to say nothing and walked down the block to Garcia's Cigars and bought a couple of newspapers. Reporters and cameras trotted along with him, still asking questions and he had to apologize to old man Garcia about the circus. The old man shrugged and asked if anybody wanted to buy a magazine.

He had a chilly feeling growing in the pit of his stomach as he walked back to Jane's house. The biggest daily in the city carried front-page stories from Beaufort and other cops under the blocky headline: HERO COP? QUESTIONS RAISED ABOUT TACTICS, SHOOTING, all quoting unnamed sources in the department. The front page had a large picture of him, clothes disheveled, standing in El Camino Grande, smoke around him, shimmering through a telephoto lens.

The other story filling the page was worse. COP SHOOTS COP: WHY? it demanded. Just like Pesce said, he thought, the department's looking for ways to save Stevie Wonder and jam all the bad shit, bad cops, bad judgment, on me. He strode past three men in suits standing on the lawn, one with close-cropped gray hair, giving a finger-jabbing interview. He jabbed at Jane's house. He stopped talking when he saw Medavoy.

Medavoy kept walking, the man came to him, and soon the whole gaggle of reporters surrounded them with notebooks, waving little tape recorders, and cameras.

"Robert Medavoy?" the man asked. His two companions,

younger and stockier, guys Medavoy had seen go in and out of the building without knowing, were stiff-faced.

"Yeah. Who're you?"

"I'm Lieutenant Gunderson, Internal Affairs." He showed his badge.

"What do you want?" Medavoy held the newspaper folded up under his arm, uncomfortable to be so visible, like an insect pinned to a board.

"I'm here to notify you that departmental charges are being brought against you and other officers and to search your residence for evidence relating to those charges."

He handed Medavoy a Santa Maria Police Department blue form, which always meant some kind of bad news. Medavoy found his hands starting to shake, and he didn't want to be seen out here, in front of his neighbors. "I don't want to talk out here. Come inside."

He started for the front door. Gunderson, a pugnacious man, asked loudly, "You giving us permission to search?"

"I'm saying you can come inside. That's all. Or you can get lost."

The reporters babbled in protest, trying to keep Gunderson or one of his men outside. But, they followed Medavoy into the house and he slammed the door. "What the hell are you doing?" Medavoy demanded. "I've been a cop for twelve fucking years and you treat me like this?"

One of Gunderson's assistants put up a hand to keep Medavoy back. "Don't cop an attitude with me, Medavoy," Gunderson said. He had even, white teeth. He and his men wore similar charcoal-gray suits. "You're the worst kind of cop there is. So just read the charges and let us look around."

Medavoy was about to do something he knew wouldn't help things, when Jane came in. Johnathan started wailing in his room. She had on a yellow bathrobe and she glanced at the men in the living room defiantly. "I hope you guys have a reason for being here and waking my son up."

Gunderson nodded. "You Jane Baird, I assume?"

"That's right. I live here."

Medavoy looked at the charges listed on the blue form. They were as serious as he could imagine. For a moment his anger was replaced with bewilderment. They couldn't really be doing this to him. Not for Stevie Wonder.

"There's supposed to be a shooting review," he said.

Gunderson shook his head. "Not for you. You got a departmental hearing in forty-eight hours. Read the notice. You can bring witnesses. You can have a lawyer. But you got to be ready." He had his hands in his pockets. He pointed to his men. "We're going to look around."

Medavoy stepped in front of one stocky guy. "No, you don't go anyplace. It's not my house."

Jane said, "I'm the owner. And I don't give you any permission to search my house." Johnathan cried more insistently. "I've got to check on my son." She left them.

"We can get a warrant, Medavoy. We can go right downtown now and get a warrant to look around," Gunderson said. He was one of those police bureaucrats on the first floor of the building, off in a room nobody ever went into. You'd see him wandering across the marble lobby sometimes, wearing a sweater, holding a coffee cup, looking like all he was doing was waiting for his pension rights to vest so he could retire on eighty-percent pay.

"You go get a warrant," Medavoy said, his mouth dry. "Just get out of the house."

The men with Gunderson looked unhappy at being denied the chance to poke around. But Gunderson said, "Sure. We have to go if you say so. Make a report you didn't want us looking around. Submit it to the review board. They'll use it at the hearing."

"Get out."

Gunderson turned to the door. "Tell your lady friend she's got an appointment at eleven today to make a full statement to Lieutenant Pomerantz in Investigations."

"Tell him to fuck himself."

Gunderson grinned sourly. "My pleasure. You can tell her the DA may decide to subpoena her when this thing gets to the grand jury."

"It's not going to the grand jury. There's nothing here." Medavoy knew he was bluffing.

"Play it any way you want, Medavoy." Gunderson stepped out with his men and the reporters crowded around them. Medavoy locked the door and stood holding the terrifying blue form in his hand, trying to make some sense of its list of charges.

Jane came in carrying Johnathan, who was cranky and sleep-creased. "What's going on, Robby? What are they here for?"

He peeked out the living room window. Gunderson again stood on the lawn giving an interview. "The son of a bitch is killing me right now," Medavoy swore. "They've got me on charges, Janie." He handed her the form.

"Reckless endangerment, failure to notify a superior, conduct unbecoming an officer," she glanced up, "that must be me.

"That's you okay. And they want you to give a statement. A real one at eleven."

She bounced Johnathan gently. They could both hear the shouted questions outside. "Holy Christ. *Murder*," she read. "They're going to say you murdered a cop?"

"They're going all out. Everything's out there." He thought about what to do, the things that had to happen right away, with only two days before he faced a departmental hearing. It was not a trial and the penalties were firing or some lesser discipline, but any findings could be turned over to the district attorney for criminal prosecution and at a departmental hearing there were virtually no procedural protections. You were guilty if accused. You had to prove your innocence. "I told them you wouldn't make a statement."

Jane sat down, putting the blue form on the couch. "No, I am making a statement. They won't like it. They're going to ask how come I was with you, right?"

"They're going to ask how I let a civilian get put at risk," he said, "among other things."

"Fuck the other things, Robby. I'm not ashamed of anything. We decided last night that nothing else matters."

Medavoy sat beside her, the kid between them. "I didn't mean that. This's got me going too many directions."

"You know what I'm going to say? I'll tell them how I found out there was an internal affairs investigation. I tell them their IAD guy is telling outsiders about secret police department investigations." She nodded grimly.

"They'll go crazy. You'll get Schroeder on the hook right away. Your pal Smitty, too."

"Robby, in this town, if you start dumping on one person you find out you've hit a lot of other people. Smitty's been around. He'll go along with me."

He kissed her. "Okay, you give them hell, Janie. Get them running around. I got to do some things, try to get clear if I can."

He left the house, driving his car along side streets and down alleys, making sure none of the reporters had followed him that far. Or that IAD wasn't tailing him either. It had been a long time since he'd tailed anyone himself and he wasn't sure he recalled how to do it best.

He'd thrown a sport coat over his sweatshirt, waited in an alley—no one coming up it—then driven to a gas station minimart and used the public phone. He dialed Zaragoza's number at the department. At least he was sure no one was listening at this end.

"Zaragoza, Robbery," was the answer.

"It's me, Jimmy."

"Yeah, hiya," Zaragoza's voice was deliberately bland. "IAD's just been to Jane's house. They wanted to search it. They got a shitload of charges they're trying to drop on me."

"Yeah, they're here now. Checking things."

"You can't talk?"

"Nope."

"How about an early lunch?"

"Suits me."

"Okay, I'll meet you at the Moon in fifteen minutes." He didn't want Zaragoza to mention the restaurant's name with IAD detectives standing over him.

"Good talking to you." Zaragoza hung up.

It wasn't even eight o'clock, so maybe he should have said they'd have a late breakfast. He stood at the gas station for a minute, then called NorCal Receiving. Geffen remained unconscious the whole night, so Medavoy had simply stayed with him for an hour before going home again. He was still out, still listed as critical. Medavoy hung up and got in his car.

The New China Moon Cafe was in the middle of Horner Avenue at the edge of the city's Chinatown. It looked more like a small market than a restaurant, with boxes of fruit for sale outside and wide, gray-streaked windows. It featured chicken-fried steak or an enormous bowl of wonton soup for lunch that day.

Medavoy went inside, the place had three or four people eating slowly, and sat in a booth. He ordered coffee and waited, trying not to think.

Zaragoza bustled in about five minutes later, slipping into the booth. He wore one of his ugliest suits, a salt-and-pepper thing with narrow lapels. Medavoy had to laugh. "You got the worst-looking clothes I ever saw, Jimmy."

Zaragoza looked hurt for a moment. "I like this suit."

"So tell me what's happening downtown. All I got is a list

of charges." He showed them to Zaragoza.

"Man. Oh, man," Zaragoza said, reading. "This is bad, Robby. I mean, there's something really bad in the department when they pull this shit." He dug out a departmental form from his coat. "Look at the list of suspensions."

Medavoy read down the nine names. "They're all Special Weapons. Except me."

"Yeah. Bad atmosphere in the building. You want to hear the rumors? They say you nailed Easter because he's cheating on some deals you guys got into."

Medavoy tossed the list back. "Jesus. Where does that leave you guys?"

"We getting some strange looks today, I tell you. You got guys coming up to you, they ask how they can get in on things with Easter's setup blown. You got guys saying you great, you an asshole."

"Sounds like the department's picking sides. Anybody talking about Stevie Wonder?"

Zaragoza ordered coffee and a doughnut. "Yeah, real tense about him. Lots of rumors he messed up. This's bogus." He shook his head, his mustache glistening with sweat. "I never seen the place so bad."

"Can I get into the building, Jimmy?"

"Negative. IAD comes down, they give us strict orders. We can't talk to you, see you, nothing until after the hearing. You got to stay away from the department. They been through your cases. They been through you locker, too."

"Man, I thought I was doing everything right yesterday. I figured a couple things with the pukes might go bad, but nothing like this."

"Robby, remember, Stan and me, lots of guys, we with you. You want us to testify at the hearing, help you out, whatever you want." He ignored the doughnut and coffee when they arrived. Chinese exclamations from the grill behind the counter filled the restaurant.

"I only got two days before the hearing. Fucking departmental hearing, and they can wire it any way they want," he said, lapsing into uncharacteristic pessimism. "Janie's got into it, too. I got to get us out of this."

"You get a lawyer. That's what you got to have now, somebody talking for you."

"How about the union guy? You like him? I can't afford a private lawyer." Medavoy tried to run up his alimony and house payments and his contributions to running the place with Jane. He was extended to the limit as it was.

Zaragoza was enthusiastic. "Go see Ronnie Chadd. He's good. He pulled me out when they tried to hose me after that Supreme Court deal."

Medavoy got up. "Thanks, Jimmy. He sounds good. You keep an eye on my hot cases, okay? Make sure nothing falls apart."

"Stan and I'll watch out for you. You want to bring Jane for dinner, get away for a while?"

He shook his head. "You'd have reporters all over your place, probably. Then you'd get IAD on your ass, too."

Zaragoza made an obscene gesture and Medavoy left him to finish eating.

He had a lot to do.

THIRTY-SEVEN

THE LAWYER FOR THE Santa Maria Police Officers Association had his office in the Library and Courts Building about three blocks from the courthouse. He shared the square, egg-yolk-colored building with two bail bondsmen, a night law school, and the city's pension-fund administrator.

Medavoy discovered he had no trouble seeing Ronnie Chadd. He gave his name to the elderly receptionist in the bare outer office, and she showed him right through.

"I was wondering when you'd get to me," Chadd said from behind his accordion-file-strewn desk.

"You know about the charges, the hearing?" Medavoy was surprised.

"I've got a lot of friends in the department." The lawyer grinned. "So sit down and let's get started."

Medavoy sat in the lone chair in front of Chadd's desk. He liked the reserved appearance Chadd presented, a tall man, gray hair and athletic, in tweeds and white shirt. Soft-spoken, too, reclining in his wide chair almost like he was about to go to sleep. On his walls were pictures taken on various sport fishing trips, Chadd always posed alongside some enormous hanging fish. As the union's lawyer he handled every case of alleged police misconduct, job accidents, pension fights, hirings and firings nobody liked, and fought like a bear when it came time to renew the cops' contract with the city. Medavoy had never met him personally or paid much attention to him as long as the benefits package Chadd negotiated was decent. Now he hoped those same feisty qualities that made the department's management detest Chadd could be used to help him.

It was mildly ironic that Chadd used to be a county public defender, representing criminal defendants and he now aggressively represented cops. He liked the juxtaposition.

"You don't know it," Chadd said, leaning even farther back in his chair, "but I've followed you for a while. You mind if I call you Robby?"

"Go ahead."

"I like a cop who'd risk everything to save some bum truck driver. That's gutsy."

"Sometimes I think it was dumb."

"Show me what they're planning to bash you with." He held out his hand and Medavoy gave him the blue form of charges.

He sat uncomfortably while Chadd read, muttered. He could hear the receptionist typing slowly. He felt like a kid waiting for the dentist, knowing it was going to hurt like hell.

Chadd looked up. "Okay. First the good news, Robby. They're scatter shotting these charges. They've got conduct unbecoming lumped with murder. That says to me they don't have any one strong charge against you."

Medavoy actually sighed with relief. "I'm glad to hear something good for a change."

"Okay. Now the bad news. They don't have to make any one of these charges stick very well. They smear you, they get your butt out of the department by making these things sound believable."

"I was doing my job," Medavoy said angrily. "I nailed a very bad guy, pulled the Chief out of his car—"

Chadd interrupted with a wave. "Turn it off. You can use it at the hearing. I agree they're trying to shaft you. And I'm going to stop them."

"Tell me what has to get done." Medavoy tried to sit more relaxed in his chair, the ancient plastic crinkling under him. He was hungry again and had ten thousand things whirling in his mind—Jane, Gef, the cases, the ignominy of Gunderson's public accusation of him. He had to focus on what Chadd was saying.

"Well, what about this assault thing? You ever arrest this Ramon Trebayo? Ever see him?"

"Nope. Never heard of him until yesterday."

"So how does it happen he picks you to point at?"

Medavoy said, "The cop I shot tried to set me up."

Chadd took out a yellow legal pad, pushed aside three or four of the bulky, paper-bulging accordion-files to make space on his desk. "Okay. You better tell me the whole thing. Everything that happened relating to this shooting."

Medavoy talked for nearly two hours, answered questions, backtracked when he missed a few details, impressed with Chadd's ability to find the pivotal fact and elaborate it. By the time he finished, there were heavy sweat stains on his shirt and he had paced back and forth across Chadd's office two dozen times.

Chadd paused, studying the pages of closely scrawled notes that filled the legal pad.

"What's the verdict?" Medavoy asked nervously.

"Luckily, I don't have to give one. I don't know what it's like being a cop, facing the choices you've got to face, Robby. I don't even pretend I'd know what to do. I think you did everything you believed was right every step, you played straight."

"Most of the guys I know do that."

Chadd sat up, rubbed his eyes. "I can see what the chiefs are doing here. They take you, dump you in with the genuinely rotten cops, roll it all up at the same time. They keep McNeill because everybody knows he's a weak sister and they can run him."

"So how do I get out of it?"

"Well, first thing, I can go demand your right to a mandatory continuance. You get one postponement, maybe for a week or two."

Medavoy shook his head. "Nope. They get that time to nail things down, prepare better. I don't want this hanging over me for two weeks. I want it over with one way or the other."

Chadd nodded, as if he expected a cop like Medavoy to want to charge ahead. "Then I've got a shitload of work to do in the next two days. You do, too."

"I'm ready. I got nothing else to do." He felt the loss of his gun and badge, even though it was supposedly temporary. He felt no more than the people he encountered, no different, subject to the same capricious fortune, without the ability to strike back.

Chadd tossed him a pad. "Write me every phone number and address of anyone who can help you—guys you work with, guys who were at the scene. Then, here's my wish list for the hearing."

He wrote as he listened. "Yeah?"

"We need Brian Reilly to come in and vouch for your good name. Have him tell the hearing board you're clean."

"Not a fucking chance. I arrested him. He's looking at joint time because of me," Medavoy said.

"We still need him. And you've got to ask him to come in as a witness. No subpoena, no force. Come in voluntarily."

"A hearing board won't believe him."

Chadd grinned. "They'll have to. They don't have the same kind of direct evidence, right? I mean, you aren't crooked. So on our side we have direct, hard testimony. So we need him."

"Okay, if you think so, I'll go talk to him." Medavoy didn't think Reilly would be interested in becoming a police department witness.

"Robby, you're the cop. You know the street. I know courts and I know hearings. This one's a free-for-all. Let me play it my way, okay?"

"Sorry. Who else is on your wish list?"

Chadd stood up and Medavoy saw he must be over six-three, like an older college basketball player. "We need your pal Geffen, and we need Steve McNeill."

Medavoy shook his head. Chadd seemed to have spun off into fantasy. "Gef's still critical. I can't drag him in. The Chief's not going to help me. His guys are setting this up."

"I said it's a wish list. McNeill could drop-kick this right out of the field if he came in for you."

"No way. No goddamn way. I bet I couldn't even get to see him."

Chadd nodded, hands shoved into his coat. He seemed impatient to get Medavoy out of the office. "You finished with those names?"

"I can probably add some." He handed back the legal pad.

"Okay, Robby. Clock's running for both of us. Get out of here and bring me Reilly."

Medavoy stood up, leaning over the desk to shake Chadd's hand. "I feel a lot better. What should I do about the lie-box test if they want me to do it?"

"You shouldn't have agreed to it," Chadd said, sitting down, snatching the telephone up. "So tell the bastards to shove it."

It was close to noon, the downtown streets filling with lunchtime crowds, as merry and confident as if nothing had happened yesterday. Medavoy, walking unnoticed through the well-dressed secretaries and office workers, knew how much of a gap lay between his world and theirs.

He was tempted to try and get into the police department, but decided against it. Zaragoza said the atmosphere was bad; he'd only poison it further by showing up. That hurt, too. He never expected to be a lightning rod for the contempt of other cops. He was glad Chadd had fired up his optimism, put him on the offense.

He called down to the municipal court, using several clerks he knew to check Reilly's file for the name of his bail bondsman. Medavoy called the bondsman's office, saying he was from city police, demanding to know why Reilly's room had been changed without notifying the cops first. The secretary at the bondsman was flustered and said his room was still the same, number 457 at Santa Maria Mercy Hospital.

He tried Jane's number at the courthouse and found out she hadn't come in, but left word she'd be at the police department. He hoped she was giving Pomerantz hell in her statement.

He drove north from downtown, crossing over the bridge, passing motels and blocks of fast-food restaurants, ending up in the gently crumbling neighborhood around Santa Maria Mercy, a granite-and-brick remnant of the last century.

Medavoy deliberately took time out to find a burger joint, have coffee and a cheeseburger, and decide how to hit Reilly. I got to make him want to come in, Medavoy thought. That's a damn tough road.

He also took enough time eating to see if any cars lingered near him. It was possible that IAD was tailing him, and even more likely some reporters would follow him. But the area looked clean.

When he got to the old hospital, he wondered why Reilly had come here. It was slowly falling apart, the stone carvings dissolving, the bricks chipped. Inside, the corridors stank of Lysol and old food and urine. The nurses strolled casually, as if there were no reason for haste in this place. Medavoy instantly got the worst case of hospital blues he'd had in years.

Worse even than the vigil last night with Gef's family. Here hope seemed to have died.

Reilly's room was spacious, empty except for him. The floor was yellowed linoleum. Medavoy closed the door. Reilly was asleep on his side. He had bottles and machines ringing his bed, and his right hand was suspended by steel wires, encased in plaster.

He heard the stale murmurs of the hospital around him as he nudged Reilly's sleeping body. He nudged again. Reilly grunted, rolled over, onto his back. A wedge of afternoon sunlight hit him and he blinked, wide awake.

"This's a shitty thing," Medavoy said. Reilly's face was blotchy purple, jaw swollen, lips cracked and raw. Around his bed were get-well cards and a large paper heart signed by his kids.

"Already gave my statement, Medavoy," he said, raspy and guttural. He licked his lips, eyes roaming for the water.

"You want a drink?" Medavoy got the water pitcher, pouring a glass. He held it to Reilly's mouth, pushing out the plastic straw. Reilly drank greedily. "How come you're here? This place's a mess."

Reilly finished, water dripping down his chin. He looked calmly at Medavoy. "I was born here. My kids were born here. I'm going to die here. I said I gave a statement."

"I'm not here exactly about what happened, Reilly." Medavoy stood now at the end of the bed so the lawyer could see him easily without moving. Trask must have given him a bad beating, judging by the visible injuries. "You heard what happened after you got beat up?"

"No. I don't care."

So Medavoy gave him a highlighted account of the chase, the shooting. "I'm up on departmental charges. They say I was in with Easter, you know, taking stuff, taking money."

Reilly's face twisted in what might have been a smile. "You're kidding me."

"I got a hearing in two days. I can get dismissed. I can have the DA file on me."

Reilly made a sighing noise. "I don't believe it. It's too damn funny. I love it."

Medavoy tried grinning, too, but gave up. "I need a favor. I'd like you to appear as a witness at the hearing."

"Saying what?"

"Tell them I wasn't in with Easter. Ever. Tell them you knew Easter's bunch, and I wasn't part of it."

Reilly struggled to sit up a little. A very white foot stuck out of the bedcovers. "Let me get this straight, Medavoy. You're asking me to help you?"

"Yeah. I am. Just to tell the truth."

Reilly started shaking, then wincing, shaking again and it took a moment for Medavoy to realize he was laughing. His suspended hand seemed to wave gently as he shook. "What do you want me to say, Medavoy?"

"I can't tell you what to say. Tell the goddamn truth. I didn't work with Easter or you."

Reilly shook a little harder. He stopped after a moment. "Are you wired? You're getting all this for my trial, aren't you?"

"I've been suspended," he snapped. "They've got my badge and my gun. I've got a hearing in two days and I need you there."

"Oh, Jesus. Jesus, Jesus." Reilly winced and shook again.

"So what's your answer?"

Reilly's eyes snapped open, bitter and cold. "Go to hell, Medavoy. Right to hell. My only hope is that we don't get sent to the same prison."

The voice stung, and Medavoy started to leave the room. So what else had he expected? What would he do in Reilly's place? Chadd was crazy to think a man facing prison would get up out of a hospital bed to help his arresting officer. I screwed this guy's life up for good, Medavoy thought, there's no reason for him to save mine.

He held the door open, Reilly sunk back in the bed watching him coldly. A black nurse strolled to the door and paused. "I did my job, Reilly," Medavoy said. "I went after the guy who beat the shit out of you. Read a newspaper, get somebody to tell you. I put that guy down. No trial for him."

The nurse blocked his way, then hastily stepped aside when he stormed out of the room.

That night, he, Jane, and the kid practiced their evasive skills, taking two cars, leading the three TV vans around the city, losing them finally, and ending up for dinner at a small restaurant on the south shore of the river, far from downtown and its troubles, where the patrons were mostly people who lived and worked along the river and levee.

Medavoy had called Chadd's office earlier that afternoon and left the news he'd failed to get Reilly. Chadd was out, making the rounds at the police department, checking out the names and information Medavoy had given him.

It was a difficult dinner, even with Jane's playful retelling of her statement to Investigations. "They had guys coming in, guys going out, whispering in corners, it was great," she said.

"You must've put a good scare into them," he said, stirring his fried clams without interest. Keeping an eye on Johnathan, who was not a good restaurant diner, didn't prevent Medavoy from feeling like he'd lost before he'd gotten to bat. His enthusiasm in Chadd's office was draining away. He had started to second-guess his decisions yesterday. That was always bad, he thought, because you couldn't go back and run it again.

They drove home in silence. The usual groups of reporters were still camped on the lawn and Jane had gotten friendly enough with some of them that she offered to bring them coffee on the cool evening.

Medavoy called NorCal again, expecting nothing. He got the news that Geffen had regained consciousness several hours before. "Gef's awake," he said breathlessly to Jane, who was making coffee for the reporters. "I got to go."

"You give him my love, Robby," she said solemnly.

He parked crudely in the hospital visitors lot, taking up three spaces, and raced to the third floor. The whole place was fluorescently white and gleaming at night, haunting, and he met Sandra Geffen, without the kids, outside the door. "I didn't think it'd take you long to get here," she said, not friendly.

"What's the story?"

"He's talking a little. We can see him for about ten minutes at a time, then he's got to sleep."

"Okay. I'll make it short."

Sandra Geffen looked quite drawn in the hospital's unnatural bright light. "Cops. Like little boys, they always talk the same. He's so worried about you, whether you got hurt."

Medavoy felt a flush of sadness and remorse. "He saved my life."

"That's all he wants to talk about. But you be careful of him, you hear me?" Her voice broke a little. "He still doesn't know he's not a cop anymore."

"I won't say anything."

She turned from him and went to the small alcove off the corridor where there were seats.

Medavoy waited a moment, working to get control of himself. He had taken a lot of bad news in his life, when the old man died, his mother, the divorce, and he could put on a good front if he had to. It was better for Geffen if he made this as simple, businesslike as possible. Like they were meeting on a coffee break.

There were more people wandering the corridor than at Reilly's hospital. Medavoy pushed open the door to Geffen's room. He was amazed anyone could sleep in such bright, unremitting light. The other men in the room, wheezing and hissing, were unconscious. Their beds were barricaded with plastic tubing and machinery.

Medavoy went to Geffen, nearest the window. He tried hard not to be sickened by the gray-green color of Geffen's skin or the array of wires and tubes disappearing into his arms, nose. There was the ceaseless click and beep of monitoring machinery in the room.

Medavoy stood beside the metal barred bed. What was he going to say? He prayed he wouldn't lose it, but the emotions whipped through him anyway.

Geffen's eyes opened. "Robby."

"Hi, Gef. How's it feel?"

"Shit."

Medavoy nodded, smiled lopsidedly. "Looks that way, too."

Geffen grinned a little. "About Easter?"

"You did it, man. Got him with one."

"You okay? Nothing?"

"Without a scratch, Gef. Like a fucking miracle thanks to you. Trask got put down, too. Both bad guys got it."

"That is great." Geffen sighed long and labored. He seemed to have radically lost substance in the last thirty or so hours, the bones sharper and more forthright, as if pressing outward through his skin. "You really okay, Robby?"

"See me? I look okay, right? It was a two-hundred-percent success, Gef. You made it work."

"Been having really weird dreams," Geffen said slowly, "like I was back there, same fighting, same thing again."

"Back on the street?"

"Back in 'Nam, like I told you." He drifted, then, "You see Sandra, the kids outside?"

"Yeah, they been here all the time. Masuda, Jimmy, and me, we come by, we been calling."

So they talked for a short while about the detail because it was familiar and took them away from this place. Medavoy had started wiping his eyes again and his hands were clenched.

This was tough, tougher even than the old man's funeral because you expected it after years of emphysema like the old man had.

There was something else, and he despised himself for thinking about it, but Chadd's wish list came into his mind. He knelt closer to Geffen's ear.

"Gef, you think in a couple of days you could talk to some guys from downtown, tell them why you drew down on Easter out there?"

"They know why," Geffen whispered sleepily.

"Yeah, but how about making a statement, okay? If your doctor says okay? Just lay it out for them?"

"Okay, Robby. Couple days. I'm going to miss this. You get some major, major narcotics." He sighed deeply and seemed to go to sleep.

Medavoy stood again, shaking with anger at himself for taking advantage of Geffen's condition to even ask about a statement. He hated the men who put him in this position. Geffen opened his eyes again. "We had guys like you, Robby, over there. Guys who'd just kind of walk through all kinds of shit, never get shot. Never wounded. You try to stay around guys like that because maybe you stay safe, too. Called them the blessed."

"Sorry I let you down, Gef. I mean it."

"Hang in there," Geffen said and closed his eyes again, breathing slowly, the green glowing screens around him registering his heart and brain and lungs without taking any real measure of the man himself.

Medavoy left without saying good-bye to Sandra Geffen. He couldn't stand her pain, too. He went to the fourth floor, saw the two uniformed cops perched on chairs outside a large suite, and knew it was impossible to get near Stevie Wonder.

On the way home again that night his thoughts were in a rapid turmoil, absolute confusion. He had always tried to do his job. He made mistakes and tried to correct them if he could. But he never set out to cause trouble or harm unless it was merited. Somehow he had brought himself and the people around him to calamity, which might have been avoided if he'd taken Easter up on the offer the night before last. The difference between tonight as it was, and might have been, was that simple.

Take the money and run, he thought. That was all.

Jane jumped from the living room couch where she'd been watching TV—more news stories about the shootings and bank robberies, and another TV station commenting on the problems in the police department. She turned the TV down.

"Chadd's tried to get you twice, Robby. He's got some news."

"What news?" he said slowly, trying to push away his thoughts.

"He said it was for you. Call him, call him." She pushed him eagerly to the telephone.

He got Chadd at the office. It was past nine in the evening.

"Robby, you are some kind of bozo. If you go talk to a man, you've got to leave him my phone number. He's got to be able to get hold of me."

"What're you talking about?"

"You must've touched some kind of button on Reilly. He tracked me down through some cops in the department. He'll come in for you."

"You're kidding me." Medavoy smiled for Jane, who stood by, listening anxiously.

"He says he's returning a favor, whatever that means."

"It's okay. I understand."

"I've got some great stuff to work with. You've got a lot of friends downtown, you know. You meet me at my office tomorrow, seven sharp. We'll spend the day getting you ready."

"I'll be there," to tell him about Geffen, too, he thought. He hung up, stood there, blankly holding his hands in the air.

"Well? What's the news? What's so great, Robby?" Jane was bouncy with anticipation.

He grabbed her fiercely. "I'm going to make it, Janie."

THIRTY-EIGHT

AT NINE A.M. Monday morning, the Hearing Board for Detective Robert Medavoy gathered on the fourth-floor conference room at the police department.

Medavoy was showered, shaved, dressed in dark-blue suit, black shoes, nervously sitting at a table near the front of the large room. Like Chadd and every other officer coming to work that morning, he had forced his way through a dense ring of reporters and cameras around the building. A line of cops in blue guarded the doors to the department because, by order of the Board, the hearing was to be closed to the press. It was a personnel matter.

The conference room was filled. Fifteen rows of chairs had been brought in for witnesses, detectives, senior department staff, and lawyers from the DA's office. Chadd insisted that Jane stay away because her presence might entice someone to call her as a witness, and he thought it could be avoided. Reluctantly, she helped Robby dress that morning, kissed him, and said she'd be at work if he needed her.

Cops Medavoy had worked with over the years made a point of coming up to him, giving him a clap on the shoulder, a brief word of encouragement. A few cops came by and cursed him.

Chadd was dressed as casually as when Medavoy first saw him. He shoved papers around in one of the two accordion files he'd worked up on the case over the last two days. He and Medavoy had spent the previous day, most of the night as well, going over the hunt for Trask and Lisio moment by moment, until Chadd said they could stop. Even so, Medavoy hadn't slept more than two or three hours. He had watched the sunrise, wondering what was going to happen that day.

"Don't look so jumpy," Chadd said, frowning briefly at a note on his legal pad. "Guilty people always look jumpy."

"You're as much of a bullshitter as I am," Medavoy said, knowing Chadd was trying to relax him.

At a table to Chadd's right was Gunderson. Two detectives, not the stocky guys at Jane's house, sat with him as assistants. He would present the department's evidence.

At nine-ten, the room growing restless, the Hearing Board entered from the Assistant Chief's office. Five senior cops: Druliner; Schroeder from IAD as chairman of the board; and Compton, Lewkowitz, and Solarzano from Vice, Narcotics, and Auto Burg. Three votes were needed to declare a charge proven. The Board was trying to look impassive, but all of them were uneasy with this proceeding and the events leading up to it.

"What you have got to get into your head, Robby," Chadd had said to him last night, "is that these guys believe you're guilty. Of some of these charges definitely. They don't think there's any setup."

"I thought this was to save Stevie Wonder's ass," Medavoy answered hotly.

"It is. But that's not how they want to see it. They can go after you feeling very righteous because they're helping the Chief and bagging a dirty cop, too."

Medavoy looked behind him. Masuda and Zaragoza

and most of the past Robbery detectives sat together, intently watching. Pesce and Hollenbeck sat apart. The department's running on automatic pilot today, Medavoy thought. All the supes are here for me.

It gave him no pleasure.

He wished Jane were there. The Board members wouldn't look at him for more than a second, and he had a sinking feeling, recalling the way jurors looked away from a defendant they had decided to convict.

Chadd had explained the hearing's rules of procedure last night. The Board would take evidence on each charge before going to the next, so Medavoy could make his defense charge-by-charge. He didn't have to wait until the end of the department's presentation of every charge before beginning. That was to his benefit, Chadd said, "because we'll know where we stand all the time."

And, the Board would take hearsay evidence, unlike a regular court, without exception. Anybody could report anything anyone else had said. "I said it's a free-for-all," Chadd repeated last night.

"Good morning, ladies and gentlemen," said Schroeder. He was wearing a dark, solid suit, buttoned completely. He fussily adjusted his glasses and piled several books and manuals in front of him on the long green cloth-covered table behind which the Board members sat.

The crowded, humming room subsided into silence. It was humid, Medavoy thought, running a finger under his shirt collar. Like after a warm shower, even with air-conditioning. A court reporter sat to the left of the Board, taking down everything. Somewhere in the mass of suits, uniforms, dresses, would be media people, undercover among the cops. Some joke.

Chadd sat upright and Medavoy took a breath.

Schroeder cleared his throat. He was like a parochial-school teacher, precise and efficient and strict. "Before this Hearing Board formally convenes, I have a few announcements to make. The funerals for Sergeant Ralph Easter and Patrolman Ellis Kozlowski will be held day after tomorrow, at ten in the morning at United Methodist on Seymour Avenue and three in the afternoon at Our Lady of Sorrows, so that you may attend both services. Full dress uniform is required at both services." He cleared his voice again. From the dead to the living. "This Hearing Board is now in session. The Board wishes to announce it will conduct a conditional examination of Sergeant Arnold Geffen at nine A.M. Friday, which is the earliest his doctors say he can be questioned. His evidence relates to charge number seven."

That was the shooting death of Easter, which the department was attempting to call murder. Chadd looked over at Medavoy with a nod. "His testimony will bag that one for good, Robby."

Medavoy clasped his hands together. Jesus, I look like one of the pukes in court, he thought, and let his hands go.

Schroeder read from a slip of paper. "The Board also announces that it will take no evidence on charge number four, conduct unbecoming an officer." So Jane's statement had worked, Medavoy thought. Scared the shit out of them that they'd have to go after a captain, too.

Chadd was on his feet. "Mr. Chairman, the defense wants it clear on the record that the Board finds no merit to charge number four."

Schroeder looked blandly back at Chadd. "I said we wouldn't take any evidence on it."

"So it is stricken for lack of evidence?"

"Yes. So noted in the record." He nodded at the reporter working at her machine. He tapped a pen on one of the manuals.

Chadd sat down. "So I've got them in a little coverup of their own," he said delightedly. "Might be useful if they try anything later."

Medavoy whispered, "Keeps Jane clear. That's all I care about."

Chadd whispered back roughly, "See the guys from the

DA's office? If you beat the charges here, you're home free. They won't prosecute a charge the department couldn't make even with this rigged show. It matters to have it *all* on the record."

Medavoy nodded. "Okay. You know what's best in here."

Schroeder read aloud the sections of the department regulations under which the hearing board was convening and its powers. Chadd was on his feet again.

"Mr. Chairman, Sergeant Medavoy strongly protests the exclusion of the press from this hearing. He feels it's his right to have the facts presented publicly, immediately. His reputation has suffered too much already from the secrecy of this proceeding."

At his table, Gunderson flipped clumsily through his copy of department regulations, but Schroeder waved a hand at him. "Mr. Chadd, this is an internal police issue. It is the Board's decision to close the proceedings. You're overruled."

Chadd sat down. Medavoy wondered what the point of that futile objection had been. "So the reporters get it out you want it opened up, Robby. You've got nothing to hide."

Medavoy decided that Chadd knew how to handle the hearing. This kind of tactical jockeying wasn't part of his experience as cop on the street, or even as an acting supervisor.

Schroeder next read aloud the seven, now reduced to six, formal charges. Failure to notify a supervisor of dangerous activity, exceeding his authority, reckless endangerment of civilians, corruption, assault, and murder. A mouthful. Medavoy couldn't look to see how the other cops took it all. The room was very quiet as Schroeder read. You could hear the steno machine.

"As departmental advocate, Lieutenant Gunderson may make an opening statement to the Board at this point," Schroeder said, looking up.

Medavoy understood how a defendant felt, listening to the smug, righteous Gunderson, like a gunnery officer, venomously describe the offenses and the evidence against him. Gunderson wandered back and forth beside his table, immersed in his eloquence, hands waving. He went on for twenty minutes.

It was a harrowing, hideous, deformed portrayal of Medavoy's actions in pursuing Trask and Lisio—in fact, of his whole career. He wanted to slug Gunderson. Chadd, glancing over notes or fooling with one of the files, seemed bored by it. "They're all going to act like they're Perry Mason," he said caustically to Medavoy, sensing his temper. "They'll blow it."

When his turn came, Chadd said simply, "Sergeant Medavoy has a twelve-year record, commendations, and a Medal of Valor. He denies each charge completely." He sat down.

"How about some more," Medavoy demanded.

"Let's let the evidence do the work, Robby. Trust me." He settled back, almost trying to recline as if in his office chair.

"Please state which charge and evidence you intend to present first," Schroeder said to Gunderson.

"Charge number six, sir. Assault."

Chadd stood up. "I want the record to state my vehement objection to the fact that neither I nor Sergeant Medavoy has been provided any evidence or access to any witnesses to be called here this morning. We're flying totally blind."

Schroeder looked at the department regulations again. "Well, as I said, Mr. Chadd, this is a disciplinary hearing, not a court of law. We have different rules."

"I wanted it clear in public who's pulling the strings." He sat down. The room bubbled with half-muttered replies and one or two people clapping. Schroeder frowned, the other members of the Board were stony faced. He rapped his fist lightly on the table.

"This may not be a court, Mr. Chadd, but decorum is required and respect demanded. I can have you barred from this proceeding."

"Leaving Sergeant Medavoy without defense counsel?"

"It's up to you, Mr. Chadd."

"I have the greatest respect for this Board," Chadd said. His sarcasm was so obvious, several people laughed quietly.

Another rap of the fist by Schroeder. Medavoy didn't think this strategy of irritating the Board was a bright idea. He wiped his hands on his pants. Sweating like a rookie.

Gunderson called Ramon Trebayo as his first witness. Two cops went to bring him in, and Chadd said urgently to Medavoy, "Get to another seat like we talked about."

Medavoy quietly rose and moved to a folding chair two rows behind the counsel table.

Ramon Trebayo was brought into the room in handcuffs. He had a brace on his neck, and his mouth was wired shut. It didn't look like he could speak until the clerk of the Board, a secretary from Homicide named Debbie with a high silvery hairdo, gave him the oath. Trebayo spoke through clenched teeth, like a ventriloquist. He wore a white shirt and dark pants and loafers without socks. Medavoy was certain he'd never seen him before.

Gunderson got up, swaggering a little. Trebayo sat in a chair between the Board and Gunderson's table. He hunched forward.

The questions were convoluted, pompous, and long. Still, it took only fifteen minutes for Gunderson to draw out the basic facts of Trebayo's attackers. "The man who broke your jaw, did he at any time tell you his name?"

"He say, Robby Medavoy. Couple times he say it. Then he whack, he break my jaw," Trebayo heaved with emotion, "while they holding my arms and I got handcuffs on."

Gunderson had his back to Chadd. "Will you point out the man who broke your jaw?"

Medavoy watched Trebayo's eyes linger on the empty seat beside Chadd, sweep the room. Schroeder spoke up sharply. "Where is Sergeant Medavoy? Is he present?"

Medavoy stood from his chair. "Yes, sir."

"Then take your seat, Sergeant Medavoy."

As he returned to his place by Chadd, Medavoy heard Trebayo say, "That's Medavoy. He the guy."

Gunderson sat down and the three men at his table

mumbled to each other. The Board members made notes and stared out at the room.

So what was Chadd doing now? Medavoy watched him walk to Trebayo. "Mr. Trebayo, you're charged with several felonies, aren't you?"

"So?"

"Haven't the police said they'll help you with the district attorney when these charges go to court?"

Trebayo sat back, head stiffly upright. "So?"

"So all you want to do is what the police tell you, isn't that correct?"

Gunderson called out, "Objection, sir. Improper question."

"I never heard that objection before," Chadd said to the Board. "I'm only trying to show a bias here."

"That's enough on that issue, Mr. Chadd. The Board gets your point, so move to another question." Schroeder made a note and the other men at the long green table looked uncomfortable.

"All right, Mr. Chairman." He turned to Trebayo, who had crossed his legs in what Medavoy recognized as the defiant puke pose. "Mr. Trebayo, these men who robbed you of your drug money, they weren't in uniform, were they?"

"No. Shirts, you know, like casual."

"And you knew they were police officers because they told you so, right?"

"They had badges, like on their pockets, too. I seen them."

"Badges, too. And did they have nameplates?"

"No. Not that I seen."

"And so the way you found out that Robby Medavoy broke your jaw was that someone told you his name, right?"

"Yeah, he say his name. Medavoy."

Chadd looked at the Board, then out to the crowded room. "Have the police showed you a photo lineup to identify the man who struck you?"

"Yeah, couple days ago when I was in the hospital."

Chadd walked to the desk and from one of his open file folders picked up Easter's personnel picture. He brought it and showed it to Trebayo. "Take a long look, Mr. Trebayo. Is this the man you identified as your assailant?"

Gunderson stood up. "I haven't seen this picture first."

"I'll show it to you in a minute," Chadd waved him down.

Schroeder cleared his throat. "Show it to him now, Mr. Chadd."

As Chadd gave Gunderson the picture, Trebayo said, "Yeah, I seen that guy that night. He hit me, busted my jaw."

"Just a second," Gunderson said. "There's no question."

"I think I got a pretty good answer," Chadd snapped. The room broke into a quick laugh and Schroeder rapped for quiet. Gunderson said he objected to the picture; Schroeder examined it and denied the objection. This seemed to surprise Chadd for a minute.

"All right, Mr. Trebayo, have you looked at any other photo lineups?"

"Yeah, couple more. Same day I seen the one with Medavoy in them."

"Did you identify anybody else from those lineups?"

"Couple guys. They was there."

"But no other pictures of the man who hit you?"

"I told you, I seen him in the first pictures. That guy, that picture you got there."

Chadd laid the picture before Schroeder. "Will the Board take notice that this is a personnel photograph of the late Sergeant Ralph Easter?"

Schroeder glumly studied it, passed it down to the other members and nodded. "Yes, it is a department personnel photograph."

Medavoy felt his pulse quicken. Chadd was hammering them and they weren't fighting back. Either he was very good or they were very bad.

"Mr. Trebayo, how is it you've identified two men as hitting you?"

"Medavoy's the only guy who hit me." Trebayo's braced head bobbed emphatically. "Check it out, man."

"Did anybody tell you where Medavoy would be sitting in this hearing room today?" Chadd asked loudly.

Trebayo pointed at Gunderson. "This dude, he say Medavoy going to be at that table over there. Only he ain't there when I check."

"No. I told him to sit elsewhere," Chadd said. "Take a look at the man seated alone at the table now. Is he the man who struck you and broke your jaw?"

Medavoy felt his gall rise as Trebayo stared at him. It was repellent to think senior cops would even consider taking the word of this puke over his. His jaw tightened in anger.

Trebayo was obviously torn between his photo identification and what the police wanted him to do that morning. Finally, he said "All's I know is that the guy in that picture, Medavoy, he bust my jaw when I couldn't do nothing about it."

Medavoy stared back in disgust. Chadd said, "Mr. Chairman, I want the Board to take official notice of the gross incompetence in the handling of this witness by the department. You have gravely compromised Sergeant Medavoy without cause by this negligent investigation."

As he returned to his seat and Gunderson rose to argue, Chadd whispered to Medavoy, "Better to accuse them of being klutzes than crooks. Gives them a way out."

"They knew this wouldn't stick," Medavoy whispered fiercely. "They knew the guy couldn't ID me. What's the point?"

Chadd nodded. "They want a smear. It's Easter's little gift. They just want this guy saying your name a lot. Anything else is a bonus for them."

Medavoy noticed the Board members all making notes. He felt some pleasure that one charge had been disarmed, but anger at the way a lineup had been concealed and evidence known to be suspect used to try to get him. Schroeder told Gunderson to call another witness and Trebayo, with a last defiant bounce in his step, was led out and back to the county jail.

THIRTY-NINE

AROUND THE CIRCULAR EXERCISE yard behind the jail kitchen, five times possible at an easy pace in the thirty minutes she was given every day for limbering herself, Carol walked alone, feet crunching on the gravel-and-cinder path, brown grass at the center of the yard. Guards watched her at the kitchen doorway and from the second floor of the jail. This was her privilege because she was an unusual resident at the jail.

Now what? she thought, trying to think, the morning sun prickling on her neck. Trudge, trudge, like the way my life's gone up until now, in a big, pointless circle. She hadn't slept well, the odd noises and routine of the jail kept her on edge.

She had to think deeply. A compact, taciturn man from the DA's office had just left her. Told her all about the hearing going on and what Medavoy faced. Told her that if Medavoy was discredited as a result of the hearing, the DA wouldn't feel bound to honor the written agreement at all. And forget any idea of immunity.

413

The deputy DA said they might be willing to make a new deal for her if she'd testify against Reilly. She'd have to do a great deal more prison time, of course, without Medavoy's arrangement. But, she didn't expect the People of California to meekly go along with what a crooked cop agreed to, did she?

She had dreamt of Kenny last night, too. Carol paused, picked up a pebble, and squinted into the sun. I do miss you, she thought. Jesus.

She walked on. I hope to God that cop can get himself free of all this.

Medavoy sat, wanting to shout back, do something, every time Gunderson called another witness. He was putting on evidence about the corruption and murder charges. His witnesses were four cops who told the Board about rumors in the locker room, Medavoy the grandstander who was probably on the take; rumors floating around the department about shakedowns, robberies, and Medavoy's name involved.

As each cop repeated the insubstantial office nonsense, Chadd would lean over and whisper, "Stay cool, Robby. You got us a big gun to fire back with."

"I can't listen to much more of this shit," he replied, a little too loudly.

It was hard to passively listen to Gunderson, playing to the Board and Schroeder particularly, deferring to them, then addressing the conference room audience like he was in a high-school play. But Chadd didn't do much with each cop, driving home each time that none of them had personal knowledge of any wrongdoing by Sergeant Medavoy. It was simply a matter of dragging locker-room speculation before a solemnly constituted police hearing board. Medavoy liked the way the senior cops fidgeted at that.

It was almost eleven before Gunderson finished, and Chadd, with a dramatic flourish, had Brian Reilly, wearing hospital pajamas and a thin blue hospital robe over them, brought into the room in a wheelchair. He put Reilly, who looked like a battered old bird, hand propped up in its cast, beside the reporter taking down the testimony.

After the oath, Chadd spoke from his table, leaning against it. Medavoy noticed that Reilly was affecting a bored expression, and sighing. He won't look at me, either, he thought. God, I hope he's not going sideways on me now.

Chadd said, "Your name is Brian Reilly?"

"Yes, it is."

"What is your occupation, Mr. Reilly?"

"I'm a lawyer in private practice in this city. Been in practice for almost twenty years."

"You must know a lot of people in Santa Maria," Chadd said easily. "Police officers maybe?"

Reilly nodded, bored, working at the pose. "I know a lot of people." He turned his head toward the Board. "Lieutenant Compton is a client. Personal matters. Lieutenant Solarzano is also a client. It's good to see them again."

Medavoy heard the twitter throughout the audience and observed the studied way Compton and Solarzano met Reilly's eyes. Chadd went on immediately, "Was Sergeant Ralph Easter one of your clients?"

"I'm not going to get into any matters about him," Reilly said, shifting his legs. He had on old brown slippers. "As you know, I'm facing criminal charges and I think I might reserve any comments about the late Ralph Easter for my trial."

Medavoy shut his eyes, felt the sweat dampen his hands suddenly. Reilly was going sideways. He's going to hang me out, Medavoy thought.

Chadd didn't appear disturbed. He nodded. Gunderson tried to make notes and watch at the same time and was only partially successful. "I'm sure the Board appreciates the right against self-incrimination. Let me ask if you know Sergeant Medavoy over at the defense table?"

Reilly leisurely looked over and locked glances with Medavoy. "Oh, yes. I know him. He arrested me several days ago and searched my office very thoroughly."

"Is that the only contact you ever had with Sergeant Medavoy? When he arrested you for breaking the law?"

Reilly smirked at Chadd's heavy-handed attempt to exculpate Medavoy. It was, Medavoy knew, strictly for the Board's benefit. "I've heard about him. I never met him."

"Heard about him? How? What context?"

"The time he got a medal for bravery or something," Reilly said, returning the heavy-handed tactic. Medavoy thought he saw a small grin on Reilly's face. He grinned back.

Chadd walked toward Reilly's wheelchair. "To your knowledge has Sergeant Medavoy been involved in any criminal activities or corrupt practices?"

Reilly shook his head. "To my knowledge he hasn't. I wish he had. I might not be here today."

As much as he could, Medavoy felt a measure of gratitude toward Reilly for that. Chadd said, "Would you have been in a position to know if Sergeant Easter and Sergeant Medavoy were criminal conspirators, Mr. Reilly?" It was asked sternly.

Reilly sighed deeply again. "Let me just say I have a wide circle of acquaintances, police and civilian. I would have known if there was anything going on."

"Thank you, Mr. Reilly. I have nothing further." Chadd winked at Medavoy as he sat down. "Enjoy the show, Robby."

Medavoy watched Gunderson flip through his notes, stand, sit, flip, then stand again and self-consciously button his coat. He didn't go near Reilly.

"So you refuse to answer any questions about the deceased Sergeant Easter? You are under oath."

"Well, ask me one. I might answer it." Reilly relaxed as if playing with a stupid child.

"Well, I might do that," Gunderson said. "Now, you say you know a lot of police officers. I'd like you to tell this Hearing Board their names."

Reilly raised his eyebrows, then began, "To start with in Homicide—" when Schroeder cut him off.

"The Board on its own motion finds this testimony irrelevant. You need to get to something dealing with these charges," Schroeder said, then cleared his throat.

Gunderson looked at his notes again, at a loss. "I was only trying to find out who he might've been talking to—"

And again Schroeder said, "Go to something else, Lieutenant. This won't get us to anything pertinent."

Like the names of a lot of very embarrassed cops who used Reilly for divorces and drunk-driving tickets, maybe even to help them with mortgages and the kids' tooth bills, Medavoy thought. He allowed himself a little wiggle room because Gunderson did seem overmatched.

"All right, Mr. Reilly," Gunderson said. "Now, you said the defendant arrested you—"

"Objection!" Chadd said in booming voice. "Sergeant Medavoy isn't the defendant, and this isn't a trial."

"Excuse me," Gunderson said hastily to Schroeder. "I wasn't thinking."

Reilly raised his eyebrows again and looked uncomfortable in the wheelchair, as if it were time to leave.

Gunderson tried again. "If he arrested you. I mean if Sergeant Medavoy arrested you, why have you come here today to help him out? Do you and he have something going, you know, some sort of arrangement?"

Reilly frowned. "I can't make any sense of your question. I can say everyone wants to do what's right. When it's possible." He looked, for a final time, at Medavoy. No more favors, Medavoy thought, he's squared everything and we're back to the way it was.

Gunderson swung and missed for another twenty minutes,

trying to establish a prior relationship between Medavoy and Reilly or to make Reilly link Easter and Medavoy even faintly. The lawyer barely exerted himself and Gunderson finally sat down. He was bright red, his gray hair sharply contrasting with his blushing. He sorted through his notes, hoarsely snapped at one of his assistants.

Medavoy whispered to Chadd, "Never laid a glove on him." Reilly was wheeled from the room again, the crowd watching him go.

"Now comes the tough part," Chadd said. "Watch yourself."

Medavoy looked up again, at the Board, every senior cop looking back at him with something between hostility and concern. He did not see any friendly faces, although Schroeder was hard to read at all behind that bland expression and the polished glasses.

Gunderson stood up. "My next witness is Sergeant Robert Medavoy."

FORTY

AS MEDAVOY WALKED the long, impossibly distant few feet from the table to the witness chair, Chadd stood up behind him.

"I want to remind the Board that Sergeant Medavoy is agreeing to appear and answer questions even though he has every right to invoke his privilege against self-incrimination," Chadd said, speaking in part to the audience, the observers from the DA's office, and other cops. "He has nothing to hide. I want the record to reflect that of the nine men suspended from duty in this inquiry, only Sergeant Medavoy has agreed to waive his constitutional privilege."

Medavoy, sitting down, thought Chadd had made a serious blunder if he hoped to make these cops and prosecutors respect him for being open and aboveboard. Waiving your right against self-incrimination sounded too much like what pukes did when they wanted to gain some advantage or con you. It was not so much an act of courage as connivance. I should've told him that, Medavoy thought miserably.

He stood again to take the oath. You've testified before, hundreds of times, this's just like that. Except you got a real no-brainer in Gunderson trying to act like a lawyer. It's not so bad. It's like you're answering questions about any arrest, any case you ever worked up and took to court. He was acutely aware of the hardness of the chair, his sweating, the dryness of his mouth. It's not so different from a regular case, not so bad.

But it was bad.

Gunderson stood at his table. The Board rustled its papers for a moment, then sat quietly and the room itself fell into a kind of stalking silence. He looked at Chadd, leaning back in his chair confidently.

Gunderson got through the preliminaries surely, quickly. Maybe Reilly shook him but I don't, he thought in fright. I'm just another cop.

"We've got ballistics back on your gun," Gunderson said, his pencil point ground into a pad in front of him. "So you did shoot Sergeant Easter on May twenty-fourth. That's right?"

"I did shoot him."

"You shot him deliberately, to kill him."

"He was aiming at me. I was defending myself. I was getting the Chief out of his car, he was injured."

Gunderson put up his hand. "Don't answer other questions. You did shoot to kill, right?"

Medavoy and Chadd had gone over this extensively. "Yes, I did."

Gunderson said briskly, "Now, you say Sergeant Easter was aiming at you. He had a rifle, he was a good shot. How about that he was aiming at something near you, behind you, something you didn't see?"

Medavoy shook his head, feeling angry recalling the scene. "My fellow detective Arnold Geffen shouted and alerted me that Easter was going to shoot me. So I shot first."

"Well, we'll talk to your fellow detective on Friday and get his story," Gunderson said. "How about that he was mistaken, too? Maybe he saw Easter pointing his rifle and thought wrong about the target."

"It wasn't possible."

"Wasn't it very mixed up out there at that point? Lots of smoke, men running around? Didn't you have a live and dangerous suspect still in the vicinity?"

"Easter didn't know about the live suspect. I didn't know it. He was aiming at me. He wanted to shoot me." Medavoy knew he was wrong to raise his voice. He looked at the rows of cops, hating the truth. It was about the most reprehensible thing possible, a cop trying to gun down another cop.

"You are telling this Hearing Board and your fellow officers that the supervisor of the Special Weapons Unit was intentionally going to kill you?" Gunderson had his hands up in front of him in mock amazement.

"That's what it looked like to me."

"You've been a cop twelve years. You used your weapon once before. You can't be so sure you did not make a terrible mistake on May twenty-fourth."

"I'm telling you what it looked like to me, what I was afraid might happen because of things I'd heard, seen recently." No point in avoiding it now, he thought.

Gunderson came from the table and strode to him. "Things you heard, things you saw? Why would Easter want to kill you?"

"Because he was dirty and I knew it."

They went around and around the stories Medavoy knew about Easter and the Special Weapons Unit. As he spoke, Medavoy thought it all sounded flimsy, as vague and hard to hold as the rumors about himself. The Board wasn't writing, just sitting and watching. Gunderson was laying a dual track for culpability. Either Medavoy shot Easter because they were involved together in criminal activities and had a falling out, or Medavoy shot him through incompetence, making a mistake at the crime scene.

Either way, I come out very badly, he thought. He discovered he had a terrific need to urinate, and sat rigidly. Even when my whole career's on the line, he thought, a couple of extra cups of coffee come back at you.

Gunderson moved to the pursuit of Trask and Lisio itself. "You know about department regulations 674.8 and 654.2 and the sections regarding notification of superiors, don't you?"

"Yes." He couldn't answer any other way. Nobody knew all the regs.

Gunderson held the bulky department manual like the Bible. "On May twenty-fourth, you didn't notify your supervisor that you had begun a high-risk investigation, did you?"

"I was the acting supervisor of Robbery that day."

"But did you try to get hold of anybody else? Check out your action plan? Like maybe with Captain McMurray?"

"I didn't think there was time. I thought action was called for."

Gunderson held the manual for the Board to admire. "No time. Well, how much time was there between the robbery of Santa Maria Federal Savings and Citizens Savings?"

"From when I found out that Citizens Savings was the next target?" Medavoy asked.

"Okay."

"Approximately twenty-five minutes."

"That's nearly a half hour."

"I had the Special Weapons Unit with me. I had choppers in the air. I was in a position to move quickly."

Gunderson stepped close to him. "And if you talked to someone with higher rank, someone who could advise or overrule you, what happens? You have to do things according to department regulations."

Chadd spoke up calmly. "I haven't objected to these editorial comments, but they should be questions."

Schroeder cleared his throat. "Sustained. Make them shorter, Lieutenant."

Medavoy saw that it was edging toward noon. Lunch, out of the sweltering conference room, away from Gunderson and a chance to talk to Chadd, call Jane. Just make it to noon.

"Your deliberate decision was not to bring in any superior officers?"

"It was my case. I didn't think I needed anybody else. I had to act quickly. Lives were on the line."

"Well, isn't it possible that a little involvement from a superior officer would have coordinated the operation better?"

"There wasn't any coordination problem."

"There wasn't? When the Chief of Police arrived at the scene, he didn't even know you'd set up a roadblock. You were so far out of the chain of command."

"Another objection," Chadd said, still leaning in his chair.

"Sustained," Schroeder said, sipping from his water glass carefully.

Medavoy wished Chadd would be more aggressive and protect him, but part of the strategy was to let the Board see how he handled himself under pressure. So you can't blow it. It's all back in your hands, he thought. He swallowed dryly again.

"You didn't know the Chief was on his way to the scene, did you?"

"No, I did not. I would have warned him or told him the situation."

"And there was no way for him to know what you were doing unless he talked to you directly, right? He couldn't get a handle on it in the regular way from a senior officer." Gunderson was flushed again, speaking in clipped, angry phrases. He looked like he wanted to punch Medavoy.

"It was pretty odd for him to show up," Medavoy said. "I had a man with explosives, armed suspects, and it's just not something the Chief normally gets in on."

Gunderson looked at the Board, one by one. "It is his department, isn't it, Sergeant Medavoy?"

Then the subject turned again. Gunderson began with the time factor once more. He hit again on the dangerous nature of the suspects, which Medavoy had freely acknowledged. Someone coughed loudly in the conference room and the sound seemed to bounce fully. There was nothing else in the dead silence while Medavoy spoke.

Gunderson looked at several report forms. "Okay, Sergeant Medavoy, you let these dangerous armed men approach a bank full of civilians, didn't you?"

"I decided it was the only option available."

"And you didn't take any steps at all to warn these civilians, did you?"

"There was no time to warn the people at Santa Maria Federal by the time I found out what was going on and formulated an action plan." Medavoy repeated the wording he and Chadd had decided on.

"You had nearly a half hour."

"That's right."

"And knowing that armed felons were about to commit another inherently dangerous felony, you did nothing at all to warn any authorities, right?"

Medavoy thought this decision, spoken out loud today, much after the event, sounded callous and even foolhardy. At the time it made perfect and complete sense, even if he recognized the dangers. "I chose to set up an ambush for the suspects instead," he said. "It was the best choice."

"You admit endangering civilians, which regulations 873 and 874 specifically tell you never, never to do?"

"Look, we all know it's impossible to be a cop and protect everybody from everything all the time."

Chadd made a note as if he liked the phrase, but Medavoy knew the Board hated it, if for no other reason than it was a truth best left unsaid. Like he told Jane about the little bribes, the unspoken truths made life possible, made things work. It was just a bitch when you had to talk about them.

The conference room clock hit twelve exactly.

Gunderson went on for a few more minutes, but he had made his points. He then picked up a thin, clipped report. "So when this whole runaround ended, you wrote it up. Like you were required to do?"

"I made my report," Medavoy said. Jesus, hold on to your water and your temper for a little longer.

Gunderson tossed the report to the floor. He must have seen the gesture on a TV show. "And you included every fact, all the information you hadn't told anybody while the thing was happening, didn't you?" He stepped toward Medavoy. "Things you didn't have time for before?"

"I made my report as I was directed to by a superior officer."

"You mean somebody told you to write this superficial document?"

"I was ordered to write a bare-bones report."

"By who?"

"Captain McMurray on the twenty-fourth. Those were his words."

Gunderson looked in astonishment at the Board, at Chadd, at everyone but Medavoy. "Captain McMurray said, Medavoy, you go write your report and leave out all kinds of facts, like what the Chief was doing at the scene, who gave the order to open fire on the suspects' car, all kinds of vital information?"

"I told you what he said."

"You're not saying he directed you to falsify or distort your report, right?"

"No." There was no other answer possible given the way McMurray put the order.

"All he did was assume that a twelve-year veteran cop would understand his simple instructions and not write a huge, repetitive report," Gunderson declared to the Board and sat down.

Medavoy started to answer, but Chadd stood up, hands in his pockets, calm and relaxed. "I'd like to take up all these matters after lunch. I'm going to put Captain McMurray on the stand, too."

"You are asking for the noon break, Mr. Chadd?" asked Schroeder, polishing his glasses slowly, putting them back on his nose carefully.

"Yes, sir." He jerked his head and Medavoy left the witness chair, his legs, he found, shaky and twitching as though he'd run hard and long. He stood by Chadd. People had already begun to get up and shift in the room. He heard the doors bang open.

Schroeder rapped twice on the green cloth. "We'll adjourn until two P.M. and resume taking testimony."

The Hearing Board officers stood and, without speaking to each other, filed back out in a line through the Assistant Chief's office.

Medavoy wanted to leave the room, but he said to Chadd, packing up a few legal pads, hefting one of the files, "I want to cut loose on that asshole, Ronnie. He's making it sound like I was playing games out there."

"We do our bit this afternoon," Chadd said, patting his shoulder.

"You think it's going okay?"

Chadd frowned. "They may be buying the endangerment charge, Robby."

"Shit. There wasn't anything else I could do."

"If we had McNeill come in here and say you were the greatest cop since Teddy Roosevelt, I wouldn't be worried."

Medavoy and Chadd walked out, the aisle thick with people. "No chance. I told you. Can't even get near him."

Chadd said, "We got a shot this afternoon. Watch out for the news-at-noon bunch." He pointed at the hungry-eyed reporters knotted just beyond the doorway, scanning faces for someone to pounce on.

Just then, Masuda and Zaragoza took his arm. "Let's go out the back, Robby."

Chadd waved and Masuda and Zaragoza hustled Medavoy through the empty waiting room of the Assistant Chief's office, down a flight of marble stairs flanked by stained white walls. "Jeez, I got to take a leak," he said, ducking into a men's room on the third floor.

"It's like a fucking sideshow, but you doing great," Masuda said. The three of them were alone in the little-used men's room on a side corridor. The crowd from the hearing shuffled and gossiped above them, like a tidal wave moving inexorably toward shore, dull and heavy.

"Chadd says if I could get Stevie Wonder, it's a done deal. I said, the guy's got guards, can't get near to ask him."

Masuda, combing his hair slowly said, "Hey, I saw Gef last night. They moved Stevie home around nine. He didn't like the hospital."

Medavoy finished, feeling better and thinking quickly. He washed his hands, ripped a paper towel roughly and dried them. He looked at Masuda and Zaragoza. "You guys want to give me a little help here?"

FORTY-ONE

DONNA MCNEILL WAS PLEASANTLY surprised by the two detectives who appeared at her front door ten minutes later. They urged her to whisper or speak quietly and wouldn't come inside. Sergeants Masuda and Zaragoza said they represented a group of men who wished to present the Chief with a gift during his convalescence and would she help them with some ideas for a few minutes?

Donna McNeill was reluctant to leave the Chief alone, but he was comfortable now and she would only be gone for a short time. She began thinking about a gift as the two detectives helped her into their car and drove her downtown.

From across the street, in a clipped hedge almost perfectly angled and tended, Medavoy watched them leave the house. He walked briskly across the wide, well-maintained street and around the back of the Chief's impressive white-brick home.

He picked his way through the geometrically precise flower beds and lawn and worked on the back door briefly. It took only a minute and a half for him to jimmy the lock and step inside the house. He was in the pantry and he walked quickly through the kitchen into the foyer, stepping over heavy carpet. There was no sound and he couldn't tell where Stevie Wonder might be. He had no more than ten minutes, according to the deal with Masuda and Zaragoza. He didn't want to waste it searching the house. He called out the Chief's name.

A moment later, he heard a hesitant voice to his right. "I'm in the study, Detective. Come on in."

Medavoy had tried to work out his appeal, but decided to simply lay it before Stevie Wonder, man to man. He went through the study, a high-ceilinged room lined with model ships. The Chief looked up from the sofa on which he lay, the TV tuned to a game show in front of him. He had several thick blankets on him and only the top of his head was visible. Dark computer screens stood on his desk.

Within easy reach from the sofa was a table with water and a multitude of pill bottles.

"I didn't hear Donna let you in," the Chief said. He blinked and looked inquisitively at Medavoy.

"No, sir. I broke in just now."

"Why did you do that?"

"I wanted to talk to you alone."

The Chief coughed slightly. "Would you mind turning off the TV? I'm only watching that shit to have some noise so I don't think."

Medavoy walked over, switched off the TV. Even though everyone called McNeill Stevie Wonder and thought little of him, Medavoy felt the awe of being with the Chief of Police. It was bred into him.

"You said you broke in?" the Chief asked. "You didn't want to come to the front door?"

"Sir, I didn't think I'd be able to see you if I did that."

"No, I'm pretty much under wraps now." He touched his head slightly. "I'm sorry I haven't thanked you personally for your effort the other day. I just haven't been up to it." His voice was already growing shaky.

"Sir, I'm in the middle of a hearing board. I'm going to get nailed."

The Chief sat up a little, making a face. A lot of banged-up guys, Medavoy thought, all kinds, too. "You performed to the highest standards, Detective. They say the same thing on the TV."

"Sir, my lawyer feels that if you came in to the hearing this afternoon, told them that, it would help me a great deal."

"I don't think I could, Detective. I am still rocky, you know." He smiled wanly, and Medavoy thought he was struggling with something other than physical pain.

"I need your help. You got to tell the Board what happened when you drove up."

The Chief studied Medavoy for several seconds. "You realize what you're asking me to do?"

"I don't think it's anything more than you can handle, sir." Medavoy jammed his hands into his pockets to hide his nervousness and impatience. Time was running away, and the Chief just lay there.

"Put yourself in my place," the Chief finally said, his hands open on the blankets. "What would you say?"

Medavoy told him candidly, blundering into an operation, causing it to blow, causing a death, risking the lives of police officers and civilians. Take the blame, Medavoy wound up, put it where it belongs.

The Chief listened, head dropping sometimes. It was strained in that paneled room, surrounded by the family mementoes and all the model ships. Medavoy finished.

"You would do that," the Chief said. "I went through your file that day. You're a direct man. That's why I'm not angry about how you got in. You saw something that needed to be done and you did it."

"Sir, will you appear at the hearing for me?" He wanted to shake Stevie Wonder, shout at him. You ungrateful son of a bitch, I pulled you out of that car after you wrecked my operation and killed one of your own men.

"I'll think about it."

"Sir, respectfully, I have to have an answer immediately."

The Chief focused a cold, oddly commanding expression on Medavoy. "I don't have any answer now. I want you to get out of my house."

Medavoy swore under his breath and left the room, the Chief sitting up partly. Gef was right about the loyalty around the department, he thought, getting into his car down the block. Christ, Reilly stood up for me, and he's a goddamn puke.

Donna McNeill was no fool and when she heard her husband tell her about Medavoy's visit, she knew she'd been tricked and was angry. She wondered why the Chief sat so quietly.

"That was an unconscionable act, breaking into our house," she said. "He should be thrown out of the department for that alone."

The Chief had gingerly moved aside his blankets and groaning, had begun to move his legs to the floor.

"What in God's name are you doing, Mac?" she cried.

"Trying to see if I can stand up. In more ways than one." He groaned again, sweat breaking out on his face.

"Mac, get right back under the covers. I'll give you some medication. You're only home because the doctors gave in when you promised to get more rest here."

He put out his hand. "Will you help me?"

"Think what you're doing, Mac. Stop and think."

"Will you?" he repeated, his hand outstretched. He trembled on his weak legs and felt sick to his stomach again, fought down the rising bile.

Donna hesitated, then took his hand firmly.

"Call for an ambulance," he said, holding tightly to her. "Get me an escort downtown."

"I gave it my best shot," Medavoy said in frustration to Chadd as they took their seats again just before two o'clock. "I thought he'd go for it. I was talking to myself." He slumped back.

"It was a long shot, Robby. You tried," Chadd said, looking up as the Board filed back to their places at the table and Schroeder called the hearing to order again. "Look at Gunderson. They were doing something over lunch. Something's going on."

Medavoy thought Gunderson looked considerably more at ease and grinned over at them. Chadd was right. The play had changed somehow.

Medavoy felt isolated when he took the witness chair again. Masuda and Zaragoza had to start their shift and in all of the crowded room, he counted few true friends.

Gunderson, laying back, imitating Chadd's relaxed posture, began on Medavoy's refusal to take a polygraph examination as he initially agreed to. It was, he said, a matter he forgot to take up that morning and Schroeder permitted him to do so now.

Medavoy gripped the chair's armrests. Chadd spoke up vigorously. "Mr. Chairman, failure to take a polygraph examination is inadmissible in any court. It's reversible error to even talk about it."

Schroeder smiled condescendingly. "Well, as you reminded me several times this morning, Mr. Chadd, this isn't a court. We can consider a great many things excluded from a trial. Go ahead, Lieutenant Gunderson."

Medavoy was going to blurt out a harsh reply when Bart, the Assistant Chief, bustled through the door, up to Schroeder, the cigar in his mouth wiggling. He was in shirt-sleeves and looked as out of place among the formally dressed senior officers as a stagehand breaking in on a matinee. He whispered something and Schroeder stood up. "A development requires the Board's presence. We'll take a short recess. Please remain in your seats." He hurried out the side door with the other officers trailing after him.

Medavoy got up, the audience loudly murmuring and glancing around. "This what you're worried about?" he asked Chadd.

"I don't think so. Gunderson looks about as confused as everybody else."

In the Assistant Chief's office, Councilman Prefach had kept the others away so he could talk to the Chief. "You're talking about the end of your career if you make any statement, Steve."

The Chief, in a plain gray suit and dark tie, sat in a heavily padded chair. He had let Donna give him a booster of pain-killer, but he felt otherwise quite alert and steady. Bart held the deputy chiefs just beyond the outer door.

"It's my career. My decision, Vin."

"Suppose I prevent you from making a real fool of yourself," Prefach said tightly. "I might have to keep you here until we can get you back into the hospital."

"In my own building? With two hundred and twenty-six cops available for me to have you taken into custody?" He smiled. "Don't even think about it."

Prefach stepped back, darkly angry. "Whatever you do, Steve, I'll have to protect myself."

"That's your business. I don't care."

Prefach walked toward the door. He paused, said, "You really are a fool, Steve," and stepped through it. The Chief motioned for the deputy chiefs, and Bart led them in.

Medavoy was startled when the Chief, looking frail, held up by the Assistant Chief and another cop, was brought into the room and seated at the green cloth table. The Hearing Board remained standing at the doorway.

Schroeder said, "The Board has unanimously voted to allow the Chief to address it and the observers present today."

"What's he going to say?" Chadd whispered urgently to Medavoy, eyes on the gray figure unfolding a piece of paper and holding it stiffly.

"I haven't the slightest idea," Medavoy said. He refused to hope.

The Chief let long seconds go by, then asked for a glass of water and sipped from it. "I'm going to order that the press be admitted for the purpose of hearing my statement. Open the doors." The cops on guard unlocked the doors and pulled them back. The reporters and camera crews, unable to sit down in the already-packed conference room, lined the walls and came down to crouch just below the green cloth table to take photographs. The Chief waited until they were in position and the room, as it had that morning, grew still.

Medavoy tried not to think at all.

The Chief lowered his head, then raised it, his glasses glinting in the TV lights. He spoke slowly at first, then gained confidence. He held the paper he read from tightly.

"Ladies and gentlemen," he said, "and my fellow police officers. I am going to make a brief statement and then I shall refuse to answer any questions."

Chadd whispered worriedly. "What's that mean?"

"Nothing we can do anyway," Medavoy said quietly. He watched Stevie Wonder on center stage.

"I appreciate the indulgence of this Hearing Board in permitting me to make an unscheduled appearance. I would not, normally, interfere in this way with the conduct of a Hearing Board, but this matter is not normal and demands extraordinary attention."

The Chief sipped again and fiddled with his coat pocket. "I have been a police officer for over thirty years. In that time I have found few men with the qualities of leadership, initiative, and bravery Sergeant Robert Medavoy demonstrated on May twenty-fourth this year."

"Home free," Chadd whispered, grabbing his arm. "Home fucking free, Robby."

Medavoy let his breath out slowly. He must have been holding it.

The Chief was speaking more calmly. "I have reviewed Sergeant Medavoy's record and it is exemplary. I believe he acted in the highest traditions of this police department when he undertook measures to protect the lives and property of Santa Maria's citizens against a brutal and cunning assault. He is, I want to state directly, exactly the kind of dedicated police officer this department must cultivate and honor."

The Chief cleared his throat and looked up at Bart, then Medavoy noticed the slim older woman, his wife, standing also at the side of the room.

"Now I must add a personal note," the Chief said. He stopped again. "It is fashionable today for men in authority to accept responsibility for acts in the abstract. I reject that idea. I believe responsibility is personal and direct. If there is a wrong, we should have the courage to accept it and acknowledge it.

"Unlike Sergeant Medavoy, I displayed a gross recklessness on May twenty-fourth, entering an area without regard for procedure, failing to alert posts in the area, and causing a fatal disruption of an otherwise excellently laid operation. In so doing, I negligently brought about the death of my driver, Patrolman Kozlowski," he stumbled at the name, his jaw tightened, then he went on, "and put at risk other police officers and citizens of this city. This was utterly inexcusable and I take full, direct, and personal responsibility for these disastrous consequences."

Somewhere during those words, Medavoy stopped thinking derisively of McNeill. He's the Chief, he thought. The guy has it.

The Chief folded his paper and beckoned for the Assistant Chief, who rushed over, and his wife who came beside him, head raised almost imperiously, but not quite. The room was silent except for the *snick, snick* of still photographers snapping off pictures.

"Since responsibility in the abstract is abhorrent, I am announcing my resignation as your Chief effective immediately." His voice broke finally. "Being your Chief of Police has been the greatest privilege of my life."

As the Chief was helped out of the room, reporters began shouting questions at him and the cameras tried to get closer. A wedge of cops, unbidden and thinking alike, pushed through and prevented anybody from getting near. The room was alive with voices and babbling.

"What happens now?" Medavoy asked Chadd. The Chief was gone, and Schroeder rapped again and again on the table.

"It's over, Robby. They aren't going to top that," Chadd said. "He just fell on his sword."

Schroeder finally called out, almost in a shout, "We will take a ten-minute recess. Ten minutes. Ten minutes." Then he darted away to catch up with the other senior cops.

Chadd had a great, easy smile and he reached up as if to grab the ceiling in a deep stretch. "In about ten minutes, Robby, I think you're going to be knighted."

FORTY-TWO

FEELING JUBILANT, Medavoy raced from the fourth floor down to the second, pushing past anybody who tried to slow him down. He thought he'd go to Robbery, see who was kicking around, and call Jane. She was probably still in court, though, because most judges during a trial didn't take an afternoon break until three.

The news of the Chief's announcement spread through the building almost instantly, and cops stopped where they were, already placing him in the ranking of other chiefs and arguing who might be coming next.

Medavoy sat at his desk, reached for the phone, and tried Department 24 at the courthouse; he found out it was still in session, so Jane was tied up. He was too excited to do anything and everybody in the detail was signed out someplace.

He started back to the fourth floor, passing Homicide, a broad office of desks and small-doored cubicles so the elite detectives had a little privacy. A flash of color caught his eye.

Gunderson was bent over a black man, dressed in a red

prison jumpsuit, manacled. The black man's head was shaved and gleamed with sweat. One of Gunderson's assistants pointed at Medavoy. Gunderson looked up, sour faced. He had been shouting at the black man. "See who we got, Medavoy?" he called out. "Flash from the past."

The black man, his Folsom jumpsuit filled out from either eating too much or weight lifting, swore at Medavoy. It was Leroy Menefee, older and having made the grade as a career criminal.

Medavoy leaned against the marble wall in the stairwell. That was the surprise Chadd wondered about and McNeill's bombshell had thrown it into confusion. The deputy chiefs were sitting back in the Assistant Chief's office right this moment arguing about what to do with the brutality evidence Menefee would give. Was it worth putting on after what the Chief just said? Would it backfire on them?

Medavoy could almost hear them.

He walked more slowly up to the fourth floor, into the conference room where some people had returned to their seats, but it was only half-filled. Chadd sat at the table, making notes, preparing to go on.

Go on to what? There was a point where you couldn't be a fugitive forever. You had to come back.

"Ronnie, I want you to go in and make a deal," he said, sitting down, lowering his head to speak to Chadd.

Chadd stopped writing. "A deal? For what?"

"Tell them I'll resign right now and they give me a public clean bill of health and drop everything. It's a wash." He kept his voice steady.

"Robby, they're going to make you a certified hero in a couple of minutes. We're going to walk away with all the marbles."

"I don't think so. I found out about Gunderson's surprise."

"We've demolished the guy," Chadd said. "What could he have that's left?"

"He's got something."

"Accusations. I can handle them. Trust me."

Medavoy licked his lips. "I don't think you can handle this one." It was said.

"Why not?"

Medavoy nodded slightly. "Because I'm guilty." He told Chadd about Baladarez and the man sitting two floors below them, waiting to pour it out in public.

Chadd listened. Then he said slowly, "All you have to do is deny it, Robby. It's his word against yours. It always has been."

"Yeah, I know. Please make the deal." And he sat back, afraid he might cry.

The ten-minute recess lengthened like a delayed airline flight, the people and reporters first becoming annoyed, then angry, then very curious. The reporters moved stealthily through the room, checking with sources, getting shrugs in return. Medavoy wasn't around. He'd gone to the Assistant Chief's office after twenty minutes.

It was the longest hour of his life, listening to the wrangling and bickering in the office. The agreement was made. To preserve the department, the compromises other men had made, and the Chief's reputation, too.

Medavoy was allowed to hold his resignation for three days so it would not appear to be part of the hearing.

At three-forty-two, the Hearing Board returned to the conference room, Medavoy and Chadd seated at their table, Gunderson throwing down his pen in fury, the hearing's reporter calmly taking everything down on her machine with the same benign, empty face.

Schroeder made the announcement to the cameras and crowd.

"In view of the extraordinary statement made by Chief of Police Stephen McNeill, the Hearing Board has voted four

to one to deny all of the charges brought against Sergeant
Robert Medavoy. We want the record to show this denial to
be with prejudice. We have found no merit to the charges."

He smiled a wintry, solemn smile for the cameras
and Medavoy.

"The Board, and this Chairman especially, want to thank
Sergeant Medavoy for a job well done." He slowly began
clapping and the applause built throughout the room, some
people rising.

Medavoy listened and Chadd put out his hand. "You're
still a hell of a cop, Robby."

"Thanks for everything you did," he said, shaking hands.
"It wasn't your fault. My mistake, that's all."

He waited outside Department 24 for a while, watching Jane
inside, tapping on her steno machine during the trial. He liked
seeing her in there, concentrating on the testimony, eyes set,
looking determined. He liked her persistence. You really can't
tell, he thought, just looking at her, how much of a fighter she is.

About fifteen minutes later, the court broke for a recess
and she strolled out with the jury. There was no audience for
this routine trial.

"It's over, Robby? You're done?" she asked when she saw
him in front of her. He realized she saw the look on his face.

"I'm not a cop anymore," he said, taking her in his arms.

"It's all right," she said gently, the jurors walking around
them, curious. "It's going to be okay."